CO

The Gates of Hel: Eschaton Cycle
Gods of the Ragnarok Era Book 8
MATT LARKIN
Editors: Clark Chamberlain, Regina Dowling
Cover: Yocla Designs

Incandescent Phoenix Books
mattlarkinbooks.com

MIDGARD

THULE

NIDAVELLIR

SVIARLAND

LAPPMARKEN

JAMTLA

DALAR

UPSAL

NIARAR

OSTERGOTLAND

SANDVIK SEA

NORREVISKE

SKANE

SIBORIA

ARUS SJAELLAND

BURGUNDAHOLMR

LAALAND

MORIMARUSA

BRETLAND

REIDGOTALAND

RIJNLAND

MENZLIN

XANTEN

HUNALAND

BAIA

SWABIA

STYRIA

VALLAND

AQUISGRANA

IDAVOLLIR

OUTER MIKLAGARD

ANDALUS

KARTUBA

MIDDLE SEA

VANAHEIM

SERKLAND CALIPHATE

POHJOLA
SAMODIYTSIA
KVENLAND
KALEVALA
UTGARD
BJARMALAND
MIDGARD WALL
HOLMGARD
QAZAN
JARNVID
HALFHAUGR
AUJUM
KIOVIA
TARAZ
HYRCANIAN SEA
BLACK SEA
MIKLAGARD
MIKLAGARD

EXTRA RESOURCES

For full color, higher-res maps, character lists, location
overviews, and glossaries, check out the bonus resources
here:
https://tinyurl.com/y47j3gcj

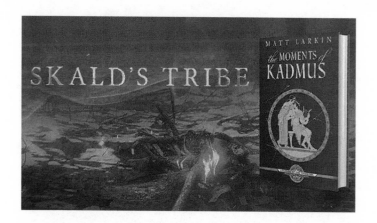

Join the Skalds' Tribe newsletter and get access to exclusive insider information and your FREE copy of *The Moments of Kadmus*.

https://www.mattlarkinbooks.com/skalds/

PROLOGUE

*W*hen Sigyn moved to empty the bucket, water dripped on Loki's face. Erratic, unpredictable drops of it. Or, perhaps not wholly unpredictable, had he had access to more variables than he did at present. Every time Loki allowed his mind to begin to calculate probabilities, a drop would splash upon his eyes.

He knew, of course. He knew that occupying himself with such conjectures were distractions, not from his present discomfort—though he certainly didn't enjoy having his feet stuck in water for days, beginning to rot—but rather from the more the painful eventuality that must soon impend.

Sometimes, in such moments, he allowed himself to question whether the inception of this cycle was truly born of necessity, or whether he—who, despite his prescient abilities and immortality, remained essentially a Man—had allowed hubris to sway him. A desperate gambit, one that, most like, managed to but delay the inevitable.

Sigyn set the bucket over his head again, grunting

slightly, her arms no doubt burning with fatigue from holding them over her head for hours on end. Pneuma might enhance one's stamina, but even it had its limits.

"Rest," he told her. "Please."

"Perhaps later. Rather, I've been mulling over the situation."

"Sigyn ..."

She sniffed. "Well, denied access to Sessrumnir, I'm instead forced to reconstruct the texts I read. I don't know that I'd call my memory eidetic, though it's certainly above average, but Mundilfari made several passing references to hearing about a technique of storing knowledge in a kind of mental library. I'd never considered such things needful until now."

"Sigyn, please ..." Please do not waste the time that was left to them. "Talk to me, rather than lose yourself in these musings."

She blew out a breath. "I'm seeking some means of breaking this chain. Even orichalcum cannot be indestructible. If it was, how would smiths forge it into aught?"

"That's before they've bound souls into the metal."

"I considered that. If the souls themselves render orichalcum stronger, it seems the key to breaking such a chain would lie in finding a way to disperse those souls. I suspect that's how Odin broke Gramr, all those years ago. Either way, that event—and many who saw the battle agreed the sword *did* snap in half—proves that even orichalcum is not unbreakable." She paused. "Alternatively, were I strong enough, I might crush the stalagmite the chain runs through, instead. It would leave the guards to deal with, but I've begun to wonder, if, were I able to infuse the entirety of my Pneuma into a single blow, I might then snap even such a thick stone?"

"Whatever happens, I love you."

She stroked his cheek. "I won't leave your side, my love. That's why I take no vengeance for what Thor did to our son."

Eons of blood had washed over the World because of Loki's choice. Not that he'd called himself Loki back then. So much blood, leading to vengeance, which necessitated more vengeance, and more blood, on and on, until an Era at last must end in fire or flood, and always, with death on a scale no Man would have imagined.

So they could start again. Buy a little more time.

"You want to talk, though," Sigyn said. "So ... you told me that Hel was *our* child, that I, in a previous incarnation of my soul, had been mother to her. I understand your perpetual reticence to discuss your dead wife and dead daughter, even if *I* was the wife."

"Too much knowledge of your past lives is like to compound the difficulty that already exists in breaking away from the patterns already impressed upon your soul."

She chuckled. "You mean I'd keep making the same mistakes, over and over? How am I to learn from mistakes I don't remember?"

An eternal question of the Wheel of Life. Loki suspected, rather, that so much knowledge would weigh a soul down, as his remained so burdened. Crushed, under the weight of losses and regrets stretched over eternity. "Perhaps to begin each life with a clean slate is a blessing." One he was denied.

"Perhaps." She looked up sharply, at the tunnel.

A moment later, the flicker of torchlight shone within that passage, and shortly after that, Odin made his slow way over, torch in one hand, walking stick in another.

Sigyn glared at Loki's blood brother as he approached,

though the man fixed his gaze on Loki and paid Loki's wife no mind.

Odin plodded over to stand just before the puddle's edge, staring at Loki.

"Come to gloat?" Sigyn asked, her voice laced with venom enough to make even Loki cringe.

Odin continued to ignore her entirely. "Despite myself and my better judgment, I could not stay away."

Loki nodded, struggling to keep his face impassive as the tumult of emotions roiled in his gut. Rage, at the awful death of his son. Guilt, at knowing he himself had wrought that, and had—at least in Odin's mind—betrayed his brother. Relief ... in knowing some part of Odin still wanted to believe in him. How fragile even Loki's ego seemed, despite his eons of life, despite his supposed move beyond such petty human limitations.

"I decided to give you *one* last chance to explain yourself, Loki."

Loki frowned. How badly he wished he could. But even if saying things aloud did not hold their own dangers, Odin was not ready. Not quite, though so very close. "You're wrong about one thing. This is not the last time you'll see me."

Odin groaned, shaking his head. "Oh, I don't think I'll be coming down here again."

All Loki could do was purse his lips.

After a moment more, Odin turned and tromped away, the sound of his walking stick hitting the stone echoing in the tunnel even after the light from his torch had vanished.

Sigyn sniffed, tossed the bucket once more, and then replaced it. "The man has gall."

Oh. Well, but then Loki had needed a man with gall. With confidence beyond even arrogance. With a willingness, perhaps even a *need*, to persevere even in the face of the certainty of defeat.

"So," Sigyn said. "You want to talk, but not to Odin. And to me?"

"Of course."

"All right. What is Tartarus?"

Loki frowned at her sudden change of topic. He'd regretted that outburst the moment he'd made it. Mentioning to Odin the torment he'd endured there so long ago, it served no purpose save to vent his wrath in petty defiance of Odin's equally petty torture here.

"Is that a name for a place?"

"After a fashion."

"No. I don't think it's a place, in the strictest sense, but rather a name for one of the Spirit Worlds. Except, I cannot figure out which. Black walls? Muspelheim?"

Loki pursed his lips. How badly she wanted to know everything. Sigyn's incessant curiosity was both her most endearing and most self-destructive trait. She wanted answers to every question imaginable, never once considering that such answers would only become burdens. Waking nightmares that would serve no end save to trouble her days and leave her quivering in the night, sleepless and tormented.

"Right. I didn't really expect you to answer that. You *say* you want to talk, to pass this imprisonment in conversation, rather than in trying to escape. As if you are content to remain here until the end of time."

Loki winced. "I will be freed, eventually."

She tossed the water from the bucket once more. "When? How?"

He grimaced as another drop fell on his face. "I told you a long time ago. Naught lasts forever, my love."

Not his imprisonment. Not his hopes. And not the World itself.

All would become ash.

PART I

Year 399, Age of the Aesir
Winter

1

---

*I*f prescience was a lie, the very essence of a self-fulfilling prophecy, then the only hope to challenge urd lay in refusing to look into the future. It was a desperate gambit, of course, because Odin could not say whether a yet worse chain of events would unfold because of his refusal. One thing remained certain, however. Every dark, soul-crushing truth he had foreseen had come about, not only in spite of his striving to change them, but because of it.

Prescience accounts for itself.

That truth he and Loki had worked out in long talks sitting before fire pits such as the one he now stared at in the back of Valaskjalf. Except, Loki had known it all along. He, a slave of the Norns, had led Odin down this path from the day they met, guiding him toward slow, agonizing revelations of his utter impotence next to the will of urd. And now, his blood brother lay chained in a tunnel beneath Asgard, awaiting Ragnarok.

The final war that must lay at their doorsteps. Odin ought to kill Loki for all he had done, but he could not bring himself to such an action. No, maybe the man had felt as powerless as Odin now felt, trapped by his own destiny even as he spun out those of others.

And now, Odin's son was dead. His wife a distraught wreck who refused to see anyone. Only Thor remained of Odin's family, and he'd seen his last child's death, as well. Seen it long ago and done so much to try to avert it—actions he could no longer count on to have the effect he'd desired.

Across from him, Freyja shifted. Having burned off most of her stored sunlight, her skin now cast only the faintest of glimmer. She'd held silent, letting him grieve Baldr, and too, grieve for the loss of the future he had imagined in favor of the one he'd foreseen.

After Baldr's pyre, he'd stormed Yggdrasil and closed in upon the Well of Urd. But the Norns who had tended it had refused to show themselves. Perhaps they had retreated to their mountain abode in the Sudurberks.

"If you're right," Freyja said, "and some great final battle for this Era impends, we must decide how to proceed. We need to call a council, as you intended when bridging Alfheim to Vanaheim."

Whether she refused to call it Asgard or simply forgot, Odin could not say. Either way, she spoke the truth. For days he'd lingered in the dark, staring at flame and shadow as if either would have an answer, whilst adamantly refusing to allow his visions to manifest. He fought them down as much as he could—though sometimes glimpses would peek through, especially in his sleep.

"We will call a council," he said after a moment more. "And it needs to include not only the Aesir and Vanir. We need the liosalfar and ... the jotunnar."

Freyja grimaced at him, shifting in obvious discomfort. "I don't know that I can convince anyone from the Summer

Court to attend. Besides, even with the bridge, they'd still need hosts."

"We'll find those."

"You mean you'll force captives to serve as vessels."

Odin shrugged. When compared to the urd of the entire World, the suffering of a few meant very little. After all, if he failed, if he lost Ragnarok, they'd all be dead. "I've reason to believe Hel herself will make another move on our world. Before that happens, we need every possible ally. Which is why I'm sending Tyr to call even the jotunnar to the council. And you, I implore you to return to Alfheim and convince as many of the liosalfar as possible to join us."

Freyja chewed on her lip. "We need to talk about Idunn and Hnoss."

Oh, Odin had thought long on the two of them. "I cannot turn the Bilröst to Svartalfheim. I'll recreate the device here to stabilize the bridge, but a bridge runs in both directions, Freyja. If I open the door to that place, I invite in the svartalfar themselves, and whatever other abominations they bring along with them. No one can afford that."

"So we abandon our daughter? Our friend?"

"I've no desire to abandon either of them! What would you have me do? I ... I made so many mistakes, my love. I thought I was saving people when I banished the Vanir. I thought I could save the future by bargaining with Volund. It's all ... I cannot take such risks again." He shook his head. "No. We'll go back to Svartalfheim ourselves, once we've secured Midgard against the impending threat. It's happening *now*, Freyja. I can feel it. I ..."

She crawled around the edge of the fire to take his hand. "You take the weight of all the worlds upon your shoulders. Be careful that burden does not crush you beneath it."

Oh, it probably would.

The wolf ...

Fenrir's jaws closing around his throat. No! Odin would no longer look into the future. He would cut through the Web of Urd by refusing to acknowledge it. Fenrir would remain chained far below Asgard, howling in impotence.

Why not give in ... to the future ...?

No.

Freyja squeezed his hand. "I'll go to Alfheim. I'll do as you ask. Promise me ... once this Ragnarok is done, we'll go back for our daughter."

"I swear, if I still draw breath, I'll find a way to reach her."

His lover frowned, clearly not pleased with his words. But—much as it tore him apart—he could see no way to dedicate himself to Hnoss or Idunn's rescues at the moment.

Give in ... Let it be done ...

No.

Odin would never surrender. He would fight until the last gasp of the World. Hel had destroyed the last Era and created this poisoned one. This time would be different. This time, he'd win a true victory.

❦

"I DO NOT HAVE ALL the details," Odin said to the small crowd he'd gathered in Valaskjalf. Frigg had refused to attend and Freyja had already left, but many others stood here now. "But Ragnarok is upon us. We have, perhaps, one last chance to ready ourselves before we are faced with the threats now impending. Tyr already knows his mission. The rest of you must act as seems needful to gain as many allies as possible. And I would see us armed against the threat. I am told the dvergar now hide, deep within their halls. But their crafts remain."

He beckoned Hermod forward, and his apprentice came, bearing a bundle wrapped in cloth. This he laid at Odin's feet and unwrapped it slowly.

A few of the gathered crowd murmured when runeblades were revealed.

Odin knelt—ignoring the pop in his knees—and took up Laevateinn. "This blade was given to Frey by the Lofdar, long ago. So I return it."

Frey might never much love him. He was, however, one of the strongest warriors they had, especially infused with sunlight. The Vanr knelt to claim his former weapon once more, offering Odin a grim nod.

He understood, of course. They need not love one another.

"Tyr."

The man trod forward, and Odin handed him Mistilteinn. The hateful blade had claimed Baldr's life—could kill any immortal, in fact. And there was no one Odin could trust more with such a weapon than his champion.

Hermod already bore Dainsleif, and Thor had Mjölnir. For Thor's daughter Thrúd, Odin offered Hrotti, a runeblade Frigg's agents had recovered after the death of Gunnar.

To Thor's son Magni he gave Skofnung, arguably the most vicious of all runeblades.

And to Syn, Hermod's wife, he granted Gramr—nor did Odin miss the look of lust Tyr gave that one, even after so many years. Frigg's people had recovered it from Sigurd's pyre, he was told.

"The last two runeblades are lost," Odin said. "At least one was destroyed, and I have not uncovered the other.

Those called upon to wield a blade must do so with the utmost care, for these are cursed things, wrought in the dark by dvergar as twisted gifts for princes of old."

"I was there," Frey pointed out.

Odin offered a nod of acknowledgment to him, saying naught more on it. "That's it. All of you prepare. The council will be held in two moons. If it can be arranged, we shall meet at the hall of Aegir off the coast of Valland. Tyr will stop there to arrange it." Odin looked to Hermod. "A word with you."

The others departed, leaving him alone with his apprentice.

Hermod folded his arms over his chest and stared at Odin, while he climbed back into his vacant throne.

With Frey and the other sunlight-infused Vanir gone, the hall seemed so much darker now, lit only by the crackling braziers.

Odin sighed, and rubbed his brow. "I must ask you to attempt something ... drastic. Something you alone have the power to accomplish, given that we need Andvaranaut to maintain the bridge to Alfheim." Oh, he'd been tempted to claim the ring and go himself. But she might even expect that. The battle had to come between him and her, and he could not deliver himself unto her doorstep. Besides, he'd have no way to bring back his son. "I need you to use your power and travel between the Realms."

"To where?"

"To Niflheim. Take Sleipnir—I suspect you can carry him across the Veil, given his nature—and ride to the very gates of Hel."

Hermod's arms dropped to his sides as he took a faltering step forward. "What madness?"

"I must have Baldr back. I ... His death begins this final

battle. I fear our only hope left of averting it would be to restore him. And you alone have the ability to reach Niflheim, and to bring someone back to us."

"You really think she'll let him go?" His voice shook with trepidation, though no one would have thought him craven for that.

No, and Odin pitied him, hated himself for placing the man in such a position. But there was no one else. "Offer her Draupnir. Offer her ... aught else that seems needful. Or sneak in, if it suits you. But find a way to bring back my son and we might yet avert the end."

Hermod shook his head. "This is Mist-madness. No one passes the gates of Hel save the dead."

We are all dead ...

Odin nodded grimly. "You are the son of a valkyrie, Hermod. You can do this."

Hermod looked away, staring at the rafters, the columns, everywhere else before finally turning back to Odin. "You truly understand the peril you place me in?"

"*You* understand a father's grief."

Hermod glowered at that.

"This is *more* than grief, though. Baldr's life might save this Realm. If there is even a chance, we have to take it."

"And do your visions tell you I will succeed?"

Odin lowered his gaze.

"So I fail?"

Now, Odin looked sharply back up at him. "I don't know." It was better that way. "But I'm asking you to try. And be wary, Hermod. The orbits of the Spirit Worlds are elliptical, which is to say you cannot judge how much time will pass here, while you are away."

Hermod groaned, then finally nodded. "I cannot deny you, my king. I must see my wife, first."

"Do so. But do not tarry long."

"One more thing ... you're seeking allies. In Hunaland I met a völva, Bergljot, who strives to uphold the old ways. She is protected by a varulf, Didrik, and well respected. You might call upon her as an ally."

Odin nodded.

Without another word, his apprentice turned and fled Valaskjalf.

Your madness sends him to torment ...

No. Hermod was strong. Maybe stronger than any of them. He'd survived passing into Svartalfheim to rescue Odin. Now, he would have to pass into Niflheim to save Baldr.

And save them all.

2

_____

The Bilröst shimmered before Yggdrasil, within the city of Gimlé in Alfheim. Freyja watched the glittering bridge as the ferryman carried her out over the waves toward the islands of Tír na nÓg, where the queen's Summer Court lay. Sunlight reflected off the waters like a field of diamonds stretching out forever—or seeming to, given that Alfheim itself had its bounds and, if one passed far enough, one would come to the other Spirit Worlds.

Exactly where ... well that was more nebulous, with the intersecting orbits of the worlds being somewhat irregular. At the moment, if she were to travel far enough out to sea she might reach the world of Noatun, whence came mer and the like, though she had never traveled half so far from shore. Only the bravest—or most reckless—of traders made such a crossing.

The islands ahead glittered themselves, so lush and green they seemed like single living beings rising up from the sea. Given the choice, she'd have advised the construction of the Bilröst there, not in Gimlé where Dellingr reigned, ineffable and unknowable. But Frey had insisted closer proximity to Yggdrasil would create a stronger connection between Realms.

The ferryman's canoe scraped up on pink, sparkling sand, and Freyja hopped over the side, landing in ankle-deep water. Always so warm here. After her time, however brief, back in Vanaheim, Alfheim seemed almost overpoweringly hot.

"Thank you," she said to the ferryman.

He kept his gaze lowered, probably unused to being acknowledged at all. Such people were slaves of the Summer Court, after all.

The path to the Summer Palace was paved with cobblestones and flanked by marble columns covered in ivy that grew overhead to create a shaded canopy. Freyja had come here oft over the centuries, and, despite the glory of the court itself, she always found the walk the most soothing. It was a kind of meditation that otherwise could become challenging in Alfheim, much less in Tír na nÓg.

Some days, the trek felt long, but this day, it seemed to end too quickly, as the queen's palace came into view. It rested on a greenery-covered mountain slope, with small waterfalls pouring down through giant arches just outside it, all leading to a water garden. The palace itself was carved from marble and pearl, with sparkling towers supported by great buttresses. Around balconies, bards played harps and lyres, the music never ceasing here, by command of Queen Áine. The Summer Queen, she called herself, and—as summer and daylight never abated here—insisted that all eternity must be passed in revelry.

A marble staircase rose up over the mountain, cut into the slope and doubled back in a zigzag as it rose. Much of the path remained shaded by palm trees, ferns, and the occasional rosewood. Three-legged sun crows flitted about in the trees overhead as Freyja passed, climbing the long stairs up to Áine's palace.

Smaller abodes dotted the lower slopes, homes and workspaces for those who served the palace but were not permitted to dwell in the grand chambers within. Freyja herself had once occupied one, before withdrawing from the court for favor of the redwood groves beyond Gimlé. Few of the Vanir had ever attained the full trust of the native liosalfar, even if her brother Frey operated with a greater leeway than most others.

Beyond the steps, Freyja trod into the grand palace itself. Great, fluted marble columns supported a domed atrium, with water trailing from the ceiling in thin falls between the columns. Within, several dozen males and females were caught up in an orgy, whilst others drank honeyed wines or smoked forest herbs designed to provoke visions.

The temptation to join them—either group, really— flooded over her like a wave, drawing her in, its pull almost irresistible.

This was *not* why she'd come here. In fact, that pull was a good reason to avoid the Summer Palace entirely. Freyja pushed on, not to the throne room—Áine herself would almost certainly refuse to help—but to the wing leading to the water gardens.

In Gimlé she had heard Saule had come to the palace, and the water gardens had always most attracted the other woman.

Massive windows flanked either side of the path up to the gardens, before the roof terminated entirely and the sun washed down over Freyja once more. Its radiance held its own kind of intoxication, though she remembered once fearing it, her skin burning and peeling if she spent too long outside the rainforest canopy. Now, though, she absorbed sunlight. The path rose up gradually, without need for stairs, before leading to an artificial plateau the queen had ordered built here.

Ponds and tiny falls dotted the surface, along with flowers of every imaginable color and a scattering of palm trees. A place of wonder and beauty, indeed, and Freyja had come here oft on her visits to the Summer Palace.

As expected, Saule lounged on a rock, gazing into a lily-covered pond where rainbow-colored fish swam within. The red-haired woman glanced in her direction, brow raised in surprise. "Come back from the Mortal Realm so soon?"

Freyja climbed atop a rock across from the other woman and settled down, pulling off her boots so she could dangle her toes in the water. So many times she'd run over what to say. Saule was a Sun Knight, a commander among the warriors of Alfheim, and if Freyja won her over, she could bring in a small army of liosalfar.

But, as with all native liosalfar—and increasingly the Vanir who'd stayed here long—Saule was removed from human culture and tended to see mortals as amusements, at best, uncomprehending of how seeming pranks might drive mortals to madness or worse.

"I've come to seek your aid."

Saule shrugged. "We lost a great many people rescuing you from Svartalfheim. I'm not sure Áine would permit another such attempt, much less for *Idunn*." The liosalf managed to instill enough scorn into Freyja's friend's name that Freyja found herself flinching.

Given the choice, yes, she would have gone back for Idunn. But maybe Odin was right. Maybe he had to stop the impending war first. "It's not about Idunn." Or Hnoss, much as it pained her. "The mortals are inviting us to their Realm, offering to find hosts."

"Games?" Saule chuckled, the sound like music and yet somehow filling Freyja with a profound unease. "They want to play games?" The liosalf licked her lips.

"It's not for games. They want us to join them in war."

"Oh! They want to fight us? That sounds enthralling! We could Stride them into the sky and let them fall into the sea."

Freyja forced her face to neutrality. One wrong word might offend Saule, preventing any chance of Odin's entreaty from working. "They don't want to fight against us. They want us to help them fight a coming war."

"Meh. Also could be entertaining. What if we blinded both sides and let them flail around trying to kill each other! The songs we could sing of such a sight!"

"Saule. They believe forces loyal to Niflheim are planning to try to claim their Realm. The mortals look to us for protection."

Saule twisted her face and rolled her eyes. "Boring."

"No one is saying you cannot amuse yourselves with human bodies. Only, make certain we are there to help stop the forces trying to enslave or eradicate them. How much fun will mortals be if they're all dead?"

Saule chuckled. "Lots. Dellingr can send the valkyries for their souls. Imagine, whole legions of dead flitting about the Penumbra, waiting to feed us."

"We're talking about the end of the Mortal Realm."

Saule abruptly pulled her dress over her head, tossed it aside, and slid down into the pond. "It happens. I've seen it happen. When you've been here long enough, you won't worry so much over it."

Freyja flinched at Saule's casual disdain for human life. It was like trying to convince a human that the life of an animal mattered in the long run. They might care about a particular animal, but animals in general seemed to exist only to serve their needs. Freyja sighed.

"You fret too much," Saule called. "Come and swim."

"I care about the mortals." Some of them, anyway. Oh, she wanted to worry over all Mankind the way she knew she should. She could feel a lingering guilt, inside her at not caring more. It niggled her, the absence of decency that might have once motivated her. But even if she could not motivate herself to more general beneficence toward humanity, she could at least care deeply about a few out there.

Od. And those following him, including now her own brother.

Frey.

Saule liked Frey. They were lovers, oft enough.

"You realize my brother could die in this war. I could die. Ullr. Others. We are *physically* in the Mortal Realm. If we lose this war, we're gone. You, you lose a host and get sent back here. Not me."

Saule turned back to her, face no longer lit with glee. "So don't go."

"I've already given my word. You're not suggesting I break a bargain?"

Saule rolled her eyes, not bothering to answer. Of course, no spirit would ever consider breaking a bargain, even one made with a mortal. "This is why you watch your words when making a pact."

"I told Odin I would fight beside him. Frey made the same agreement. We're doing this, even if you refuse to help us. You say you've seen these Era-ending wars before? How does it end?"

Saule frowned. "Fine. I'll call those loyal to me and we'll come to aid the mortals. But you should never have made such a bargain. I don't know that I can protect you from what will happen, if this truly is the forces of Niflheim unleashed. Her power ... She will bring the Mistwraiths, snow maidens, and who knows what other fell creatures from that icy world."

Freyja nodded. She had Saule, now. She could almost see it as the battles played out in her friend's mind. Glorious entertainment, she would think it. Well, let her think as she would, so long as she brought warriors of the liosalfar.

"Thank you," Freyja said.

Saule shrugged. "One way or another, I'll see you back in the Mortal Realm."

Yes, and Freyja should get back there. Little time might remain, and whatever was left to her, she'd want to spend with Od.

3

_A_s ever, Syn guarded Yggdrasil against any trying to steal the apples, though so few of those grew these days. Perhaps that made protecting them even more needful. Men he'd have judged well deserving had not received apples, and had thus withered and died, ravaged by time. Hermod pitied them, of course, though sometimes he wondered if immortality was as much a blessing as they had first thought.

He endured, while many of those he'd loved had vanished into shadow.

Sif.

His parents.

And so, so many friends.

Syn sat against the root wall, half dozing, but she rose when he drew nigh, frowning. "What is it?"

He grunted, hardly sure how to relay the magnitude of Odin's request. The sheer temerity of it bordered on hubris. On madness. If he truly believed Baldr's death would cause Ragnarok, and that bringing the man back might avert this war, then Hermod had to try. No matter how Mist-mad it seemed. How perilous to his very soul.

"Odin ..." He shook his head and grunted again. To give voice to the idea was to make it real. "Odin wishes me to ... Oh, fuck me." He sighed.

Syn folded her arms over her chest. "If Odin wishes to fuck you, remind him you are already married."

He grimaced but didn't bother responding to that. He had no mood for levity. "What if it was possible ..." He raised a finger. Pointlessly. A jitter rumbled in his stomach. "What if it was possible to bring someone back?"

"Back from what?"

Just say it. Say her name. And draw her gaze upon him. That was what völvur used to say. Don't name any vaettir, for names held power. To name a thing was to attract its attention. In the years he spent training Hermod, Odin had not precisely contradicted that. Indeed, sometimes he seemed to imply a grain of truth lurked behind the fear.

"Back from the gates of Hel."

Syn's hands dropped to her sides and she took a faltering step toward him. "That's impossible. The only things that come back from death are draugar."

Eh, well. Draugar were ghosts, in truth, still dead, just possessing their own corpses. At least, that was how Hermod understood such things now. Much the same as vampires, in fact.

"Suppose someone could be given a body and returned to the Mortal Realm? Actually living."

"Y-you mean Sif?"

Hermod gripped his wife's arms tight. Odin wanted Baldr back. But if that was even possible, then so too should it be to recover Sif. Hermod had to believe that.

"Odin wants his son returned to him," he said, his voice barely a whisper.

"Well, I want my daughter!"

Hermod nodded. "Before now, I never imagined ... never thought anyone could do this. But Odin believes I can. So I have to try. If ... If I don't return ..."

Syn traced a palm along his cheek. She didn't speak, but her eyes said enough. Promised that her heart went with him. Begged him to return. Said ... all their hopes lay in his hands.

Hermod kissed her, and pressed his forehead against hers. "I don't know how long it will take. Maybe a long time."

"I'll be waiting."

A hollow terror writhed in his gut. More profound than even what he'd felt in deciding to go after Odin in Svartalfheim. Overwhelming dread.

And if he did not start on the path, he feared he'd never have the courage to do so.

ODIN HIMSELF BROUGHT Sleipnir to Hermod, on the bridge before Yggdrasil, below the city of Asgard. Sparkling towers and gilded roofs stared at him. A final beacon of light before he descended into shadow.

The king grasped his forearm in his own, tight, and offered him a nod of encouragement. "You alone can do this. I know you can."

"You've seen the future?"

Odin grimaced. "I dare not look."

Which was to say, Odin didn't know that Hermod would

succeed. He didn't know even if he would live out the day, much less make it to Niflheim and back alive.

Behind Sleipnir's saddle, the king had stocked extra furs and numerous torches. Plenty to stay warm—in mortal cold. Would aught ever prove enough to hold back the icy bite of Niflheim?

"I've placed a kingdom's worth of gold, silver, and jewels in the saddlebags, and plenty of dried food. Eat naught you find beyond this Realm, son."

The look on Odin's face had Hermod's stomach lurching in a jumble of emotions. He, more than most, understood some fragment of the burdens Odin had taken upon himself. And if Hermod had possessed the ability, he'd have lightened those burdens far more than he had. Odin had chosen Hermod, even over his own true sons, as a protégé and apprentice. But Hermod had never done enough, not to avert Ragnarok, not to help Odin save Midgard.

Maybe this ride was the only way he could ever make up for that failure.

The old man drew him into an embrace and patted him on the back. "I'll keep you no longer, my friend. Ride swift and stay safe."

Hermod suspected his destination precluded the latter, but he nodded, and swung a leg up over Sleipnir's back, then patted the horse's mane, grateful for any companion on such a sojourn.

It was almost dark. Twilight would make the passing easier. While Hermod would seldom have concerned himself with it, trying to pull a horse—even one of Otherworldly heritage—across the Veil would add a complication to his passage. Better to wait out these last few moments, watching the sunset.

Indeed, who knew if he'd ever see the sun again?

HE WAS ALONE on the bridge when the sun had finally dipped below the horizon. Odin had left him to his thoughts, and Syn had retreated inside Yggdrasil, perhaps not even wanting to see him leave this world. Most people couldn't handle the idea.

With a long sigh, Hermod nuzzled Sleipnir behind his ears. "I suppose we've delayed long enough, yes?"

The eight-legged horse neighed fiercely.

Hermod supposed it was as much answer as he was like to get.

Kicking Sleipnir into motion back toward the city, Hermod allowed himself to push sideways, through the Veil and into the Penumbra. All warmth bled from the World around him, colors muted into shades of black and blue, and shadows came alive, dancing at his periphery. The buildings remained ahead of him, finely wrought halls and columns carved with facades, but the pale half-light of the Penumbra seemed to infuse them with a sense of decay, and, at the same time, to give the carved faces a hint of malevolence that belied their inanimate nature.

Sleipnir neighed in disquiet, shaking his head so furiously Hermod feared the horse might try to buck him free.

"Easy ..." He stroked the horse's neck. "Easy."

Ghosts were always fewer in Asgard, but here and there, shades flitted about, some drawn to him now that he had entered their Realm. Most did not dare approach as he rode forward, though a few trailed him, bemoaning their urd in senseless whispers that seemed to carry on a non-existent wind.

The hairs on the back of Hermod's neck stood on end, and a chill had him shuddering. This place was always cool, and not even the apples of Yggdrasil offered much protection against it. It was the chill of the grave.

He rode forward further, seeking for a deepening of the shadows that might present ingress into the Roil. Despite his many treks through the Penumbra, he'd never really found a way to wrap his mind around the geometry of the Astral Realm. It was a place of shadow, divided into at least two layers—the Penumbra and the Astral Roil. The Penumbra was a dark mirror of the Mortal Realm, that much was obvious, while the Roil was a nebulous domain of seething darkness that seemed to exist between the Mortal Realm and the Spirit Realm.

Exactly *how* the two Astral domains related, he couldn't say, except that moving from the Penumbra to the Roil seemed akin to how he thought of entering the Penumbra itself. More a step sideways than up or down. Hermod doubted even Odin understood much more than that.

Sheer force of will allowed Hermod to cross the Veil and move between the Mortal Realm and the Penumbra. But the Roil ... well, for that, he needed a liminal space. And those spaces always seemed like a darkness within the darkness.

The city had grown to such an extent that some halls seemed practically built atop one another, with small alleys running between them. Finding one such alley that seemed to repulse him—the moans of the restless dead grown deeper, the darkness more oppressive—he turned Sleipnir toward it.

The horse balked, pulling away.

"I rather mislike it, myself," Hermod admitted. "But Odin has commanded us to travel to far darker places than that."

Again, Sleipnir jerked his head to the side, trying to take Hermod down another path.

Hermod sighed. "I have no choice, and I know you can understand that. If you will not accompany me, I'll return you to the Mortal Realm and press on myself." Not a choice he relished. The horse's presence, even if he could not speak, at least served to mitigate the pervasive loneliness that filled this Realm.

Another snort, then Sleipnir finally turned down the alley.

Hermod's breath frosted the air, though even that lacked color—as if he breathed out faint smoke.

Sleipnir's hoofbeats clapped on the hard-packed dirt of the alley. Slow, almost timid. Hermod swore he could feel the horse's heartbeat pounding through his legs. Never could he recall Sleipnir showing such trepidation. Odin had ridden Sleipnir against an army of trolls and the horse had not faltered. But this ... this the animal clearly misliked.

Nor could Hermod blame him.

All the hair on his arms stood on end. His stomach lurched and his ears popped, the deeper he rode into the alley. Reflexively, one hand went to Dainsleif's hilt over his shoulder. Yes, they had drawn nigh to the liminal spaces that bounded the layers of the Astral Realm together.

Dust began to swirl at the bases of the surrounding buildings. It gathered beneath Sleipnir's hoofs. It twisted, melding with shadows to give the illusion of a column of billowing black smoke that rose up in a choking cloud like the sandstorms of Serkland.

Sleipnir snorted frantically, trying to back up, his head snapping up and nigh catching Hermod in the face. Hermod squeezed his legs, guiding the horse forward, into the darkness.

It rose up around him, obstructing his view. It felt like a physical substance—lighter than water—yet still washing over his skin, cloying and oppressive as it seeped in through his eyes and ears and nose.

They passed into a twisted landscape that no longer resembled the city they had left behind, but rather seemed carved from stone that had warped back on itself at impossible angles, like some nightmarish reef beneath the sea. A profound sense of having stepped into an alien landscape settled on him, as it always did when he began to enter the nebulous Roil. He could not even say for certain that the ground itself did *not* move—he suspected it did, though he'd never dared to linger long enough to be certain.

The billowing smoke had not dissipated, but rather formed up ahead of him, a column of it that dwarfed the obscene stone formations, rising to ten times his height. Atop it, a purplish light crackled within the smoke cloud, like a hundred eyes all gazing down at him. Was it ... alive?

"Fuck me," Hermod mumbled, jerking Sleipnir aside from the cloud.

Indeed, a tendril of it almost looked like ... an arm. Ending in a clawed hand bigger than he was.

Hermod kicked Sleipnir into a trot, the fastest he could manage given the rocky outcroppings that jutted up at so many perverse angles. The horse's fear became an almost palpable thing. Or perhaps Sleipnir sensed Hermod's own dread. The horse darted between rough-edged stone coral, not half so agile as a man, and unable to bring the whole of his speed to bear in this place.

"Shit." Hermod glanced over his shoulder.

That enormous smoke *thing* watched him. Seemed to watch him—hard to say where it looked when its whole head seemed a mass of eyes. But it spread its clawed hands wide, almost as if welcoming him into this nightmare.

Sleipnir broke free from the reef, into an expanse of

rolling, obsidian hills that stretched out into the distance. Without prodding, the horse broke into a wild gallop.

"Wait, wait!" Hermod shouted, but Sleipnir kept running, so fast that the wind of his passage tugged on Hermod and threatened to yank him from the saddle. All he could do was lean forward and hold on.

Somewhere, a bridge should span the space between the outer edge of the Penumbra and the true Roil. An entity called Heimdall watched that bridge, but he'd never barred Hermod's passage, and by taking the bridge, he might have hoped to orient himself. After all, he didn't actually know how to reach Niflheim, though he'd heard it lay beyond the nether river Gjöll.

None of that mattered, as Sleipnir ran and ran, his hoofs clattering upon the obsidian ground. They drew nigh to a river—which one?—but Sleipnir just kept charging forward, riding over the water as if it were solid ground.

Hermod's gut lurched at it.

Yes, he'd known the horse could do that.

Didn't change the profound unease that seized him on riding atop a liquid surface. He clung on all the more tightly, as vertigo took hold of him. More than aught else, he wanted to close his eyes. He dared not, though.

Only when the horse's hoofs again clacked on a rocky surface could Hermod even allow himself a full breath. A gasping pant. "Whoa, whoa, easy!"

At last, the horse slowed to a walk, allowing Hermod to gather his bearings.

This side of the river, the landscape looked more like a cracked, dusty wasteland, empty save for rocks, some of which ... were flying? Yes, a few pebbles and some larger rocks hovered ever so slightly off the ground, driving about the dust clouds.

"Ugh." What madness had created this Realm? Was it, as Odin had once mused, possibly formed *literally* from the nightmares of the living and the dead?

A cloud of dust and shadow melted up before him once again, taking on the head and torso of a man—and man-sized this time—while its legs remained half-formed and fluid, merging in and out of the darkness around him.

Hermod jerked Dainsleif free and pointed it at the entity. A wraith? Those fell shades were drawn to the darkness of the Roil, seeking dead souls to devour. "Stay back."

He could not say with utter certainty that the apparition was a wraith—or any other form of ghost—but it hissed at him, a sound that made him want to run and hide like a damn craven.

Rather than allow the sensation to grow, Hermod urged Sleipnir forward. "Back!"

The entity spoke, the words hateful, and alien, bombarding his mind and leaving him even more disquieted. A few, though, he recognized, or thought he did.

"I do not speak Supernal."

And why would a ghost use the language of spirits? Because it was timeless, eternal?

The apparition melted away, only to reappear closer. Sleipnir jerked against his reins in terror and Hermod brandished Dainsleif.

How the fuck had it done that? Ghosts that could manifest visibly in the Mortal Realm could achieve that by moving quickly through the Penumbra, as he did. Within the Penumbra, perhaps some shades could achieve that sort of thing by crossing into the Roil and back. But—so far as Hermod knew—he was already *in* the Roil. Where had it gone?

The entity breathed out a long, discordant breath and

Hermod barely managed to stay his hand. He had no idea what it was or how powerful. Dainsleif could kill it, he suspected, but if he could avoid being drawn into battle with the thing, he would prefer to do so.

"Mortal ..."

Now he faltered, allowing Sleipnir to fall back a step. "You can speak Northern?"

"Mortal ..."

In the sense he had come from the Mortal Realm, yes. Hermod had not come to debate semantics with a ghost. "What do you want? I've no time to fret over the last wishes of the restless."

"Passage ..."

Passage? Oh. It wanted to ride him back to the Mortal Realm. It wanted him to allow it into his body. "No."

"What do you seek ... in dark lands? Do you know how to find it ... in the shadows?"

Hermod glowered at the dusty ghost. No. He didn't know where he was, and even if he did, he did not easily know the way to cross into Niflheim. Nor after that how to find Hel's abode within the World of Mist.

It was a significant issue, in fact, and one he'd fretted over on his way to meet Syn. There had to be a way, for he'd found a way to Svartalfheim. But he'd paid a ferryman for it ... with pieces of his very soul.

"I seek the gates of Hel," he finally said.

"Oh ... I know them well ..."

"Because you are damned."

"We are all damned ... You cannot reach the gates alone ..."

Hermod grimaced at the shifting apparition before him. Its very nature seemed as fluid and alien as the landscape that surrounded him.

Never trust vaettir. They lie. All the time. About everything. Odin had warned him, over and over. And yet ... yet the king himself relied—at times—upon the two vaettir he had bound to him.

Hermod wasn't a sorcerer. But he did know that, much as vaettir lied, they could not easily break a pact.

Stifling a tremor, he dismounted, and sheathed Dainsleif, instead drawing a dagger. "Your oath that you will guide me to the gates of Hel and will not, under any circumstances, attempt to possess my body or feed upon my soul."

The ghost's answering hiss sounded annoyed.

"In exchange," Hermod said, "so long as you remain true, I'll grant you the chance to return to the Mortal Realm."

He'd be unleashing a dead thing upon the world of the living. But then, the World was already in turmoil. There was always a price. Odin had told him that, too.

He slid the dagger along his palm, then squeezed out several drops of blood. "My oath." Flipping the blade around, he offered it to the ghost. "Now yours."

The creature reached out, a hand of shadow brushing over Hermod's fingers with a graven chill. Despite feeling less than whole, the ghost had substance enough to grasp the blade, and it drew it along its own hand. Rather than liquid blood, motes of dust flitted up and drifted along in the air before vanishing into oblivion.

"I swear to abide by your terms ..."

Did that seal an oath? Unfortunately, Hermod would never know enough about this place to be certain. Nor did he much wish to learn more.

The ghost returned the blade, and Hermod sheathed it, then the creature held out a waiting hand. Waiting for him to take it.

Damn.

He could not stop the tremor in his hand as he reached for the ghost's grasp. His fingers brushed so close, he could feel the creature's chill without even touching it.

This was a mistake.

Never trust a vaettr.

Never.

Hermod's hand closed around the apparition's wrist.

"The pact is made ..."

At once, the ghost yanked him forward, while flowing toward Hermod itself. Dust and shadow rushed over him, flowing into his mouth, eyes, nose, and ears. The cloud of it choked him. He tried to cough, but coarse shadows continued to scrape down his throat.

So cold!

Wracked with convulsions, he stumbled to his knees, hands at his own throat. In utter panic, Hermod clawed at the edges of his mouth, trying to pull the creature back out, to stop it from diving inside of him. It was like trying to hold a sandstorm. It brushed roughly over his fingers.

Sleipnir began backing away.

The last of the ghost flooded into Hermod. He sucked down a painful breath then broke into a fit of agonizing coughing. It felt like his lungs were aflame. Like his throat had been shredded from the inside out. Then frozen solid.

Sleipnir continued to edge backward.

"Wait," Hermod rasped.

And then another convulsion wracked him. An awful, unspeakable pain, as if something wormed its way through his insides, crawling along his spine, burrowing up into his brain, and squirming around behind his eyes.

In horror, he tried to scream, but his throat had seized up and refused to obey his command.

What had he done? What had he agreed to? What a fool he'd been!

Yes ... To seek the abode of the damned ...

The hollow voice now sounded within his own head, hateful. A whispering gong in his mind, one he could never hope to ignore.

Hermod pressed his palms against his temples, unable to fight back the pain of this *thing's* presence.

Keuthonymus ...

What? His breaths came in pants, his chest heaving, but slowly, his brought himself under control. He had chosen this. Had chosen to agree to Odin's request, and had agreed to his alliance with this creature.

Keuthonymus ...

Its name?

Yes ... Long I wandered in the dark ... Waiting for one like you ...

Keuthonymus. Rather unwieldy name.

Then use Keuthos ...

Shuddering, Hermod forced himself to his feet. Sleipnir continued to back away. Hermod raised his hands. "Easy."

Finally stopping, the horse allowed him to touch its face.

Hermod blew out a long breath, then mounted up. "All right, Keuthos. Show me the way to Hel."

4

The vargar couldn't have passed beyond the old fortress at the breach that Hrungnir had built. Narfi's advisors had warned him, of course, said that tearing open that fortress and widening the breach might get looked at as an act of war. The way he reckoned it, so would leading an army of jotunnar across Midgard intent to storm the gates of Asgard. Taken that way, Narfi didn't see how it much mattered, him riding a varg across Bjarmaland.

No one dared bar their way, of course. Frost jotunnar had tamed other vargar. Nine of the wolves, in total, rode beside him. The greater part of the army trailed days behind, but they'd made good progress.

Ironic, really. Frigg had given him the means to hold together the fracturing jotunn alliance. Didn't reckon that was her intent, but there it was. It had come to him, in a vision, the way the queen had ordered his brother ripped to pieces. The bastard Thor had done it, and he'd pay for it, too, or Narfi would be damned. Oh, but the real guilt fell on the Queen of Asgard, and it fell hard, like Narfi's axe would fall on her skull.

Some of the jotunnar, they'd be itching for another war. Them what sat around too long got restless as a snow rabbit in mating season. Locking hips or locking weapons won't so different, when it came down to it. All about getting the blood flowing. They wanted to avenge themselves for the loss, some of them, but mostly they just couldn't abide the boredom. The different tribes, they'd been at each other's throats before he called for this march.

Better part of all Jotunheim must lay empty now, what with thousands of jotunnar all converging on Bjarmaland. Oh, some numbers, they set about sieging Gardariki and taking slaves and what not, true enough. But Narfi didn't give a trollshit about conquering petty mortal kings, nor even much about whether Miklagard held sway wherever. That weren't his style, even if he didn't see much point in arguing with the jotunnar who set about it.

No, he'd come for vengeance, plain and pure as fresh snow. For blood. The Queen of Asgard had murdered his brother, and done it vilely at that. Then the king had shown up and had Narfi's father imprisoned.

Maybe Odin could see him coming, maybe he couldn't. Didn't much matter, he reckoned. Either way, Narfi could see it, in his mind, when the messenger would meet him and invite him to sit and talk and so forth. A waste of time, his men would say, but Narfi figured he owed it to those trollfucking Aesir to look 'em dead in the eyes and tell 'em he was coming for their blood.

The varg beneath him was panting heavy now, so he called for a halt, reckoning this must be Aujum. Past here they'd run into Hunaland, and more civilized lands, or so men claimed. 'Course, by *civilized*, they just meant some Men thinking themselves better than others, and the rest having to ask permission just to have a shit.

Probably they'd be meeting a deal more resistance from there, though. Men were touchy about their *civilizations*.

They passed a few groups of Miklagardian soldiers in Bjarmaland, true, but none fool enough to try to take down a band of jotunnar mounted on vargar. Just as well. His quarrel weren't with them.

After rubbing the wolf's head, he slid down, his feet sinking in the snow, then made his way to where the rest of his band were doing the same. Gangr, the eldest, the others always seemed to defer to him, which was half the reason Narfi had brought the old jotunn. That, and he gave good advice, time to time, while still respecting Narfi.

Gangr patted his varg and sent the animal off scrounging for food. "Didn't reckon the Fimbulvinter would've hit so hard already."

Narfi nodded. Old Vafthrudnir, he'd claimed it was coming, the bitter cold what would swallow the summer like the wolves chasing the moon. Since the better part of his forces were frost jotunnar, Narfi reckoned it worked in his favor, even if it was Hel stretching her power in the Mortal Realm. Mother—his real mother, not Sigyn, much as Narfi loved her—she'd said Hel was Father's daughter, which Narfi figured made her his sister. He liked to think she'd called up the Fimbulvinter on account of knowing he'd be needing it to cover the march of his army.

Wishful thinking? Sure, could well be. Still, they were kin, and he'd make an ally of her, if it came to it.

"It's time Asgard fell. I'm thinking of raising a throne there."

Gangr sniffed. "You like to tell the others this is about Asgard's corruption. Maybe about how Brimir fell and they took our legacy from us and the time had come to take it back. We both know that ain't half of it."

"Never denied I wanted vengeance on top of the rest."

"Nah. Not on top of it. You've been holding the peace with Asgard for three hundred winters, while they was getting fatter off the World's praises. Now, though, now they killed your kin, and you'd have us all believe this is war for our rights."

"Can't be both?"

"Sure. Just sayin'. Old Vafthrudnir tells it like our kind had great empires before Brimir, too. But those fell, and Menfolk came to take the World. Over and over, if you can believe that. Great circles of history or whatever. Lots of jotunn empires rose and fell. Strains the mind, it does."

Narfi snorted, his breath frosting the air. "Reckon it's about time we took another turn at it. Few thousand years ought to do for Men. Maybe a few thousand for us, now."

Hyrrokkin stomped her way over to them. She was the real tamer of vargar, the one who got the wolves for his little advance band, and she weren't half inclined to let anyone forget it. The others, especially Gridr and Leikn, they respected her almost as they did Gangr. A shame, really, since she'd never got on over well with Narfi. "What are you arse-faces jabbering about? Sökkmimir caught a pair of Men a few miles back. Plan is to fill our bellies, but he won't let us get a taste without your damn say-so."

Narfi grimaced. All these years, he'd discouraged the eating of Man-flesh. Now though, the rules had changed. They said a jotunn, even a half-jotunn like him, what ate the flesh would always crave after it. Always want more, to get stronger and bigger. 'Course, them what ate enough of it got twisted up like Thrivaldi.

Still, he couldn't well be seen to pass it up now. It would undermine his position, and naught could be allowed to interfere with him avenging Hödr. Shit, Narfi scarcely even liked his brother, but the matter remained, he was dead, and died awful. Some things couldn't be borne. So he followed Hyrrokkin back to where Sökkmimir was poking a stick into the foot of a tied up Man, while the Man's comrade stared and whimpered.

"Gonna eat your toes, one by one," Sökkmimir said.

"Well, I claim his stones," Baugi said. Everyone paused to look at him. "What? You eat enough Man-stones and you might grow another cock. You ain't heard that?"

"What the fuck you need with another cock?" Leikn asked. "You don't hardly know how to use the one."

Suttungr chuckled and punched his brother's shoulder, though Baugi himself frowned.

"Why don't you show me how, Leikn?" the offended jotunn said. "I hear one grew up between your tits for you to suck on when night goes on too long."

Narfi snorted, and settled down beside the captives. Shit, but he didn't much want to do this. Truth be told, though, it was for the best. Eat them, he'd absorb their Pneuma and get all the stronger. He reckoned he'd want all the strength possible when it came time to fight Thor or Odin or the rest of that family of giant arse-birds.

Thor might've had a head the size of the Midgard Wall and the brains of a dead mushroom, but Narfi reckoned no Man had killed more jotunnar in all the scope of the World.

So he pulled out his axe and grabbed one of the Men by a finger. Immediately, the prisoner set to screaming. "Relax," Narfi said. "I ain't gonna eat it while it's still attached. Not that savage."

"Well, I am," Hyrrokkin said.

"Shit, yeah," Baugi said. "Don't know if eating the stones would work if I cut them off first."

The man whimpered, a stain began to yellow the snow between his legs.

"Ugh," Baugi said. "That's offensive."

Narfi sighed. Poor unlucky bastards. Well, he could spare them a little of this, then. He leaned in and swung his axe, planting it cleanly between the Man's eyes, crunching bone and splattering his face with blood.

The Man's companion set into a fresh bout of screams.

With a grunt, Narfi jerked the axe free, then lopped off the hand he still held. First time was the worst, he'd heard it said. Bleh. "Kill the other bastard, would you? No need to make him suffer."

"I like the suffering," Hyrrokkin complained. "Seasons the flavor."

"Fucking kill him!" Narfi ordered. Wouldn't do to push his authority too far, no, but there was a time to make sure everyone knew he still commanded the jotunn alliance. Maybe he could make another Brimir, maybe not. But whatever he made, it would be *his*.

Grumbling, Sökkmimir slit the remaining Man's throat.

Satisfied, Narfi carried the severed hand away from the others a bit and settled down. He was still staring at the macabre thing when Gunnlöd made her way to his side and settled down. The last and youngest of their band, she was Suttungr's daughter and Baugi's niece. Course, Narfi mostly just wanted her around because she was keen to spread her legs for him every night.

"Best just be about it." Actually, she was holding a severed femur, dripping with blood and flesh.

Narfi blew out a breath. "Sure this is really what jotunnar are meant for? Eating Men and killing and so forth?"

She shrugged. "Meant by who, exactly? Them Norns?

43

Why should we care what they want, anyway? Don't much care about Vafthrudnir's wild musings on urd, myself. Eating flesh gives us power. Ain't naught more to it than that."

The woman had eyes like a cave lion. She didn't used to, did she? He could have sworn they were less feline when he'd first met her, a few decades ago.

Well, but they let her see better, she claimed.

And he *did* need power. The Aesir, they had that. And he aimed to see them all rotting before the gates of Hel. Let his sister deal with the bastards, and the World might even thank him. Well ... maybe not the Men he ate, nor their kin.

Some things, though, just had to be done.

With a grimace, he stuck a finger in his mouth and bit down.

5

*T*hose stupid, trollfucking, arse-licking jotunnar!

Thor's mother sighed. "You'll wear a track in the floor with all that pacing."

Grumbling, Thor cast his mother a glare, not pausing in his stride. Let him wear a fucking hole, then. Dig a pit with his feet. Then throw the fucking jotunnar inside and stomp on them. "He's invited *them*."

Mother leaned forward on her throne. "Why do you think that is?"

"I don't want to think!" He *wanted* to smash some jotunn skulls, and he'd scarce been allowed to do that for centuries. Just the ones who passed across the Midgard Wall without permission.

And Father had now given them *all* fucking permission!

Oh, Hel. Spots began swimming before his eyes. Already the headaches were coming. Jotunn-sized headaches, in fact. Coincidence? Thor didn't fucking think so.

"Need to pummel something," he grumbled.

"Thor—"

Whatever Mother would've said got caught off when

Father entered the great hall, walking stick clanking off the stones. The old man ought to use the apple's Megin all the damn time and save himself the pain. When he wanted, he could move like a northern breeze—Thor'd seen it plenty of times. But Father, he just trudged along like an aged mortal, knees creaking so bad they seemed apt to just pop right off. How an Ás immortal got so old, Thor didn't know. When he'd asked, Father had just gone into some unmanly nonsense about the Art.

Hel, it was bad enough that his mother had to go meddling with that Otherworldly business. But his father doing it ... anyone but the king would get ... uh ... what was that damn word? Exiled! Exiled for that sort of thing.

Father nodded at Mother, and she returned the gesture. Barely. Not that Thor could blame her. The old man didn't even bother to hide that he'd taken that Vanr bitch as a lover. These days, he all but treated Freyja like *she* was the queen.

Thor'd had more than a few words with Father about that, too. The old man listened to no one, though. Not since he'd imprisoned Loki. Probably should have killed him, for that matter.

"Well?" Thor demanded. Father cocked his head as if to ask what Thor was on about. "Oh, don't give me that troll-shit. You know what I'm going to say before I even think it, don't you? Hel, you knew what was going to happen here before I got out of bed. So why don't you just out with it and tell me what I want to know?"

Father pursed his lips in a tight smile, looking even older than normal for a moment. Weary as if he hadn't slept in a century. And had taken a beating as oft as he took a shit.

"What?" Thor spread his hands. "Vanr woman keeping you up all night?"

"*Thor*," Mother said. Oh, damn it. Mother could make her tone as hard as a dverg's arse when she wanted.

Father cleared his throat. "Speak plainly, boy. I've no time for games."

Thor folded his arms. Fine. Sure. "We lost a lot of lives beating down the jotunnar. Breaking first Thrym, then Narfi, then Skadi, and a bunch of other trollfuckers whose names I wouldn't trade a steaming pile of shit to know. Dead Aesir, dead mortals. So we let Narfi keep them under control all this time." Thor shrugged. Had to show them he didn't care so much about that. "Whatever. But now, you've gone and let them back into Midgard and invited them over for the night meal. Maybe we ought to build some fucking houses for them? Let them drink all the mead. Ask them if they'd like to borrow our women? Maybe offer them massages?"

Now Father just looked at him, almost expressionless. Or if he had an expression, Thor figured it said something like, 'shut up, you imbecile.' Bastard could say a lot with one damn eye. Finally, the man sighed. "Thor, it might be too late to stop Ragnarok. I can't say that for certain. But if the battle comes and the jotunnar are not on our side, they're like to fight against us."

That sounded fine to Thor. He liked cracking jotunn skulls. Especially the Man-eating ones. They had big, thick skulls that were so satisfying to crunch. "I'd kill them."

Father stared hard at him. "We need every ally we can arrange. Like it or not, we share the Mortal Realm with the jotunnar. The Vanir tried to divide the Earth between Midgard and Utgard, and I am no longer convinced they made the right choice."

Oh, what the fuck was this? "Are you seriously suggesting the whole Midgard Wall was a bad idea? What, like we should just let the jotunnar tromp around wherever they damn well please, never mind if they want to eat a farmer here or there? Hel, instead of hanging criminals, why not just—"

"Do *not* mention her name. As for the rest, do you have any control over the words coming out of your mouth, boy?"

Thor grimaced. Of course he did. He didn't say a fucking thing without meaning to. Most of the time.

Some of the time.

"What do you want from me?" Thor demanded.

"I want you to try to be a little more like your brother," Father snapped.

"What?" Thor asked. "Dead?"

Mother flinched at that, and Father's face grew darker than ever. Thor threw up his hands and stormed out of the throne room. Old man didn't listen to anyone! Thor didn't even know why he bothered trying to talk to him. No, he'd sent Tyr to go welcome in the jotunnar. Next thing any of them knew, some frost jotunn's teeth would be lodged onto Thor's arse. He didn't need any of that ... what was the word? Prescience. Didn't need prescience to know this would end about as well as throwing a feast in the middle of Muspelheim.

Beyond the great hall, Thor came within a hair of blundering into a slave carrying a decanter of something. Thor snatched the pitcher from the slave and shoved him aside, taking a long swig.

Ugh. Wine.

Wine was for people who didn't know how to make mead or ale. Growling, Thor flung the half-full decanter at the wall. It shattered gloriously, and the slave flinched, arms half covering his head like he expected Thor to take a swing at him.

Which made Thor snort. As if hiding behind his arms would have done the man a damn bit of good had Thor intended him harm.

Well, maybe he had to stay positive about all this. Thanks to Father, Thor would no doubt get the chance a crack a bunch more skulls. Maybe all the skulls in Jotunheim.

6

_____

For days, Hermod had ridden in the tumultuous shadow lands of the Astral Roil. He'd dared not sleep, though he'd dozed in the saddle, trusting to Sleipnir to stay alert. Other times, he'd dismounted and allowed Sleipnir to rest.

Much of the Roil seemed composed of frozen waves of obsidian. Or half-frozen, given that they moved, albeit in slow gyrations. Other places, though, the land fell away into an expanse of stormy starlight, as if Hermod rode along a coastline.

Apt ...

Keuthos's voice in his head had him cringing. The wraith—he felt fair certain Keuthos was a wraith—did not speak oft, and when it did, the suddenness of it gave him a horrific start.

He followed the coastline—a precipice, really—gazing out at the storm clouds that swirled below, crackling with purple lightning. Out there, in the gaping void, islands of jagged rock floated, held aloft by forces Hermod could not comprehend. Amongst some, eruptions of fire scorched the sky for brief instants. From others issued icy mists like those that drowned the Mortal Realm.

"What is this madness?" he finally asked.

The Roil draws its name from its shifting nature ... Here, the World shapes and unshapes in patterns the mortal mind cannot fathom ... Here, we brush the edge of even the Roil ... into the dark beyond ...

"What's beyond?"

Hermod felt his gaze craned, almost against his will, to the side where, among other clouds and a shifting swirl of cold colors, there gleamed too bright stars. Crystal spheres that represented the Spirit Worlds, larger, and brighter than they usually seemed.

Sleipnir must have sensed his distress, for the horse slowed his pace.

"We're nigh to the edge of the Spirit Realm."

Yes ... Or, were you to pass the great shifting chaos and weather the cosmic storms ... you might delve yet deeper into the Astral Realm ...

He was almost afraid to ask what he'd find.

Oblivion ...

Of course, the wraith seemed able to hear his thoughts.

Not wanting to linger, Hermod urged Sleipnir forward.

He'd lost any sense of time, as always happened if he spent too long in the Astral Realm. Nor could he guess how much time had passed in the Mortal Realm. Less than had here, yes, but how much?

The shadows, the darkness, and the clouds did not allow him to see but so far ahead. Yet, it looked like ... in the distance ... an obelisk?

A watchtower ...

Hermod swallowed, unable to quite wrap his mind around that. Someone had *built* something here, in this place of seething chaos? How could anyone find materials with which to build? How could they hold back the writhing of the land itself in order to stabilize a foundation?

Was it built ...?

What would the alternative be? That ... that the tower had always existed here on the Roil's edge? That seemed madness. Structures were created by sentient minds, not nature itself.

Where, precisely, do you behold nature ... as you mean it ... in this Realm?

Huh. Well, perhaps Keuthos had a point. Naught about the Astral Realm seemed natural.

As THEY RODE CLOSER, the tower grew larger. So tall, in fact, that its upper reaches disappeared into the churning storm clouds above, preventing Hermod from even harboring a guess as to its height.

Hundreds of feet, without a doubt. A wider baser tapered along a slow arc to the narrower central spire. Though cut from stone, the watchtower showed no indication of separate blocks, as if it had been hewed out of a single mountain. The stone itself did not resemble any he knew from Midgard, though perhaps if he drew closer he could—

You do not wish to draw close ...

Eh. Well, perhaps not. "What lives inside?"

"Watchers."

He scoffed at that. So watchers dwelt in watchtowers. It seemed Keuthos actually had a sense of humor.

He'd expected a response, but the wraith said naught else.

Thunder and lightning rumbled and flashed among the upper spire, while mist seemed to seep out of openings around the base, concealing any entrance that may have existed. And yes, it terrified him, but still, he could not deny the curiosity that pulled him to this place.

Even so, Hermod guided Sleipnir wide around the edge of the tower, trusting that if even a wraith feared what lay within, he ought to avoid it entirely. He had not come here to explore the maddening depths of this Realm.

And they were maddening, threatening ever to consume his mind.

The landscape nearby seemed desolate, inhabited by only the rarest of shades, ones which seemed to wander in torment, more shadow than man. These entities, too, Hermod gave a wide berth.

Experience had shown that worse things than ghosts dwelt out here. His experience with the living bog-thing still haunted his dreams. But since he could not guess where such an entity might dwell—and could only hope Keuthos would guide him around them—the best he could do was avoid running afoul of other shades.

Still, the loneliness of this desolation had him.

Maybe it was just the isolation, or his fatigue, but he almost felt like he was losing bits and pieces of himself the longer he dwelt here. Was it the Lethe, or was that merely his fear? It would steal his memories, he knew. This place fed on them.

Yes ...

How strange, that his solitude should feel so complete that even the hateful, hollow voice of a wraith was almost a comfort.

It eats you ... The further you travel from the Realms of Men ... the closer you get ...

"To what?"

Truth ... We are all damned ... Even the one you seek ...

Hel?

Yes ... Even she is prey to the fell gyrations of Fate ... She is the periphery of terror, that eclipses your view of the greater expanse ...

Hermod shuddered, hardly knowing how to respond. Of course Hel was damned. She ruled the damned. But if Keuthos meant more than that, he was not certain he truly wished to even know.

Wise ...

What was worse? To dwell forever in ignorance and yet find some measure of peace, or to begin to uncover the secrets of the World, even if they were terrifying and would forever haunt his dreams? Perhaps every sorcerer struggled with that question, until finally they tipped over the precipice and lost themselves in the darkness that consumed minds and souls. Odin had said something to that effect, long ago, though Hermod could not remember the specifics of the conversation.

Indeed, so many conversations now seemed muddied, their flavors diluted, their words swallowed by ennui.

If such unfathomable horrors surrounded the Realm of Men, how had Mankind ever arisen in the first place? How had they survived?

If Keuthos had an answer, the wraith did not offer it.

EXHAUSTION FINALLY FORCED Hermod to dismount and allow both the horse and himself a proper rest, even if for only a few hours. How many more days had passed now? A total of seven, he thought, though he was starting to lose track.

Settling down onto dusty ground, back against a boulder, he riffled through a saddlebag until he found an apple Odin had packed for him. While the apples of Yggdrasil were precious beyond measure, the Aesir prized even the ordinary apples they could grow in the few orchards of Asgard. Some common folk were lucky if they could taste a few such apples a year.

Odin had packed three for Hermod, and this was the last of them, so he supposed he had better savor it. He bit down, letting the juices soothe his dry mouth and aching throat.

Even the pleasure of eating was dimmed by the effect of the Astral Realm, as if everything vibrant, even flavors, could not survive the graven chill that so pervaded this existence. Still, a sweet apple—even one with diminished taste—was a blessing after at least a day without food.

Finding Niflheim was proving even more difficult than reaching Svartalfheim had. Perhaps he should have sought a nether river and found a ferryman or ferrywoman to carry him to the World of Mist.

Hold on to your soul ... if you can ... naught is more precious ...

Hermod swallowed his bite. Was that what happened to Keuthos? He had lost too much of his soul?

The Art ...

The Art? "You were a sorcerer?"

The wraith did not answer further. But what he *had* said ... did he imply that the Art had done this to him? Or ... that it did this to all sorcerers? Was practicing sorcery enough to damn one to this lifeless existence for eternity?

If so, did Odin know it? Hermod's mentor avoided the Art when he could, but he had certainly cast his share of spells using it.

Hermod blew out a long breath before taking another bite.

Somehow, the apple had lost even more of its taste.

THE PATH before Hermod stretched twenty feet wide and spread out over an endless, rumbling void beyond which lay some reality—or lack thereof—he did not truly wish to contemplate. Nor did he much wish to dwell on the road itself beneath Sleipnir's hooves, which looked rather like a fleshy tendon stretched out over the abyss. The horse's steps didn't clack as they had on the obsidian that composed so much of the Roil, but rather thumped like blows on solid muscle.

The tendon joined with a convoluted mess of others like it, forming a web that spread out at all angles, a maze of horror that set Hermod's gut churning to even give consideration to for more than a moment.

Far below all this, eruptions of fire and cold crashed together and flung up curtains of steam that concealed the depths of … a creature? He seemed to tread upon a living being, but how, he didn't dare imagine. For naught could survive having bits of itself stretched out into such extremes. Indeed, his mind wanted to reject the sight utterly.

Madness in the dark …

Yes. How could a man look onto this cosmic void where life itself seemed unbound by the laws that ought to have governed it, and not thus find his mind broken by the sight? It defied reason—it devoured sense.

So sheltered … your Realm … thinks itself … hidden from the greater World … from darkness eternal …

Keuthos's voice so rarely proved a comfort. Besides,

Hermod had begun to suspect not even the wraith truly knew what lay out here. Rather, the ghost itself was caught in currents of primal horror, writhing in eternal fear, but trying to bury its terror beneath its rage. For the vaettr dwelt on the fringes of this utter insanity and knew instinctively that not even one such as it could survive long by passing this threshold.

As you mean to do ...

Hermod meant but to find the river Gjöll and pass into Niflheim. The World of Mist no doubt held its own terrors, but at least he could dare to hope some semblance of logic must govern its existence.

Hope is a lie ...

So spoke a ghost that—unless Hermod missed his guess —had damned itself to this hateful existence by its use of the Art. Oh, he pitied Keuthos, yes, but he could not forget that the wraith had wrought its own urd.

Perhaps you do not understand ... Fate ...

Perhaps not.

&.

A LONG TIME MORE, Hermod rode on, reaching another twisted, obsidian plain, before he caught the sound of blades clinking together. A battle? Out here?

But no, as he rode closer, beneath the sounds of clinking blades he heard the murmur of a swift river.

Was this it? Did he draw night to Gjöll?

Yes ... We had an accord ...

So Keuthos had truly guided him to the edge of Niflheim. This nether river would form the boundary?

The thought both offered comfort—to think he might

actually reach his goal—and terror at the thought of truly coming before Hel herself.

Sleipnir broke into a swift trot, perhaps as eager as Hermod, or, at least, sensing his desperation. The horse drew up short as they reached the river, though. Water surged past in relentless rapids, and the river stretched so far he could scarcely make out the far side through the darkness, though ... yes. It did look like mist over there. But beneath the water's surface surged thousands upon thousands of frozen blades, clanking together, bouncing apart, and—as the rapids hit—breaking the surface for a heartbeat before crashing back down. A cacophony of death that would tear Sleipnir's hooves to shreds if he tried to ride across this.

The river Gjöll ... Beyond here lies the world of Hel ...

So at long last, after nine days of riding, he had reached the boundary of Niflheim.

"How do we cross this madness?"

The bridge ... Golden roofed ... it crosses between Realms ...

"Which way?"

Hermod felt a tug at his arms, pulling Sleipnir along to his right. Taking Keuthos's advice, he guided the horse along the banks of this river of knives, watchful, though he had seen few beings of late. It seemed the deeper he trod into the Roil, the fewer ghosts dared enter these spaces.

A long time more he rode, until at last coming to a covered bridge, its roof thatched with gilded sheets, its peak easily ten times his height. The bridge spanned the river, but within lay a pervasive darkness that seemed almost alive, and, melding with those shadows, a mist that crept halfway across the bridge.

Frost coated the golden roof on the far side, removing any doubt that remained of what lay beyond.

Niflheim.

World of Mist. Domain of Hel and the damned. The world of desolate cold. Odin had speculated that Hel—or Niflheim itself—eventually rounded up most of the dead that wandered the Astral Realm. Few had the strength to evade the dark goddess forever. Thus, wraiths and draugar and perhaps even vampires eventually found themselves drawn to her, though they were not native to her world.

And now Hermod willingly rode into this place of damnation.

Hermod rode up to the bridge's threshold. High windows allowed in tiny beams of light that failed to quite drive back all the shadows lurking at the fringes, and only served to reflect off the mist.

Sleipnir shied away, and Hermod had to force the horse's head back around.

"I'm sorry," he said. "I don't want to go, either. But Odin has ordered us to retrieve Baldr, and we must do so, whatever the cost."

The arrogance of it …

Perhaps.

Hermod squeezed his legs and, finally, the horse began to ease forward. Sleipnir's eight hooves clanked noisily on the wooden boards that made up the bridge's floor.

They will not let you enter … living …

"Who?" Hermod's voice sounded a whisper in his own ears. Even then, it seemed too loud, apt to draw unwanted attention to himself in this haunted place.

The guardians …

Hermod's pulse hammered in his temples. A cold sweat dribbled down the back of his neck. More than aught else, he wanted to turn away, allow Sleipnir to flee. To ride back to the Mortal Realm …

Baldr. Odin swore that Baldr's death heralded the end of the World. And if they could recover Baldr ... and *Sif* ... Hermod had to try.

For a bare heartbeat, he shut his eyes, trying to steady himself. He dared keep them shut for no longer, though. Not even Odin knew what horrors would lurk in his path.

He clenched his fists so tightly around the reins his hands hurt.

"A little more," he whispered to Sleipnir.

She is watching you ...

Who? Hel? Hermod tried to swallow but found himself unable to do so. Whatever else she had become Hel was ... Loki's daughter. She had been just a woman, a mortal woman, before this. And now, she was ... what? A draug? Hermod had fought draugar before. Now, he wasn't going to fight, but rather to bribe her. To negotiate.

He could do this.

So why did the thought of looking upon Loki's daughter leave him half ready to piss his trousers?

Sleipnir's hoofbeats continued to echo off the bridge, loud enough to almost drown out the tumultuous river below.

Ahead, the wind howled too, as if a feral beast, sweeping over misty mountains.

In his youth, Hermod would have prayed to the Vanr gods. It had been a long, long time since he had so missed the comfort of his faith. Now, he had no one to call on.

Maybe there were no true gods. The Vanr were men and women become immortal, as were the Aesir. Hel was a ghost. Maybe ... maybe just the so-called Elder Gods that seemed to rule the Spirit Worlds. Somehow, he doubted they held much interest in his prayers.

As he rode further, the mist grew thicker, swirling

around him, seeming more alive than the foul vapors that permeated Midgard. As if the mists themselves saw him, judged him unworthy and an interloper here. He, a Man not dead, trespassed in Niflheim, the mists seemed to say.

Thicker and thicker, until he could make out no more than a dozen feet ahead of himself, if that. But at last, he reached the terminus of the bridge, and found himself stepping into a world saturated by mist. It was dark here, almost as dark as the Astral Realm, but, amid mist growing ever thicker, he saw shadows of trees. Twisted, misshapen silhouettes, barely visible through the vapors. The trees had only hints of leaves, and all were bent in unnatural angles, as if writhing in agony.

Worse still, they lacked ... substance? Bits of them appeared hazy, bleeding off into the mists, unforming and reforming from the corner of his eyes, though he could catch no movement if he looked directly at any given silhouette.

Transitory lands between shadow and cold ...

Keuthos meant this was a liminal place, somewhere between the Roil and the greater expanses of Niflheim.

She's coming ...

Hel?

The guardian ...

Hermod grasped Dainsleif's hilt, but did not draw the runeblade. If he could cross this expanse without a fight, he'd prefer to do so.

The hateful mist had begun to whisper, nonsensical, sibilant sounds that felt like claws digging through his skull.

And there ... in the depths of the mist, the blurry form of a naked girl, passing through the shadows. Disappearing behind a tree, only to reappear from another, like a flickering shade, half-formed.

Perhaps he could get through this place without a fight, but Hermod doubted he'd pass without at least confronting this guard. He eased Sleipnir forward, though the horse tried to back away once more. It knew something truly foul lurked nigh.

As Hermod approached the trees, he realized some of the trees were further warped out of shape by chains that grew out of the bark and stretched down into the frozen ground. Locked within these chains, something squirmed beneath the tree's wood.

A ... face?

Oh, fuck. Hermod couldn't lurch away while in the saddle, but he jerked back. An incomplete human form pushed out from the trunk, for a moment, wriggling beneath the surface.

Bound within ...

A soul. Locked here in eternal torment. Literally chained inside a tree. The joints of several fingers reached out toward him, straining against the bindings, begging him to touch them, to offer the comfort of warmth and life.

Unwise ...

Mercy was unwise? Sympathy?

You do not know ...

Didn't know what would happen if he touched that hand. Would the damned soul within be able to pull Hermod into its prison? Those fingertips gave over and melted back within the tree trunk, vanishing, save for that slight burrowing beneath the surface.

Grimacing, Hermod pushed on, until the hint of the woman he'd seen before passed beside him, silent as death, seen only from the corner of his eye. And much larger than he'd first suspected.

Close to eight feet tall, he'd wager. A jotunn ghost?

Hermod spun on her, but she'd vanished back into the mist once more.

Well, damn it. That was more than enough of this.

Hermod leapt off Sleipnir's back, drawing Dainsleif in the process. He paused only to grab a shield.

Modgud ...

Her name? Was Keuthos telling him her name?

Yes ...

He grimaced. All right then. "Modgud!" he bellowed. "Modgud, come and face me!"

A profound silence settled over this twisted forest. To find a wood with no birds or insects or aught else save those hateful whispers, it left him squirming. Slowly, he turned, seeking the—

The woman stood to his side, not three feet from him, gaping down at him. She was stark naked, her flesh yellowish brown, and she had three pendulous breasts and a mouth that was slightly too wide.

Her half smile exposed misshapen teeth with no sense of alignment. "Who are you, living Man? Why do you dare to cross my bridge?" Her voice was at once sensuous and resounding, leaving his skin crawling.

He opened his mouth, but his throat was so dry he found it hard to form words.

Tell her ...

He swallowed. "I am Hermod Agilazson. I have come seeking the gates of Hel for an audience with Hel herself."

The woman—or creature—snickered, and cocked her head to the side. A hair too far to the side, in fact, for a human neck ought not to have bent so far. She ran a segmented tongue over her upper teeth. "I do not allow the living to enter nor the dead to leave."

63

"And yet, you must allow me to do so. I have come to bargain with the Goddess of Mist."

Offer her something ...

Oh, damn it. He'd brought wealth with which to bribe Hel, not her minions. "I can offer you gems and jewels from across the Mortal Realm."

The creature blinked and, for a bare instant, Hermod would have sworn her pupils had become slitted discs. Yet when he looked again, they seemed normal. "I don't need rocks."

Hermod nodded, slowly. Whatever he gave this Modgud would be one less thing he had to offer Hel, and he didn't even know for certain if the goddess would accept his offerings. If she refused, then what? Was he to give up on Baldr? On Sif?

Or perhaps he ought to simply run Modgud through with Dainsleif. Could this oversized guardian survive a runeblade through her heart?

The ring ...

Draupnir? He'd intended to offer that to Hel, as well. But if it meant surviving this encounter, maybe he had no choice. Grimacing, he lowered his shield to the ground, then slipped Odin's ring from his finger and held it up in his palm so she could inspect it. "Orichalcum."

The creature leaned down to inspect the ring a moment, then plucked it up with her thumb and forefinger. "And thick with souls. Mmmm." She snickered. "Very well. Ride on, north, to the wood's edge where the Hoar Caverns are cut into the glacial wall. Pass through the caverns and beyond the mountain, following the river to its source in the spring of Hvelgemir. Thence flows another river, one that cuts through the Helwind Chasm and leads you to the gates of Hel."

Hermod hardly trusted himself to speak. Or to keep from fainting at the impossibility of her words. He had truly passed into Niflheim, the most feared world in all the World. "Thank you."

How timid he sounded.

Modgud didn't answer, but rather, stepped back into the mist and disappeared once more. All around issued forth the sound of wood cracking, warping. Trees bending into further unnatural shapes at her command.

Much as he misliked parting with Draupnir, Keuthos had given him a way past Modgud.

Yes ... But greater peril lies ahead ... You will not love this land ...

An understatement.

Hermod mounted Sleipnir once more.

Whatever lay ahead, though, he'd face it. He had not come so far to turn back now.

7

*W*alking along the Bilröst seemed surreal, even after having taken it several times before. Saule drifted beside Freyja, with the Sun Knight's retinue trailing behind. The closer they drew to the Mortal Realm, the less substantial the other liosalfar seemed. Despite the bridge's power to allow passage across the Veil, it couldn't allow non-physical beings to retain substance in the Mortal Realm.

Perhaps the Veil itself ensured that remained impossible.

As promised, Odin had arranged numerous hosts on the far side, all bound and kneeling, probably having no idea what awaited them. The sight made Freyja frown. Only the strongest of spirits could claim a totally unwilling host. Most of the time, a host unknowingly invited the spirit in, often as they drew nigh to death and sought for any recourse to avert that end. Even those spirits who could claim a host without a faltering of the subject's will could most oft only do so if they were already across the Veil.

Thanks to the Bilröst, Odin had arranged just that.

Victims, hale, and yet about to lose themselves. Would they see it coming? Oh, they stared at her as she descended the shimmering arc and stepped down before Yggdrasil. When she looked back, though, she could no longer see Saule or those who had sworn to her.

Freyja embraced the Sight to look across the Veil, and, sure enough, there Saule was, treading among the kneeling victims, examining each in turn, even as her people did the same.

She'd want a female, of course. Most spirits preferred hosts of the same gender, and they were easier to claim, according to most sources.

Odin's prisoners comprised a roughly even mix of male and female hosts, a score of them, though Saule had only brought a dozen liosalfar along. Still, more than half her followers were female too, so the majority of the women here were like to lose themselves this day.

Centuries ago, Freyja would have objected. Even as a Vanr, immortal, she'd have stood in outrage at such an affront to humanity, as unwilling subjects were offered up to spirits as vessels. Yes, she had made such sacrifices when working sorcery, and yes, it had bothered her less and less with each passing offering. Now, though ... now she found it hard to even hold on to the feelings of indignation she knew she ought to have felt. She could remember the sensation, but she couldn't quite pull herself out of the apathy that had her transfixed.

Even as Eguzki selected a girl Saule had passed up, one probably with no more than sixteen winters behind her. Eguzki placed her hands upon the girl's head and her victim shuddered. She wouldn't feel the touch as a touch, so much as a chill, a profound sense of wrongness brushing against her. Eguzki leaned in and kissed the girl, deeply, and the host stiffened, moaning in distress.

The liosalfar's form turned to light and melted into the girl, who began thrashing, her moans became frantic, wordless cries of terror, like a victim caught in a nightmare, desperate to scream but unable to get it all the way out.

Freyja stood, hands on her hips, watching, even as others began to undergo the same convulsions, overcome with fear and discomfort as alien presences entered their bodies, beat down their consciousnesses, and feasted on the fringes of their souls. Why could she not look away? Why could she not still feel revulsion at this spectacle of mass possession that ought to have terrified the most jaded of mortal criminals?

The answer, of course, was obvious. She'd lost that part of herself, through her sorceries as a mortal, and through her transformation into a liosalf. Maybe one day, she'd even lose the ability to take on corporeal form as she did now. Maybe her only remaining recourse would lie in taking a host, just this way. Damn, how badly she wished that could horrify her.

Instead, she watched, impassive, as Malakbel forced himself inside a scarred warrior. As Malina selected a woman with a single streak of gray in her hair and lines around her eyes. As Saule herself took a sandy-haired shieldmaiden and drove her into convulsions as she struggled in vain against a foe she could not see or touch or ever hope to overcome.

Face dark, Odin moved to Freyja's side, continuing to watch the spectacle himself. Her lover hardly seemed moved to pity over it, and yet, he did not seem well pleased to witness such a thing either. Driven, not by the self-absorbed lack of empathy of spirits, but rather by the perhaps even more merciless whims of necessity? He had bemoaned the Web of Urd many times to her, steadfastly refusing to look into the future in the vague hope that might somehow allow him to avert it.

She had pointed out—and he had acknowledged it as if he'd known all along—the flaw in that logic lay in the assumption that the Web did not already account for his choosing not to use the Sight at the present juncture. That, just because he did not look at the future, did not mean it did not exist in a fixed progression.

"How to win a game when the rules demand you lose?" he mumbled, as if reading her mind. Or, perhaps, simply caught in the question that never seemed to offer him any respite. It drove him to the brink of madness, whether waking or sleeping. It tormented him, the thought that all he'd become and done and would do had been decided by urd.

He had said, once, that he'd long accepted a certain inevitability within the visions. But in coming to the realization that such a set course had come from the Norns, from figures who themselves had written their Web of Urd, it had vexed him beyond endurance.

Or rather, Freyja feared, it had broken him, something that neither a millennium in the Tower of the Eye nor all his sacrifices and losses had managed to achieve. Odin teetered on the edge of utter despondency, such that Freyja feared to add to his burdens by pushing the issue. His mission carried him forward with a desperation and momentum that, alone, kept him from toppling to the ground.

"I don't have a good answer to that," she finally said.

"Hmm. I do. Find a way to break the rules."

Oh, but if the rules themselves accounted even for such an attempt? To think of it made her want to despair, so she dared not give voice to it. The Web of Urd had them all. But Odin seemed to believe that, given an audacious enough play, he might yet sever the strands that bound him.

And that, at least, allowed Freyja to move beyond the profound apathy that settled upon her when she tried to feel for these victims.

When it was done, Odin had the possessed hosts freed from their bindings, while the others were led away.

He laid a hand upon Freyja's shoulder. "I've a few things to see to. Your brother awaits you in Sessrumnir. We'll have to leave for the feast soon, though. Before the day is out."

Well then, she supposed she'd have to call upon Frey.

SESSRUMNIR WAS the only part of Vanaheim Freyja yet recognized. Oh, she could look and imagine where old halls had stood, where the brilliant forests had flowered. But the old halls had been replaced with new ones, and spires she didn't know, while forests had been cut back only to grow in new directions.

Everything had become like a dream, faded, different, and yet, still drawn from the same canvas. But Sessrumnir, oh, that at least she knew. They'd told her that a woman named Sigyn had kept the library in her absence, though they'd done away with the aspect of Sessrumnir as a school for the Art.

She could not decide whether that decision represented wisdom or willful ignorance. Pretending the Art did not exist, that it did not represent the single greatest threat to the Mortal Realm—that delusion did not obviate the reality of the danger. Still, using the Art had, perhaps, caused the Vanir far more woe than weal.

She passed into the foyer, where inverted waterfalls still created curtains of beauty, and lilies still sat upon graceful ponds beneath arching bridges. Upon the rail of one such bridge, her brother sat, staring at her as she approached, arms folded across his chest.

"He had the temerity to ask if Mundilfari made a mistake, so long ago, when he banished the jotunnar to Utgard."

Freyja sighed and settled down opposite her brother. Given all that had happened, she just ... she didn't even know. She'd helped Mundilfari raise the Midgard Wall, not so very long after the man had taken the throne, and it had all seemed so needful at the time. Or perhaps, she'd been taken with her teacher, convinced of his brilliance even as the man descended into madness.

"He has bargained with Aegir," Frey said.

"So did Father."

"Yes, I don't begrudge him that. But the sea jotunn has agreed to host the delegation, and it includes representatives from Utgard. All Mundilfari wrought crumbles. They have torn down our great civilization and replaced it with a place I cannot hardly recognize."

While she had just had much the same thought, Freyja didn't see any benefit in admitting that. Frey had never much liked Odin, and this line of reasoning wasn't going to smooth things over. What they all needed was unity. "I'm not sure there is any question of who was right or who was wrong anymore. We all failed the World—Vanir, Aesir, jotunnar. We all tried to rule urd with arrogance, with hubris, when we saw ourselves as gods. Where did it all lead? This final war that Odin calls Ragnarok? Idunn warned us, thousands of years ago, she warned us that Hel might return. That we had not done well by Midgard. None of us listened."

"Idunn was always an agitator who never fit well in any society. She undermined the Vanr kingdom. I half suspect Father made her the keeper of Yggdrasil in the vain hope of keeping her out of trouble. Father's murder falls upon her head as much as Odin's."

Freyja sighed, rubbing her hands on her knees. "Odin killed Father in single combat. It wasn't murder. And don't even start with claiming I never mourned him, because you damn well know I did. As far as Idunn ... her mistakes are no worse than our own. I don't *care* whether or not her svar-talf blood led to her perpetual discontent. She was my friend and I will find a way to save her."

"What would you have me do, then?"

"Exactly what we came here to do. Attend the council Odin has arranged. Find a way to fight back against Hel and stop her from turning the Mortal Realm into a second Nifl-heim. That is what's at stake, is it not? Whether your loyalty lies with Vanaheim or Alfheim, it does not benefit us to see the Earth fall to Hel."

"You still call it Vanaheim."

Yes. She refused to refer to this place as Asgard. That just didn't ...

Frey snickered. "It's not like our ancestors didn't rename this place when they claimed it. What was it called back then?"

Freyja rubbed her head, trying to even remember. "Ugh ... Atlantis. Maybe other names, too. What does that matter? Are *you* on the Aesir's side now?"

Her brother broke into a chuckle. "Weren't you the one asking me to set aside my grievances with the man?"

Yes, damn it. And she didn't much appreciate having her

own double standards pointed out, either. "Maybe he's right. Maybe joining the Aesir, Vanir, jotunnar, all of us flawed would-be gods together is the only way to stop Hel."

"A true goddess."

"Odin claims she was once mortal. That she died and somehow gathered enough power to challenge the original Elder God of Mist."

"How the fuck do we challenge someone with enough power to overthrow an Elder God?"

Freyja slid off the rail, shaking her head. She wished she had a better answer, but the only one she could see was simple. "She was defeated, more than five thousand years ago."

"At the cost of the World itself. At the cost of blanketing the Earth in freezing mist. What will victory cost this time?"

Freyja wasn't sure she even wanted to know the answer to that.

8

*A*egir's castle rose up from the sea, towers so tall they pierced the mist and touched the sky. Odin had seen this place in his visions, before he had turned from them, and though he had not known for certain it was Aegir's, he'd suspected. It didn't matter. This, he had seen already and thus could not turn from it.

While numerous towers rose from the main structure, still more spires jutted up directly from the sea, the greater portion of the architecture concealed by the waves. Aegir had married Rán, a mermaid queen, and the two were famed for their nine daughters. Wave maidens, tale called them, though Odin had never seen them himself.

A mighty bridge of stone stretched over the ocean, from the beach to the castle. Now, ice covered much of the shoreline, making the beach aught but inviting. Still, this place would serve the needs of the council. Aegir had maintained neutrality in the wars and not even the self-important emperors of Valland dared risk his wrath. Not anymore, though some had tried in the past, and lost a great many of their warriors.

Odin trod at the head of the procession, Freyja to his left and Frigg to his right. Many others trailed behind. Thor, petulant over him inviting the jotunnar, had refused to attend and no doubt still lingered up on the cliff. If the boy threatened Odin's alliance by attacking the jotunn delegation ... No. Odin wouldn't dwell on that, not when he had so many other worries weighing upon him.

An archway almost ten times his height led into the castle itself. Inside, fluted columns supported a vaulted ceiling carved with reliefs of sea creatures, and—perhaps—one of the ancient mer kingdoms that had now dwindled. Fleeting memories of past lives flitted through his mind, of days where the sea inundated the land and the empires of mer dominated the Mortal Realm. Fragments and names came unbidden, of the battles of Hiyoya and Mu, and other sprawling undersea kingdoms.

Odin blinked, forcing it from his mind. If he looked back, the pull of time, the currents of it would seize him. Because the past was, in a sense, a refraction of the future, with prescience serving as a bridge that allowed causality to warp, not only in chains, but into loops. He must attend to the now, first, and find a way to sever the strands of the Web of Urd once the immediate situation had resolved itself.

Focus. Let him keep his mind grounded in the present.

To either side of the main walkway, the ground dropped away into pools of water that no doubt connected to the sea. Mermaids and mermen swam about there, perhaps even including some of the daughters of Rán.

A woman met them halfway across this walkway. She wore naught save a wrap around her waist—a mermaid in human form, perhaps, for she did not shiver in the least—and her skin had a slight aquamarine tint to it along her neck and ribs. Her eyes were deep as the ocean, almost mesmerizing.

"Kólga?" Freyja asked. "Is that you?"

"It's true, then," the mermaid said. "You are much changed by the World of Sun. And, yes, I've a new host now, of course, but my features begin to show through. Come." She inclined her head for them to follow, and began to lead without waiting to see if they would.

While numerous paths led down the steps and through the pools of water, Kólga was considerate enough to take them along other walkways and thus allow them to remain dry. In some areas of the castle, waterfalls poured down from overhead, spilling from the mouths of carved benthic creatures, serpents and other undersea monstrosities.

Kólga led them on into a great chamber with a stone table at least forty feet long, and vaulted ceilings that rose high above. Arched windows twice Odin's height let in a hint of sunlight from high above.

At the head of the table sat Aegir, a veritable wall of corded muscles at least nine feet tall, shirtless, and with a long white beard. Faintly luminous runes covered his arms and chest. Odin had heard from Sigyn, long ago, that the sea jotunn could increase his size to the point he could walk on the seafloor outside his castle and still stand only waist-deep.

Beside him sat Rán, who herself seemed pushing seven feet tall, with glittering blonde hair that hung down to cover her otherwise naked breasts. A hint of fish scales peeked out from beneath her flesh. An old host, being slowly transformed into the more fishlike true nature of mer.

Odin took up a seat opposite Aegir and beckoned his entourage to fill in around the table. Frigg sat to his right, and Freyja to his left. Tyr, Frey, Ullr, Eir, Syn, Thrúd, and

Magni all took places as well. Bragi, though, walked around the table for a time, before coming to sit closer to Rán, casting a slight glare at Odin in the process.

They had never got on well, Odin had to admit. He'd asked Bragi how the man had gotten to Alfheim—it had taken Odin decades and cost more than he'd ever have imagined—and Bragi had revealed that he'd merely embraced his heritage as the child of a liosalf, and become one in truth, much as Volund had embraced his svartalf heritage. Odin couldn't say he liked either man better for having done so.

Sunna and Mani came in next, followed by Gefjon, Saule, and her contingent of liosalfar.

While Odin had dared to hope his invitation to the jotunnar would have brought more of them, none had arrived as yet. Perhaps they would soon, but he wasn't certain they could afford to wait much longer.

Already, the gathered guests had begun murmuring. Kólga and her sisters directed slaves who brought forth wine, then raw fish laid atop beds of seaweed. Most of the others seemed disinclined to try the fish, but Odin saw no harm and wouldn't risk offending their host. More like than not, Aegir had ordered the fish served thus as a test. Peeling back scales, Odin tore a chunk of flesh off and bit into it.

Wet and cold and slimy. Not really enjoyable, but he could stomach it if he must.

Tyr and others followed his lead and poked at their own fish, and the liosalfar seemed much less reserved in doing so.

After forcing down a fair portion of the fish, Odin threw back his goblet of wine. A Vall vintage, though not one he knew. He'd been so long away. After a moment, he banged the empty goblet on the stone table, and everyone else fell silent. "Thanks to our host for feasting us here," he said, raising the goblet.

As if on command, Kólga was at his side, and filled more wine from an engraved pitcher.

Everyone raised their own goblets, then drank.

Strange, really. He'd spent centuries preparing for Ragnarok, and now it was upon him, he hesitated. As if, to actually speak now, to say the words, would make it too real. How deeply he wished he could turn away from this. Return to Asgard, cross the Bilröst, and retreat to Alfheim to linger under the sun.

Craven ...

No. Audr was wrong. Odin was no coward. He'd do what he must, what'd he'd always been preparing for. That did not mean he had to like it, nor rush forward with mad glee.

The image of Fenrir tearing out his throat came unbidden to his mind, and he forced the visions down lest they overwhelm him.

Give in ... Let the future unfold as you know it must ... You cannot deny urd ...

He could try. "We all know why we're here. Midgard ... The whole Mortal Realm is in chaos. Winter never broke, and we can see Hel's hand in that. She stretches forth from her prison, eager to escape it as she has done before."

Will you perpetuate the cycle ...?

No. He was going to end it. "Ragnarok is upon us." Maybe, if Hermod succeeded in restoring Baldr, maybe that might avert the end. "Our enemies are manifold. The Deathless priests are a blight upon our world, servants of undead masters that spread a vile faith. But even they are an inconvenience compared to the power Hel must soon unleash against us."

"Our great and glorious leader must forgive me," Bragi

said, "yet I find myself compelled to ask if he has any evidence other than a long winter? The World fares ill, you say, and the cause falls at the feet of Hel herself? Could it not be that Mankind is simply a wretched race, lusting after power and treacherous?"

Part of him wondered if Bragi antagonized him simply out of habit, despite the reasonable points the poet raised.

It was Saule who answered, though. "Those of us who survived an Eschaton before know it is a cycle that plays out in the Mortal Realm. One can see ample signs of the rising chaos in the last age of an Era. From what I gather from the natives to this Realm, those signs abound. As to whether the final conflict will come with Hel or with another power, does it truly matter?"

"It will be with Hel," Odin said.

"Your visions?" Ullr asked. "I was given to understand you no longer relied on them."

Odin grunted. "Nevertheless, I do not doubt their veracity. Hel has worked for four centuries to stir the currents here. It would not surprise me to learn she has even aided the Patriarchs of Miklagard, though we have no way to know for certain. I have called you here not to debate whether Ragnarok impends, but how we are to face it. These may be the last days of this world, but no matter what happens, I will not surrender our Realm to *her*. We have endured five thousand years of her cursed mists, but I will not see Midgard become a second Niflheim."

"We don't have enough warriors to hold back the Deathless legions," Frigg said. "Waging war against them will surely weaken our forces further. The vampires among them oft have enough power to challenge even an Ás immortal, to say naught of the Patriarchs, should they get involved directly."

Saule chuckled. "We have a small army of liosalfar to help swing the balance of power back in your favor, if it comes to fighting vampires."

"Nor do I think they'd fare well against Laevateinn," Frey added.

Odin folded his hands. Yes. This was what they needed. The three factions working together. If only the jotunnar would have come then ...

The great double doors to the hall swung open and Narfi strode in, stern-faced, and flanked by jotunnar from the frost, sea, and wood bloodlines. Everyone fell silent, watching. The jotunn king turned his grim gaze on Aegir first, before finally looking over the others gathered.

Bragi drummed his fingers on the table. "Perhaps the lord is hungry? Sadly, we've no Man-flesh to offer you."

With a sneer, Narfi pushed his way in beside Magni and Thrúd and settled onto the bench, staring at Odin. "Strange I don't see my father here, nor my mother, when you named them kin, Odin Borrson."

Odin pursed his lips. So Narfi knew. Hardly a surprise, given he possessed some degree of the Sight, though how powerful his visions had become, Odin could not say.

One of Rán's daughters brought him a goblet, and Narfi raised it in salute. "Hail, Aesir! Lords of Midgard and Asgard." He looked to Bragi. "And hail to the rest, discounting that glowing buffoon who thought to bandy words with me. Reckon he don't realize I'd just as soon feast on *his* flesh?"

Bragi cleared his throat. "All right, all right, don't take it amiss. Surely the lord doesn't want to undermine the peace Odin strives for between us."

"Wary of war?" Narfi asked. "Hiding a bit of craven under that gleam, are you?"

"Mind your tongue, lest you find your head held in my hand."

Narfi snorted. "You? Who is this bench-ornament?"

Odin wanted to groan. He'd dared to hope Narfi might come here in goodwill. It seemed otherwise.

Gefjon stood. "Please don't argue, either of you. Whatever happened with your father, it need not come between the rest of us who were not even here."

Narfi pointed at her. "I know you, don't I? Ain't you the one who fucked her way through Reidgotaland after the Old Kingdoms fell? I reckon you must have the hungriest cunt in any Realm."

Odin lurched to his feet and slammed his palms on the table. "Enough! We are not here to debate Loki's misdeeds. You have truly gone mad if you plan to insult every last member of this gathering while we are here trying to discuss the Fate of the World. Of all the worlds, perhaps."

"Because you are so innocent, great king?" Narfi sipped at his wine. "Did you not use valkyries to decide the outcome of wars, betraying those most loyal to you? All of you play at honor and grandeur while sneering down your noses at the jotunnar. At least we don't keep false airs. Your schemes and machinations wrought death and destruction around the North Realms, and yet you so abhor my father for his having had his hand forced by urd."

Odin glowered at the man. He would not listen to this ... Shit. Was he a fool for having refused to look forward and foresee Narfi's belligerence? If he saw the future, did that set it, or was it set from the beginning? All he had to do was let his mind wander, see the outcome of this ... No! No, damn it. There had to be another way about this.

Narfi believed his kin betrayed, and Odin must salve that wound if he was to hope the jotunnar would join his alliance. Finally, he slunk back down into his seat and rubbed his brow. "I'm told, Aegir, that your daughters have lovely singing voices. Perhaps we might lighten the mood with a song or two?"

Aegir spread a hand toward Kólga and the mermaid did move to the back of the hall, beckoning her sisters closer. They exchanged a few words, then broke into a haunting melody, one that echoed off the vaulting ceiling.

They sang of the collapse of the undersea kingdom of Mu, of the loss of the World. Of the end of an Era.

9

─────────

The beautiful song had Freyja swaying in place, left almost as if in a dream. One that she found herself jolted from when Frey elbowed her.

"What is it?" she whispered.

He leaned in close. "Who is that jotunn woman beside Narfi?"

"How would I know?" What was he on about now?

"She's radiant ..."

Oh, by the blazing Sun. "You can't be serious. You've only just laid eyes on her, and she's come with Narfi. Things are not apt to go well if you—"

"Go to her for me. Ask for her hand on my behalf."

Freyja groaned. Her brother and his obsessions. "This is unwise."

The singing had ended, and now the Wave Maidens set to refilling goblets with more wine.

"After the feast, please. Ask her ... at least entreat her to lie with me. I must ..."

Freyja rolled her eyes. "I don't think that—"

"So," Narfi said. "Here we come to your so-feared

Ragnarok. On account of this battle, you betrayed your followers and your kin. You worked sorcery in the dark, calling upon Art that ought to have stayed forgotten. In so many guises you wandered Midgard, caring naught who your schemes undid. And now ... now you find the battle impends not only in spite of your efforts, but because of them. Reckon that's irony."

Frigg shook her head slowly. "You speak as if you know the weave of urd, boy. Your tongue reveals the depths of your ignorance. Odin is here, offering you the chance to join our alliance—"

"Oh, silence yourself, witch. What, you think yourself blameless in all this shit? You had my brother torn apart."

Frigg rose slowly, gaze turned icy. "He earned it for the murder of Baldr."

"What do you mean, 'because of my efforts,'" Odin asked.

Narfi wasn't looking at the king, though, but at Odin's queen. "You coddled your son and built an arrogant cur in place of a prince. Man who thought the whole World his due. Not so unlike his father."

Oh, this did not bode well. "Narfi, I don't know you—" Freyja began.

"No!" he snapped. "No, but I know you. How truly magnificent your trench must be, that Odin would risk unraveling all the worlds for another chance to plow it. If your cunt is that legendary, perhaps you ought to share it widely? I don't reckon you're much opposed to fucking every last man in the hall? Or do you deny having lain with half of Svartalfheim to get back to Odin?"

Freyja flushed, unable to quite form words. How in the blazing Sun did he know what went on in the World of Dark?

"Oh, come now," Narfi said, leering. "You fucked your way through Alfheim and when there won't a liosalf left who hadn't pounded into you, you started on the svartalfar. Well, when you're done with them, may I recommend jotunnar? We'll give the biggest cocks in all the—"

Odin rose again. "You are dangerously close to losing your guest-right."

"Oh, but I ain't *your* guest, dear Odin." Narfi looked to Aegir. "I came for my own kind. I am here, announcing that Ragnarok, that you so feared, is upon you. And you wrought it yourself when you betrayed my kin! So what of it, Aegir? Will you fight along the sea jotunnar, or will you turn your backs on your own progeny?"

Frigg sneered at him. "Lord Aegir has received tribute from us for centuries in exchange for our friendship."

"Yes," Aegir said. "But that does not mean I can deny the call of my fellow jotunnar. I must think on this development."

"Do not do this," Odin said, though whether to Aegir or Narfi, Freyja couldn't say.

Narfi spit on the table. "Me, I'll await your answer, Benthic Lord. As to the rest of you ... well, in Hunaland we passed the Deathless legions. Reckon they're closing in on any fool enough to yet follow the Aesir. This winter ain't gonna end, neither. How long have you got before your foes are burning down the halls of Asgard? Not long, I reckon."

With that, Narfi turned and stormed out, leaving a few jotunnar behind to await Aegir's answer.

Freyja let her head slump down into her hand. That could've gone better.

Frey elbowed her again. "She's still here, Sun be praised. Tell her I await her."

Gaping, Freyja turned on her brother. "Are you mad?"

"Yes. Mad with lust that must be sated. Find out who the jotunn woman is and send her to me."

All she could do was groan.

AEGIR HAD CONTINUED to extend his hospitality to the Aesir, Vanir, and liosalfar, though many had departed once the feast was concluded, including Odin himself. Freyja had promised to catch up with him in Hunaland, after he insisted he must verify Narfi's claims of the Patriarchs moving on that land. Od adamantly refused to use the Sight to do so.

It seemed utter madness that Frey wouldn't give over his desire for the jotunn woman—Gridr, her name was—but her brother insisted that a relationship with her might help maintain the peace.

For her part, Freyja doubted aught would do so now, not after all she'd heard about Baldr and Hödr, and Narfi's parents. Odin may have tried to plan everything so intricately, but from her perspective, it was hard not to see merit in Narfi's accusations that her lover's own schemes had created this disaster.

Now, Freyja plodded along inside Aegir's castle, to the chambers granted to Gridr, and rapped her fist on the door.

A moment later, the door swung inward to reveal a spacious room complete with a pool. Probably it connected with the sea, but, given Gridr was a frost jotunn, the cold would have had no effect on her.

It took her a moment to spot Magni, sitting on the jotunn woman's bed. Had she *already* taken a lover here?

"What do you want?" the jotunn asked.

"May I enter?"

The jotunn waved her inside and shut the door. On Alfheim, if you wanted to lay with someone, you simply said so. The liosalfar were even freer about such things than the Vanir had been, and Freyja saw little point in being circumspect. If the woman refused, maybe Frey would give over this madness and join Odin in fighting the Deathless.

On the other hand, Magni's presence made it more difficult.

Perhaps noticing her watching him, he rose, and stretched. "I'll see you before I leave, Mama."

Mama? Better than finding he was a lover, yes, but ... Well, that was unexpected.

Freyja nodded at him as Magni left. Once he'd shut the door, she turned back to Gridr. "My brother, Frey, is taken by your beauty. He wishes to lie with you."

Gridr snorted. "Wouldn't be the first Ás in my bed."

"Frey is a Vanr, not an Ás. He's willing to give you gifts of silver or gold for your favor."

She grinned, exposing teeth that still seemed mostly human. "Wouldn't take that amiss. Him's one of the ones what was glowing?"

"Yes."

"Eh. Does his cock glow, too?"

Freyja arched an eyebrow. "I'm sure it does." Other liosalfar's did.

"Reckon that'd be a sight."

"Shall I take you to him? You can decide for yourself about his ... endowments."

Gridr shrugged. "Ain't got aught else to do to pass the time, waiting for Benthic's say-so."

These creatures were vile. Mundilfari had done right in choosing to banish them. And now, here they were, thousands of years later, begging an alliance from the jotunnar. Except, war now seemed more like than not.

Well, let Frey enjoy himself then. There would be blood aplenty, soon.

ATOP one of the towers rising from the castle, Sunna sat on a windowsill, staring at the ocean, though Freyja didn't imagine her friend could actually make out the waves through the mist. They could hear them, though, breaking against rocks below, beautiful and soothing.

"I miss Alfheim, actually," Sunna said. "I mean, I had missed Vanaheim, too, though it has changed so much. My home is gone."

"Mmm." Freyja didn't recognize the place anymore. "You don't like it out in Midgard."

"No, not really. Not half enough sunlight here. So dark, and cold. It's like staring into Niflheim. Your parents did well, declaring this world off-limits."

It was a strange thing, their friendship, Freyja had sometimes thought. After all, both of their fathers had once served as monarch of Vanaheim. For that matter, so had Sunna's grandmother.

Freyja rubbed her hands. "And yet, here we are, planning to fight for the mist-filled iceberg."

Sunna clucked her tongue. "Is it worth saving? Even if we could win, would it be worth the lives we'll lose to do it? I'm not sure we should have ever come back."

Freyja knew the feeling, yes, but she had to believe in the cause. "I know it doesn't feel like it, anymore. I mean we were born on Vanaheim. But Midgard is still our world. Our ancestors came from here, or at least from east of here."

"Well, some ancestors from north of here, and the others ... I mean, that's out in Utgard, technically. Kind of makes the whole wall thing seem contrived." Sunna looked back at her sharply. "Oh. Damn, I'm sorry. I ... I had forgotten you were involved in that."

Freyja bit her lip. What was she supposed to say? That it had seemed a good idea at the time? That it had been to end a war, back when they still thought Midgard worth fighting for? So much changed over time. They'd overthrown Brimir and destroyed the jotunn civilization in the hopes of letting Mankind rise into its own. But they'd gotten what later generations called the Old Kingdoms instead.

Lines as corrupted by the Art as Brimir had been, if not more so.

Freyja sniffed. "If you really want to go back to Alfheim, no one will stop you."

"Eh. My brother won't go."

"I doubt that's the only reason you're staying."

Sunna chuckled, shaking her head. "Honestly? I just don't want to see all the people I care about die in this icy wasteland. You and Gefjon and even ... Saule and the others."

Freyja patted her friend on the shoulder. "For whatever it's worth, I'm glad you came with me."

No sooner had the words left her mouth than her brother came tromping up the stairs and blundering into the room. "She's gone!"

"Who?" Sunna asked.

"Gridr! She left while I was sleeping."

Freyja snickered, shaking her head. "Well, it sounds like you got what you wanted anyway, so I don't see what the—"

"She took the sword!"

Sunna glanced from Freyja to her brother and back. "You mean ..."

Freyja groaned. "You mean you let her steal Laevateinn." She Sun Strode from the window to her brother and grabbed him by the hair with both hands, pulling his face down to hers. "You let the jotunn bitch take away a runeblade!"

"Gah!" He grabbed her wrists and yanked them back. "I didn't think ..."

Freyja released him, barely forestalling the urge to slap the man. "I hope she was worth losing one of our greatest weapons, you cock-brained cretin."

Frey had the sense to flush, backing away.

Shit. They needed to find Odin and let him know. They couldn't afford to waste any more time.

PART II

Year 399, Age of the Aesir
Winter

10

The crush of two shield walls, smashed together for the third time, created a heaving mass of bodies. Men grunting, shoving, pushing forward with their shields in desperation to drive the enemy back, while thrusting spears over or under the wall. And while getting spears thrust back at them.

Little Odin could do would make much difference in such a press of warriors, so instead, he stood motionless behind his line, glowering at the Miklagardian army beyond. Oh, and it *was* an army, many times over his numbers—though the mist had prevented him from getting exact counts. It looked as though the Miklagardian commander had deployed two ranks of infantry, each pressing in together, while lighter warriors guarded their flanks.

Warriors out of Gardariki, in fact. North Realmers who ought to have served him rather than the vampiric Patriarchs.

Continuous snow flurries—enough that a layer of frost had built up on Freyja's gilded armor where she watched by his side—further impeded vision, making it almost impossible to gauge the Miklagardian's true strength.

They had spread out through the Rijnland valley, and could have—had their commanders been willing to wage a battle of attrition—overwhelmed Odin's dwindling numbers at almost any time. The Miklagardians seemed intent, rather, to fight slow, careful, conserving their men for the no doubt impending invasion of Reidgotaland once Rijnland fell.

Saule's armored, golden Sun Knights scattered through the valley struck an impressive sight, but even they had not turned the tide of this war.

"You cannot win this," Freyja finally said. His lover's breastplate and manica actually resembled the armor worn by Miklagardian commanders, though polished gold plated hers. Her armor left her sides bare, exposing her glowing skin. Impractical, yes, but the more skin she had exposed, the more sunlight she could absorb. Odin had already had to dissuade her from Sun Striding behind the enemy line and killing a few to disrupt them. She carried a thin-bladed sword that she'd admitted served better against lightly armored foes than armies, and thus had also acceded to bring a light mace. With her alfar strength, Freyja could certainly crush a man's armor and his chest cavity beneath using such a weapon.

But using such powers might have alerted his greater foes to her presence, and Odin could not risk that. Not yet.

Odin spared her a glance, but found his gaze drawn back to the crush, where handfuls of men continued to fall, after getting spears jammed into their faces, or their ankles cut out from beneath them.

"Your opponents have superior armaments, superior numbers, and, from the look of it, superior training. It's only a matter of time ... unless you choose to find a solution."

"No." No, he would not look into the future. Were he to do that, he'd willingly step into the Norns' trap and would find his actions bound by their whims.

"You have no way to know for certain that simply refusing to use their powers frees you from their Web of Urd. Are not the rest of the World who lack such gifts still bound by their strands?"

Odin shook his head. Freyja said naught that he hadn't considered, over and over, from the day he rejected his visions. He had no solution, but he refused to be a pawn. Except ... the obvious objection then became, that perhaps their game ran so deep as to have accounted for him not using the visions. How to contend with such beings? Loki had once implied that they existed outside time, and thus did not perceive it the way Odin did.

"The light infantry has continued to flank around us," Freyja commented.

The only way she could have known that was to have embraced the Sight. Reluctantly, Odin did so, as well, allowing the battle to become a haze. The mist and snow vanished from his view, though, as he peered through shadows. The battlefield was thick with shades, flitting about, bemoaning their deaths. By looking through the Veil, he became more solid to them, and many began to draw closer, drifting toward him and Freyja.

Perhaps they had served Miklagard in life and now meant to continue their fight, or perhaps they merely deluded themselves into thinking he could abate their suffering. Even had he possessed such a capacity, Odin could not have afforded the time to attend to the dead. Not while the living so quickly joined their ranks.

He followed Freyja's gaze. Without the weather obscuring the valley, he could indeed make out two more Miklagardian units, one to either side, flanking around. A few more moments and his forces would find themselves caught in a pincer. The strength of a shield wall lay on one side alone, and an attack from the rear would collapse the wall almost immediately, turning the already hopeless battle into a bloody rout.

Worse, beyond the Gardarikian mercenaries, mounted archers rode, moving into position.

Shades now drew up mere feet from him, flailing, moaning, shrieking inane pleas at him in a maddening cacophony of lamentation. Hundreds of them, pressing against one another, almost like their own shield wall.

Odin blinked the Sight away before any ghosts decided to force the issue. "We have to stop those archers, and the mercenaries, as well."

Freyja frowned. "The horses."

Odin nodded. Yes. Her sunlight allowed her to influence the minds of animals—even a hydra once, Hermod had told him.

Freyja spread her hands, and her eyes began to glow.

Out in the valley, beyond the immediate press of battle, Odin could have sworn he heard fresh screams. Despite the risk, he had to know. He embraced the Sight, just for a moment.

The archers' mounts had suddenly charged right into the ranks of the Gardarikians, trampling them underfoot, ignoring the commands of their riders. Rampant chaos.

Releasing the Sight once more, Odin looked back to Freyja. Her eyes continued to glow, but the light in her skin rapidly dwindled. She could not keep up such an effect for long.

In another lifetime, as another man, Odin had tasted such glorious powers ...

Bah! Such nostalgia served no purpose at all.

Finally—perhaps having realized their reserves had come under attack—the Miklagardians pulled back their shield wall, creating a perilous gap between the two armies.

The Hunalanders took the opportunity to limp backward, dragging the wounded away as they did so.

The whistle overhead was the only warning.

"Shields!" a Hunalander shouted.

And then arrows rained down over his army. They jerked their shields up into a clumsy shell overhead. A barrage of *thwacks* resounded off the boards, punctuated by grunts and screams as no few shafts found flesh.

Odin cringed at the hideous slaughter of his army. There had to be some way to push back the tide, but he could not see it. "Kára," he called, though he knew the valkyrie would already be doing all she could to gather the most valiant souls for Valhalla. In truth, he was lucky the valkyries obeyed him at all, given he'd handed over Draupnir. Perhaps they did not know he no longer possessed it.

Maybe he ought instead to use Kára to fight, directly. Valkyries had incredible power. She might slaughter dozens of Miklagardians. But she wasn't invincible, either, and couldn't protect herself against so many foes. All he'd get for his trouble would be one more dead valkyrie.

The day had dragged on, and at last the Miklagardians allowed the Hunalanders to pull back.

They wouldn't attack at night. Not with the army. But the fall of darkness would bring other, more terrible woes upon Odin's people.

❦

As Hermod had advised, Odin had found Bergljot and her varulf protector, Didrik, on his arrival in Rijnland. The pair had greeted him with awe, then, and—in the days since—it had only partially faded. Under other circumstances, Odin would have concealed his identity. Now, with the end of the World upon them, such games seemed pointless, or even self-defeating. If he could not save the Hunalanders, at least he could let them see him, there among them, while the Age of Man died.

Now, they sat around a campfire, watching the sun set with palpable dread. Every night, the mist thickened, and death stalked the camp.

Oh, the vampires avoided varulfur and liosalfar, for the most part, preferring to seek out prey that could neither detect them nor fight back. Sadly, the Hunalanders had less than a dozen varulfur left to them, and maybe twice as many liosalfar.

One among the varulfur, Vebiorg, was a gray-haired, weathered shieldmaiden the rest seemed to defer to. Odin had said she seemed too old to fight anymore.

"Coming from you, old man," Vebiorg had retorted, "that claim means very little."

To see a varulf so old, she must have lived for centuries. Vaettir could sustain human hosts much longer than a normal human lifespan, but not forever. Vebiorg had reached her last days and probably sought a means of dying with glory. She had not denied it, when Odin implied such a thing.

Maybe, though, death with glory was all any of them had left to hope for.

"We saw this in Gardariki," Vebiorg said, staring into the night as if the vampires already stalked the mists, though

Odin suspected they'd wait until the last rays of sunlight had vanished.

Sunlight stripped their powers, and thus, they rarely chose to walk beneath it. Varulfur were stronger in moonlight, as well, though not so powerful as vampires. And liosalfar … well, they could not replenish their powers in darkness.

You will die … accept it …

"I'd still be there, maybe," Vebiorg said after a moment more. "If Gevarus hadn't bled out in Sviarland, I'd be there, prowling the night, trying and failing to protect the people. The armies came every morning, and every night, those vampires would …"

A low growl built in Didrik's chest, the only answer to Vebiorg's musings. Nor did she seem to expect or want an answer. Melancholy had seized the whole valley. All these people, they knew they had a few days left of life, at most. This would be their last stand.

Here, Hunaland would fall to the Deathless legions of the Patriarchs.

Freyja's hand fell on Odin's knee. "You can find the answer."

Only by inviting yet worse urd upon them. Odin said naught, staring into the campfire while deliberately avoiding looking for patterns. Were he not careful, it would draw in his mind, and force the visions upon him.

Didrik doffed his shirt and tossed it aside. Preparing to shift. The moon was rising.

Ironic … you embrace the varulfur … even knowing their kind will end you …

Fenrir.

No. Odin would change it all.

"I fought vampires even before this," Vebiorg said. "I

went to Miklagard ... the city, itself, back before we knew what the Patriarchs were. The vampires were horrors I'd not have dreamed of, but the Patriarchs ..." She shuddered.

Few things frightened a varulf. Did she know Odin had been the one to arrange her ill-fated trip to Miklagard back then? He'd thought to claim Mistilteinn from the Patriarchs. How poorly he'd planned that, never even imagining the runeblade would be turned against his own son.

Indeed, every time Odin had contended with Miklagard, it had brought woe to him and those he favored. He'd lost Gungnir. He'd brought the instrument of Baldr's death to the North Realms. He'd even lost Starkad to them.

"Why did Hermod not come himself?" Bergljot asked. She had asked as much before, and Odin had evaded the question.

What answer could he give? That he'd sent Hermod to the gates of Hel in a last, desperate gambit to reclaim his son and somehow forestall Ragnarok? In truth, while he knew Baldr's death had begun Ragnarok, he could not say with any certainty that his return would end it. Still, how he longed to look upon his son once more.

The boy's death had opened a terrible void in Odin's chest.

Even knowing it would come, having seen it from way back, it crushed him.

With a groan, Vebiorg rose, pulling off her own shirt to reveal wrinkled breasts Odin studiously avoided looking at. She and Didrik stalked from the camp as the last of the sunlight dipped behind the hills.

With the Sight, he might have found vampires, stalking the camp. The problem, however, remained the over-whelming press of dead souls that would descend upon him. And the vampires were yet a few more ghosts among the many.

Freyja squeezed his knee. "Look into the future and find a way to save us."

"The Norns are not interested in saving lives."

"Then what do they want?"

Naught good. Odin had tired of their game. He'd make his own, no matter how grim it turned things.

⚓

THE SCREAM SHOT through the camp, making Odin cringe, despite him knowing it would come sooner or later. The screams always came. Men found the bodies of their comrades exsanguinated, or torn to shreds by something beyond inhuman.

He shared a glance with Freyja, then the two of them took off at a run, racing toward the sound.

Sunna met them halfway there. The liosalf's skin had become a lantern in the darkness, a beacon to vampires—one they always seemed to avoid. Odin had tried to use this to his advantage, posting a liosalf from Saule or Frey's contingents with every major group of the Hunalander army. But he had not nigh enough of such warriors to go around, and besides which, it meant they had to conserve their sunlight for use at night, meaning by the time the thick of the fighting had settled in during the day, his greatest weapons could not join the fray.

Together with the two liosalfar, he blundered toward one of the other campfires, and there came to an abrupt stop.

He smelled it, even before he saw it. The stench of death. Blood and viscera and shit—ruptured bowels. The creature that had attacked here had strewn the intestines of a dozen or more men about in a twenty feet radius from the fire. Guts lay tossed atop the tents. Splatters of blood formed twisted patterns in the shadows, as if created by some Mistmad painter. An arm—ripped off, not severed—lay before Odin's feet.

A leg crackled and sizzled in the fire, the stench of burning flesh nauseating.

Every living man in the camp was dead long before he'd arrived.

No single vampire could have so annihilated a band of soldiers in so short a time. A group of them, at least two or three, must have descended on a fire unprotected by liosalfar, and utterly slaughtered everyone.

Grim-faced, Odin trod among macabre wreckage where his warriors had once rested. Or tried to rest, rather, given everyone now knew nachzehrer—as the Hunalanders named them—stalked the night. Legends come to horrifying unlife. Embodiments of the worst nightmares of all men. Something somehow worse than draugar.

Other warriors had begun to cluster around the perimeter, none daring to tread within. Whispers of the land being cursed, damned. Men made signs of warding, invoking the Aesir, perhaps unaware one already trod among them and found himself nigh as sickened as they did.

"Why do this?" Sunna asked.

Odin cocked his head at a cluster of warriors backing away, mumbling prayers—to him, no less. In their midst, someone retched. "They think to destroy our morale and make it easier for their soldiers to break our shield wall."

He left it unsaid that this was probably retribution for Freyja seizing control of the horses during the day. A painful retribution. Now, the Miklagardians would be afraid to use their cavalry or mounted archers.

The vampires' answer to that—make the Hunalanders afraid to even take the field.

As if it were not bad enough. A loose war band of Hunalanders, even a levy, they had ferocity, but not the discipline of a Miklagardian army. In a small cluster of men, they could fight like mad. Fifty, sixty men, maybe a few more. A Miklagardian legion comprised a thousand men, so far as Odin could tell. Facing one required the Hunalanders to smash together any number of war bands who had no experience coordinating their efforts like that.

The Valls might have, maybe, from their days fighting the Serks. But the Valls seemed to worship some version of the Miklagardians' Deathless god-emperor, even if they didn't quite realize it.

"Whatever the cost," Sunna said, "if you want to survive this, we're going to have to—"

The mist coalesced behind her. Mist, or a cloud of dust that had melded with it. A feral roar broke through the night an instant before an undulating blade burst through Sunna's chest, hefting her off the ground. The liosalf flailed, an explosion of blood bursting from her mouth.

The vampire behind her snarled and flung its blade, hurling her body into one of the tents so hard it toppled over.

That was Gungnir. The vampire held Odin's spear.

All at once, more vampires appeared amid the gathering warriors. One heaved a man into the air then brought him down upon its knee, breaking the man's spine with an audible crack.

Freyja instantly appeared beside the vampire holding

Gungnir, swinging her mace. The vampire melted into dust, then reformed behind her.

"No!" Odin shrieked, driving forward. "No!"

The vampire caught Freyja's neck with one hand and flung her through the air. She vanished before landing, though, and Odin couldn't see where.

He thrust with his own spear, but the vampire knocked the attack aside as if Odin moved in slow motion, despite him pulling on his Pneuma. Snarling, it lunged forward, intent on impaling Odin with his own damn spear. He blocked, again and again, but the vampire was stronger and faster. Furiously fast.

A Patriarch.

The dark closes in ...

Growling himself, Odin whipped his spear at the vampire's legs. The Patriarch melted into dust for an instant, shifting his position just to Odin's side. His elbow took the snarling creature in the face. The blow stunned the vampire, if only for a bare instant, enough for Odin to get his own spear back into position. To knock aside another vicious lunge.

He'd never keep this up.

Freyja appeared at his side once more, this time the sword in one hand and mace in the other. The vampire whirled Gungnir so fast she couldn't close in though.

Dimly, Odin heard the screams all around him. The vampires slaughtering their way through every last human nearby. He could not help them, though. Not with the Patriarch here. Surely this vampire commanded all four Miklagardian legions. Now was his chance.

Odin lunged again, as aggressive as he could be. His spear gouged the vampire's side.

Gungnir slashed through Odin's throat.

He collapsed in a heap, hot blood bubbling up through his fingers.

A snarling wolf launched itself through the air at the Patriarch. The vampire caught it by the throat, then vanished into dust, reappearing an instant later ten feet back.

Odin could scarcely make them out. Everything going dim ...

The vampire grabbed the wolf's jaws and ripped them apart, tearing off half the wolf's skull.

The varulf fell to the ground, slowly turning back into a gray old woman.

Gurgling, Odin tried so furiously to staunch the bleeding in his neck. Warm hands were on him.

But still, all went dark.

"OD. Can you hear me, my love? I pushed more of my Pneuma into you."

"He'll live. Unlike so many others."

Odin couldn't make his eyes focus. Everything writhed and twisted about him.

Freyja.

Freyja.

She was there.

Trying to reach him.

But his mind kept slipping ... pulled out as if on the tides ... pulled under ...

A SMOKE-FILLED HALL. Aflame, burning to the ground.

He knew this place. Valaskjalf. His hall. The royal hall of Asgard.

The thrones empty.

No, not empty, Odin realized, as he blundered through the smoke. Upon a burning throne sat Frigg's head, empty eyes staring accusation back at him. He had failed her. He had failed Asgard and Midgard, both. Everywhere, the World died.

"You said we'd do better than the Vanir," Frigg said, her voice broken, hollow.

Not real. Odin shook his head, backing away.

This was a nightmare.

In the darkness, a massive jotunn stalked through Odin's home, chuckling, knowing Thor would come there.

His son!

No, not merely a nightmare, much though he wished to believe it. In his weakness, the visions had flooded into his mind like crashing waves, pulling him back under the surface. Ready to drown him for denying them for so long.

ODIN LURCHED UP, gasping, his breaths painful, throat raw and feeling apt to burst apart from the force of the air he sucked down into his lungs.

Freyja held his hand in both of hers. "Easy. You almost didn't make it. I had to give you so much Pneuma ..." She'd grown so pale.

So weak.

Doomed ... like Frigg ... like Thor ... like everyone you love ...

No! Odin tried to scream the word, but only managed a painful rasp.

All you build will turn to ash, your children shall die, and your dreams shall burn.

No ... the Odling ghost had cursed him ... Or the Norns had ...

Had to stop the visions. If he didn't look, maybe he could still ...

§

FREYJA WAS THERE, standing in the snow, the dead all around her, staring at him, a mixture of hatred and love and fear and hope. Maybe none of those things, for Odin could not read her eyes.

Except for the fear. Maybe that was certain.

Her face was beaten bloody, and no hint of sunlight remained in her skin.

And Odin rammed Gungnir straight through her heart. Not even a liosalf could survive without head or heart.

He held the spear tight, as her eyes grew cold and died. As she slipped away from him once more.

Dream of one who dreams of you, never the two dreams to meet. Still you wait for the one to hold your heart.

All a dream. And now he must wake.

§

ANOTHER PAINFUL RASP, as Freyja drew him into her embrace.

"It's all right. Stay with me, Od. I've got you."

No. No. No. No.

This was not happening.

Just a nightmare. It wasn't the truth. He would *never*, ever strike down Freyja.

You know better by now ... Urd cannot be changed ... You have seen the future ... The Mad Vanr walked from his throne ... he claimed an Oracle had shown him things he could not endure ...

No. No!

You know how this ends ... With the wolf tearing out your throat ...

"Od?" Freyja asked. "Od, you'll be all right."

He realized he was squeezing her so tight—even drawing Pneuma to do it. Maybe she couldn't scarcely breathe.

Fuck.

Fuck!

He pulled her back to arms' length, staring into her face, trying to form words, but unable. Just wheezing.

"Shhh. Don't try to talk. Not even an immortal could have lived through that, but I poured into you all the Pneuma I could give and still live myself. Between that and the apple, you've pulled through, but I doubt you'll be able to speak for several days, if not longer."

Sunna came to settle beside Freyja, patting her on the shoulder. The liosalf had lived? Gungnir must have missed her heart. Now, she wore no shirt, rather most of her torso was wrapped in bloodstained bandages.

"We had to bring you away from the front," Freyja said. "Saule has command, and she's decided to unleash the liosalfar upon the Miklagardians. They set upon their shield wall in a torrent of slaughter. It's not enough to break them, but it certainly ended their assault for the day."

The words washed over him, hardly making sense.

Frigg was dead, or would be soon. And he'd seen himself kill Freyja. He'd seen Fenrir kill him. He'd seen Thor dead, slain by some sea serpent. Everything he'd ever loved destroyed. Turned to ash, even as the Odling ghost had promised him long ago.

First, the burning child ignites a pyre you cannot staunch.

The Norns had said that to him, before all this. Child ... Loki's child. Hödr, once possessed by a Fire vaettr, burning. Hödr had started this. A pyre for the World.

The Norns had orchestrated every moment, hadn't they? They'd set the prophecy before Odin four hundred years ago, and he'd played into it. Even Loki, the Nornslave, seemed powerless to do aught save play his role in their schemes.

Refusing to play the game had not stopped it from unfolding around him.

Because maybe he had not yet made a desperate enough gambit.

He stared into Freyja's beautiful, bright green eyes. His soul mate. She'd been torn from him, oh, so many times. Not this time.

No, whatever it took, Odin would break the Norns' plans. He would end the cycle of destruction. He would ensure Hel would never rise again, never take Freyja from him again. And most of all, he'd protect those he loved, no matter the cost.

Had his gambit not yet been desperate enough?

Well, then it left him one choice.

He would destroy the Web of Urd. By destroying the Norns who had created it.

THE BANDAGES around his throat itched. Rubbing at them, he stared at Freyja across the large tent. Outside, the skirmishes were already beginning, and Saule had left to hold back the Miklagardian army.

"The vampire raids were worse last night," Frey said. He rubbed his arms. "I should get back out there."

"No," Odin rasped. "No, I need you to go back to Asgard. Take a few of your warriors, and go back. I've seen ... I think the war is already there."

Frey groaned. "If I leave this front ..."

"Sun Striding, you can make it there faster. Please."

Freyja's brother nodded, dour, and trod from the tent.

Freyja squeezed Odin's hand.

Beside her, Sunna picked at her own bandages. Odin found it hard to believe she had even lived through getting impaled by Gungnir. Whether her nature as a liosalf, or having had an apple long before, he'd count it as a blessing to have such hardy allies at his side.

"This time," Freyja said after a moment, "the vampires seemed to target the varulfur directly. Didrik tells me we lost four last night."

Their numbers dwindled. How many varulfur remained to them? Six? Seven?

It hurt to speak, so Odin held his peace, instead, watching the two women. Once, long ago, they had been human, and thus Odin trusted Sunna over Saule. The liosalfar—the *true* liosalfar—flitted from fancy to fancy, sometimes seeming as glorious and grand as their beautiful bodies implied. And sometimes seeming capable of Otherworldly cruelty without the slightest pang of conscience. Indeed, any semblance of morality appeared incomprehensible nonsense to them.

Odin could not forget that Saule had fed on his life force, the same as a vampire, and had done so in the midst of making love to him.

Desperation had led him to ally himself with these creatures, but he could not allow himself to forget, they were not people.

"Perhaps we ought to withdraw back to Valland," Sunna suggested. "Certainly, we cannot hold out much longer."

Freyja shook her head. "From what I've heard of the Valls in this time, they'd be more like to attack us than welcome us. No, we'll never move the Hunalander army there, though we might manage to retreat into Reidgotaland. Unfortunately, that would mean moving through the Myrkvidr, which exposes us to any number of dangers and prevents us from keeping the entire army together."

Odin cleared his throat, even that a painful, scratching sensation. "We have to kill the Patriarch."

Both women paused, looking at him now. The sadness in Freyja's eyes unsettled him. Like she knew they would all die soon. He'd not allow it. He would save her, save them all.

"Even if we knew where to find him, we have no means to destroy such a foe. Supposing we could, though, the Patriarch has shown himself only once. He moves in and out of the Penumbra, where we cannot follow, nor prepare in advance for his arrival."

They could. They could if only Odin would look into the future. Doing so drew him back into the Norns' bitterest trap, yes, but perhaps that would not matter. Not if Odin destroyed them and thus severed their web. He could see no alternative to doing so, but nor could he set out to find the Norns while the situation here remained so very volatile.

"I will determine where to find this Patriarch."

Freyja looked at him sharply now. "You said ..."

How easily you justify ... even to yourself ... any action ... Oh, stepping across the line ... must always seem needful, yes ...?

You contend with the very thrones of Fate, Valravn said. *You push limits mortals cannot hope to surpass.*

Mortals?

Nor vaettr, either. Even we must abide by the bounds of time and space, and thus cannot act against these entities you name Norns.

Not even vaettir ... No. Odin refused to believe it hopeless. He would not fulfill the prophecies the Norns had given him.

Odin grimaced, rubbing at his raw, aching throat. "I know what I said. But I see no alternative. We must kill the Patriarch. It should throw them into disarray, enough to allow the Hunalanders to retreat to Reidgotaland."

Freyja and Sunna exchanged glances, but each nodded in turn. They would find a way to do this. They had to.

11

*A*s the bridge guardian had said, Hermod had found a cavern carved out of a glacier. Given the incredibly dense mist outside, he could not even harbor at a guess at the glacier's size, for it disappeared in all directions. Inside, once past the first few hundred feet, the mist lessened enough he could at least see the surrounding cavern.

Walls of irregularly cut ice stretched up twenty or thirty times his height, with the tunnel oft wide enough an army could have marched through. If Niflheim had armies. Other than Modgud, Hermod had seen no sign of any living creature in his time in this frozen waste.

Before entering the cavern, the wind had whipped through the forest, scalding his face like a flame. Once, he dared lean up against a twisted tree trunk, just to keep its bulk between himself and the cold, an effort that had offered him limited success and left him even more certain the trees themselves moved, slowly writhing and perhaps intent on grasping him.

Ever-present snowfall had his beard blanketed in frost within moments of entering this world. He'd wrapped a cloth around his face, only to find that had frozen solid. Too, he'd wrapped his hands in linens, but despite his precautions, his fingers had felt apt to freeze and snap off at the joints. Hermod couldn't imagine any living man who hadn't tasted the fruit of Yggdrasil could survive that bitterness.

Once he'd trod inside these caverns, the wind no longer gnawed at his flesh. The coldness down here remained deep, though, permeating everything in any direction.

Cold, manifested as a building block of creation ...

Sleipnir didn't complain—Hermod had wrapped wool blankets over the horse, as well—but he could feel the animal's relief to have found shelter from the weather. Inside, the cold went from apt to kill an immortal, to only enough to freeze a man's stones into solid blocks of ice.

His breath still frosted the air, and now, Sleipnir's hooves clomped down on solid ice rather than hard-packed snow. It created ethereal echoes that bounced back through the massive cavern and could have fooled Hermod into thinking an entire war band rode through here.

"Is it better than the shadows of the Roil?" he whispered to Sleipnir.

The horse snorted, whether in acknowledgment or denial, he couldn't say.

Niflheim. World of Mist, land of cold. Even if not inhabited by the primordial abominations that seemed to dwell in the Astral Roil, this world was ancient beyond the ken of Man, and Hermod could not help but feel that timeless power that saturated it. Primal, unknowable, and far from benevolent.

Keuthos cackled in his mind, a terrible, gut-wrenching sound that made him want to cut his good ear off. Not that it would have helped against a voice in his head.

She is old beyond your reckoning ... And she rules this world, absolutely ...

Every world of the Spirit Realm had its horrors from before the dawn of time. Still, he could not help but think of some as worse than others, even if that came down to ignorance. He'd seen Svartalfheim, Alfheim, and now Niflheim. Of the three, he'd have chosen to visit Alfheim any day over the others.

Hateful Sun ... Do not think of it ...

Huh. So the wraith didn't even want him imagining memories of that world. Well, Keuthos, thus far, had served as a passable guide, as it had promised. The least he could do was try to avoid thinking of things the wraith feared.

Hermod rode forward until a wall of ice several times his height blocked his passage. The cavern ceiling rose much higher, vanishing into darkness his torch could not begin to light, but he could see no way forward save scaling the ice cliff.

"Unless you can jump that," he said to the horse.

Sleipnir snorted and began to back up.

"Whoa, whoa." Hermod dismounted, pulling Sleipnir to a stop. Then he tightened the girth and checked the straps on his saddle bags—which had grown precariously light as his supplies dwindled. Only when everything looked secure did he remount. "All right. Let's see how high you can really jump."

Sleipnir turned, trotting back a hundred feet or so from the ice wall. The horse snorted, scuffing one hoof on the ground. Then he broke into a gallop that sent a rush of bracing wind sweeping over Hermod, forcing him to lean low over the horse and hold on desperately.

His stomach lurched as Sleipnir's hooves left the ground. Freezing air snared the hood of his cloak and jerked it off his head. Everything whooshed by, and the ice wall passed clearly underneath them. Then they were falling, Sleipnir's eight legs flailing in midair. Hermod's gut in knots.

The horse's hooves crashed down on ice, forelegs first, cracking the floor for a dozen feet in all directions.

"Fuck me." Hermod finally dared to breathe again. He shook himself. "All right. Well done."

Before him, someone had carved what looked like a mighty temple into the glacial wall. Up high, it melded with the rest of the rough ice, but for forty feet or so, a facade displayed architecture of impressive—if haunting—talent. The pillars rose at irregular angles and, the longer he stared at them, the more they seemed engraved with watching faces. Indeed, now that he looked closer, he caught sight of reliefs of human visages, twisted into expressions of terror or agony.

Yes ... a shrine to damnation ... in this world, so many souls are brought ...

For judgment?

Judgment is immaterial, for we are all damned from before our births ...

"He sees it ..." The sibilant voice came from just behind him.

Feeling his heart clench for an instant, Hermod twisted around in the saddle and jerked Dainsleif free. Sleipnir, too, pranced about, bringing the entity into view.

The woman had porcelain white skin and even whiter hair, though she looked young. Or, at least, timeless. Her eyes were the palest of blues, and her fingers ended in nails as long as his hand and looking sharp as claws. The woman wore a dress that seemed made of mist, ever shifting about her figure, even as she slowly drifted about the cavern without seeming to walk.

"Snow maiden," he said.

Bean sí ... lampades ...

Hermod had no idea what that meant, but he couldn't worry about the wraith at the moment, regardless.

The snow maiden's smile held such malevolence it chilled him to the core. "I see your death ..."

"My death? You mean to kill me?"

"No need." Despite the seeming glee on her face, her voice sounded sad, almost on the edge of tears.

They revel in it ... but, given the choice ... prefer to allow the terror of impending death to creep upon you ... it ripens your soul for feasting ...

From the corner of his eye, he caught sight of another of the snow maidens, drifting out of the tunnel. He glanced in her direction. Several more followed after her.

"Shall we weep for you? We so oft weep for those soon to join us. So they will know what urd awaits them." She whimpered. "They called us weepers ..."

They pretend to bemoan your suffering ... only to enhance your own dread ...

Hermod raised Dainsleif a hair, to ward her off. "I have no quarrel with you."

A half dozen of the vaettir drifted around him, surrounding Sleipnir, seeming half made of mist, half women clad in pale dresses. "We have not come for your soul just yet," another of them said.

"Hardly needful, when your death draws so very nigh."

"Oh, he rides to *her* abode."

"Do you think that's how he'll die?"

"Passing few have made it so very far."

"There is yet farther to go before he can reach her."

They spoke in such rapid succession, Hermod found

himself constantly twisting about to keep the speaker in view. "What do you wish of me, maidens?"

"Naught."

"We've no quarrel with you, either."

"But we hope to see you again."

Do not attempt to strike them ... or they will freeze your heart ... They will not attack first ... least of all with a wraith inside you ...

A snow maiden had attacked Sif, in Jotunheim.

Provoked ... or compelled to it ...

That, Hermod didn't know, exactly, though the experience had terrified his daughter. So, should he sheath the runeblade?

No ... Keep it in hand ...

In case someone *did* compel these vaettir.

"Let me pass, then," he finally said.

Whimpering, two of the snow maidens drifted apart, clearing a path which he immediately guided Sleipnir through. The more distance he could put between himself and these chilling abominations, the better.

The horse broke into a trot the moment he had cleared the snow maidens, and Hermod encouraged it, riding deeper into the cavern while casting occasional glances back over his shoulder. The vaettir had vanished, though, perhaps becoming one with the mist wafting around outside the temple.

By the Tree, he misliked this place.

Worse than the Roil ...?

That was like comparing being flayed with being boiled alive. A pointless distinction between two abominable ends.

What he missed was Midgard.

Where the World is ending ...?

Yes. Even so.

❧

A GOOD MANY hours more he rode through the cavern, having twice passed shades making the same march as himself, each group guided by a snow maiden. The dead here seemed solid enough, and had looked to him with imploring eyes, as if he might spare them their urds and keep them from having to pass the gates of Hel.

Keuthos had advised against it, not that Hermod had felt overly tempted. His mission here mattered too much to allow himself to be swayed by sentiment for strangers. Those who died—those he could—he'd guided to Valhalla through the valkyries and ...

Oh. Well, fuck.

He hadn't felt any different for having given away Draupnir, but ... Odin had used the ring to bind the valkyries. Now it was gone, would they yet serve Odin or Hermod? He'd not bothered summoning them or issuing them specific commands in many decades, had almost forgotten about them, as they went about their assigned tasks. But without the ring ...

Desperation leads us to difficult choices ... one must sacrifice one thing or another ...

Except, Hermod hadn't made a choice, specifically. He'd been so obsessed with reaching Baldr and Sif, he'd not considered the consequences of giving up Draupnir.

And it was far too late to do aught about it now.

Grimacing, he continued to ride forward.

Besides the rare, wordless encounters with the dead, he'd seen no one. His only company in this desolate place was the horse and a wraith inside his head. After days in the dark and at least a day in the cold, he felt he might soon go mad from the isolation.

Are you not mad, already ... you, who willingly ride to Hel's abode while yet alive ...?

Keuthos might have a point, but still, Hermod would've killed for someone real to talk to.

What dwells here ... you would not wish to converse with ...

He snorted at that. Again, perhaps the wraith spoke the truth.

And so, Hermod rode through endless icy caverns in profound silence, edging ever closer to his terrible destination.

The snow maidens had claimed he would meet his end soon. Perhaps they taunted him. Perhaps they lied.

But given that he sought the gates of Hel, he could not help but suspect they truly did foretell his doom.

Will you then turn back ...?

No. There was no going back. Hermod was finding his daughter. No matter the cost.

12

The way Narfi reckoned it, Asgard looked better inundated. The sea jotunnar had come to him, finally flocked back to old Aegir's banner, and flooded the valleys. They brought the sea crashing down—especially Aegir. Whole ocean seemed poised to obey his whims, and his wife's too. Crusty bastard had betrayed the Elder Council, true enough. Sided with Mundilfari when the Accursed One raised the fucking wall. Gone then, and married a mer instead of one of his own kind.

Well, but he'd had a seat on the Elder Council, was a progenitor to the sea jotunn race. Didn't matter if someone was man or jotunn, really. They always came back to their parents.

Just like Narfi. Avenging his brother and come to see his father and stepmother.

Actually, just like Leikn, too, and her rage might almost have matched his own. She didn't talk too much, but she'd demanded to come on his first war band. Always thirsting for vengeance for Vörnir, a wrong done by the Aesir before

Narfi was even born. Done by Thor, no less, same as just about all the other wrongs they laid on the Aesir.

She wanted blood for her dead father, and Narfi couldn't half blame her for it.

Now, he watched from across the new lagoon, while Leikn set into another of the Asgarder war bands. Weak-looking, in fact, probably hadn't had apples, the poor wretches. She tore into them, with help from Hyrrokkin, riding one of her vargar.

Couldn't well have gotten the giant wolves across the sea without Aegir's help, so Narfi reckoned he owed the old jotunn that, too.

"Should be over there," Gangr said. "Should be helping."

Narfi didn't bother with a response on that one. They all knew they had to strike all over the both of the islands, and hard and fast. Catch the Aesir unawares, much as they could, and prevent them from mounting a real counterattack. It meant he'd split his people all up, with Suttungr taking his brother and daughter to the east island, and Narfi breaking the jotunnar into groups to strike all abouts on this isle.

By now, Thrivaldi ought to be wreaking some havoc inland, and Hyrrokkin's wolves were terrorizing the woodlands, while Narfi himself set to securing the coasts. Sea jotunnar were making sure no one came to help the Aesir, true, but Narfi won't taking no chances of letting his prey escape. They'd scuttle every boat they found, kill the sailors, and make damn certain Asgard didn't have much more than a fortnight left to live.

An enormous crash of thunder resounded out across the lagoon, followed by exploding trees.

"Oh, fuck a mammoth," Gangr complained. "Don't tell me that's him."

Narfi had reckoned the man would show up now. Hadn't much liked it none, of course. No, but he knew what the sacrifice bought him.

While Thor was here, fighting Leikn—killing her, as Narfi had seen in a vision, sad as it was—it meant Odin's son won't anywhere else. Not guarding the halls of Asgard up on those mountains, like a man with half a head for strategy might've done.

No, Thor was too damn proud for that. Him, he'd want to be in the thick of it, always on the attack, pushing back against the invaders. And why not? Word would've reached him about vargar, and who better than Thor to put down giant fucking wolves, right?

Stupid shit-brained buffoon.

So, Narfi had sent Gunnlöd to the other island, safe from the rampaging prince of Asgard. Had waited until Odin was well and gone before he even risked his invasion. Oh, he'd deal with the damn king, of course. Once the Man had lost his home and the better part of his warriors.

Across the lagoon, Thor came crashing out of the woods, swinging that damn hammer like a shooting star, bolts of lightning leaping from jotunnar to vargar to trees. Burning his own damn forest down in the process, though he probably didn't have brains enough to notice.

Narfi nodded grimly.

"Steaming sack of walrus shit," Gangr snarled. "Best we get around the lagoon and deal with him."

"No."

"What?"

Narfi scratched at his beard. "Won't ever a chance we'd take Asgard without losing some of our own, were there?" The other jotunn glowered. "No, 'course not. So, what matters most is, taking more than we lose. Right now, their best two warriors—Thor and Tyr—are both engaged, dealing with our ..." Well, he'd been intent to say *pawns*, but didn't reckon Gangr would much like hearing him talk thus. Besides, would've made him sound a bit too much like Odin. "Our most expendable forces."

"Hyrrokkin ain't expendable, and Leikn—"

"Wants vengeance against Thor, same as me. Only difference is, I'm planning farther ahead." And Hyrrokkin, well, she'd never been the best at following orders, had she? Wouldn't hurt his cause overmuch, her getting splattered on Mjölnir.

Still grim-faced—maybe the sacrifice didn't sit well, and regardless, he sure as Hel better look like it didn't—Narfi turned away and pushed deeper into the wood, knowing Gangr would follow.

By now, Leikn was dead, and Hyrrokkin would follow her, along with a bunch of wolves that would take down a few dozen Aesir before they died.

They weren't the point, though.

Because while Thor busied himself with the pawns, his home turned to rubble. Narfi almost wished he could see the look on the bastard's face when he realized it.

Well ... *if* he realized it.

Thor really was dumb as frozen mammoth shit.

13

They'd always thought the reef would protect Asgard. That, and their deal with Aegir. Well, now the sea jotunn had turned on them, and the waters had risen well over the reef, inundating the shore and washing away any halls in the lowlands.

Whole valleys had become turbulent lagoons swarming with sea jotunnar, and Thor couldn't well fight them in the water. Nor was the flooding the worst of it. The waters had carried in ships that had swarmed over Asgard's paltry navy and unloaded an army of frost, wood, and mountain jotunnar.

Those last oft stood fifteen feet tall or more, with hides almost as rocky and tough as trolls. Everywhere Thor looked, fires spread over the mountains of Asgard. While the valleys drowned, braziers overturned in the halls had set them alight. Mountain jotunnar flung boulders bigger than Thor himself, sent them crashing through walls and demolishing the city.

Women and children fled into the woodlands only to get

skewered by wood jotunn arrows the size of spears. Like those Thor wended among now.

A little girl, maybe five winters old, pinned to a tree by a shaft as long as Thor was tall, her insides spilled out below her. Grimacing, he shook his head. Fucking child-murdering savages.

Just thinking about it had his head pounding. Damn little spots flying about!

Everywhere he turned, the dead dangled from those shafts. A macabre forest of murdered non-combatants. Hundreds of them, the stench of their shit and blood overpowering. Some few, here and there, were still moaning, filling the wood with the sound of torment, making the place seem like something out of Naströnd.

Thor was going to feed every last fucking jotunn in the World to Mjölnir. He'd crack their skulls and let the hammer devour their souls.

More moaning sounded ahead, sending those spots swimming before his eyes.

"Not ... now ..." he growled at the damn spots, making his way closer.

A woman had a tremendous shaft impaled right through her bowels. Despite it, she still tried to crawl along the ground. Thor glanced around until he spotted her goal. A dead boy, six, maybe seven winters, hung upside down from branches overhead.

"Fuck these jotunnar," Thor mumbled. He leapt up, grabbed the boy, and yanked him down, heedless of the blood and guts that spilled over him in the process.

The boy's limp body hardly weighed aught. Holding him like that, it sent a void opening in Thor's own gut. Grimacing, he yanked the arrow out. The shaft squelched, tearing out more flesh in the process, but that hardly mattered to the dead. He carried the corpse over to the woman—his mother?—and laid the body down beside her, putting a hand on her head.

"You cannot be saved."

Her eyes trembled when she looked at him, but they didn't show any sort of shock. Instead, she just grabbed the boy and pulled him close.

There was no reason for the jotunnar to kill people like this. People who couldn't have fought them. Fuck them all. They wanted to eradicate the entire Ás race? Well, Thor would do it to them first. When he was done, all Midgard—and Jotunheim too—would be drowning in jotunn blood. This whole world would belong to Mankind, he swore it.

"I will send you to him," he said to the woman. Her eyes met his again, and she didn't object. Didn't even try to speak.

Deaths like that, they'd be reaching the gates of Hel. But what could Thor do about it? Not a fucking thing. He drew a knife and slid it along the woman's throat. Mercy. Not much to offer, but that—and vengeance—were all he had to give.

He'd come back to burn the bodies later. There were no mists on Asgard, so no draugar. Those who still lived, they needed his attention first.

ASGARD DIDN'T HAVE enough warriors left. Not nigh to enough to face down a threat like this. The remnants of several war bands lay strewn upon the mountain slopes, while other warriors remained engaged with dozens of frost jotunnar.

Thor wended his way among the melees, smiting with Mjölnir when any jotunnar came into range, but heading ever upward. Valaskjalf burned atop the greatest peak of

Asgard. It was like a great pyre, lighting the evening sky, billowing a cloud of smoke a man could see from miles around.

Growling, Thor smacked Mjölnir into a frost jotunn's face. A crack of thunder resounded, and a blast of lightning sent that trollfucker tumbling backward into a rock. The jotunn pitched over sideways and rolled down the slope.

Thor would've spit after him, were he less fatigued. What energy remained to him, he needed to save for killing whoever dared to defile Valaskjalf, so he kept charging upward, relying on the apple's Megin to give him speed and endurance.

How dare these bastards destroy the greatest work on Asgard? How dare they—

The silver-plated tower where Father's High Seat rested cracked, the sound like a gong. Sheets popped out sideways, bent and twisted, leaving Thor gaping in horror. For more than three centuries the tower had served as a beacon to the court of Asgard.

An instant later, another crack resounded, and the stonework beneath the plating began to crumble inward. The ground beneath Thor's feet rumbled as the entire tower collapsed into itself, blowing out walls and and sending a shower of debris down the mountain.

Those trollfucking ... Wait. Mother might have been in that tower!

Drawing on as much Megin as he could, Thor broke into a mad sprint up the rest of the slope. He didn't stop even as he reached the threshold and the blaze within. Just blundered right through the doorway, arm out before himself.

Flames shot up along the rafters, and clouds of black smoke concealed the better part of the hall. Almost immediately, Thor fell into a fit of choking coughs, and had to hold the back of his hand over his mouth. Tongues of fire licked at his exposed arms.

"Mother!" he bellowed. "Mother, where are you?"

No answer. The flames had become a roar, a cacophony accompanied by the continuing collapse of the once-glorious hall. Thor would *have* to pull back. For all he knew, his mother had already withdrawn. And joined the other women and children in the woodlands?

Fuck.

Thor pushed forward once more. He had to be sure she wasn't in here before he—

His foot thumped into something wet on the ground. Thor glanced down and almost retched.

An arm. A woman's arm, not severed, but ripped out in a gory mess. Only once had he seen something like that.

Hödr, when Thor himself had done it.

"Mother!" Thor shouted. Fuck! No! Shit! Fuck! He stumbled forward, half-blind from the billowing smoke. "Mother!"

A rafter behind him snapped in half and crashed down.

"Where is the queen?" he shouted, though he knew it unlikely anyone remained in the hall. She'd be fine. There was no proof that arm belonged to her.

But there, on the floor, lay another arm, this one having caught fire.

Beyond it lay a leg ripped off at the knee.

And ... on the throne ... sat his mother's head. The pulpy mess, the trailing spine, it meant something had ripped her head off.

Thor sank to his knees, arms dropping to his side. His mind refused to focus. Like that ... had she been alive ...? Had she felt ...? No.

A nightmare.

Mother ...

He was haunted by a ... ugh, what was it ... a mara? Had to be a mara? A nightmare.

Wake up! *Please*, let him wake from this. Please do not let this macabre end have befallen his invincible mother. Please ... someone ... say ...

More crashing sounded around him.

A monstrously large shadow stepped through the smoke, so tall it almost brushed against the flaming rafters. Shoulders too wide.

A head poked through the dark cloud.

Then another.

And another.

The creature that stepped through looked like a mountain jotunn, gray, rock-like skin, carved with strange sigils, and mighty bull-like horns jutting from its head. Except, there were too many heads. Three about its shoulders, and then two more torsos jutting from its waist, each with three heads.

Nine? Nine heads?

Thor gaped at the monstrosity. He'd seen jotunnar with two heads, sometimes even three. But this ... this unfathomable abomination ...

It had killed Mother. It had wrought this destruction.

Snarling, Thor climbed to his feet, Mjölnir raised before him. "I'll send you to Hel!"

Two of its hands grasped a hammer bigger than Thor, with a stone head.

As Thor closed in, the jotunn swung the hammer. Thor leapt aside. The blow shattered the floorboards, breaking through down to stone foundations and sending up a shower of ash and dust.

Roaring, Thor raced back in, dove between the massive

creature's legs, and came up in a roll. The jotunn reached down with another arm and giant, rocky fingers closed a hair away from Thor's ankle. He scrambled up, swinging Mjölnir. The hammer roared like a thunderclap, knocking a chunk of rock from the jotunn's calf and sending lightning bolts leaping about the hall.

The jotunn stumbled a step forward but didn't fall.

Not the effect Thor had hoped for.

Two-handing Mjölnir, he brought it around for another swing. A hand the size of his torso smacked into his chest and sent him flying. Everything whooshed past him and Thor crashed through a wooden support column, splitting it in half. His momentum carried him on, into a roaring flame that ignited his hair, beard, and furs.

Desperate, he rolled to extinguish the flames, and managed to come to a stop on ground not yet aflame. Gasping, he lay there for a heartbeat. Whole damn room kept spinning. Thor tightened his grip on Mjölnir.

Let it give him strength for this. For at least one more battle.

Blood dribbled down his brow as he stumbled to his feet, stinging his eyes and further blurring his vision. There were times, with his Megin drawn and Mjölnir's fury raised, when even the spots no longer bothered him. When all he could see was rage, focused in a singular direction. Absolute, unbridled fury.

Maybe Hel would pity the object of his wrath. Thor had none.

The nine-headed jotunn came blundering toward him, its weight crushing more of the floor and sending ashes tumbling down from above.

"Welcome to your pyre," Thor growled. And he raced back in.

The jotunn swung with that hammer. Thor leapt up, over the weapon, and came down swinging Mjölnir not at the jotunn, but at the other hammer's haft. Mjölnir shattered the wood in the jotunn's grasp, sending bolts of lightning coursing along it, even as shards of wood exploded. The stone head flew free and crashed into another support column.

Bellowing, the jotunn stumbled backward, gaping at a sliver of its own weapon that had wedged into the crook of one of its elbows.

"Mine's better," Thor said, wiggling his hammer.

The jotunn lunged at him, and Thor couldn't fall back fast enough. A pair of hands grabbed him around the waist and hefted him into the air. They squeezed, pressing all wind from his lungs while holding him up into the smoke, choking him. It felt like a mountain pressing down on his sides. Those arms guided him toward a massive head, jaws lined with wolf-like fangs that seemed carved from stone.

Bastard intended to literally bite his head off.

Unable to get enough air to even scream, Thor whipped Mjölnir around in a clumsy arc. The hammer slammed into the jotunn's jaw, knocking it off in a shower of blood and rock and bone.

A chorus of eight other heads bellowed in agony, even as the jotunn dropped Thor to the ground. He landed in a crouch, but rose immediately, swinging up over his head to crack Mjölnir into a kneecap. Lightning lit the hall, leaping over rocky hide and across the jotunn, who stumbled backward, leaving a shower of blood in his wake.

"One head for mother's head," Thor said, panting. He hefted the hammer. "How many appendages did you rip off, you trollfucking, stone-headed, rock-cocked piece of linnorm shit?"

The jotunn fell into a battle crouch, eight heads all roaring at Thor, six arms raised, drawn back in threat.

Thor didn't give a fuck. "You killed my mother!"

He whipped Mjölnir around to slam onto the forefinger of one hand, then back up to catch the wrist of another. Blasts of lightning erupted around him, but Mjölnir protected him from it.

Thor pushed in, swinging over and over, each blow knocking out chips of rock and drawing forth springs of dark blood.

Roaring, the jotunn grabbed a support column with four hands and yanked it free, splintering wood in the process.

Huh. That didn't seem like a good—

The tree-sized club caught Thor in the chest and sent him hurtling. Everything blurred in a haze of white. A rush of wind. Something slamming into his back. Stealing what breath remained to him.

A vague sensation of falling. Over and over, spinning round and round.

Then stillness. A ringing filled his ears, drowning out all other sounds.

He blinked, but the white light covered everything. That and pain. Vast oceans of pain, limitless, as if everything within him had broken.

"... ince ..."

Someone shaking him.

"My prince!"

Slowly, his vision began to clear. Tyr was standing over him, slapping his cheek. Blurry though, as if seen from behind a waterfall.

Tyr rose, growling, and jerked free a runeblade stuck into the ground. What ...? Everything kept fucking spinning.

Thor wanted off this damn boat, wherever the fuck it was bound. He wasn't interested in a ride.

That nine-headed jotunn had crashed through the main doorway to Valaskjalf, taking out half the wall in the process. And Thor lay on the mountainside, halfway down the slope. With Tyr racing up there, runeblade in hand, to engage the monstrosity.

"Thrivaldi!" Tyr bellowed.

Thing had a name. Oh. Of course it had a fucking name. Thor just didn't care.

Grunting, he pulled himself up to his side. Pain threatened to crush him. Pain like every rib was broken. Desperately, he seized the apple's power. It pushed down the pain a bit. Just barely.

Mjölnir. The hammer lay two dozen feet away. Without that, he'd never be able to stand.

Shit. Fucking jotunn. Groaning, Thor began to drag himself toward the hammer.

He glanced up. Somehow, Tyr stood on the jotunn's shoulder, ramming that runeblade down through one of its necks. How the fuck had he done that? Most of Thor wanted to sit there and watch, try to figure out how the man pulled such stunts. Mightiest warrior in the World, they called Tyr. Most of the time, Thor found that insulting. Sometimes, though ...

Shit. He needed Mjölnir.

Teeth grit, Thor continued to crawl toward the hammer. Felt like knives dug deeper into his guts with each foot he managed like that. Felt like something crushing him. Ruptured internal organs? Was he going to die, despite the apple? If so ... he'd die on his fucking feet. Ramming his hammer down all nine of Thrivaldi's throats. At the same fucking time.

His fingertips brushed Mjölnir's banded haft. Even that faint contact fed a lick of energy into him. It didn't help his injuries. It just let him ignore them. His fist closed around it. Power flooded into him. The power of hundreds of damned, tormented, fury-filled souls eager to visit their suffering upon any and all they might encounter. Eager to devour that jotunn who'd murdered Mother.

And Thor would feed it to the hammer.

He gained his feet. And then Tyr hurtled through the air to crash down beside Thor, tumble end over end, tearing up the grass and dirt, and continuing onward.

Just as well. This ugly bastard belonged to Thor.

"I own you," he panted, forcing himself to take one stumbling step forward.

Tyr had decapitated one head, blinded another, and impaled a third. A whole torso's worth, rendered dead weight for Thrivaldi.

Well, it still left five heads for Thor. Five heads, and probably a single mighty soul. He closed both hands around Mjölnir and let its power suffuse him. Lightning crackled along his arms. It leapt over him in a torrent. Building into a storm.

The jotunn came blundering toward him.

Good.

Thor didn't have the strength to charge.

He had the strength for one thing. One he had never tried. Maybe the last thing he'd ever do.

Those souls within writhed. Twisted. Raged. Like Thor raged. Pent up to the point they could all explode. So furious it would consume them.

Roaring, Thrivaldi seized Thor up with a pair of arms. Keen to try eating him again. It wanted his power.

Well, it could have it.

With a bellow, Thor released the stored energy from Mjölnir.

All of it.

It erupted outward in a deafening blast. A curtain of lightning exploded in all directions, a sphere that rushed over Thrivaldi, leapt along the jotunn's arms, torso, legs, and heads in a crackling tempest that drowned out the sound of the jotunn's screams and of Thor's own roar.

Thrivaldi's arms exploded into showers of rock, and Thor dropped down to the ground. The jotunn's opalescent eyes melted beneath the lightning storm. Heads popped like rocky pimples. The lightning leapt from the jotunn to corpses and sent them jittering and spasming. It surged into the ruins of Valaskjalf and the hall exploded.

The jotunn fell to its hands—what remained to it—and knees, smoke rising from its smoldering, spasming body. Dead, and it didn't even know it.

Spent but refusing to quit, Thor hefted Mjölnir. Lightning no longer crackled along it. He had completely drained its stored power. But it would still serve, as it had in days past.

Swinging up above his head, he cracked the hammer into Thrivaldi's middle jaw. The blow sent the jotunn tumbling over backward, crashing down like an earthquake.

A steaming corpse.

Thor slumped to his knees. Black surged up to catch him.

Mjölnir slipped from his grasp.

14

*T*yr groaned. Everything hurt. Not unusual. Everything always hurt after a battle. If you were lucky. If you still felt aught.

Frey was there, hefting him to his feet. Man was strong. Would've been nice when Tyr was fighting that jotunn bastard. Now he needed ... Shit.

Shit. The prince. Tyr shrugged off Frey and trotted back up the slope. Legs hurt. Not enough Megin left. Using that much meant he'd feel this for days.

Thor lay there, in a pool of mud. Plenty of blood, too. Breathing, though. Lots of bruising.

Tyr knelt and prodded at the man's ribs. Definitely broken. Maybe every last one of them.

"Does he yet live?" Frey asked.

Tyr grunted in assent. Praise the Tree for that. "Can't move him. Injuries. Best send for Eir."

The liosalf knelt by the prince's side. "Well ... never let it be said I didn't come to Odin's aid despite our differences, then." He laid a hand on Thor's chest, then grit his teeth. A sheen of sweat built on the liosalf's forehead.

Come to think of it, man hadn't really sweat from the sun.

His world must be hotter than even Asgard. Didn't sound pleasant to Tyr's thinking.

Tremble shot through Frey. Bad one, like he was about to swoon. Otherwise, Tyr didn't see much.

All he could do was grunt. "Doing that life-force thing Eir does?"

"Yes." Frey almost growled it, through clenched teeth.

Thor groaned under the man's palm. Good sign, Tyr supposed.

Prince gasped, then. Sputtered. Coughed.

Frey pitched over onto his arse. Not hardly looking godlike the way men thought of alfar as. Then again, Thor himself got more worship than most. And he was lying unconscious, half-dead.

"You can move him now," Frey said, between pants.

Tyr grunted again. "Heard doing that gets someone lustful. Dying for it, even." People, they always wanted more of wherever it came from. That's what he'd heard, leastwise. Had gotten Vili killed, in fact, going after Frigg like that.

"Yes, well, if the prince wishes to suck my cock, I'll not stop him."

Shit. Normal times, Tyr would've laid Frey on his arse. Talking like that about the prince. It didn't hold with him. Not in the least. Even if Thor was an arse himself, most times. Some things, a man just didn't say. Hardly fitting to punch the man who saved the prince's life, though.

Instead, he just slipped a hand under Thor's legs. Another under his shoulders. Hefted the man up and trod down the slope.

"Got to find a safe place," he said.

Frey huffed a moment more. Then the alf came trotting

after him. "Your people have rallied around Mani, who mounted a defense by Thor's hall."

"Ugh. Thrudvangar. Not far. Just on that peak over there. Defensible."

"Yes," Frey said. "But we have nowhere to retreat from there. With the mountain surrounded, the jotunnar will breach those defenses, sooner or later."

"Cost 'em. Especially once I get there."

He'd not let more Aesir die. Not without the jotunnar paying in blood. Paying heavy, for every life taken.

"WE'VE LOST MORE than half the island, already," Frey said. "Saule and many of her liosalfar remain engaged with the Deathless on behalf of Odin, so I doubt they even realize we are so besieged here. Odin only sent me because he sensed danger to his wife."

Danger. Putting it mild. Tyr had failed Queen Frigg. Plain as day, failed her, and failed Odin in the process.

Hadn't much thought about feeling old since he'd tasted the apple. But Tyr felt old now. Tired.

They sat inside Thrudvangar. Mani had taken command. Thor came in and out of consciousness. Not fit to challenge anyone. What with Eir missing, one of Frigg's maids attended to Thor at the moment.

Tyr could have protested. He had authority. But Mani seemed to do well enough. The Vanr focused on defense.

A good sign, given hundreds of non-warriors had holed up here. Like to get slaughtered if things turned ill.

Frey cleared his throat. "Ullr and Magni hold out on the bridge to Yggdrasil, but I don't know how long they can maintain their position."

Oh. Well, trollshit. Tyr hadn't even considered what would happen if the jotunnar got apples. Naught good. Be swimming in immortal jotunnar.

"Got to reinforce them," he said.

"With what?" Frey asked. "I share your concern, I do. I might be able to Sun Stride through enemy lines and aid Ullr, though it would take a significant amount of my stored sunlight to do so."

"Ugh. One man won't make the difference."

"Rather my point." Frey had begun pacing the hall. "We've lost contact with the other island. We have no idea who remains alive there, though fires have been spotted, so they're certainly under attack. Or they were. Maybe they're all dead."

Tyr didn't want to dwell on that. "Damn jotunnar. Too many of them."

"That would be why Mundilfari built the Midgard Wall."

A jab at the Aesir for failing to maintain it? Tyr didn't have patience for that kind of shit.

"If you can get to Yggdrasil, you can get to the Bilröst."

"Another issue," Frey said. "If the frost jotunnar seize the Bilröst, they might turn it from Alfheim to Niflheim. Odin believes Hel will make a play for this Realm. The last time she came to Earth, she flooded the Realm with the mists using a similar device."

Tyr stared at the liosalf. Hardly knew what to say to that. He opened his mouth. Shut it. "King ... gave Hel a way to our Realm?"

Frey folded his arms. "Not intentionally, but we may find ourselves left with no choice save to destroy the device and shatter the bridge."

Well, trollshit. "Not what I had in mind. Got to get rein-forcements."

Frey grumbled something under his breath. "You mean from Alfheim."

"Seeing as how you already lost us a runeblade." A man thinking with his stones was naught new. Losing a runeblade for it? Pretty new. Had to figure it made Frey a giant walking cock.

Liosalf actually winced at that. Good. Still felt shame, then. Good sign, that. "There's news from the mainland, as well. The Serklanders have crossed the Andalus Marches and moved on Peregot."

Ugh. Not again. Bastards must know the Aesir found themselves pressed. Figured, maybe, no better time would come. Damn caliphate wanted to own the World.

Didn't see how he could do a damn thing about it now, though. "Valland belongs to the Deathless. No better than the Serks."

Frey shrugged. "I'll do as you ask, though I cannot promise any liosalfar will come to our aid. My sister already won over those most inclined to aid us, and I used up much of my goodwill in Áine's court when I brought our warriors into Svartalfheim."

Couldn't hardly picture that. Didn't much want to, either. Battles in Otherworlds? No. Shit, but no. Tyr had enough problems on Midgard.

"Go, anyway," he said. "Have to try."

Frey frowned. "If we lose the Tree while I'm gone, if they alter the bridge, I'll have no way back."

"Best hurry, then."

The liosalf's frown turned into a glare. Didn't object, though. Knew better, Tyr figured. What with having lost Laevateinn.

Not an hour after Frey left, the prince was groaning on his cot. Tyr moved to his side. Settled in a chair.

Took a fair bit before Thor actually opened his eyes. Blinking. "Mother."

"Gone."

"She's ... that nine-headed trollfucker killed her ... tore her apart ..."

"Thrivaldi." Tyr had long heard tale of that one's savagery. Even back with Hymir. Strange thing, knowing Tyr's old master was dead. Maybe even his father. Never knew for sure. Didn't hardly know how to feel about that. Easier not to dwell on it at all. "You avenged her, then."

"Tore her apart ..."

Right. Prince had to figure it happened that way on account of Hödr. Queen ordered Thor to savage Narfi's brother like that. Tyr would've died to spare her from that urd.

Still could see why it happened that way.

"Narfi's got to die," Tyr said.

Thor grunted in assent.

"Don't figure you'll be in the shape to do it. Not for days, still."

"Every day he draws breath ..."

Tyr shrugged. "Say the word and I'll hunt him. You go now, you'll fail."

"I never fucking fail!" Thor gasped at his own outburst. Even speaking probably hurt.

Prince was damn lucky no rib had gone through his lungs. Tyr didn't bother arguing with him. "We're losing Asgard. Don't know if they knew Hermod was away. Scout would've helped. Now I need someone else looking for survivors."

"Where are my children?"

Tyr grunted. "Magni's at Yggdrasil with Ullr. Holding it for now. Thrúd's here. Been checking in on you every few hours. Figure she's sleeping now, though."

"Send her to scout." Looked to Tyr like saying it pained the prince. Maybe his wounds. Maybe the thought of putting his daughter in danger.

Didn't much like the idea himself. Tyr had all but fostered Thrúd. Maybe the prince had the right of it, though. Had to send someone. Had to be someone who knew woodcraft.

Grumbling, he rose, then made his way to Thrúd's chambers. Knocked.

"Enter."

Girl stood staring out the window. Probably couldn't see much from here. Just mountains. Warriors outside, watching for another press of jotunnar. She glanced his way, then looked back outside.

Those burns on her face never had healed. Girl didn't blame him. She said she didn't, leastwise. Tyr couldn't help but blame himself, though. Should never have left her alone at Peregot. Possessed or no, Hödr had ... Well. Man deserved whatever Hel did to him now.

"Need someone I can trust."

Now Thrúd did turn to him.

"We don't know if anyone else yet lives, save those here and at Yggdrasil. Could be survivors all over. Someone needs to find them, bring them here."

Thrúd nodded once. "I'll do it."

Right. He'd known that, of course. "Listen to me. Finding others, it's important."

"Of course."

"Not half so important as you getting back to us. Your father needs you." Part of him wanted to say he needed her too. Part of him wanted to claim to be a second father to her. Fostering wasn't official, though. Words like that, to the king's granddaughter ... just not proper.

Maybe she saw it on his face, though, because she embraced him before she left.

With Starkad and Vikar long gone, Thrúd was like to be the closest Tyr got to having another child.

And here he was, sending her out to face jotunnar while Asgard crumbled around her.

Ragnarok. All the king's efforts, and still it had come to their shores. And Tyr didn't know if he could save anyone from it.

15

The glacial caverns had seemed to stretch on forever, such that, when Hermod at last came to stone steps carved into the floor, it had taken him by surprise. The builders had bored down into the ice in order to expose a staircase leading up into what, he could only surmise, must be a mountain.

Yes … The Mountains of Fimbulvinter …

As in the name given by völvur to the Era of mists on Midgard, and later to this prolonged winter?

Yes … Her reign began here … Her sorcerers flocked to her banner … defied death … to shape Niflheim in her image … They called her a goddess of sorcery …

Hel? Keuthos spoke almost as if he had personal knowledge of these events. Did that mean the wraith had known Hel before her mortal death?

But now Keuthos fell utterly silent in Hermod's mind, as if rejecting this line of inquiry. The truth was, unlike his sister or even Odin, Hermod did not much care about such knowledge for its own sake. Wisdom mattered only insofar as it served to achieve an end. Knowing which plants he could eat or use for poultices might save a woodsman. As Odin's apprentice, knowing how to drive off vaettir became indispensable. But unraveling the secrets of Hel's or Keuthos's mortal life didn't make overmuch difference to Hermod's mission, so far as he could see.

If the wraith wanted his secrets, or—perhaps even more likely—had lost his memories to the Lethe, it concerned Hermod little.

These stairs, though, bore extensive, faintly glowing glyph lines along their length, traced in strange, Other-worldly arcs and angles, as if someone had intended to work sorcery on a grander scale than ever Hermod had beheld thus far. That, of course, bespoke utter madness. If any sorcery was apt to cost the sorcerer's soul—perhaps trans-muting it into something like Keuthos—then to attempt mystical workings of such a magnitude must represent hubris only men like Mundilfari had ever mastered.

Of course, if Hel had truly usurped the original goddess of Niflheim, her arrogance must have dwarfed even the Mad Vanr's.

Mist billowed in from the top of the stairs. Which meant they led back outside.

Grimacing against the bone-chilling cold that must soon return, Hermod climbed up, into the mist, walking Sleipnir behind himself. The stairs ended in a landing. A tunnel, really, one that he followed for another twenty or thirty feet before coming to an archway twice his height. From this, another staircase descended the mountainside, disap-pearing into mist that, while less thick than what he'd seen before, still concealed much.

Hermod glanced back at the horse, who snorted. Above them, those glowing sigils spread out over the nigh vertical cliff they had emerged from, stretching dozens of feet. More, perhaps, given the mist prevented him from seeing their end. Someone had engraved an entire mountain with sorcerous markings.

"Fuck me."

Indeed, similar glyphs—not glowing—lined the stone rails that flanked the stairs and even covered the landings where the surface leveled out here and there.

What did all of it mean?

You don't care ...

Hermod snorted. No. He didn't care, true enough.

Ice had crusted over those steps, and he didn't trust himself riding down that. Instead, he released Sleipnir's reins and allowed the horse to descend at his own pace, while making his own careful way down the slopes.

The sky above looked like night, lit by faint stars and brighter, swirling bands of iridescence like those found above Nidavellir or Kvenland in the winter. No moon, though. Just mist covering the ground and dancing lights in the sky.

And everywhere, endless snow-drenched mountains.

IT TOOK the better part of two hours to descend the stairs and into a valley, where the mist grew thicker than ever. On the trek, he'd glimpsed numerous mountain peaks creeping out of the top of the mists and seeming intent to scrape those lights in the sky.

No way to know how far these mountains went on or how long he'd have to navigate the passes to reach his destination.

Modgud had told him to follow the river to its source.

Except, Hermod didn't see or hear any river.

Continue forward ... take the left branch of the pass through the canyon ...

Ah. Well, that was the first Hermod had heard from Keuthos in a while. His guide had proved true, thus far, but Hermod couldn't say he truly missed that hissing, hollow voice in his head.

With a sigh, he stretched, then remounted Sleipnir. After wrapping a cloth around his face once more, he kicked the horse forward. With Keuthos's sporadic guidance, he did move from the pass between two mountains to a canyon that seemed more a crevasse in a glacier than aught else. Icicles three times his size dangled from overhangs, looking like teeth in the maw of a linnorm.

Come to think of it, Hermod truly hoped no dragons dwelt in this abyssal place.

Not abyssal ...

What?

Not abyssal ...

Sure. Yet another random comment the wraith seemed disinclined to elaborate on. Maybe Odin or Sigyn could have taken these fragments and pieced them together into some meaningful snippet of knowledge. Hermod had not the cleverness nor patience to bother.

Mist filled the crevasse, too, until Hermod could scarcely make out his hand in front of his face. Overhead, a howling wind must have whipped some of the mountain slopes mostly clear of the vapors, but here, Hermod couldn't escape.

And the longer he breathed in these mists, the more lightheaded he felt. The Aesir had long held that immortals were immune to the degenerative effects of the mists of Niflheim. But then, they'd never traveled to Niflheim itself.

Hermod coughed once. His throat felt frozen solid. Raw

and apt to crack. Just thinking about what these vapors were doing inside of him had his mind reeling.

Perhaps sensing his rising panic, Sleipnir increased his pace.

You cannot outrun the air itself ...

Unable to glare at the wraith, all Hermod could do was draw his linen tighter around his face and hope it offered some protection from the poison mists as well as the cold.

❧

WHEN HE AT last emerged from the glacial crevasse, he heard it: the crash of ice hitting against ice, mingled with the rush of water. Keuthos guided him on, around another slope, until he caught sight of the river.

It cut through the pass, carving a path through the valley. Ice shelves slammed together, cracked, and continued onward in a frozen cascade that disappeared into the mist. How so much of the river remained unfrozen, he didn't know, but clearly, its source lay some distance ahead.

Far ahead ... Hvergelmir ... The Well of Cold ... from which the icy Elivagar rivers flow ...

Elivagar. He knew that name. Poison rivers from the dawn of time.

Yes ... From poisons come all things ... Life itself is a toxin ...

The wraith had a blissful conception of reality, Hermod had to give it that.

He tugged on Sleipnir's reins, guiding the horse along the riverbank, careful not to draw too nigh. If this *was* one of the Elivagar rivers—nether rivers, perhaps?—he didn't want to know what would happen if it splashed on him or the horse.

This river ... Sildr ...

MATT LARKIN

Good to have a name for it.

She bid a jotunn lord drink the waters ...

Drink it? From Sildr? From Hvelgemir?

Drink and ... should the jotunn survive ... become infused with the powers of Niflheim ...

Did Keuthos speak of Ymir? Odin had said something to that extent, even mentioned that Vafthrudnir had claimed Ymir would walk once more, though he'd been dead for centuries.

We are all dead ...

Odin had also claimed having a wraith in his mind was a torment akin to getting sand in one's trousers, constantly chafing one's stones.

Audr Nottson ...

Hermod jerked around, though, of course, he could not see Keuthos inside of himself. But his wraith ... knew which wraith Odin had bound. Because he knew what Hermod knew? No. It sounded as if Keuthos knew, or at least, knew of, the other wraith. Friend?

Now, Keuthos's mad cackle had him cringing.

Friendship is an illusion for the living ...

Oh. Of course.

Audr touched the power of Nott ... Long after my death ...

So Keuthos was older than Audr, who had been a prince of the Lofdar. That fit, if Keuthos had actually known Hel while she lived.

Not her name ... at the time ...

So, *now* the wraith wanted to share information?

But Keuthos fell silent once again, leaving Hermod to trek along the Sildr's riverbank alone with his thoughts.

HERMOD FOLLOWED the Sildr's course for what he judged to be an entire night and the better part of a new day. The sun never rose and those lights in the sky never went out.

Once, he paused in the faint shelter of a grove of leafless trees. They served to cut down on the wind, if only just, and he allowed himself to doze, trusting to Sleipnir to wake him if aught approached. He'd seen the dead moving on mountain slopes, but down here, in the mist, he couldn't make out much more than a few feet, so who knew what might draw nigh?

No, he had to rely on his—and Sleipnir's—ears, rather than their eyes.

After the rest, he'd ridden on.

On the far side of the river, concealed in the mist, he'd seen several pairs of faint red gleams. Draugar eyes, perhaps? The creatures either could not see him, had no way to cross the icy river, or did not care about him. A strange thought, that last one, for draugar on Midgard attacked most living beings unfortunate enough to happen across them.

Here, though, in a world filled with the dead, perhaps they had other aims. Or no aims at all.

They serve ...

Served Hel? Or whatever her name was.

At last, the river led him to a massive depression where the mist thinned enough he could catch a glimpse of what lay ahead. A bubbling spring set around a massive root that descended from the sky. The mist banked away from that root, forming around the well in a circle. A root of Yggdrasil? From this well rose nine rivers, bubbling up with enough force they flowed up over the twenty feet from the water's surface to the top of the depression, then cascaded away. Rivers of ice and knives and chaos, pulsating like the icy veins of a primal abomination. The beating heart of Niflheim.

Yes ... Hvelgemir ... The Well of Cold ...

Hermod grimaced, transfixed in mute horror by the scope of it. He could not judge how far across from one side of the well to another, but easily two or three hundred feet.

Around the edges of the well, shards of ice jutted up like spears the size of longships. Longer, even, piercing into the mist cloud bubbling above the well.

And one of these rivers would lead him to the gates of Hel.

Gjöll ... Through Helwind Chasm ...

Wait. The same river he'd passed through on the edge of Niflheim?

Yes ...

"Then why the fuck did we come the way we came?" he demanded.

There is no passage that way ... None a living man could survive ...

Hermod groaned, rubbing his face. So Gjöll, the River of Knives, both formed a barrier around at least part of Niflheim, and also cut through it. A half circle, perhaps?

Yes ...

Damn it. He was bitterly tired of this place. In fact, he was just plain bitterly tired. He'd not slept properly in almost a fortnight, unless his sense of time had entirely fled him. Which was possible.

Hermod grabbed the wrap over his mouth and squeezed, crunching frost off it, then pulling it down to breathe in air where the mist wasn't so thick. A strange thought that, though Hvelgemir might be the source of the mists, the well itself remained exposed through Yggdrasil's power.

Still, the air stung his throat and he felt like his eyes would freeze solid in their sockets.

They will ... Leave this place with haste ...

No feller land could exist. After drawing his wrap up once more, Hermod kicked Sleipnir into motion, skirting the edge of the well until he came to another river. Not Gjöll, though.

Hermod looked around. The mighty root of Yggdrasil stretched down from a mountaintop, and though the Tree itself repelled the mist, the vapors blocked his view and prevented him from judging how different it might look from the Tree on Asgard.

Seeing no alternative, he backed Sleipnir up to have him jump the river. Here, at least, they were narrower than further out. The horse broke into a gallop, crunching snow under his hooves, then leapt, flying for a heartbeat, before crashing back down once more.

This jump Hermod had to repeat once more before at last coming to a river where shards of metal clashed together in a chaotic jumble.

Gjöll.

And if Hermod followed the river's course, he would find the gates of Hel at long last.

16

The island had become a giant conflagration, half of it aflame, while amid many of the mountains, snowstorms raged. Snow, on Asgard, for the first time in living memory.

Loki's guards had whispered to each other, perhaps not realizing Sigyn could hear every word. They'd spoken of an attack on Asgard itself, and this Sigyn had to see for herself. Neither of them had tried to stop her from leaving the cavern.

But their words had not begun to prepare Sigyn for the catastrophic destruction that ravaged her home. She had climbed up the mountain slope for a better view, having to skirt her way around wood jotunnar. Her enhanced senses made that possible, though if she had not heard the guards mentioning it, she'd never have imagined jotunnar could reach these shores.

After centuries of alliance, Aegir had betrayed the Aesir.

On hands and knees, Sigyn crawled higher, to the very peak of this mountain. On the lower slopes had rested halls, though they had become pyres now, smoldering. Up here, icy winds blew, and snow dusted the slopes where none should have reached. The strongest of frost jotunnar could control the weather. They were bound to nature in a primal way, and it would obey them.

Which explained the flooding in so many of the outer valleys.

Atop a rocky slope, Sigyn at last rose to a kneeling position. Snow flurries whipped against her face, but she ignored them, peering through the storm and outward to the eastern island. It too lay besieged, and she couldn't see a single structure not ablaze, buried in snow, crushed, or flooded.

A thunderstorm raged above that island, clouds so dark they probably made it seem night over there. What could cause such a tumult? Storm jotunnar? Vanr writings had mentioned them, but their kind were few, and they'd not taken much interest in Midgard since their war with the Vanir.

The devastation encompassed this larger island, too, and the cataclysm seemed to be compounding rather than abating. Leaves fell from Yggdrasil in great droves, a curtain of them, with each falling leaf meaning someone had died, here or out in the greater World.

Armies of jotunnar lay siege to Yggdrasil, trying to claim the World Tree for themselves. If that happened, Asgard would truly have fallen.

As it well deserved.

Sigyn hadn't had any way to send word to Narfi about Hödr's brutal murder, but her adopted son had clearly learned of it. Perhaps his Sight had even revealed the horror Sigyn herself had witnessed.

Yes, Narfi must lie at the heart of the ruination now raining upon Asgard, though she had not found sign of him.

He kept himself well hidden, working from the shadows. Even if she did see him, though, she wouldn't have dissuaded him from this course.

Frigg and Odin had brought this upon themselves when they betrayed her family. Sigyn tapped a finger against her lip. If she *could* find Narfi, however, he might find a way to free Loki, and the three of them could escape Asgard together.

Still, the armies of jotunnar indiscriminately slaughtered any Men they came across and Sigyn could not trust they would recognize or spare her. She could not risk roaming the battlefields in search of her son. She'd need another way to find him.

Maybe Loki could help with that.

THE GUARDS scarcely seemed to notice her return.

Loki, though, watched her as she drew nigh, though he flinched when another drop of water fell from the stalactite and dribbled down his face. Sometimes, he crawled backwards up the stalagmite that bound him, enough to hold his feet out of the water for fear they would rot. He could not keep himself aloft thus for long, though, and always splashed back down.

Watching it made Sigyn want to weep. Or rage against Odin's petty cruelty.

"He thinks himself betrayed," Loki said, as if reading her mind.

Perhaps her expression plainly wrote her thoughts. Sigyn had found, over time, she had learned to read people almost as easily as he did. Tiny variations in facial muscles or posture, flitting eyelids, tone—all gave away hints to a person's inner world. Loki was harder to read than most, but not impossible.

"Odin can think whatever he wishes," she said after slumping down in front of him. "Far be it for me to try to alleviate his delusions at this stage. You and I, we know the betrayal runs in both directions at the very least."

Loki sighed. "If I did not say it enough ... I want you to know how much I love you."

His words triggered a sudden pain in her chest, and she lurched to her feet, putting her hand to his cheek. "Why are you saying this?"

Though she knew what he would answer.

"Because I'm sorry for all that's happened. And all that still will happen. I ... I would have changed it all, if I could. If I could break the cycle ..."

Well, she had not foreseen that last bit. "You told me that the World has to end. That was why you started all this."

"I've seen it end six times already, my love." He sounded almost ready to weep himself. "But I didn't want things to go as they have. I just ... I am powerless ..."

"The Norns placed this burden upon you?"

Loki sputtered as more water fell on his face. "They are ... intermediaries."

"To *what*?"

He shook his head suddenly, as if changing his mind about whatever he'd been about to reveal. Something out there used him, used even the Norns, with an agenda Loki either didn't understand, or could not bear to share with her. Without doubt, this somehow involved the cyclical end of the World.

Sigyn tapped her lip, taking a step away from Loki. "Fifty-two centuries ..."

Loki looked up at her, pain on his face.

"My calculations, based on the Vanr records, seem to indicate that approximately fifty-two centuries have passed since the mists came to the Mortal Realm. Five thousand two hundred years since Hel last walked our world."

Their daughter.

"She was already dead," Loki said. "She needed a human host. A foolish sorceress unwittingly provided one."

Sigyn paced around, not bothering to respond to that. The specific variations within an iteration of the World probably didn't matter so much as the overall pattern. The cycle, Loki had referred to it as. She looked over at him. "Is it always fifty-two centuries?"

"More or less."

Some fragments of Mankind had survived that cataclysm and headed for here, naming the islands Vanaheim. At the same time, a jotunn empire had risen and taken control of most of the World. Civilizations rose ... and they fell.

Trying to hold the puzzle pieces in her mind was surreal, like trying to map a dream, when the landscape defied linearity by its very nature. If she could disengage her mind from grounding in the present, she could almost see it all, on an intellectual level. But to try to reconcile time on such a scale, events of such magnitude, to do so strained the limits of comprehension. She could know it, but not quite understand it.

And Loki's words ... implied not much time remained.

"Narfi's come," she said at last. "He's destroying Asgard in revenge for what they did to his brother."

Loki stared at her, his crystal blue eyes looking ready to break apart, as if they could not contain the torment of whatever he'd seen in an impossibly long life.

He said he'd seen the World end six times. "If this is the

seventh iteration of the cycle, and each cycle endures for approximately fifty-two centuries ... you've been carrying this weight for ... more than thirty-six millennia ..."

"Sigyn. Please. This doesn't matter. Narfi coming here, it does not presage aught we should rejoice over. I need you to know how much I love you, how sorry I am that I cannot stop what's happening."

His words left her shivering, more than any snowstorm had. "I ... I love you, too. We need to find Narfi. He can help us escape from here."

Loki lowered his head and groaned. "Sigyn. Run from here. Do not wait for Narfi. Just ... find a way off these islands. Escape anywhere you can."

"I won't leave without you."

"Sigyn—"

"No! I'm not losing you."

At her outburst, the guards glanced in their direction.

Sigyn held up a finger. "Narfi will come for us."

She knew he would.

17

It sat amidst broken mountains with jagged peaks pointed inward like fangs. The fortress, if fortress were even the right word. Rather, Hermod might have called it a city, or even another mountain. It rose up from the mist, tall beyond his fathoming, a twisted wonder of stonework coated in millennia of ice that jutted from the walls in vicious spikes. Amid the stones lay supports that looked like bones, albeit bones larger than the tallest of trees.

A screeching wind swept down over the mountains, its wail *almost* enough to cover the lamentations of the dead lurking within the fortress itself.

Carved monstrosities overlooked the walls, hanging from skeletal buttresses, poking out from the ice upon spires wider than a king's hall, and lurking within the triangular gable that rested above the infamous gates of Hel themselves. And those ... Fuck. A path cut from the ice and stone rose up the mountainside to double doors that must have stood twenty times Hermod's height. Iron-banded stonework, complete with rime-crusted spikes and strange sigils half-concealed beneath the frost.

An entire force of jotunnar would've found it hard to open those doors.

"Fuck me," he mumbled, then patted Sleipnir's face. "We truly made it."

The rumble in his gut told him it was, perhaps, not something to rejoice over.

All of this was lit only by those ephemeral bands of light in the night sky.

The path leading to the gates broke off in several branches, and from those, a procession of shades marched. Many bore horrific wounds or burns. Some, Hermod could see where they'd been decapitated, leaving little doubt that, despite their trudging pace, they no longer lived. Or, perhaps, they lived here now, in the ultimate necropolis.

He saw few guards among the shades, besides the occasional snow maiden ushering them onward. They marched, not under the whip, but perhaps, because they realized they had nowhere else to go.

Grimacing, Hermod eased Sleipnir forward, joining the procession that headed in. A small throng had gathered before those enormous gates in the distance, awaiting the chance to enter the last place they would ever see. How many of the dead lurked beyond? Did the souls of all who had passed in every Era dwell within?

Not all, of course, for some had become vaettir, while others, according to Odin, were drawn back into the World Tree and spun out again in the Wheel of Life—an idea Hermod found hard to wrap his mind around.

Feral howls erupted from somewhere ahead, echoing through the pass, melding with the wailing wind.

"What the ...?"

The hounds of Hel ...

Oh. Damn.

From a cave he'd not even noticed in the path, a trio of massive dogs surged forward, each the size of a horse, but dead-looking, composed of rotting flesh that sloughed off to expose muscle and bone beneath. Fell bone spikes jutted at irregular angles from the hounds' backs, and their eyes gleamed red like draugar's would.

Hermod grabbed Dainsleif's hilt, but the runeblade held fast in its sheath.

"Oh, fuck me."

Fumbling with it, he caught the sheath with one hand and heaved with the other. A coating of ice cracked and the runeblade lurched free an instant before the closest hound bounded straight into him. The weight of it hit him like an avalanche, sending him toppling off Sleipnir, while the horse himself crashed down beside him, neighing in pain or fear.

Snow broke his fall, but the snarling hound—fuck, it stank!—bore him down. The claws on its foreleg dug into his left shoulder even as slobbering jaws dribbled acid-like saliva over his face. Screaming, Hermod rammed Dainsleif up through the hound's chest. Its blood sprayed over him like a scalding geyser blinding him.

Everywhere, screaming. Sleipnir's wild shrieks. The dead fleeing in terror. Howls of those hounds.

Claws raked Hermod's shoulder, snapping the links of his mail, shredding his gambeson like plain linen. Gouging his flesh almost to the bone. Roaring in agony, he twisted the runeblade, then yanked on it. It sheared through decaying flesh with ease, and that massive weight collapsed atop him, knocking his breath out.

Grunting with the effort, Hermod drew on his Pneuma and heaved. His muscles strained. He could scarcely use his left arm. Trying felt like his tendons were apt to snap in half.

"Gah!"

An agonizing hair at a time, he pushed his way out from under the yelping and somehow not dead—or still undead —hound. Dizziness swept over him in waves as he finally yanked his legs free. Unable to use his free hand, he scrubbed the blood from his eyes with his arm, though they continued to sting.

Swaying, he managed his knees.

The other two hounds of Hel now flanked around him. Beyond them, they had torn Sleipnir to shreds. Half-devoured legs lay strewn over the snow. Flesh and tendons were flung over a space of forty feet or more. A lake of blood drenched the snow, and steaming entrails lay flung in all directions, reeking.

Hermod's chest clenched at the sight. Odin's precious horse. His companion for centuries. And over this long ride, Hermod's own truest ally. He couldn't control his breathing, though his own wounds scarcely hurt anymore.

"Fuck you all ..." Panting raggedly, he advanced on the nearest hound at an unsteady gait. They would pay for this slaughter. He would cut down every last one of these monstrosities ...

Beyond the perimeter of blood, the shades had formed up in a ring, some of them even kneeling to scoop up hand-fuls of bloody snow and devour it. The sight further turned Hermod's stomach.

These abominations deserved to rot within Hel's fortress.

But his view of them quickly dimmed as the mist thick-ened just behind the hounds. In the space of a few breaths it grew so dense he could make out naught else, like an almost solid wall of the vapors. The shades shrieked in terror, though he could no longer see most of them. Those he could, turned and fled toward the fortress with such abandon that even Hermod faltered.

What now?

Empousai ...

What?

Mistwraith ... Her ancient servants ...

Indeed, within the mist, a darkness seemed to take form. Clad in scaled shoulder guards like the plated manica sometimes worn by Miklagardians, whilst further armor seemed lurking beneath a shroud that bled off into the mist—or perhaps formed that very mist. No hint of a face was visible beneath an equally ethereal hood. The Mistwraith bore an axe with blades so wide it ought not have been able to swing it.

She can ...

She?

Beneath the shroud and scaled armor, Hermod could not have begun to guess at a gender. Nor would he have attributed one to any sort of ghost.

Fool ...

The hounds moved to flank the Mistwraith, which advanced on Hermod, seeming to float through the vapors rather than walk. It drifted close enough that Hermod found himself taking an unconscious step back. This *thing* seemed composed of the very fabric of Niflheim, and gazing into its empty hood was like falling into a well of cold darkness that would swallow him whole.

The ghost hefted that massive axe.

Damn it. Not too welcoming of the living, then. Teeth grit against the pain in his shoulder, Hermod backed up, raising Dainsleif to ward off the entity before him. Between the darkness and the thickening mist, he could barely make out where the Mistwraith began or ended. It almost seemed to encompass the entire fog bank, closing in all around him.

"Walk ..." Its voice was hollow, like Keuthos's, seeming to waft in around from all angles.

She will grant you an audience ...

Even as the thought of beholding Hel terrified him, Hermod hoped Keuthos had the right of it. Indeed, the Mistwraith pointed that hideous axe at the gates. Ushering him forward.

Not wanting to turn his back on the fell ghost, Hermod cast frequent glances over his shoulder. Though he could still feel the hateful presence setting the hairs on his neck and arms on end, he could no longer see the Mistwraith. This thing was something of a combination of a snow maiden and ghost, wasn't it?

Yes ... That, and more ... Ancient ... Trapped here from days when the World was ... young ...

Like Keuthos himself?

Yes ...

At last, he came to stand before the mighty gates, and they stretched taller than he had even realized from a distance. The gathered shades retreated to the fringes as the mist beside Hermod congealed and formed up once more into the vile Mistwraith.

Hermod's blood froze to even look upon this entity. This *thing* Odin had never prepared him for.

The truth was, there remained so very much even the king had not known about the Otherworlds. How many fell kinds of abomination lurked beyond the Veil? Each of the Spirit Worlds seemed to have at least one form of sentient vaettr, but these Mistwraiths were something else entirely. Or, at least an amalgamation of two already vile kinds of vaettr.

The sound of iron grating over stone rumbled from within the fortress. Like chains, massive beyond imaging, tightening around gears. Slowly, almost painfully, those gates began to creak open, exposing a darkened vestibule within. A wide staircase descended into that darkness.

Grimacing, Hermod sheathed Dainsleif and set about lighting a torch. Managing it with one hand half limp proved no easy task.

A hissing whisper undulated out of the Mistwraith and wafted around the mist itself, snarling with hatred.

Hermod jerked the fragile torch up between himself and the entity. It didn't like fire.

Of course it doesn't ...

Fire banished the mist. Fire is life. Every child learned that. Never let the fires go out. Hermod's father had admonished him of it, back when they'd lived on Wolf Lake, so many lifetimes ago.

"I cannot see in the dark," Hermod snapped at the Mistwraith.

Whether or not that appeased the creature, it hissed once more, then drifted forward, into the opening gates.

Well. The gates of Hel. Warriors across the North Realms swore by these things. And here he was, actually entering them. Alive. At least for a little while longer.

He followed the Mistwraith down the stairs, to a lower landing. In alcoves to either side, massive chains did indeed loop around gears—those pushed by dozens upon dozens of ragged looked shades. Ghosts of Men and jotunnar, both.

The Mistwraith did not pause, though, instead leading him to a colonnade flanked by enormous columns with statues almost as tall. The statues looked bronze, but they wore strange clothes, styled their hair oddly, and otherwise seemed alien to him. Nor did he recognize ... Wait.

Was that Loki at the end of the colonnade? Hermod stepped away from the main path to raise his torch and inspect the statue more closely. If it wasn't Loki, it still resembled his features, the cut of his chin, his gaze, with sapphires set in his eyes, catching the torchlight. No other statue had gemstone eyes. And this one stood apart from the others, along with a woman across from him.

Hel's mother and father?

Keuthos remained oddly silent.

The Mistwraith, though, hissed in irritation, and Hermod dared not test the limits of its patience, so he chased after the ghost, but glanced over his shoulder to see that the other shades did indeed file inside, guided by a snow maiden.

The colonnade ran a long distance, with side exits the Mistwraith bypassed, though the snow maiden guided her charges down one. Hermod's guide, though, paused before another set of doors. While the ghost gave no command Hermod could hear, the doors began to creak open of their own accord.

Pale light filtered in as the doors drew wide, revealing another long hall, this one with upper arches exposed to the frost. Ice coated everything within, from the floor to the vaulted ceilings, to the columns supporting that roof. Icicles the size of spears lanced down, as if the entire hall was a fanged maw of an immense dragon, waiting to clamp down upon any foolish enough to tread within.

The thought didn't much appeal, but the wraith wafted through the doors the moment they finished opening, forcing Hermod to continue onward. Chilling mist billowed in through the open arches, seeming to meld with the vapors emanating from his guide, turning the entity in a cloud that seemed to suffuse the entire passage.

Indeed, the mist clung to his legs, making walking more like wading through a bog.

Hermod jerked the torch around and the worst of the vapors thinned, recoiling from the flame as they did in the Mortal Realm. In response, a silent anger seemed to creep into the air, a wrath that threatened to swallow him.

This long hall led to yet another set of gates, that, once again, drew open when the Mistwraith paused before them.

The doors opened into another long hall, one that swallowed the light of his torch and dimmed it much as Svartalfheim had. Hermod took a step inside, and his torch crackled out, as if even fire itself could not survive in this place.

Instead, he found the chamber lit by braziers that burned like pale blue flames but radiated not heat but coldness, casting the mighty hall within in distorting light. Hermod tossed the useless torch aside.

Once again, columns flanked the hall, but these were not stone. That was ... bone. Even the vaulted ceiling was supported by giant curving ribs too large to even have come from a linnorm. About the ceiling flitted ephemeral shades.

The Mistwraith allowed him no further time for inspection, though, forcing him forward. Skulls crunched under his feet as he moved, drawing a wince from him. Skulls and broken bone formed the walkway and, beyond the columns and arching ribs, the floor dropped away into darkness. Within the walls of that pit, shadowed bodies writhed, half dead, and locked in eternal torment. Their moans filled the chamber, and they reached out to him with skeletal hands, as if he might somehow yank them free of their prison.

A pit composed of the damned. The cold braziers did not light deep into the abyss, but with his keen eyes, he could make out that more tormented souls squirmed within a wall of corpses and bones. Hundreds of thousands of shades, drawn into this prison.

The Mistwraith led him up to a vertical circle of bone flanked by two more of the pale braziers, and there fell to one knee, offering no indication of what it expected Hermod to do.

Keep walking ... You came to see her ...

Yes. He had.

Of course, he had to clench his teeth together to keep his mouth from trembling, and his heart was hammering so loud he suspected the wraith could hear it.

But he stepped through the archway.

Beyond, stairs of writhing corpses led up to a dais upon which rested a throne of skulls and bones. On this sat a woman, naked and with her legs spread provocatively, though there was naught sensual about her. For half her body had rotted away, exposing muscle and skeleton within. It was like someone had sliced her down the middle, and her entire left side had rotted away, decaying and reeking, even from ten feet below her. One eye was missing while the other gleamed faintly red despite the lack of firelight to reflect it.

Her auburn hair—threadbare on her decaying side—looked rather like her father's. She was large, too, at least six and a half feet tall, larger even than Loki, who was no small man.

"Hermod Agilazson." Hel's voice echoed through the chamber, as hollow and mind-rending as any wraith or draugar's. More so, perhaps, and Hermod could not quite contain his wince. "I cannot say a living Man has come before me ... in long ages ... Come to taste the honey of my trench?"

She traced a lazy finger over her sex, but half of it had

rotted away like the rest of her, gray and necrotic and exposing raw flesh beneath, while part of her pelvic bone jutted free of loose skin.

Hermod wanted to retch. Vaettir delighted in making mortals suffer, Odin had told him, time and again. They would taunt Men in whatever way they could, horrifying them with word and deed and feasting on the disquiet their actions engendered.

And Hermod refused to give her the satisfaction of a response, verbal or otherwise. Instead, he strode to the edge of the stairs, just shy of where grasping fingers reached to snare his boots. "I have come for the soul of Baldr."

"Have you? I rather think ... you wish to see another ..."

Sif. Now he couldn't quite suppress the anticipation that crept onto his face. "S-she's here?"

"Oh ... yes ..."

"I can offer you tribute of gold and silver and gems." All of which had been on the saddlebags.

Hel grinned, the half of her face with flesh twisting into a sickening smile while the other side remained disquietingly still. She knew his tribute lay outside. Maybe she'd already even retrieved it. Her laughter was a cackle that made Hermod want to curl up into a ball and weep for his parents and beg forgiveness for all his misdeeds in life.

Finally, the dark goddess shook her head. "Well, then, Melinöe. Take him to see those he would bargain for. Let it not be said I deal in bad faith." With that, she waved her hand.

Hermod spun to see the Mistwraith—Melinöe—rise from its knee and beckon him forward.

Yes. Let him see them. Let him see Sif, at long last. And he'd pay aught imaginable to have her back.

18

The temptation to create a paradox and thus begin unraveling the Web of Urd kept rustling around in Odin's mind. His visions had revealed Didrik's death here, at the fire beside Bergljot, where Odin sat watching them. Should he not, then, send the varulf away, to safety? Not merely to save the man's life, but to forestall the designs of urd.

Except, his very plan now hinged upon allowing the future to play out precisely as he had envisioned it. The Patriarch—Thurkell, Odin had learned its name was—would come to kill varulfur this night, Didrik included. And he would succeed. If Odin saved Didrik by hiding him, as he had hidden the liosalfar, he might save the varulf, yes, but Thurkell would not come.

Or rather, more damning, Odin had seen the vision, which meant he *would not*, rather than could not save Didrik. He needed to let the future unfold, sacrificing a few lives in the fragile hope of saving this world.

Self-delusion ...

Yes. Odin wanted to save Freyja and Thor and those he

loved. Saving Midgard was secondary, in his heart. Did that make him a monster as much as the ghost that prattled on in his mind?

We are all dead ...

Oh, Odin knew he had lived and died so many times. He did not need Audr to remind him of that. Those lives were a constant murmur in the back of his mind. An endless collection of skills and talents and experiences, all waiting to bubble to the surface.

The crackle of the fire was a small comfort. It would begin so very soon.

This plan sacrificed not only Didrik, but another varulf —Petra—and dozens of human soldiers. So, yes, he knew what he was, allowing others to die for his plans. He'd had a great many years to justify his actions to himself. The wars he'd started. The men he'd used and betrayed. All toward a greater purpose, or so he told himself.

Thor would judge him harshly, if he understood half of all Odin had done. As for the liosalfar, it had almost bothered him that they did *not* judge him. Because they placed so little value on life, much less mortal life.

But poor Didrik. Brave, and loyal, and worshiping Odin, even now, having no idea that Odin had planned his imminent death.

"Whatever happens," Odin finally said, "know that Asgard honors you for all you did. You fought for us, even as the faith died around you."

Audr cackled in Odin's mind, the sound drawing Odin's lips pursed.

Didrik grunted, then looked up sharply. An instant later, he leapt to his feet. He'd smelled his foe, closing in. "Arise! Nachz—"

The varulf finished no more before a form stepped from

the shadows of the Penumbra, appearing like a cloud of dust rising from the ground. The vampire Patriarch lunged at Didrik with Otherwordly speed, Gungnir bursting through the varulf's back and out his chest.

Bergljot shrieked in terror, in horror at seeing her friend slaughtered. Her cries of anguish were the signal Odin had told the liosalfar to wait for, hiding beneath blankets inside a tent, concealing their sunlight.

Thurkell caught Didrik's skull with his free hand and jerked so forcefully Odin winced at the sound of crunching vertebrae. The sound he'd heard in his visions.

He rose, staring down the vampire lord.

"It's you," Thurkell said, chuckling. "Still alive?" He jerked Gungnir free, whipping it around and splattering Odin and the others around the fire with Didrik's blood.

An instant later, a dozen naked liosalfar appeared in a circle around the campfire, their bodies glowing like miniature suns, arms outstretched, fingertips not quite touching. They were flaring their sunlight, not to fuel any great Manifest Art, but rather, for its own sake. So bright, they had created a tiny ring of daylight. They could not maintain such for long, but, it would be long enough.

Odin advanced on Thurkell. "Sunlight suppresses vampiric powers just as it does those of draugar, does it not?"

Thurkell's face betrayed its sudden surge of panic. Here, a ghost that had lingered on Midgard from the early days of mist. Ancient, powerful. Doomed.

In Odin's mind, Audr cackled in perverse joy at seeing another's dread. A distant sound, though, for the wraith also disdained sunlight.

Thurkell lunged at Saule, Gungnir raised.

Pulling on his Pneuma, Odin moved faster, charging in.

He caught the spear's haft with one hand and heaved, flinging Thurkell back around like a doll, casting the vampire straight into the campfire. Shrieking in unaccustomed pain, the vampire blundered from the flames, flailing as they spread over its arms and back.

Odin kicked it in the chest, sending it sprawling and yanking Gungnir free of its grasp. "Your kind think yourselves gods. An arrogance I am all too familiar with." He thrust his ancestral spear straight down, right through the vampire's heart. It punched through ribs and out Thurkell's back, embedding in the slushy ground. Odin twist the spear, shredding muscle and bone.

His prey flailed wildly, refusing to die despite the flames and the blade through its torso.

Odin jerked Gungnir free, then swiped it across Thurkell's neck, taking its head clean off. The snarling, fanged thing continued to hiss even as it hit the ground. Odin kicked the head into the flames.

Almost as one, the liosalfar's lights winked out, and they sank to their knees.

Odin planted Gungnir in the snow and trod to Freyja, drawing her up, and kissing her on the lips. "You did it."

She blew out a long breath, nodding. He held her close a moment more, then looked to Saule. "Give the signal. We pack up the camp and make for the Myrkvidr while the Miklagardians are overcome with chaos."

ONCE MORE GARBED in her gilded armor, Freyja walked at Odin's side. "You seem far away."

He leaned on Gungnir as he walked, missing Sleipnir.

The horse would have proved a boon for the trek ahead, though Hermod had needed him more. "I ... I am not coming to the Myrkvidr. Send a few liosalfar to see the Hunalanders through the wood, but the rest should return to Asgard. Your brother will have need of them in the defense of the isles."

Odin had tried not to see the future, but he could not deny what he'd seen for Frigg. Could only pray Frey would get to his wife and save her.

"What are you talking about?"

He placed a hand on her shoulder. "I have a last, truly desperate hope to fix everything."

"Then what are we waiting for?"

Oh, he had not needed prescient visions to know she would react thus. "For this ... I must go alone. I cannot risk bringing anyone else along on my quest, nor do I dare even speak aloud of my intentions. Others would call it audacious. Arrogant." Perhaps it was. "But I have to try. And I have to know you and the others I love are safe in the mean time. Please, go to Asgard. My wife and child are in danger. Protect them, if you can."

Freyja grabbed him, jerking him to a rough halt. "You truly think I'm going to let you walk into danger for your *audacious* plan? Alone?"

"Don't fear for me. This is not how I end."

Oh ... now you lie to both yourself and her ... Forgetting the entire purpose of your sojourn ... to break the chains of urd ... to change that which you have foreseen ... Your success might very well mean your death ...

Perhaps the wraith speaks a truth, at long last, Valravn said. *Your only hope may lie in failure.*

Odin struggled to keep their debate from warring across his face.

"We have not been through so much to lose one another now," Freyja said.

Odin stroked her cheek. He was doing this *for* her. Even if it meant his own death, if he could undo the Norns' designs, buy her life, it would be worth it. "Please trust me."

Freyja jerked away and threw up her hands. "Because you've never made mistakes before, have you? Discounting banishing the Vanir, bargaining away your daughter, and risking the entire damn World to try to correct your mistake. Had you been here, things might not have grown so dire."

Odin flinched at her tirade. It was true ... even if it wasn't urd. He had to fight now to give them the freedom to have their choices be their own choices. "Forgive me, I ... Well, I have no excuses. Only a promise—I'm going to try to save us. All of us. And I ask you to protect my family while I'm gone."

Freyja groaned before finally waving him away.

Not the parting he'd had in mind.

19

_M_elinöe led him through winding corridors filled with the lamentations and moans of the damned. Places where the walls squirmed with souls absorbed into the surface. They passed a door where hundreds of gray, rotting hands stretched out of a crack too small to allow their bodies. Those fingers grasped at Hermod, silently imploring him to somehow free them from their torment.

Or worse, perhaps they wanted him to join them.

So many vaettir sought to make Mankind suffer, as if the whole of the dead—caught in misery—thought sharing their torment with others might slightly obviate their own. Odin had taught him that, even before the first time Hermod had stepped across the Veil. Many, if not all, of the vaettir of the Spirit Realm had lived once, as men and women in the Mortal Realm.

They had lived, and they had died, and found damnation waiting for them. And through the passing of ages, some of the ghosts transmigrated into spirits dwelling beyond even the Astral Realm.

Half truths ... clouded perceptions ... Conclusions drawn from observations with gaps ... One of you sees much ... but does not understand everything ...

Perhaps not. But Hermod's own observations lined up with Odin's claims. Vaettir—ghosts and spirits if there were truly a difference between them—by and large hated mortals. So many of the Otherworldly creatures seemed locked in agonies and all too eager to share those pains with Mankind. Perhaps they resented the living for possessing what they themselves had long since lost.

Keuthos said naught more, but Hermod could feel the wraith inside him seething, enraged by Hermod's insights.

Though he spoke naught aloud, Melinöe slowly craned her head around toward him, as if somehow sensing his line of thought. Or ... feeling the disquiet of the wraith inside him? Could one vaettr detect another?

Keuthos, though, refused to answer that, perhaps out of spite.

The Mistwraith guided him down a flight of twisting stairs with no inner wall such that to one side he could see a drop of hundreds of feet. At the bottom crackled another of those dark braziers, casting fell blue-green light but failing to provide even a bit of warmth.

In the world of Hel, even fires burned cold.

Numerous hallways broke off the staircase, and Melinöe took one just before the bottom landing where the brazier sat. Bones and rotting flesh composed this corridor, its reek of decay so overpowering that Hermod couldn't help but gag. It was like stepping inside the putrefying throat of a sea serpent big enough to devour a ship whole. Shreds of gray meat dangled from above in gory ribbons that swayed ever so slightly as Melinöe's mist wafted through the passage.

Hand over his mouth to keep from retching, Hermod stepped around these bits of flesh. Had Melinöe brought him this way to further discomfit him, or was this truly the only way to reach the souls Hel had promised him an audience with?

Either way, the Mistwraith took an exit formed by a cross of curving bones, one Hermod had to duck his head to sneak through without touching any of the necrotic filth. Beyond, the Mistwraith continued down another hall of bone before eventually coming to rest outside an archway of overlaid, curving bones. Those bones bent backward as Melinöe raised a hand to them, lurching open with the sound of cracking joints.

"The son of the Destroyer has been afforded a place of honor ..." The Mistwraith waved her hand for Hermod to step inside the chamber beyond.

A cell, in truth, he realized as he ducked his head to enter.

Baldr waited within, stripped naked, pressed up against the walls of his bone cage and whimpering, arm covering his eyes. His flesh had swollen and turned sickly yellow, and hundreds of small cuts and bruises covered him. They had tortured him?

"Baldr ..."

The man moaned, but didn't look up.

From the shadows, another entity sashayed out, a female, her movements sensuous even as her visage repulsed. She was lithe, naked. Bat-like wings flapped lazily behind her, and a serpentine tail twitched in time with her movements. Small, spiraling black horns jutted from her head. Her leering mouth revealed irregular fangs and a bulbous purple tongue at least a foot long.

"Come to join the fun?" Her voice conveyed such lasciviousness that Hermod felt himself begin to harden despite her horrific appearance.

"What the fuck is this, Baldr?"

Panting, breath so fast he seemed like to faint, Baldr turned to him, peeking at the creature, before cringing. "Y-y-you can see her? S-s-she's real?"

Hermod's hand closed around Dainsleif's hilt. "What are you?"

Alp ... Mara ... Nightmare manifested ... lust ...

A nightmare spirit. Did these creatures come from Niflheim?

Well, it hardly mattered. "Leave him be." Hermod eased the runeblade free of its sheath.

Melinöe hissed outside the cell, but made no move to enter. And if the Mistwraith wasn't going to stop him ...

The mara cocked her head to the side, slathering that tongue over her chin and down, to the skin between her breasts. She purred, the sound somehow causing a vibration in Hermod's cock that had it up and ready in an instant. Every instinct in his body—to his horror—demanded he pound into the mara's trench over and over.

And lose your essence ... one carnal gratification after another ...

Teeth grit, Hermod pointed Dainsleif at the mara. "Whoever or whatever you are, leave Prince Baldr. Now."

That serpentine tail twirled around before her face, coated with dried blood, Hermod now realized. "He likes it," she purred. "He likes it when I slither up his arse and use him like a woman. Would you like that?"

Baldr whimpered, actually weeping.

Fucking abomination.

Hermod lunged in. A swipe of Dainsleif severed that tail, and the detached piece landed on the ground with a wet *thwack*, then flopped wildly around of its own accord. The mara gaped—exposing those mismatched fangs—at her injury as if unable to believe any mortal would dare strike her.

Snarling, Hermod thrust in, intent to ram Dainsleif through her hideous heart.

The mara moved so fast he barely saw it. She twisted away from the blow, caught his sword arm by the wrist with one clawed hand, and caught his chin with the other. Like a savage wind she hefted him off his feet and slammed him against the wall with such force his vision dimmed a moment.

Her distended tongue slapped against his neck. It crawled over his face like a slithering worm. It brushed over his lips then pried them apart, slipping into his mouth. Then it kept going, forcing its way down his throat until it cut off his airways. Hermod gagged, flailing, desperate for a breath.

He bit down hard, but the mara only tightened her grip on his wrist and neck.

Everything started to go hazy.

His free hand, ravaged by those hounds, beat ineffectively against her arm.

Like this ...?

You thought to fight her ...?

Baldr slammed shoulder first into her midsection, jerking the mara off Hermod and sending himself and the creature sprawling to floor. Hermod dropped to his knees, gasping. His throat felt scoured as if by sand.

The mara shoved Baldr off her, then hefted him up by his hair, screaming.

Hermod's hand closed around Dainsleif's hilt once more, desperate for its strength to beat down the pain.

While the mara focused on Baldr, he lunged in, not bothering to gain his feet, but swiping at her leg.

The runeblade slashed through her flesh and embedded in her shin, drawing a feral shriek from the vaettr. She pitched over, wailing. How had Dainsleif failed to sever the leg? No time to think on that now.

Hermod struggled to his feet, rose, and planted a boot on the mara's leg. Then he jerked the runeblade free with a shower of black blood. The mara snarled at him, wells of swirling blackness in her eyes. Hermod dropped down atop her, driving the runeblade clear through one of those eyes.

The creature flailed, her mind-splitting cries worse than ever. She flung him off her with her gyrations and somehow managed her feet, despite having a blade run clean through her skull and poking out the back.

How the fuck did such an abomination die?

Baldr leapt up, grabbed the runeblade, and yanked it loose with a sickening squelch that splattered brain and bone and blood in a gory mess. With a battle cry, Baldr swiped the runeblade across her neck. Again, it failed to sever the bone, instead embedding itself in her spine.

And she caught Baldr's wrist and twisted until he released the hilt.

"Fuck me," Hermod rasped.

"Don't say that!" Baldr screamed, clutching his bruised wrist.

The mara grabbed the edge of the runeblade with both hands and began to slide it free of her neck. Black blood dribbled down her fingers but it hardly seemed to disturb her.

How did he kill this thing?

Cut off the head ...

Baldr had just tried that.

Hermod kicked the mara in the gut, grabbed the hilt as she fell backward, and jerked it free, managing to sever one of her fingers in the process. The mara hissed.

Roaring, pulling as much strength from his Pneuma as he could, Hermod swung at the same angle Baldr had. The blade sliced through already shredded flesh and into the bone once more. This time, it punched through, scraping down against her collarbone. The creature pitched over backward and landed on her arse, flailing wildly.

He'd severed her fucking spinal column and she was still fighting?

Growling, Hermod dropped atop her and began to saw with Dainsleif, working the blade up, away from her collar. Three great heaves, and her head popped free of her shoulders. Now her ichor bubbled forth from the stump of her neck like a hot spring. It gurgled, dribbling down over her body. Her corpse slowly began to dissolve as if sprayed with acid, turning to ash.

Well done ...

Huh. Hermod wasn't half sure whether to thank Keuthos for its advice or admonish the wraith for failing to do more than it had.

Save your recriminations for mortals ... Your ire is a feast to those bound to the Otherworlds ...

Coughing, Hermod finally managed his feet. Utter madness. After cleaning Dainsleif with a cloth—one he tossed aside given it had turned black and putrid—he sheathed the runeblade, then offered a hand to Baldr.

The prince took it and rose.

"Let's go," Hermod said.

"He cannot," Melinöe said from the threshold. "While freed of the mara, he remains, in fact, dead, and thus under the thrall of Queen Hel."

Hermod was damn tempted to draw the runeblade again.

Considering how well that went against the mara ...

Yes. Diplomacy then. "I did not come through all I endured to leave Baldr behind."

"You have yet to strike a bargain with the queen."

Hermod glanced at Baldr, who nodded in grim acceptance of his urd.

Damn it. Damn this whole abominable place.

Yes ...

He shook his head in disgust. "Then take me to my daughter."

❦

MELINÖE LED him back to the staircase, and down to the landing. The exit from there led into what looked to him like an ice cave, perhaps cut beneath the fortress itself. The Mistwraith guided him through a maze, a warren of passages that housed chamber after chamber of tormented shades.

Some were actively tortured by the snow maidens in service to Hel or even by other shades that had become overseers of this torment. He saw men and women flayed. Saw them eviscerated so slowly it might take hours. The screams ravaged his mind as souls were cast into freezing waters and thrown into ice-blue flames. They were pierced by spike-like icicles, stretched upon hooks, and had their insides scooped out.

No matter what depraved violations were visited upon them, the shades seemed unable to die.

They are already dead ...

Could ghosts not be despatched?

Souls can be drained of their essence ... sometimes to the point they cannot hold together self image ...

What did that even mean? Bah. Such esoteric musings suited Odin better than Hermod. What mattered here was that the victims suffered these sporadic torments merely at the whims of those around them. Out of a desire to share their own suffering. The thought of it turned his stomach.

Behold the fate of all who live ... Locked in torment ... reliving the wounds that felled them ... awaiting the cessation of torment found only when something stronger devours their souls ... We eat ... or we perish ... not so unlike you ...

"I don't torture animals before I eat them."

Melinöe looked to him, perhaps curious at his sudden outburst. Hermod found himself disinclined to explain himself to the Mistwraith.

Without comment, his guide led him onward, up a slope and out of the ice warrens, into a chamber of stone. A tower, perhaps, for stairs led dramatically upward, disappearing into the darkness far above him.

It felt liked he'd walked for hours since leaving Hel's throne room.

A speck on the vast tapestry that is the fortress ...

A billowing cloud of mist, Melinöe drifted up the stairs with ease, and Hermod chased after her. His shoulder throbbed with pain, though he could feel the apple at work, using his Pneuma to knit together the wound. Too, his throat hurt where the mara had half-crushed it. He'd have recovered more quickly with a good night's sleep and a proper meal, though Odin had advised him to eat naught offered in the Otherworlds.

After twelve flights of stairs they came to a landing, a doorway that popped open for the Mistwraith. It led to an enclosed bridge from one tower to another, with great arching windows that let in the howling wind. The moment the door opened, a blast of cold surged over Hermod and chilled him to the bone. Inside the fortress, he could have frozen to death in his sleep, he imagined. Outside, and up at least a hundred feet in the air with naught to cut down on the bitter winds, it felt as though he might freeze solid mid-stride.

He hurried across, or tried, but Melinöe continued to drift along at a calm pace, and Hermod could not bypass her without wading through her own chilling mist. The Mistwraith tormented him, he suspected, but didn't see how he could do aught about it save endure it silently.

So, shivering and in pain, he waddled across the sky bridge.

At the far end, the Mistwraith urged open another door, leading into a second tower. Actually, was the Mistwraith taking him on a circuitous route in a deliberate attempt to exhaust him? To confuse his sense of direction? Or was Hel's fortress simply so sprawling it had become a maze incomprehensible to the living?

They went down one flight of stairs, then paused before yet another door. When Melinöe didn't open it herself, Hermod grabbed the handle and eased it ajar so he could peer through. The room beyond was dark, lit only by a small, iced-over window, and even then, the eternal night of this world didn't offer much illumination to begin with.

Hermod slipped inside.

Something in the back corner snarled, and he spun, hand going to Dainsleif's hilt. A pair of gleaming red eyes rose from a crouch and took a faltering step in his direction. Her beautiful, golden hair had become threadbare, clumps of it sticking to her decaying scalp. The skin around one of her glowing eyes had rotted away, and the gleam came not from the orb itself, which was missing, but from a hollow within.

A raw, bloodless gash separated her throat, the edges peeling apart.

Hermod's heart clenched in his chest. His breath caught, and he couldn't form a word.

The draug—his daughter—lurched toward him, hand raised as if she intended to go for his throat. She paused a hairsbreadth from throttling him and cocked her head to the side. Perhaps shocked he had not retreated.

"What has she done to you?" His voice was a whimper, barely audible even to his own keen ears.

Kept her soul from fraying into pieces ...

No. No, Hermod refused to look upon Hel transforming his daughter into a draug as a mercy.

Willful ignorance ...? But truth, nonetheless, for naught of mercy survives the mist ...

Hermod reached a trembling hand up to stroke Sif's cheek. Her flesh was cold as ice, and clammy. "I'm so sorry ..."

Sif touched a hand to the wound at her throat. Then she drew up the edge of her tattered shirt to reveal another decaying injury in her side. Where the Serk had first stabbed her, Hermod judged, though so much had rotted away, he could read little detail.

"It still hurts you?"

Her low growl seemed to fill the air with rage, and she nodded slowly.

The wounds would never heal. So they pained her, and would for as long as her soul held together. Most draugar—at least those that came to Midgard—possessed their own corpses. He didn't know what happened to them when those bodies finally fell. But Sif ... she had no body. She was just ... a soul. Trapped in torment.

Her wounds ... manifestations of a tormented mind ...

Not real? But how to explain that? "I ... I killed so many Serks hoping to offer you vengeance, hoping it would ease your suffering." Her dark growl set the hairs on his neck on end, but he forced himself not to step back. "I'd have done aught imaginable to save you. Would have killed them all, even after Odin bid me stop, if I thought it might have spared you this. If I'd known ... my precious daughter."

"It wasn't a Serk." Her voice had gone hollow, and it wheezed through her rent throat, raspy and grating. Still, he dared to hope he heard some semblance of her true self beneath the pain.

"N-not a Serk? Who else would strike you down?"

Sif leaned in close to his face. So close he could smell the putrefaction of her skin and the rot on her breath. "Aunt. Sigyn."

***

A RAGE HAD TAKEN him and, despite all Keuthos's imploring that he control himself, he had barely managed to bring it down to a simmer in the long walk back to Hel's throne room. It boiled in his gut, fresh, as if Sif had died this very day rather than hundreds of years ago.

No, not died. Had been *murdered*.

For centuries, he'd believed his daughter taken from him in war. Murdered, yes, but murdered by enemies intent to eliminate a military threat. Not by ... by Hermod's own sister.

Foster sister.

Fuck. His parents had taken her in, made her part of their family. Raised her, sheltered her, loved her.

And this ... this atrocity was the repayment for their kindness?

Sigyn had betrayed him in the worst possible way. And then she'd continued to converse with him, as if naught had happened, as if she was still his closest kin.

His feet threatened to give out beneath him on the threshold to Hel's audience chamber. He slumped against the bone arch, forcing down a sudden clenching of his heart.

Sif.

She had endured torment the living could not imagine. Felt the pain of death in every moment for three centuries and more ... much more, perhaps, depending on the flow of time so far from the Mortal Realm. Hel's minions had tormented his daughter further, transformed her into that mockery of existence.

Melinöe paused in front of him, looking back in his direction, unspeaking, though Hermod could have sworn he felt mirth wafting off her, filling the cloud of mist she emanated with her joy at his despair.

Yes ... Gaze unto infinity ... and know you are a speck of dust ... caught on the wind and swirled for the fleeting merriment of fathomless horrors ...

No. No, Hermod might have seemed insignificant compared to the timeless entities that lurked beyond the Veil. He might have seemed thus, but he was a Man. A husband. A father. And, unlike an animal, a Man might be driven to motives beyond base instincts.

He pushed off the bone arch and strode toward Hel's throne, forcing down his pain and his momentary despondency.

Few vaettir seemed to enjoy any reminder that they too had once been mere men and women. And yet, from all Hermod and Odin had learned, most were. Hel was. Loki's daughter. She clawed her way from the abyss of death up, unto a throne from which she might terrorize all the worlds for eons.

But, in the end, her wretched soul had come from much the same stuff as his own.

"I want them back," he said, when he at last came to rest before the steps leading to Hel's perverse throne. "I want them both back."

Hel drummed the rotting fingers of her left hand upon the exposed bone of her knee. "And yet, the trinkets you brought me would not buy release for even one soul." She snickered, a hateful, wheezing sound, like the raspy voice of a draug. Like Sif's voice. "What is it you think I would do with bags of silver or gems? What value do such things hold in a world where trade comes in but two forms—Pneuma or souls. Which would you give to me?"

"I will you give my Pneuma, then."

Now she leaned forward. "Surely, you know there are but two ways I could claim that. I could draw it out through enduring nights you would spend in my bed, as you poured life out with each loss of your seed. Or ... I could devour your flesh, piece by piece, bringing you inside me another way." Yes, as she leaned forward, he could almost have sworn that telltale flicker of red lurked behind her eyes. A kind of draug herself? She was, after all, half rotten.

Your mind treads dangerous paths ... toward answers you might not welcome ...

Hel chortled softly. "Either way, you'd be dead and welcomed into my embrace for eternity, while I would have gained hardly enough power to even notice it."

"I am an Ás immortal."

She turned over her decaying hand as if inspecting the spots where her skeleton poked through. "A man who has tasted the fruit of Yggdrasil would provide a feast of power to spirits of lesser magnitude. But I am an Elder Goddess. My power is already limitless."

Lies. She was neither the Elder Goddess nor did her power exist without bounds. She'd fallen, defeated in the last Era, even if the cost had been great. Odin held back so many things, but he had explained enough for Hermod to know Hel could be bested.

The delicious failing of supreme arrogance ... Built up like a simmering feast ... before your fall ...

Keuthos could think as it wished. Hermod knew the truth, or enough of it.

"That leaves us," Hel said, when it became clear Hermod wouldn't answer, "but the option of devouring your soul, complete and entire. I could leave you a withered husk, unfit for the Wheel to spin up again, save perhaps as a worm. Condemned to lifetime after lifetime of meaningless, animal existence in an eternal quest to fortify your soul enough that it might take human form once more in some distant Era. Is that what you would offer me?"

Yes. If that was what it took to restore Baldr and Sif. In so doing, he might save Midgard. If his very soul was the price of so many lives, then he would pay it. He had grown weary, either way.

He opened his mouth to admit it, to accept her offer, if offer it was, but she continued, almost as if talking to herself.

"Oh, hmm. But you have asked me to release two souls from their prisons here. And you, dear, little Hermod, have but one soul to offer, and one already tattered at that."

No. She intended to make him choose between Baldr—

whose restoration might save the World—and Sif. His beloved, precious daughter? Hermod worked his mouth, unable to form words. The impossible choice was a weight upon his chest, denying him breath. Crushing him to a pulp.

Yes ... As it does us all ... Choice ... or the illusion thereof ...

"I ..."

"Suppose," Hel said, "that I offer you an alternative bargain."

"What?" His voice was a whisper now. Lightheadedness seized him and he swayed a little, unable to maintain his facade of strength a moment longer.

"Offer me sacrifices. Many, strong souls to feed upon. When you have granted me nine souls, I will free the two souls you so desperately seek after."

Hermod's throat hurt. He couldn't swallow. "H-how do I know you speak the truth?"

"Pacts bind the living and the dead alike. Lying is one thing, little Hermod. But I would not break a bargain nor an oath. Surely, you know this."

Melinöe seemed to melt up beside him, a bronze-bladed dagger held toward him in her outstretched hand.

"Nine sacrifices to feed me, and you'll have the souls you wish. Or let all the World weep and still you shall not have any who have ever passed beyond my gates."

Hermod set his jaw. And he closed his hand around the dagger's hilt.

PART III

Year 399, Age of the Aesir
Winter

20

hrudvangar had never seemed so confining. Oh, Thor hadn't wanted to spend much time here since Sif died. The bright light and noise made the headaches worse, and he couldn't stand to linger in the hall he'd once shared with his wife. But now, this place had become a fortress, a last bastion where more and more of the Aesir had begun to gather.

Now, he paced in his great hall, the motion sending tiny lances of pain through his ribs. Thor didn't care. Pain meant he lived. Meant he'd be able to share more of the same with the jotunnar.

Thrúd had sent refugees here from all over.

She even reported on the continuing battle over the bridge to Yggdrasil.

That trollfucker Narfi knew he needed to claim the Tree. Maybe he knew about the Bilröst, maybe he just wanted the damn apples. Thor couldn't let him get ahold of either.

Besides.

Besides ... he owed that bastard *pain*. An ocean of torment to come crashing down on his head. Even that wouldn't make up for what he'd done to Mother. Thor would kill him nine times if he could. Rip the fucker out of the gates of Hel just so he could throw him down there once more.

"I'm going to eradicate every last jotunn in Midgard and Utgard," he grumbled.

A few of those gathered looked at him, but no one commented.

Well, except for Tyr, who rose from his seat and stalked over to where Thor paced. In the damn way.

"Move!" Thor bellowed.

"Need to calm your mind. Moment you could stand you were out here. Wearing out the floor."

"I don't give a troll's rocky cock about the floor!"

"Not about the floor. About you, letting rage cloud your judgment."

Thor grabbed the man's tunic and shoved him aside so he could trudge past. "All I have is rage. All-consuming, crushing *wrath*. Enough to destroy their whole race."

"Mist-madness." And there Tyr was again, tromping along beside Thor like he'd asked for company. "All you'll do is get yourself killed. You, and anyone who follows you. They are too many, just on Asgard. We have no idea what unfolds on Midgard. Have to focus on survival first."

Thor spun on the other man, caught his shoulders, and flung him sideways, into a column. "I am your *prince*! I say what we focus on, you sniveling wretch! We focus on vengeance! They murdered our queen!"

Damn, but those spots were everywhere, flitting around the hall. A splitting headache started at his temples and built and built, expanding outward, like a fucking nail driven sideways into his brow.

"Already avenged her," Tyr said. His voice was grating.

"Need to think on what she'd want from you."

Oh. Oh, he presumed to speak of what Mother would have wanted? Fuck him. Thor slammed his fist into Tyr's face.

The thegn's head snapped into the column with enough force to crack the wood. Roaring, Thor grabbed the man, hefted him over his head.

Drawing on the apple's Megin blunted the growing pain in his ribs. Thor heaved Tyr, sending the man flying into a table. The thegn hit hard, rolled over, and groaned.

Wouldn't daze him long. Thor needed to kill some fucking jotunnar. Oh. That was it. Tyr was half-jotunn, wasn't he? Son of that trollfucker, Hymir.

Thor climbed onto the bench, straddled Tyr, and slammed his fist down into the man's face. Again. And again. And again. Until the table split beneath them and they both crashed down to the floor.

The impact jarred him, sending another painful lance through his sides. But at least the spots had vanished. Pure rage helped with that. Snarling, Thor grabbed a goblet and bashed it against Tyr's brow when the man tried to rise.

"You dare to fucking question *me*? My mother is dead! My mother is fucking *dead*!"

He reared back to bring the goblet down again, but someone caught his arm and hurled him aside. Thor spun through the air before crashing into a different table.

Mani. Vanr arse-lord had stones like a mammoth if he thought he could—

Several other men seized Thor's arms and hauled him up. Aesir men, not even immortals.

Fools.

With a roar, Thor flung three men free from his right arm, then hurled loose those holding his left.

He stormed over to where Tyr was moaning, looking half-conscious, if that. Thor pointed a finger at the man. "If I say I'm going to wipe out the jotunnar, only thing you ask is how you can fucking help!" With a growl, he kicked a spilled bowl of broth over at the thegn, sloshing what remained of its contents onto the man's trousers.

Then he spun and stormed from the hall.

He didn't need these weak fuckers. All he needed was Mjölnir. That, and a bunch of skulls to crack.

THOR SWEPT the mighty hammer at a tree. No lightning surged out from it, though the wood did splinter with a satisfying crunch. Hammer really had used up its power.

Well, it had fried Thrivaldi, so Thor would call that fair enough.

Even if he'd have preferred to shock Narfi with it.

"I'm sorry, Mother," he mumbled.

Oh, he'd have to satisfy himself with beating the bastard into gooey ... uh ... goo. Before Thor was done, he'd see every last bone in Narfi's body broken. Only when the man knew unrivaled agony would Thor crush his skull and let his suffering end.

Then he'd go and kill all the other trollfucking jotunnar who dared to defile Asgard with their filthy hides.

With a grunt, he spit on the ground.

He stood on the lower slope of a mountain. Below him, where farmers had once raised crops in the valley, now lay a lagoon filled with sea jotunnar. Across, on the next peak, raged a fucking blizzard. And smoke still rose from dozens of raging fires across the island. Probably the other isle looked much the same.

The jotunnar had ravaged Asgard, maybe worse than this land had ever seen.

Well.

It was a fair trek from here to Yggdrasil, especially with the floods and snowstorms. Still, Narfi would go for the Tree, if he wasn't already there. The greatest power in all the World came from Yggdrasil, even before Father had built the damn rainbow bridge.

Narfi would go for it.

And Thor would be there to … uh … what was that word? Annihilate! Thor would annihilate him, his army, and anyone else on hand. By the time he was done, he'd have fed Mjölnir enough jotunn souls to bring the lightning back.

Actually, that was a damn fine plan. Then he could use the hammer at full power to knock down Thrymheim itself. Send those towers and walls crumbling. The jotunnar wanted to murder children? Well, fuck it. Thor would feed their children's souls to Mjölnir, too. Let it shit out baby lightning bolts.

They had earned the utter end of their existence.

A FELLED TREE trunk floated by, not three feet from where Thor stood waist high in waters. It was like fording a river just to reach Yggdrasil. If he recalled right, a small river had once run through this valley, tumbling down from the mountains above in gentle falls.

Well, now the river encompassed fields that had once grown wheat, as well as an apple orchard. Many trees still stuck out of the new lagoon, but Thor didn't imagine they'd last unless the flooding retreated soon. The saltwater would have to kill them, wouldn't it?

Eh. Thor was no farmer, but he'd heard saltwater killed stuff.

Except for fish. And whales.

Oh, and uh, the kraken.

Well, Thor had never seen the kraken, but maybe once he'd killed all the jotunnar, he could feed that thing to Mjölnir, too. It had to have a strong soul, assuming he could find the damn creature.

Ahead, a scaly-legged sea jotunn trudged amid the dying apple trees.

Well. Thor hadn't specifically come hunting these bastards, but if he was going to wipe out all jotunnar, no reason to let such an opportunity pass him by. Besides, the hammer was probably hungry.

He eased Mjölnir free from the loop on his belt. Just holding it dimmed the pain in his still healing ribs and sent a rush of power seeping through his arm, pumping through him like a second pulse.

In truth, he couldn't say whether him or the hammer liked killing jotunnar more. Either way, they were in complete agreement on it being a good thing.

Thor sloshed toward his foe. Paused. No real way he could sneak up on the scaly bastard like this.

Eh. Well, whatever.

"You there!" he bellowed. "Cockless fish-fucker! Get over here so I can smite you!"

The sea jotunn turned abruptly toward him, looking suitably vexed. They hated when you called them 'cockless.'

Another sea jotunn rose abruptly from underwater, this one female, and standing not more than twenty feet away.

"Oh." Huh. That made two of them. "Guess you really *are* cockless, huh?"

The jotunn didn't respond save to surge at him, snarling and brandishing a trident in her slightly webbed hands.

The other came racing through the lagoon as well, moving much faster than he ought to have been able to. Like the waters didn't even impede him. Bastard.

Thor whipped Mjölnir up to block a jab from the trident. The point scraped along the metal of his hammer, snapped up, and gouged Thor's left shoulder. Growling, he lunged in.

Only the water slowed his steps, and the female had plenty of time to fall back, bringing her trident to bear once more.

Shit. That hadn't gone well.

The male closed in now, a few breaths away.

The female thrust her trident again. This time, Thor deflected on his hammer and surged forward, not at her, but to grab her weapon's shaft. The jotunn grunted in surprise, and Thor jerked the haft up into her gaping mouth. The female stumbled backward and pitched onto her arse, hand to her face.

Just before the male reached him, Thor flung Mjölnir at his head. The hammer cracked into the jotunn's face, splattering bone, brains, and bloody mess as the creature toppled over backward.

Growling, Thor reversed the trident, then jabbed the prongs into the female's throat when she tried to rise.

Mother.

They had murdered his mother.

Still snarling, Thor hefted the shaft up, lifting the jotunn female into the air. He planted the butt into the silt below the water, leaving her as a warning to the rest of them.

A sign. He was coming for them. He was coming for them *all*.

21

*H*is legs had gone numb. They had moved beyond the aching, beyond the bitter, all-consuming cold, to the point where sheer will alone kept him going. Well, will ... and desperate fury at the terrible urd that had befallen his daughter. Part of Hermod had not wanted even to leave the gates of Hel and head back into the desolate wastes of Niflheim, but if Sif was to have any chance of escaping that dire fortress, Hel must have her sacrifices.

So, on foot, he trudged on and on. Rime had frozen his face wrap to his cloak. The snows tugged at his senseless feet. And while no blizzard further impeded his progress—perhaps Hel actually wanted him to succeed—still the mist allowed him to see no more than five or ten feet ahead of him. Oh, he could make out mountain peaks, here and there, but not much else.

Even an Ás immortal ought to have died under these conditions. Ought to have, yes, but Hermod refused. He would not die, could not, until Sif and Baldr were freed from their damnation.

Not this way ...

What? Keuthos's voice in his mind—silent for so long—caught him off guard and he stumbled to one knee, catching himself on his hands. The deathchill kept trying to claim him. He'd be lucky if he didn't lose any fingers or toes to frostbite. He'd be lucky to live at all.

There are ice caves ...

Yes. That was where he was heading back to.

Others ... Closer ...

Fine.

He allowed the wraith to guide him, not the way he'd come, but to the southwest. It took him into a valley, and from there, Keuthos offered but sporadic directions. When Hermod at last found the caves the wraith had mentioned, he stumbled inside, made it a few dozen feet, and then collapsed onto the cold surface.

His lungs burned. His body was giving out, no matter what his will demanded. The fingers on his left hand refused to open from the clawed fist they had curled into.

And Keuthos could not offer warmth, he supposed.

I am ... a Mistwraith ...

What, like those *things* that served Hel? Like Melinöe?

Once ...

What did that mean? It ought to mean something, but he couldn't make his mind work. Groaning, he managed to pull his knees up to his chest.

Teeth were chattering ... a good sign ... it meant his body hadn't given up. Yet.

So ... cold.

TINGLING WOKE HIM. Like tiny bolts of lightning surging through his extremities. He found himself wrapped in a foul-smelling fur that *might* have come from a snow bear, laying in a room carved from a block of ice.

With a groan, he managed to sit up, keeping the fur tight around his shoulders. It may have stank like a dead hound, but it was the only source of warmth he had. His hands shook as he tried to make his way to his pack. A few torches remained, if he could get a fire lit, maybe he could save his fingers.

He dug through his now meager supplies to find one of his last torches.

"Don't." The voice was whispery, and somehow sensual and terrifying at once.

Hermod spun to see a woman—or a female, at least— standing at the doorway. She wore a slitted, low-cut, ice-blue dress that concealed very little. Mist wafted off her dark hair in etheric clouds, with more emanating from her fingers, her breath, and even her dress, as if vapors somehow composed the fabric. Her eyes had a faint opalescence, and her skin was pale, almost pure white.

And Dainsleif rested against the wall beside her.

"You're a snow maiden."

She chuckled lightly, billowing forth fresh puffs of frost and mist. "If you prefer that term. Lampades, snow maidens, yuki-onna, bean sí ... whatever you wish to call us."

"The native vaettir of Niflheim."

The snow maiden shrugged. "When the World was young, my kind served the Elder Goddess of Mist. But our numbers were few, back then, and have only grown in the ages since ... Hel, as you call her, came to power. Now, most of us serve the new Queen of Mist."

"Most?"

Some remain loyal to the first ...

"You're rebels?" Stifling a groan, he managed his feet. "What do you wish of me?"

Had Keuthos known they were here when he brought Hermod to these caves?

Yes ...

So the Mistwraith wanted him to meet these snow maidens.

The snow maiden followed his gaze to where his runeblade lay resting against the wall, then smirked and stepped aside. "Take it. If you wish. If you are well enough to heft it, you are well enough to walk."

Keeping his gaze locked on the snow maiden, Hermod edged around her and grabbed the runeblade, then slung it over his shoulder. Maybe he should draw it, but if they'd wanted to harm him, they could have done much worse than give him shelter and a blanket. In fact, Hermod rather thought he'd hold on to this fur draping for the moment.

"Who are you?"

"Khione, a disciple of Achlys."

Hermod sniffed. His nose still burned. "That's the original Goddess of Mist?"

The snow maiden nodded. "Keuthonymus can answer your questions best. Walk, if you are able, and see the truth."

What the ...? She *knew* Keuthos was inside him.

She knows ... It took us a long time to plan this ...

Keuthos was working with the rebels. He was a Mistwraith, like Melinöe, but not in service to Hel?

Finding it hard to fathom these things—this knowledge should have come to Odin—Hermod followed Khione.

I failed my goddess ... swayed by the call of another ... I helped her forge the seals ... Helped her siphon Achlys's power ... I ought not to have ... But madness claimed me ...

Madness? Did Keuthos mean he had *lusted* after Hel? The wretched, rotting queen of death?

Before ... she was beautiful ... intoxicating in her intensity ... Voracious in her pursuit of ever greater knowledge ... Hardly the first sorceress ... but perhaps the greatest in history ... And how was a sorcerer like I to deny her ...?

It was hard to tell, given that the wraith's voice always sounded hateful and hollow, but now, Hermod fancied a profound sense of self-loathing had seeped into the vaettr's words.

Fool ... Do you believe ... any wraith, who are beings of undying hatred, might exempt themselves from their vehement disdain ... For ourselves, we reserve the deepest of all enmity ...

Khione led him through more ice caves, oft with small holes in the roof allowing beams of starlight in. They came to a grouping of a dozen other snow maidens. Actually, some few of them were *male*, so the term maiden hardly applied.

A mortal appellation ... perhaps spawned because ... both Achlys and Hel ... were most apt to elevate their female worshipers ...

So primarily female, but some males. What else had Khione called her kind? Lampades? The word tasted odd, clearly not from the North tongue.

Older ...

Well, whatever. It hardly mattered. Each of the lampades watched them, seeming almost expectant. Yes, these sorry rebels wanted something from him. Hermod's meeting with Keuthos had been no accident. The Mistwraith had waited for him in the Astral Realm, waited for the chance to make his offer to escort Hermod to Niflheim.

Because these followers of Achlys thought he might somehow aid their mission against Hel?

Well, that was not like to happen.

Do not judge so swiftly ...

No. No, Hermod had a deal with Hel.

She will betray you ...

He faltered a moment, then continued after Khione. Keuthos himself had claimed not even Hel could break an oath.

Perhaps not, but you will still regret dealing with her ...

Not if it meant he got Sif back.

Fool! You cannot trust the Queen of Mist ...

He snorted at that, drawing a glance from Khione. No, he didn't trust Hel. Nor Khione, nor Keuthos. Vaettir lied. That, alone, he knew with utter certainty. The only time they didn't lie was in a pact, such as the one he'd made with Hel. Let the queen have her sacrifices and feast on a few more souls. From what he'd seen beyond her gates, a handful of souls would make no difference in her endless banquet.

These rebels had not a fraction of her numbers. Hel had ruled Niflheim for Era after Era. It was hardly Hermod's errand to help anyone overthrow her. Besides which, how was he to believe Achlys would prove any better a mistress of the damned than Hel?

In his mind, Keuthos growled, confirming his suspicions. The vaettir could scheme and plot against each other all they wished. Hermod had no desire to get involved in such things.

"Just see me out of this place," he said.

Khione paused, turning to him. "We saved you."

"I can't help you."

She shook her head. "We saved you," she repeated. "And all I ask in return is for you to come and see and listen. Do that, and I will show you the way out from here."

He misliked the thought of forming another bargain with a vaettr, but this one seemed harmless enough. And Khione spoke at least one truth—they had saved him from the bitter cold of Niflheim.

Agree to her terms ... and I'll show you a faster way back ...

He grimaced. Well, the sooner he got out of this frozen nightmare, the better. "Fine. Take me to Achlys."

KHIONE LED him deeper and deeper into the ice caves, until he could see rock behind the ice, though he could not judge how thick the coating over it was. Clearly, though, they had moved beneath the mountains into a true cave where the ice had somehow continued to spread over the walls.

Below them stretched numerous chasms, some spanned by narrow ice bridges, with ten-feet long icicles dangling from them. Rime coated everything, as if a blast of the bitterest cold had swept over the cavern.

And ever deeper they pushed, until he found himself descending a steep slope into a cloud of chilling mist that numbed his legs on contact. A place as cold as Hvergelmir itself.

We are not so very far from there ... Beneath it, the worlds align and the dark dragon feasts on corpses ...

Naströnd. The shore of corpses where Nidhogg dwelt. Hermod shuddered at the thought. Naught Odin had ever mentioned compared to the horror of the dark dragon. Something whose malevolence dwarfed even that a wraith could manage.

You wanted a shortcut ... We shall take the very one your king used ... some centuries back ...

Oh. Odin had said he'd climbed up Yggdrasil's roots to

escape Naströnd, when he'd hung himself from the World Tree, back before he banished the Vanir. And now it came back to that. Hermod seemed ever following in his mentor's footsteps.

The thought of it, though, of passing in that most terrible of places ... it had his hands trembling, and not from the cold. He could not do this ...

Another bridge of ice spanned a drop into darkness, descending slowly to a landing Hermod could not make out but assumed must lurk there, for Khione plodded gracefully across the bridge. Surely they had not brought him this far to shove him into a pit.

Not well pleased, Hermod pressed onward after the snow maiden.

A clammy sweat had built up between his shoulder blades. One that had him shivering.

As if sensing his discomfort, the snow maiden raised her hand, and a blue-green flame sprang up from it. It cast light, but no heat, nor did it drive back the mists. Still, it was better than the almost total darkness that kept creeping in around him. None of the locals seemed much inclined to let him have real flame, either.

Flame is an enemy of Mist ...

And in the World of Mist, no one seemed to embrace their enemies.

This was madness. Mist was also the enemy of life. And here Hermod was, plodding along, one slow, agonizing step at a time, toward ... *something* ancient beyond words. Something that had existed perhaps from the dawn of time.

Existed in hatred.

At last, they reached the bottom, a cavern that—by the echoes, at least—seemed massive. A billowing cloud of mist swirled about his feet, somehow seeming to pull him along in its wake. It carried him about a circular path, ever toward its center, until at last he came to stand in the eye of the storm, Khione beside him, though the snow maiden fell to her knees and bowed her head.

Within the heart of that eye—which stretched for some hundred feet, he'd guess—a cloaked figure rested upon her knees, arms out to her sides. In the heart of swirling mist, a being *of* Mist.

Hermod's heart hammered within his breast, and all instinct told him to turn, to flee from this place at once and never, ever look back. The hairs on his arms stood on end, and his face tingled. Some inexorable pull tugged at him, forcing his steps forward. Though he could see naught unusual about the woman, save her concealed face and pale shroud, he could not help feel a sense of overpowering wrongness to the figure before him.

She was ... tiny.

She is not ... The aspect is a guise ... A form designed to keep from overwhelming your fragile mind ...

If so, it barely managed the feat. For his breath tried to freeze in his throat. His heart wanted to seize up. His blood to cease to flow.

And yes, he could feel it. That this thing before him was far more than she seemed. As if her presence seemed to warp reality around it.

The pull carried him up to within a dozen feet of the entity, who finally lifted her face. Her visage was deathly pale, sunken in like a draug's, and yet holding a hint of youth. Or perhaps timelessness. As if, had she wished it, she might pass for beautiful.

Or terrible enough that you would tear out your eyes for having beheld her majesty ...

"There're no chains," he managed, his voice sounded a weak croak in his own ears. "Naught holds you here."

"Naught you can see," Achlys said, her voice like a whisper, seeping from her lips into his mind. Timid, and yet so immense he had to wonder if she could kill with the force of her words alone. Mist seeped from her mouth as she spoke, vile and no doubt toxic. "Invisible chains bind me, nonetheless. Keuthonymos and Hekate wrought their treachery with exquisite care, such I would almost have to admire, circumstances being otherwise."

Hekate?

"Hel, if you prefer. Rangda. Milu. Anput. Whatever she wishes to call herself. As if she were truly one of us, she is host to myriad names, down through the Eras. But we are older still, and we saw when your kind first rose from the seeds."

Seeds? Was she deliberately speaking in riddles?

Hermod opened his mouth, but words failed him. His tongue felt frozen solid, so dry he could scarce move it.

"You wish to know what holds me here, on the threshold of Hvelgemir, where Hekate can gorge herself on eldritch power she does not fully understand? The bindings stretch along the roots of Yggdrasil. Six seals that hold me here and thus offer her a limitless font of vigor from which to draw on. One here, in my world, my followers have already destroyed, as well as the one guarded by Nidhogg. But the other four lie in worlds not so easily reached by my children."

Hermod felt as though his skull would crack and burst apart from the concussive energies buried in her sibilant voice.

"In your Realm, beyond the Veil, lies one seal. Another

rests in the hateful World of Sun, and in the equally loath-some World of Fire. The last, in the World of Storms."

Hermod pressed his palms against his temples, desperate to keep the pain contained within, and yet further to keep from saying—or even thinking—aught which might offend this entity. He could not imagine the audacity that Hel had in thinking to bind Achlys. Yet ... his bargain remained with Hel, not with the Elder Goddess.

Perhaps she heard his thoughts, or perhaps not, but she leaned forward, twirling her fingers—and a spiral of mist—beneath his chin.

"You, child of a psychopomp, can pass between Realms and between worlds. You can walk in sunlight and stand the presence of fire. *You* can go where no other can."

"No." Growling out that single word felt like lifting a mountain. Any defiance of her will seemed utter madness.

But then, Achlys was the Goddess of Mist. Madness was her purview.

"I have other tasks to attend to. Only when those are done will I consider your ..." Request sounded like a poor choice of words. "Plight." Speaking took so much out of him, he slumped down, catching himself with his hands.

"Refuse me and I shall have Keuthonymos seize your body."

"We ... have a different ... bargain."

Besides. Keuthos couldn't maintain control of him in Alfheim or Muspelheim. Odin's tales made that seem fair certain. No, the Elder Goddess needed his *willing* help. And Hermod would not give it until he had returned to Midgard and fulfilled his pact with Hel. Until Sif and Baldr were released from her prison.

Fool ...

No. He wasn't going to break an oath, either.

"Then take him back to his fragile Realm," Achlys said, at last. "Take him, and let him see what his oath buys him."

At once, the pressure holding him down abated, and Hermod scrambled away, half running, half crawling back into the swirling mist. This was the power wielded by the *bound* Elder Goddess? He did not even want to think how terrible she must seem when freed.

We go to Naströnd now ... Prepare yourself for the darkness that coalesces between the Realms ...

Yes. And then Midgard.

22

_____

It was far to the Norns' mountain, through Bjarmaland and almost to the Midgard Wall, and Odin dared not rely too heavily on the Sight to help him avoid the Deathless legions, jotunn armies, or other dangers along the way. In desperation for speed, he'd risked taking a small ship—none would crew it for him, so he had to do it himself—from Rijnland up past the Jarnvid.

From there, he'd had to pass through the trackless winter wastes of Bjarmaland by dogsled. Some few vestiges of the former colony of Holmgard remained, and in those villages he'd acquired the dogs. In the past, he had ridden upon Sleipnir's back to reach his destination, and the miles had passed in a dreamlike blur. Now, he'd have given almost aught to sit astride his old friend once more, claiming speed dogs could not hope to match.

They probably couldn't see too far ahead, given the incessant snow flurries and mist. Still, he kept the dogs guided true. This much, he could trust to the Sight for.

With no one to discuss his predicament, he spent the miles touching the edge of the Sight for other purposes, as well. Yes, now he knew the trap of prescience, and thus he forced himself not to look too deeply, not to peer into the distant future and thus, to hope to prevent himself from becoming locked into any particular course.

You still assume that's how this works ... That your course was not set either way ... That your very refusal to look does not also lie within the Web of Urd ...

Odin grit his teeth, trying to ignore Audr's grating sibilance along with his discomfiting point. Yes. Perhaps all of it, even this, fell within the Norns' schemes. If so ... if even such a plan as this had been accounted for ... then perhaps he was truly powerless to change aught.

But.

But, there seemed one sure way to unravel their designs. To prove, to himself and to them, that free will was no illusion, that he *could* choose. Loki might have argued the fact that, because he did not happen to have made a given choice, did not mean he did not *have* a choice.

Odin wanted more than semantic validation of his existence.

How to prove the Norns did not control him?

Create a paradox. A decision, an action that so totally undermined a vision as to prevent it from becoming true, and thus, sidestep the truism that prescience must account for itself. Yet, he and Loki had long ago settled upon the agreement that he simply would not see aught which would create such a system.

It had seemed more palatable when he had not known the Norns were the ones pulling the threads. To know a mind, other than his own, governed the fabric of his life, created an enmity within Odin that he could not suppress, could not name, could not deny. Like an ember in the back of his mind, searing his brain, undermining every thought and deed of his existence.

Heavy snowfall caught in the bitter winds and whipped over his face. Twilight was settling in, and the dogs must surely be on the brink of exhaustion. His supplies for them had run low already, and, despite the light woodlands all around, game had become scarce.

Everything had begun to die in this Fimbulvinter.

Warmth would not return to Midgard. Not this time. Hel had thrown all her fury at the World. Odin had not yet foreseen the totality of her plan, nor could he keep his mind focused on the Queen of the Mists when yet direr foes lay soon before him.

After pulling the dogs to a stop, he leapt from the sled and sank ankle deep into fresh powder. Grumbling, he trudged over and loosed the dogs. "Go on. Hunt if you can."

Beneath a weathered, dying fir tree, he cleared enough snow to make a patch of ground for a fire. Getting one started in this weather might prove impossible, but he had to try. Both he and the animals would be in need of the warmth this night. Besides, fire might keep snow maidens and ghosts at bay. Odin had no desire for their company.

He sniffed, striking flint in the hopes of drawing a spark. The wind swept away what few he got going. A mortal would have frozen to death days ago. Even now, Odin was not quite certain *that* urd was beyond possible. Maybe it was too much to hope for, in fact, to imagine he had already broken free of the Norns' game simply by moving against them instead of against his foes in this world.

Indeed, he gambled now, desperately hoping they would show themselves in the mountain where he'd first met them. If not, he would have wasted this trip.

A paradox ... he needed a paradox to begin to unravel their web.

And if you unravel the very timeline ...?

Odin groaned. "You mean if the Web of Urd ... is the timeline? Is history?"

Yes ... Break it ... And none of us have the experience to harbor a guess what would happen ... Suppose history collapses upon itself ... The foundations of reality sucked into a maelstrom of nonexistence more complete than the Roil ...

No. No, damn it. Odin refused to surrender, to give in, for fear of what *might* happen if he took a stand against the Norns.

You cannot change Fate, Valravn said. *Fate is Fate. Even the greatest of spirits must bow to the eldritch powers that dwell beyond our Realms.*

Odin didn't bother responding to that. The claim was the very reason he was out here. Because he demanded control of his own destiny. Was that not the essence of will? He refused to allow those he loved to suffer and die when he could do something to preserve them.

Loki had guided the course of history straight toward Ragnarok. But he was a slave to these Norns. Which meant, *they* wanted Ragnarok. They had worked, perhaps even from the time of the last Eschaton, to bring history back around to this moment.

Naresh—Odin—had fought Hel and defeated her, at terrible cost, and so little of the World had survived their battle. And now, fifty-two hundred years later, it was all playing out once more. How many times had the World ended?

His memories were not so clear, but he suspected he'd always be there, in one incarnation or another, playing out these cataclysmic battles against Hel.

Fuck that.

One way or another, the cycle would end.

So give in ... die ...

Paradox. Yes, it came back to that. Whether or not Odin could find the Norns, much less defeat them, he had settled on one way of making absolutely certain their prophecies could not unfold as they had woven them.

Fenrir could not kill Odin, nor could Odin kill Freyja, if Odin first killed himself. Suicide. Let them resolve *that* paradox.

Perhaps Loki had felt trapped by their web for eons, but if so, he had clearly missed the one way out. Oh, Odin knew he'd be born again, spun out once more by the Wheel of Life. Except, if he wasn't there to fight Ragnarok, if the Norns' vision became impossible to fulfill, would that paradox then reverberate through the Web of Urd and ...

Something drew nigh.

Embracing the Sight, Odin looked into the Penumbra, and yet, while he saw ghosts in the distance, none had wandered too close to where he still struggled to light a fire. So what ...?

A woman moved through the shadows, luminous, and yet Etheric. Odin blinked away the Sight and rose, grabbed Gungnir. Indeed, the woman, clad only in an unadorned, loose white dress that whipped about in the wind, drifted ever closer. She had white hair, and opalescent eyes, and her feet left no impression in the snow, though she appeared at least partially present in the Mortal Realm.

As she drifted closer, he could not look away from her face. It was ... timeless. Like she was neither young nor old. A statue, with a billowing gown that blended with the mist and snow.

"Who are you?" he demanded, when she at last came to a stop some distance away.

"Dís. A warning." Her voice was soft, sibilant, but not loathsome like Audr's. Rather, distant, almost dreamlike. "Desist from your musings and return to the course of urd as it lays before you."

Odin balked. They *knew*. "You serve the Norns. And if they sent you ... does that not mean they fear I might succeed?" That Odin was, in fact, a threat to them. And why not? If the Destroyer could bring down dragons and vaettir and even Hel, why could he not break the hold of three old women?

"Desist. The only warning."

Shaking his head, he pointed Gungnir at the apparition. Was Dís her name? A title? Well, it mattered naught, in the end. "I think I understand. You're afraid of what will happen when I succeed. Well, allow me to send a message to your mistresses."

The entity cocked her head to the side. Her mouth slowly opened too wide, her cheeks splitting apart into strands of sinuous flesh with horrifying gaps between.

What ... the ... fuck?

Now, Odin fell back a step, raising Gungnir higher.

The woman's dress vanished like mist, though the flesh it revealed beneath was aught but sensual. Rather, it looked weathered, ancient, yet muscular. She jerked violently from side to side and her flesh began to rupture. From between her ribs crawled free four segmented appendages like the legs of a spider.

His mind screamed at him to strike now, before the madness continued, yet he found himself transfixed, staring in rapt horror at the spectacle.

Her eyes popped out, and in their place grew faceted, pupilless lenses.

The creature uttered a hideous, chittering growl, shaking her arms and legs and gyrating wildly.

The sound shook Odin from his paralysis, and he leapt backward, even as the creature flung itself airborne. The dís landed in the spot Odin had vacated, its spider arms lancing downward like spears that would have pierced him in four different places.

Odin lunged back in with Gungnir, thrusting, screaming in fury and absolute horror at the abomination before him. The thing batted away his spear with one hand and Odin scrambled away, even as it lunged in with another. A spider arm sliced upward, gouging his shin, and sending him stumbling away, barely maintaining his feet.

Another chittering roar that seemed to shoot through his mind and rend it into tiny pieces. Until he could no longer tell where the thing was. Or when.

Odin thrust Gungnir forward and hit naught save air. The creature's form broke apart.

The entity was all around him. Her form blurred, seeming to occupy a dozen places at once. Places she'd been or was now, or would be, all in a mind-shredding blur.

Odin screamed, flailing wildly with Gungnir, desperate to keep it at bay. Audr and Valravn had begun to shriek within his mind, somehow sounding even *more* horrified than he was at this *thing* that jittered in and out of time.

In the most profound desperation, Odin tugged at his visions. A reflex. He caught images of himself melding with the afterimages—or fore-images—of the creature in a wild dance. Still shrieking, he moved in time with his own apparitions, fending off the abomination with desperate swipes of his dragon spear.

He was giving in to the visions. Allowing the tide of them to pull him back into the trap.

Or ...

Gungnir clanged off a spider leg, sheared along it a moment. Then Odin twisted the spear and thrust up, burying the undulating blade inside the creature's hideous maw. The dragon spear punched through the back of the abomination's skull.

All blurred images vanished in an instant, leaving only a single, impaled monster. One that thrashed violently in some mix of convulsion and rage, before at last falling still.

Grunting, Odin placed a boot on its chest, then heaved the creature off his spear.

Immediately, it began to warp back into itself, like linens folded into a bundle, before breaking away into loose strands that vanished in the wind.

Odin slumped down to his knees. What the fuck was that?

He'd ... he'd ... given in to the visions. Played into the Norns' trap ... or he had used the visions against their own servant ...

Of course. How else did one overcome an entity that existed outside of time?

So, then. Had he failed, or had he found the answer? A means of turning the very weapon of his enemies back upon them?

Either way, the Norns knew he was coming for them. And they were scared enough to have sent that *thing* to stop him.

Which meant, above all else, he was on the right track.

The one way to change the future.

23

Rustling came from behind the undergrowth, on the slope descending toward Yggdrasil. The sound had Thor spinning around, Mjölnir in hand, ready to smack down any wood jotunn fool enough to test his patience.

Only, it wasn't a wood jotunn, but Tyr who came stumbling out, bruises still marring his face, crusted blood coating his beard.

"What the fuck, man?" Thor demanded. "You want another beating? You want me to rip off your other hand and slap you with it?"

Tyr spit. "Want to stop you from getting killed." His words wheezed through his still broken nose. "Stop Odin's last child from dying. Figure that's worth doing. Even if you are a troll's arse."

Just looking at the thegn had those spots swimming before Thor's eyes again. Man was ... ugh, what was that word? Provocative? No. No, that wasn't the word he was looking for.

These days, Thor couldn't even remember what having

his head working right felt like. Just so ... Vexing! Like the damn thegn.

Thor pointed at finger at the man. "Now, look. I aim to smite every last trollfucking, arse-sniffing, bushy-browed jotunn from here to Thrymheim. You can either help, or you can watch." Huh. "Or I guess you could leave. But what you can't do is stop me. Mother's ghost will rest easy knowing I sacrificed the army that murdered her."

"Still figure you're invincible, don't you?" Damn, that wheezing grated on Thor. That, and Tyr shook his head like Thor was still a fucking child. Vexing bastard. Deserved to have that fastened as his name. Tyr the Vexer.

Thor glowered at him. "I'm going down to the valley and hammering my way through the jotunnar. Not hardly letting those jotunnar claim so much as an apple core. The way I see it, Mother is dead, Father's away, and that makes me in charge of Asgard."

"Asgard's aflame."

Thor threw up his hands. "Fuck, man! You want me to command it to stop burning? I mean to say, I'm in command of *you*. And I'm ordering you to help me break the jotunn lines. Are you with me?"

The thegn cracked his neck, then grimaced. "I'm with you. Not much chance of success, is all."

Thor refused to believe that. Mjölnir was hungry, and he was going to feed the damn hammer.

"Would've helped if you hadn't smashed my face. Right before such a battle."

Thor shrugged. "It's what I do. I smash faces. And skulls. And heads."

Not giving Tyr another look, Thor slunk forward, down the slope. In the valley below, at least three score jotunnar had camped at the close side of the bridge, with more on the surface itself, lobbing occasional arrows in the direction of the Tree.

From what Thor could make out, the defenders had set up barrels and debris for extra cover, with a shield wall behind that. Archers of their own returned sporadic arrows, but the jotunnar remained out of range.

Judging by the corpses littering the space in between, Narfi's warriors had made a few pushes toward the Tree already.

"Long time back," Tyr said.

"What?"

"Was on the other side, defending the Tree. Frey trying to reclaim it. Back when you were still sucking on a teat."

Thor glanced at him. "I *still* suck on teats." Every chance he got.

"Got no chance against that many jotunnar. Maybe we kill four, five of them. Maybe not even that many before they swarm us."

No. Thor refused to accept it. He was killing Narfi. In fact ... that looked like the trollfucker there in the midst of his warriors. If he was here, he had to be planning an offensive soon. Even if Thor wanted to go back to Thrudvangar and seek reinforcements, he had no time. If they lost the Tree, they lost—

One of the jotunnar reared his head back and screeched like a fucking hawk. The jotunn—a big one, and less pale than frost jotunnar—spread his arms, dropping his loin cloth. Then he began to sprout feathers. A shifter? A jotunn shifter?

From his hiding spot, Thor couldn't hear the nasty pop of bone and muscle, but he could see it happen, as the jotunn's form became that of a giant eagle. A beat of his wings sent the creature aloft, hurling a whirlwind beneath it

—one powerful enough to send his fellows tumbling away. Screeching again, the eagle flew up, high above the defenders, circling the tree. Arrows flew at the eagle, but it was too high and too fast, even for such a large target.

Tyr grunted.

The eagle banked around again, turning in midair. A buffet of its wings sent a gale down on the defenders that hurled aside their barricades and broke their shield wall as though they were children's toys scattered with a savage kick.

"Shit," Thor said. "You have to bring down the eagle."

Tyr grunted again. To his credit, the thegn didn't balk at the order, though Thor didn't a clue how he'd manage it.

The point was, the defenders were about to break, but right now, the eagle had both sides distracted. Growling, Thor hefted Mjölnir and charged forward, down the slope, the angle adding to his momentum. He'd be an avalanche on those bastards. But damn, did he miss the hammer's thunder.

Surging forward, he jumped up and cracked Mjölnir against the back of a jotunn's skull. Fucker dropped like a stone, never having even begun to turn. The next one did, though, as Thor landed. Roaring, he slammed Mjölnir into the back of its knee before it could get around to him. Bone exploded out from flesh in a shower of blue blood. An overhanded swing between its shoulder blades felled the creature.

"Narfi!" Thor roared. "I'm coming for you, you murderous goat trench!"

The next jotunn had spun on him, but was still bringing his weapon to bear. Not fast enough. Mjölnir's upswing caught the jotunn right in the stones, hard enough to lift the bastard into the air and send him flying backward.

Oh, how the hammer sang with pure joy at—

A jotunn club slapped into Thor and sent him colliding into the midst of a dozen more jotunnar. Groaning—his Megin only half blocked that much pain—he rose to one knee and waved Mjölnir wildly in front of himself. Not good.

Not good at all.

The closest jotunn moved in, intent to skewer him with a spear. Out of nowhere, Frey stood before the jotunn, swinging a broadsword. The blade slammed into the jotunn's side but wedged into the bearskin hide the jotunn wore.

Damn. Man should have had that runeblade.

Thor gained his feet just in time to block another thrust from a jotunn. A spear caught him in the shoulder, punched through his mail, and sent him stumbling to the ground, dropping the hammer.

Desperate, Thor lunged at Mjölnir, caught its haft, and tried to raise it. The jotunn that held the spear twisted, sending a spiral of pain wracking through Thor, bloody spots dimming his vision.

Someone grabbed his ankle, then everything shifted without warning. The sudden change in orientation had Thor's stomach heaving, but he lay on the ground among the scattered defenders.

The jotunn who'd pinned him was there too, turning about in obvious disorientation. Frey pulled a knife and rammed it into the jotunn's gut, yanked it free, and, grabbed the creature's beard to yank its head down. A vicious slash cut out the jotunn's throat before it could even find its bearings.

A shieldmaiden—Syn!—grabbed the spear in Thor's

shoulder, braced her foot on his arm, and jerked it free. "Sorry, my prince."

Thor groaned, and rolled over to look at the battle.

Down the bridge, at least two dozen liosalfar had engaged the jotunnar. Flashes of light, glowing bodies, and men and women appearing and disappearing, all while moving at superhuman speed. Utter madness.

But the liosalfar only had so much sunlight. And when that ran out …

24

_D_ead Aesir lay strewn over the bridge. Corpses intermingled with dead jotunnar. And fallen liosalfar. Bloody mess that Tyr had to slog through. Mistilteinn fair sang in his hand, as he closed in on the defenders.

Blade had tasted blood of a half dozen jotunnar this day. And it knew more was on the way.

That eagle still soared above. Hurling wind like javelins. Here and there, it swooped down and snatched up Men in its talons. Flung them into the abyss around Yggdrasil.

Tyr had a shield strapped to his arm. Didn't like fighting thus. Couldn't drop it if he had to. But at the moment, he kept it raised. Poised to deflect spear thrusts that might've skewered him.

As now, when a jotunn spun on him, jabbed with a trident. He batted aside the blow. Stepped inside and swept Mistilteinn up in an arc that severed the jotunn's leg at the knees. Runeblades didn't care about thick hides or even armor, much less flesh and bone. Cleaved through aught as if it wasn't even there.

His foe toppled over, wailing, maybe not even realizing he was dead already.

Tyr didn't bother running him through. Didn't have time. Instead he pushed on, the quickest trot he could manage amid the chaotic melee.

The liosalfar had saved him. If not for their sudden, tumultuous attack disrupting the jotunn lines, Tyr would've never survived this.

Still might not.

He didn't have a clue how he ought to fell a bird circling above.

Ullr? Wasn't he here? Aesir used to worship that Vanr as the god of archery. Ought to mean he could handle a bow as well as Hermod. Tyr hoped.

Tyr hacked and hewed his way closer, then, past the jotunn line, broke into a run.

The blond bearded Vanr kept nocking arrows, but never got much of a chance to loose before one gale or another sent him toppling over. Almost over the side of the bridge, in fact.

Shit.

Tyr pumped the apple's Megin into his legs. Pneuma, Hermod called that. Odd word. The moment he reached the far side of the bridge, a fresh whirlwind hefted him off his feet. Flung him bodily against the trunk. The impact dazed him. He crashed back down onto the bridge with an *oomph*. Mistilteinn skittered along the stonework, out of his grasp.

Couldn't catch his breath. Everything hurt.

His senses had gone wild. Whole bridge seemed to spin. Still, he pulled himself forward toward the runeblade. Couldn't afford to lose—

His fingers snared the hilt an instant before another gale

sent him tumbling end over to end, back into the tree's interior.

Gasping, Tyr wedged the runeblade into the ground and used it to gain his feet. How the fuck did Thor expect him to fight a storm jotunn of such power? In his days with Hymir, this sort of thing was a legend. Seemed a bit too real now.

A glowing liosalf—Malakbel, was it?—stumbled toward him, a grimace on his face. "I've no weapons that can fell such an enormous creature."

Tyr snorted. "Can't get to it anyway."

Outside, men shrieked. Others tumbled over the side into the waiting chasm. One damn storm jotunn was destroying their whole army.

Screeching, the eagle dove, swooped against the bridge. Snatched up Ullr with its beak. That maw snapped closed around the Vanr's torso.

Fuck.

A brief scream. Then legs came splattering down on the bridge in an explosion of gore that had even Tyr wincing.

They couldn't fight this. They were all going to die.

"I can get to it," the liosalf beside him said, panting slightly. "But only to annoy the bird."

Tyr spun on him. Liosalfar popped in and out of wherever they wanted. "You can get me to it?"

Malakbel nodded.

All right then. Tyr unstrapped the shield and tossed it aside. Wouldn't do much good in midair anyway. Then he hefted Mistilteinn. Cracked his neck. This was going to hurt. Right up until it killed him, more like than not.

But they couldn't lose the Tree. Odin's bridge device was whirring right behind them. Needed a gambit. Even a bad one.

"Let's do this," he said.

The alf had a hand on his shoulder. Guided him out to the threshold. Maybe he needed to see that eagle jotunn.

"Ready?" the liosalf asked.

Tyr grunted.

Everything shifted. Wind shot over Tyr in a cascade that threatened to strip him from his feet and hurtle him into the void. He stood on the eagle's back, between wings the size of houses.

Didn't know how high he was.

Didn't matter.

Roaring, he reversed his grip on Mistilteinn and drove it straight down into the jotunn's back. The runeblade tore trough feathers, flesh, and bones with ease. So much ease, Tyr lost his footing and slid backward. The sword rent flesh, not hardly slowing his descent as he slipped toward the eagle's tail feathers.

The creature bucked wildly. Shrieked.

Pitched over sideways and whirled upside down. Tyr fell free, screaming himself, as he tumbled through the air. The wind stole his screams and his breath, both.

Then—still plummeting—an arm wrapped around his waist.

Everything shifted again. He appeared above the bridge, still falling just as fast, but now at an angle. The stone rushed up to meet him. Slapped him like a hammer. Sent him skittering along the surface like a stone skipped over a lake.

His view whirled round and round, blow after blow knocking him senseless.

Darkness swallowed him before he even came to a stop.

25

*M*jölnir slammed into a wood jotunn with force enough Thor heard the creature's spine snap. The blur of liosalfar amid the jotunnar had begun to slow. Already, several of them had lost their glow. When that happened, the jotunnar oft felled them in the space of heartbeats. As broken corpses, they looked no different than Men.

Actually, they probably were Men once more, vaettir having fled the dead bodies.

"Narfi!" Thor roared. "Get over here and face me like a man! You want vengeance, boy? *I* killed your brother!"

A cluster of melees separated them, but Thor still saw it when Narfi drove his axe into a liosalf's skull.

Bastard was quick. Strong. And seemed to know how to pick his fights whenever liosalfar ran out of sunlight.

He caught another one by the throat and drove his head straight down into the stone lip warding the edge of the bridge, leaving a stain of bloody brains.

Thor cracked Mjölnir against another frost jotunn's temple.

As he turned back, Narfi's axe buried itself in an alf's belly. The half-jotunn didn't jerk his axe free so much as bodily fling his victim off.

"I'm gonna hew you limb from limb!" Narfi shouted at him. "Gonna hack your men into bits. And I'm gonna laugh til I piss, when my sister claims your soul, oaf."

Thor shoved a stumbling jotunn out of his way. "You want to see Hel? I can arrange a personal meeting for you!"

And then Narfi closed in on him. Thor swung Mjölnir, a blow that would cave in the bastard's chest.

Narfi sidestepped, jerked the haft of his axe into Thor's still bruised ribs. That drew on *oomph* and had Thor stumbling back. Narfi's knee caught him in the chest and sent him sprawling.

A heartbeat later, that axe descended for Thor's head. He barely got Mjölnir up for a clumsy block. The axe blade scraped along the hammer. Narfi lunged forward, grabbed Thor's hair, and heaved.

The motion sent him flying, feeling like his hair was ripped out by the roots. He tumbled end over end, hit the rail, and barely caught its lip as he pitched over the side.

Fuck! Thor's legs dangled over an abyss he didn't even know how deep.

Surging Megin to his arms, he flung himself upward, back onto the bridge and—

Narfi's axe slammed into his side. The mail and gambeson beneath took the worst of it, but the blow still sent him reeling, tumbling back to the ground. Gasping. Felt like his ribs had broken anew.

He tried to rise. Narfi's boot caught him in the gut and flung him into the air.

Only to crash back down a heartbeat later, knocked breathless.

Unable to even groan for the pain of it.

Fuck a walrus, the man was strong!

"Reckon I'll take my time with you," Narfi said. "You didn't give Hödr no clean death, so you ain't gonna have one neither."

Shit. Where was Mjölnir? His hammer ... It lay behind Narfi. May as well have been a mile away from him at this point.

Thor staggered to his feet, desperately clinging to the apple's power to blunt the pain.

Narfi lunged in with that axe. Thor swung with a haymaker, but Narfi ducked under it. The axe slammed down into Thor's left foot.

It took an instant for the pain to hit him.

And then he bellowed in agony, stumbling backward. Without any of his toes. A fair chunk of his boot lingered in a bloody mess. Fuck! Fucking fuck!

Thor reeled. Narfi's knee snapped up into his stones, the blow hefting him off his feet and sending him tumbling to the ground.

Snarling, Narfi placed his foot on Thor's right wrist. Then grabbed his little finger. And yanked with such force Thor could only shriek in pain and terror. The bones snapped apart. His skin tore free.

Narfi released his foot, allowed Thor to see his blood-dripping finger now sitting in Narfi's palm. The half-jotunn grinned a moment, before popping it into his mouth and beginning to crunch on it.

"Gonna eat you alive!" Narfi slurred even as he chewed.

Thor screamed in horror.

Everything was dimming. Too much blood loss.

Sorry ... Mother ... He'd tried ...

Mother.

She was there, flitting about, between the jotunnar. Head hovering over her form, torn to shreds. A ghost?

Shit. Maybe he was seeing things. So much blood ...

"Mother ..." he moaned.

"Shame I couldn't kill her myself," Narfi said, bits of Thor's flesh dangling from his lips, blood dribbling into his beard. "Reckon she suffered plenty, though. I'll settle for you."

Frey appeared beside Thor, kneeling at his side. Pressing Mjölnir into Thor's bloody hand.

The hammer's energy rushed into him like a flood of strength, driving down pain to some distant thought for another time. Because that was its greatest power. More than thunder or cracking skulls. To make a man feel no pain. Only rage.

And Thor had a lot of fucking rage.

Teeth grit, he stumbled to his feet. His balance was off without toes. It made each step a staggering, awkward move, but Thor didn't fucking care.

He didn't know where Frey had gone, though he heard the clang of metal behind him. If the Vanr kept the rest of the jotunnar occupied, Thor would attend to Narfi. He owed him that personally.

He owed him vengeance.

He owed him terror.

He owed him agony.

26

$\mathcal{N}$arfi balked, falling back a step. He sure hadn't reckoned on Thor being able to mount a defense. Much less rise and seem intent to *attack*. Fury was painted all over the man's red-bearded face.

Well and good. Narfi knew plenty about wrath.

He hefted his axe. "Which part you want I should eat next? Got a favorite?"

Even the small taste of Thor's flesh—flush with Pneuma —it flowed through him. Gave him strength and speed. Made him so much more than a man. Yes, devouring the Aesir would make Narfi a god.

A fool, though. That's what he'd been to deny himself Man-flesh for so many years.

Oh, how he'd worked at being a good son. Good ally to Asgard. They'd forgiven him for what he'd done under Skadi. Mostly forgiven, maybe. But he'd promised himself he'd be worthy of their trust.

Only, they broke that themselves. Frigg. Thor. All the others, when they'd betrayed Hödr and Mother and Father. And now Asgard was a smoldering ruin. Weren't but one hall left standing, so far as Narfi knew. And that one probably lay besieged this very hour.

"My people are burning your house, if you was wondering on that. Not that you'll be around long enough for grieving."

Thor didn't answer, except for a snarl. A lunge with that vicious hammer.

Narfi fell back a step. Let the bastard exhaust himself if he wanted. Wouldn't last more than a few moments with those wounds. No man could, not even after an apple.

So he let Thor come on, making those wild swings like a buffoon. Fool couldn't have managed a strategy if you gave him one.

No, Thor just kept on advancing, swinging away. Clumsy and oafish.

Narfi stepped in, swinging his axe at Thor. The blade crunched through mail and bit into the man's upper arm. Thor's hammer fell limp at his side, but he didn't release his grip.

The man's other hand shot up and closed around Narfi's throat, though, and squeezed with strength what would've made a jotunn jealous. Narfi's vision blurred. Couldn't draw a breath. Thor kept pulling him closer.

Then he slammed his brow into Narfi's nose. The sick sound of cartilage crunching filled Narfi's head. Couldn't focus. Not without air. Everything began to dim. The haze of death, like Hel's mists.

Flailing, Narfi caught hold of his axe heft, still wedged in the Ás's other arm. Grabbed and heaved.

Thor bellowed in pain and dropped Narfi, who slumped down to his knees, gasping. Breathing felt like lances of fire. Each breath a blessed agony. Glorious, searing air.

Thor dropped to one knee, closing his hand around

Mjölnir. Narfi hadn't even seen him drop the hammer, what with being unable to breathe and so forth.

Rubbing his throat, Narfi scrambled back several feet. Maybe toying with the man weren't his best idea.

Gasping down his painful breaths, he hefted the axe even as Thor rose, snarling. Raising a hammer with an arm what shouldn't have worked at all. How could the man tolerate such pain? Such profound injuries? Was it the hammer itself? If so, all Narfi had to do was hack off the prince's hand, and things would shift well back in his favor.

Thor half lunged, half fell forward, swinging that hammer. Narfi sidestepped. Or tried to, but moved sluggish, his body not answering the way it ought to. The hammer clipped his arm. Even that glancing blow spun him around and sent him stumbling to the ground.

Frantic, he scrambled away from Thor. An instant later, the hammer shattered stones in a tremendous explosion that flung up a cloud of debris.

Grunting, Narfi managed his feet. His heel brushed against the low rail at the bridge's edge, giving him nowhere else to retreat. He had to reckon that meant he needed to switch tactics and take to attacking.

Not surprisingly, Thor's rise was clumsy, off-balance. It gave Narfi the chance to lunge in, an axe-blow aimed at the man's head.

The Ás swept that hammer up, deflecting. A shard of Narfi's axe snapped off, hurtling out into the void. Snarling, Narfi swept what remained of his weapon down. The point of it jabbed into Thor's shoulder, scraping over the man's collarbone.

Thor roared in obvious agony, but still didn't fall.

What in the gates of Hel would it take to fell this bastard? Teeth grit, Narfi twisted the axe blade, grinding it against Thor's bone. The Ás's other fist snapped up and caught Narfi in the chest. The blow knocked his wind out, and he stumbled back, losing his grip on the axe haft. Gasping.

Sternum felt crushed. Couldn't ... breathe ...

Slobbering like a bear, Thor yanked Narfi's axe free of his shoulder and tossed it aside.

Narfi managed to catch a breath. This was impossible. How was the man still standing? Not even an Ás immortal ought to have ... Narfi's heel tapped against the rail again, and he glanced back. A tangle of roots grew out over the abyss below, descending into darkness and running who knew how deep.

Thor switched Mjölnir to his off hand.

Narfi had to reckon this was it. Except, he weren't the kind to give up and die. Not when Hödr still needed avenging.

Shit.

Another glance at his foe, then Narfi leapt the rail.

For a breathless instant, he fell, twenty feet, maybe, then landed on a curving root. The impact shot fresh pains through his whole body, and he twisted, swayed. Almost fell.

Above, on the bridge, Thor railed in wrath.

Probably just angry enough to try jumping down here, too, even when he hadn't any way back up.

Desperate, Narfi peered over the edge of the root. Another crossed under it, so far down he almost couldn't see it. Way down.

Well, he seemed bound for his sister's hall either way. Narfi rolled off the root and fell once more, the rush of air tugging at his clothes for the bare instant before that root slapped him in the face like a damn fist.

Everything swayed, going dark.

Maybe he'd have passed out, if it weren't for Thor's mad howling way above, echoing through this void.

Groaning, Narfi pushed himself up. Just enough to spit out a gob of blood.

Up ahead, this root seemed to twist into a nest of others. But it had to burrow through earth somewhere. These roots, they spanned the whole World. That meant if he crawled along one long enough, maybe he could reach the chasm's side, even find a way to climb out.

Just had to survive, he reckoned.

Live. A little longer, then rejoin his forces, rearm himself. Maybe not fight Thor by himself.

Either way, Asgard had fallen.

Groaning with pain and effort, Narfi pulled himself along the length of the root. Its fibrous surface tore at his skin, caught his clothes, and ripped fresh tears in them.

So tired ...

No. Couldn't let himself sleep. Not yet.

IT WAS A VARULF, in wolf form, running over snowy woods, faster than aught else Narfi could've imagined. Faster, and him running with it, wind whipping over him.

And then the varulf finding Odin, that Ás bastard what started all this, and what spawned Thor in the first place.

A pain in his chest told him the truth. Narfi wouldn't be the one to kill Odin.

But the varulf would. Would sink his teeth in the man's throat and end the reign of Asgard for good and all.

If he'd seen the future, it meant it couldn't change. Visions, they weren't always clear, no, but they didn't lie, neither.

This varulf, Fenrir, he was the key.

❧

THE ROOTS bent and wrapped around one another, having forced Narfi to drop down twice more, before finally digging into the side of the chasm. Given the overhang, he didn't much see himself climbing out.

No, but gaps in the wall created a tunnel. Maybe it went nowhere. Maybe it was just a burrow for rabbits or something. But ... maybe it led out.

Yggdrasil's roots connected all over. This world, the Otherworlds. Anywhere might give him a chance to survive.

Somewhere, far below the island, Odin had bound Fenrir not far from where he'd bound Father. So if the tunnel led beneath the island, that was where Narfi needed to go.

And he'd find the varulf.

Because there was yet a few more Aesir what needed killing.

27

*T*he tips of Yggdrasil's roots had bored through the glacial wall of the ice caves, and now burrowed down a hole where thick mist had coalesced, preventing Hermod from glimpsing even a hint of what lay below. It was a chasm of unknown depths, drowning in a maze of roots and poison mists.

"You want me to jump down *that*?" Hermod demanded.

Yes ...

Khione had led him up to the tunnel, refusing to go further once it began to descend, claiming such places were not for her. Unless Hermod missed his guess, such places were not fit for *anyone*, much less someone who was, for all intents and purposes, still mortal.

"I can't see aught."

There is naught to see, regardless ... It is a transitory space between Realms ... one that will lead to the depths of the Roil or, perhaps, even to what lays beyond ... And in that dark place ... all Realms become conjoined ...

Sorcerers, Odin had told him, tended to think of the Mortal Realm as the center of the World, around which stretched fathomless darkness. But reality, such as Hermod witnessed it, seemed to defy easy classification, refusing to fit into any clear model.

At the precipice he paused, watching his breath frost the air. Utter madness. He'd be like to break his neck, jumping into such a void. "You believe Naströnd lies below?"

Were you to bore down ... far beneath the frozen shelf to the east ... you might find the World of Water ... what you call Noatun ... Or beyond these ice caves, in shadows deep beyond measure ... there lies spaces that abut Svartalfheim ...

Meaning what? That the different Spirit Worlds not only overlaid one another, but existed adjacently at the same time?

When things align ... just so ...

Except, Keuthos's answer sidestepped his original question, even if it implied that Nidhogg's foul abode did lay down this abyss.

I told you not to use that word ...

What, *abyss*? "Why not?"

But, once again, the wraith offered no answer.

"Well, fuck me," Hermod said after a moment more. He pulled his last torch from his satchel, jammed it into his belt, and drew in another breath.

He didn't expect to enjoy this. He stepped off the edge.

His stomach dropped out from under him as wind rushed over his body, tugging at his clothes. For an instant. Then his feet hit hard on a slick, inclined surface—he couldn't see a damn thing down here—and skidded forward. He slipped, slamming his arse on that surface, and continued to slide down, faster and faster, not daring to grab aught for fear of wrenching his still aching shoulder. Instead, he crossed his arms over his chest.

A horrible rush of speed swept over him, pulling him so

quickly he'd surely slam into a wall and turn his bones to goo. And then the surface disappeared from under him and he was falling once more.

Flailing.

Screaming, though the wind stripped his voice away.

His hip banged against something—a root?—the impact drawing a shriek from him, even as it spun him around. He twirled around in the air, unable to control his angle. Nor brace for an impact when he hardly knew—

Bloated flesh smacked into him with the force of Thor's hammer. The bodies gave way an instant later, plunging him into a mire of filth. Flailing, flinging reeking muck in all directions, he managed to keep from going under. Caught his breath. And then retched so violently his knees gave up, and he plunged neck-deep into the corpse sea. That only worsened the stench. He slapped around, trying to steady himself on something, but corpses came apart under his blows, failing to offer the least bit of support.

Something large and sinuous brushed across his spine. At once, Hermod froze in place.

Oh, fuck.

Nidhogg's brood of serpents. Odin had never gone into much detail, save to mention nigh limitless numbers of these things dwelt in the corpse sea.

Shit. Fuck. Oh ...

Calm yourself ...

He couldn't fucking see! His torch was wet, coated in Hel wouldn't even know what, and he was in the middle of a place so horrible it terrified even Odin.

I can see ...

The corpses sloshed, disturbed by the passage of some-thing immense beyond measure. Far away, by the sound of it, but probably able to close the distance with horrifying speed should it detect him.

Oh, Hel. Oh, fuck. His stomach clenched and his heart felt apt to wilt away in the most profound terror imaginable. Part of him almost wanted to weep.

It knows you have entered Naströnd ...

Shit. This had to be the most Mist-mad thing he'd done thus far. And maybe the last he'd ever do, under the circumstances. Someone please help him ...

Calm ... yourself ... Turn slowly to your right ... Good ... Take care to disturb the waters as little as possible ... Move forward ... slowly ... Do not give in to the temptation to flee ... You are covered in decay ...

Wonderful. Hermod knew that much.

It works to your advantage ... masks your scent and body heat ... While you move slowly ... Nidhogg might not be able to spot you ...

Wait, *might* not? What the fuck was—

Calm yourself ... do not allow your elevated heart rate to draw its eye ...

Oh. So all he had to do was slosh through a sea of corpses, surrounded by enormous serpents, without moving the waters, or getting nervous. Never mind that, even if he did all that, the dark dragon might still discover him and devour him, body and soul.

I am not ... in the habit ... of coddling self-pitying mortals ...

Hermod wasn't in the habit of visiting Hel or wading through Naströnd. He was pretty certain his ordeal was the more trying of the two.

Behind him, something sizzled, and with the sound came the acrid stench of rapidly eroding bodies. Had the dragon sprayed them with some kind of acid to make them easier to digest?

Keep moving ...

That, Keuthos need not remind him of. Hermod had no desire to linger here for a moment. Certainly not for eternity.

"My son ..." A faint whisper, almost imperceptible.

Do not speak!

Was that ... Mother?

"Do not linger ..."

Oh. No, please no. How could Mother be here? Now, tears had built in his eyes, to think his mother endured this abominable torment. She had broken her oath. In order to stay with him and Father, mother had broken her oath.

A sick crunch of bones turning to mush—and slurped down with flesh—resounded through the cavern.

Just ahead ... A little more ... Control your breathing ...

His hand brushed over something fibrous. A frayed root. A root of the World Tree, except it was damaged. What could harm Yggdrasil? What *would* harm the World Tree?

The dragon gnaws upon the roots to curtail its fury ... It imagines itself breaking free ...

So it was eating the fucking World Tree? What would even happen if the Tree died? Would all the worlds collapse?

Keuthos said naught. Either it didn't know the answer, or the wraith considered that information too terrible to share. Perhaps worrying it might further set his pulse pounding or some such fear.

Which it probably would.

His mother. He had to save her.

Focus ... You cannot save the damned ... The frayed roots offer you, alone, egress ...

No. No, he couldn't leave her.

Remember your daughter ...

Sif. Damn it. Damn it!

Climb the root. Right. Hermod eased himself to a standing position, then gripped the root in both hands. With agonizing slowness, he pulled himself up, out of the muck. Despite his best effort, he could not quite prevent the *slurp* of muck as he yanked himself free.

His heart lurched and he froze, dangling just above the putrefying corpses until his arms burned. Though he could see naught, he swore he could hear serpents swimming around, a hair below his feet. His arms began to burn. Any sudden move and one of those things might sense his presence and lunge at him.

He'd need to use his Pneuma just to—

No ...

What?

Flush your body with Pneuma and they may ... sense ... it ...

Oh, damn it.

For a few heartbeats more, he hung suspended like that. Then he reached up, caught another bit of frayed root, and pulled himself upward. Hand over hand, until he could wrap his legs around the root and take some of the pressure off his arms.

Chill sweat beaded on his face as he made his slow, silent way up the root. A painful process, with slivers of stray fiber oft scraping his face or scratching his hands as he felt around for something to grasp onto.

He paused, and cast a final glance into the darkness, though there was naught to see. Was Mother really down there? Was this the price she'd paid to return to his life? A few decades with him and eternity in the corpse sea?

Whether truth or manifestation of your fears ... you cannot change aught that exists here, either way ...

Damn it. With no other choice, Hermod resumed his painful climb.

Finally, he reached a place where the root branched, and pulled his legs up and over that branch, giving himself some support. Up here, the fraying had stopped, leaving the World Tree mercifully whole. Hermod let his head fall against the side of the root, willing his breathing to slow. His hands felt worn raw, slick enough they were probably bleeding, in fact.

If he continued up this way, if he could find the Penumbra, he could pass through and enter the Mortal Realm once more. From there, he had but to find the sacrifices for Hel, and she would release Sif and Baldr.

Forget them ... Destroy the seals and free Achlys ...

No. Not until he had his daughter back.

Vile ... ignorant ... wretched ...

The wraith's anger bubbled inside him like a seething cauldron of tar, scorching his mind. Hermod suspected only Keuthos's oath not to try to possess him held the wraith at bay.

For a time, he held still there, forcing the Mistwraith's mental assault to subside. When Keuthos finally gave it over, Hermod resumed his climb.

How long had he moved among the roots? Hour after hour, it seemed, until he'd had no choice but to call upon his Pneuma to enhance his stamina and bury the pain in his hands. Now, he knew for certain they bled. Keuthos had made no further objection to Hermod using his Pneuma thus—after all, they had left Nidhogg behind long ago.

Now, he'd found himself navigating a maze of roots in

total darkness, and Keuthos—spiteful—had refused to offer any further guidance.

Hermod could have sworn the texture of the air changed. A subtle shift in the darkness, as if the shadows became less substantial. Enough, he could feel the Veil. He pushed through that, teetering on the roots as he fought with the sensation of falling, and the momentary loss of breath. Once he'd steadied himself, he drew the torch, and set to wiping the filth from it.

He had to wedge his shoulder against the fibrous surface to get leverage, and even so, managing to spark off the flint took him painfully long. When that torch finally caught, its sputtering flame seemed blinding after so long in total darkness.

Keuthos hissed in his mind.

The torch cast shifting shadows all about him, partially illuminating a knotted cluster of roots that bent and twisted around each other, pierced earth and rock walls, and stretched off in all directions. The maze extended far below him and, so far as he could tell, equally far above him. Endless.

Climbing one-handed because of the torch, he eased his way upward until the roots led to a tunnel. A cave, perhaps, and though it looked low enough he'd have to crouch, at least he could rest. On hands and knees, Hermod crawled forward until he reached the tunnel, then collapsed against one wall of it, panting.

He wedged the torch between the root and the stone floor, and released his Pneuma to rest.

WHEN HE WOKE, the torch had dwindled down to a pathetic flicker. Grunting, Hermod snatched it up. Better to make it as far as he could with what light remained to him.

So he crawled along the tunnel, following it even as the roots disappeared below ground. If this all led nowhere, he would find himself pretty well fucked. But … he could swear he heard water dripping somewhere ahead. Water *probably* meant a way out.

He continued forward until at last he came to an opening into a large cavern. Six or seven feet below, the last of his torchlight reflected off water, still, save for the occasional drop falling from recesses far above.

This was … the underground lake. Odin had bound Fenrir on an island in this lake, and after that, he'd chained Loki there, on the far shore.

Something lurks … in the water …

Odin had hinted as much. More serpents, perhaps. But other than swimming, Hermod had no way forward.

Chancing whatever dwelt in that lake was his only means of getting back to Asgard. Drawing a deep breath, Hermod eased his legs over the ledge, then slipped down into the waters with a slight splash. The lake was cold, but not half so cold as the murk of Naströnd.

Now, he could see naught, save the flicker of a torch on a pole, standing on the far shore. If aught swam around him, he'd have no way to know it. So he drew his Pneuma and swam, as quickly as he could without causing noise or disturbance, toward the shore.

Hermod swam for the torchlight. Before he'd even reached the shore, a pair of guards were looking at him, and standing beside them was Sigyn.

"Hermod?"

Here. His foster sister. Of course. She'd chosen to join

her husband in his imprisonment down here, and Loki, too, stood nearby, chained to a stalagmite, standing in a puddle.

"What in the Tree's shadow are you *doing* here?" a guard demanded, as Hermod pulled himself up onto the shore, panting.

His hair hung down over his face as he stared up at Sigyn. His beloved sister. The girl he'd seen raised from a babe, had always tried to look after.

Her betrayal stung worse than aught else, save losing Sif. And Sigyn had covered it up for centuries. Compounded the betrayal with lies of love.

A guard offered him a hand up and, slightly shaky, he took it, gaining his feet, then brushing his hair from his face.

These men didn't deserve it.

He *knew* that.

Fuck, but Hermod needed sacrifices. And he would not delay Sif's release. Not for a moment. Besides, they would try to stop him.

"Forgive me," he said. Then he drew his Pneuma and jerked free the dagger of Hel. With a swift motion, he rammed the blade into one guard's chest, slipped it loose, and slashed the throat of the other before the man even seemed to know what was happening.

"Hermod!" Sigyn fell back several steps, hand up in warding.

Hermod grabbed her cloak and slammed the dagger's pommel into her nose, crunching her cartilage beneath it. "You murdered her!"

"No!" Loki bellowed. "No, stop!"

Blood dribbling down her face, Sigyn started to crawl away. Hermod lunged at her. She caught his wrist in an iron grip, obviously Pneuma-enhanced. Hermod strained, pulling his hand free. Pneuma made her stronger than a man. Not as strong as him when he was flushed with his own Pneuma, though.

"I'm sorry," Sigyn wailed. She reached to raise the hood of her cloak and Hermod slashed Hel's dagger across her hand.

She shrieked, doubling over and clutching her hand to her chest, blood oozing between her fingers. Hermod caught her cloak and kicked her in the stomach, the impact flinging her back and snapping the clasp on her precious swan cloak. It came off in Hermod's hand and he tossed it away behind himself.

"You murdered my daughter!"

"Stop this!" Loki shouted. "I beg you, please, leave her be!"

"I'm sorry ..." Her sobs were muffled by her broken nose and short breath. Maybe he'd cracked her ribs. "I'm sorry ..." She raised her good hand in warding.

Ignoring Loki's pleas, Hermod stalked closer to his former sister, shaking his head. He grabbed her by her hair and yanked her up until her feet dangled just off the floor. "I loved you as if you were my own true sister. And you betrayed me!"

"Hermod, I—"

He rammed Hel's dagger in between her ribs. Her hot blood shot over his hand. It dribbled from her mouth as she looked at him, eyes wide in pain and fear and ... betrayal. She knew how he felt, now. He jerked the dagger free then drove it up under her chin. Now, blood exploded out over his face in a hot geyser. "You'll help me get her back." Her eyes went dead almost instantly.

"No!" Loki bellowed. "No! No! I'll kill you!" The man flung himself against his chains, straining as if he might break orichalcum, slurring his words in apoplexy. "I'll destroy you!"

Hermod dropped Sigyn's limp form and she collapsed in a heap at his feet.

"Fitting," he said, now turning back to Loki. "Fitting, that you too should pay for her crimes, and be sacrificed to your daughter."

"You cannot kill me." Shuddering breaths and sobs muffled the man's words. "But *I* ... will *end* you for this ..."

A shuffling behind him drew Hermod's gaze. Sigyn moved, pushing herself up.

What the ...? Hermod fell back several steps as she shambled to her feet.

Fool ...

She moved *wrong*. Her head lolling side to side, neck cracking loudly.

Hermod brandished the dagger between himself and ... *whatever* Sigyn had become. No draug had ever risen on Asgard, so far as he knew. But ... maybe it was the torchlight ... Still, he could have sworn that a red gleam lurked behind her eyes.

Sigyn's left eye seemed to freeze in its socket. It cracked and split, shards of it showering down over her cheek, even as she stretched, a macabre spectacle that had Hermod's empty stomach lurching. "Oh ... I could not have asked for a better sacrifice."

He knew that voice: Hel.

Slowly, his gaze drifted down to the dagger in his hand. Her dagger. Repulsed, he let it clatter to the cavern floor. It was impossible ...

"What have you done?" Hermod asked, half stumbling over his own feet as he retreated from the Queen of Mist.

The skin on the left side of her face had begun to slough

off, seeping down like tar. It turned her bloody smile all the more grotesque. "Why ... taken the offered sacrifice ... one so grand I'll hold your bargain fulfilled even though you've offered but three sacrifices instead of nine."

Behind them, Loki roared, straining against his chains, but Hermod could not tear his gaze from Hel.

What had he done?

No ...

She was ... *here*.

What the fuck ... had he done?

He was *in* the Mortal Realm. And *he* had done that. Odin's worst fear, the thing he had struggled against for so very long—Hermod had caused it.

"If ... you hold my oath fulfilled, then restore Sif and Baldr."

"Restore them?" She snorted, a wheezy sound that sent the side of her left nostril flapping. "I promised you I'd release them. Even as we speak, they are now free of their cells ... free ... even to leave my palace should they so wish."

"What?"

Betrayal ... forewarned ... and still it surprises you ...

"I wanted them to *live!*"

Hel drifted toward him, her malevolent smirk never faltering. "Then perhaps you ought to have been more specific in your bargain." She reached out and snatched his chin in her hand. Her touch was so cold it froze his breath in his chest. Her strength so immense he couldn't move. "Still, you've done well. So I give you your life, or what remains of it. Let none question my generosity."

Icy mist wafted from her, thicker even than Melinöe's, and the chill of it left Hermod frozen in place. When Hel released him, he slumped to his knee. The Queen of Mist drifted through the cavern, and out, up toward Asgard. Her cloud trailed behind her like a swirling sea of toxic vapors. The power of Niflheim made manifest.

More than ought else, Hermod wanted to weep. To curse Hel and curse urd and curse the entire World.

Sif.

Sif.

Fuck! What had he done?

"You'll die for this." Loki's voice sounded so raw. So broken. Like Odin, the man had some gift of prescience, leaving Hermod to wonder just how much Loki had foreseen of this moment. Had he known it was coming all along?

The workings of Fate lie beyond your ken ... You took your vengeance on the sister that betrayed you ...

Keuthos. Keuthonymos ... The servant who betrayed Achlys for Hel, and now regretted it.

Oceans of regret ... they shape the World ... All of existence is grief compounded upon damnation ... And the darkness seeks to draw us back into its embrace ...

Hermod struggled to his feet, finding it hard to even breathe. He'd kill Hel for this betrayal.

Imbecile ... She will crush you like an ant ...

He didn't fucking care. Hermod started off after her, breaking into a trot as he drew Dainsleif. Hel had broken her deal—the essence of it, at least. He'd not go to Odin and tell the king that his apprentice had released his bitterest enemy from her prison. No, he'd cut her down.

Even if you succeed ... she would hop to another ... If y‸ *to repay her treachery in kind ... I have already sho·*
way ...

His steps faltered at the edge of the t‸·

Keuthos wanted him to release‸
seals. To let one horrid abomination g‸

And why not? Could the one truly be worse than the other? It was Hel who had so crossed him, not Achlys.

Yes ...

Did it mean he ought to trust the first Elder Goddess? No. But at the very least, her freedom would give Hel something to concern herself with outside the conquest of Midgard.

It was a start.

28

It was a long trek up the Norns' mountain, especially without Sleipnir, and twice Odin paused to rest. He could have burned his Pneuma to enhance his stamina—indeed, he had to use a little to make it at all—but he thought it best to conserve his strength for what lay ahead. He had no way of knowing if aught like the dís would guard the Norns.

Perhaps they would have hid themselves away, refusing to show themselves, as they had done when he went to confront them beneath the roots of Yggdrasil. Perhaps ... save, if he spent the rest of time hunting them from one corner of Midgard to the next, had not their schemes still failed?

No, with a bitter certainty, he knew they would await him this time. A prescient knowledge, yes, but one he refused to look directly at for fear of what it might mean. That stubborn denial left him feeling a bit like a petulant child, willfully ignoring the adults and pretending they did not exist. But still, he could not deny that, on some level he had to wonder if aught he did not see, in a sense, truly did not exist yet within the tapestry of time.

Crouching atop the mountain, with lashing snowstorms all around, his mind kept circling back to a desire he hated himself for. The desire to discuss the implications of self-fulfilling prescience and whether, by choosing to turn away from prescience, he might thwart the workings of these non-temporal entities. The desire to circle round and round the topic, coming ever closer to the elusive center, with the one person whom Odin *could* discuss such things.

With Loki.

The very servant of the Norns Odin now went to destroy. The man who, on their behalf, had wrought all the chaos now descending upon Midgard. Maybe Odin ought to have killed his blood brother for such a complete and utter betrayal of Asgard.

Nornslave.

Because Loki, too, was trapped by urd. Perhaps, even, a victim, as much as Odin.

Trembling, Odin finally bestirred himself to press on.

Sitting alone in the cold would not avail him. If answers existed, they dwelt deep inside the hollow beneath this peak.

TORCH IN HAND, Odin trod into the tunnels leading down to the Norns' sanctum. The mighty iron doors had already stood open, awaiting him. Just as well. He and the Fatespinners had business together, and none of them could deny it any longer.

The braziers were unlit, this time. No crackling flames to hold back the darkness or the chill or the niggling sense of dread in his gut that he so wished to pretend did not lurk there.

The only sound was the soft padding of his boots over the stone floor, and the clank of Gungnir's butt upon it, as Odin descended ever deeper. So very long ago he had first come here. Back then, he'd been so young, so very naïve. The World had been a place of mystery, where the unknown and the mists held horrors. Where the supernatural was best left alone. Sometimes, Odin missed those days.

Now, he himself had passed on into the Realm of the supernatural. Now, he contended with forces he once had no idea existed, and for a prize beyond imagining. The very fate of history.

For all the allies he'd made along the way ... Odin did not recall ever feeling quite so alone.

Loki's betrayal had left him bereft.

Then, at long last, the path leveled out and led him to the chamber of the Sisters of Fate. His first visit here, he had not looked so carefully about himself. The Norns stood there, before the well once more, illuminated by a single brazier. Peering through the darkness, now Odin could make out the hints of a root of Yggdrasil above.

It was the same chamber as the one below Asgard. The same, or very similar. Odin knew better than to assume limitations of time or space existed in this hold. They were everywhere and nowhere, and he had, perhaps, even stepped outside time now.

Odin trod up, until he stood a dozen feet from the sisters, then flung the torch at their feet. It squelched down into the loam around the Well of Urd. "You betrayed me."

"Conceptions," one said.

"Of betrayal," the second said.

"Presuppose loyalty," the third offered.

Odin sneered at them, shaking his head. "So you never had our interests in mind. Fine. Nevertheless, you have brought ruin unto the World. You have wrought the deaths of those I loved." He pointed Gungnir at the closest of them. "You forced others to turn on each other. I don't know why. And I don't fucking care. It stops *now*."

"Ignorance."

"Impudence."

"Impotence."

Well, maybe not that last one. Snarling, Odin lunged with Gungnir, intent to skewer the Norn closest at hand. Her form broke apart like the dís's had, and he missed, for her images appeared all around. All three Norns had become a blurring mass of overlapping images, seeming to fill the entire chamber.

Odin grasped for his own prescient visions to counteract their temporal manipulations, but found the Sight hard to catch hold of. Were they blocking him?

As one, the Norns flitted away, into the darkness beyond the edge of the brazier's light, to the far back of the cavern.

Pausing only to snatch up the torch, Odin raced after them. "You'll not escape me! Today I free Midgard from the chains of your ..." But he faltered, as the torch's light adumbrated a stalagmite that seemed to stretch from floor to ceiling at a crooked angle.

Stalagmites didn't form like that. They were vertical ...

The shaft moved, chittering slightly. As he took another step closer, he realized coarse hairs covered the stalagmite. And it was a leg. A spider leg, big enough to fill the whole fucking cavern.

A hollow pit opened in Odin's gut, and—almost dreading what he would see—he flung the torch out into the darkness. It bounced off a bloated body the size of a king's hall. Spider-like, yes, save instead of eight legs jutting from its sides, dozens and dozens of legs erupted from the body at all angles imaginable. Those legs grasped the floor, the ceiling, the walls, the roots of Yggdrasil, in a skittering manifestation of nightmare.

Within the body itself glinted a hundred faceted eyes, spread out all over, such that the creature could no doubt see in any direction. It was an abomination beyond description, and from it exuded a timeless horror, eldritch and unknowable. Gossamer strands of reality wafted in and out of existence around the entity, visible manifestations of time and space warping around it.

A sudden, almost irresistible urge seized Odin. The need to fall to his knees and worship this being beyond the scope of even gods. To beg its—or their—forgiveness for his hubris in even thinking to come here.

His soul recoiled at the sight before him, refusing to even grasp the ultimate shape of this thing. Indeed—as it crushed all hope within him by even moving forward—its legs seemed to vanish and reappear all at once, shifting its location without the need for pathetic mortal movements.

It simply *was*.

It was everywhere. Anywhere. Any time or place it chose to exist, it was there.

The Norns, the Sisters, were but a guise of an entity that the mortal mind simply could not comprehend.

Bow down. Beg forgiveness from the lords of time. Give in. To the inevitability of history.

For history is merciless.

All he had to do was drop the weapon. Yet ... his hand would not open.

Give in.

Give in ...

You were a fool.

Fear laced even the voices of Audr and Valravn. Even vaettir knew they looked upon something so far beyond their ken.

Except ...

Odin refused to accept defeat. Refused to back down.

Roaring, lunging forward before wisdom could dissuade him, Odin slashed with Gungnir at the chitinous leg before him. The undulating blade smacked hard into the surface, but gouged deep, tearing out a chunk of exoskeleton and a spray of black-green ichor that must have passed for blood.

The Norn-thing chittered, the sound a thousand times more potent than that uttered by the dís, and sending the whole cavern reverberating with a sound that seemed to unmake reality. Those gossamer strands flitted in and out of existence.

Before Odin's very eyes, the ichor *reversed* its momentum. It sucked back up from the ground, from midair, and flew back into the leg, followed by the skeleton he had cut away, locking itself back into place as if his attack had never happened.

It had ... turned back time?

For a moment, he could only gape.

Well, how fast could it do that?

The Norns had wanted a Destroyer. They'd *fucking* get one.

Growling, Odin lunged forward, whipping Gungnir around in vicious arcs, slicing into leg after leg as he made his way toward the bulbous central body. Legs slammed down around him, vanishing from one place and appearing right where he'd stood an instant before.

Desperately, Odin caught hold of prescient Sight—it kept trying to slip from his grasp!—allowing him to predict where a leg would appear and dodge around it. His growl had become a roar of defiance. A refusal to accept Fate.

Ichor had washed over him, though it continually flowed back from his clothes in all directions, sucking once more inside the creature's dozens of wounds.

Odin dashed around one leg and drove Gungnir straight into one of the Norn's multitude of eyes. The lens exploded in a shower of gore and the creature bellowed, for the first time seeming more pained than simply enraged.

With a snarl, Odin yanked the blade sideways, tearing out flesh, cutting straight into another eye.

"I'll hack you into a thousand pieces! Can you turn back time when I cut out your fucking brain?"

Again and again, he hewed into the abomination. So fast, even the creature could not seem to turn back time quickly enough to heal all the wounds he dealt. Nor did it seem half so easy for it to fix the damage he'd done to its central core.

It kept thrusting at him with those spider legs, and only his own prescient insight allowed him to avoid getting skewered. He leapt over a leg just as it appeared and thrust Gungnir out, once more impaling the Norn.

All he had to do was cause so much damage its brain gave out. At least, he hoped all he had to do—

Another dís appeared from nowhere. Space bent around her, and she stepped out, almost like stepping through the Veil, only she had not come from the Penumbra. Before Odin could react, a spider leg thrust down, impaling his shoulder.

Gungnir slipped from nerveless fingers.

With a shriek, the creature jerked the leg up, flinging Odin free of it and sending him bodily tumbling through the air. One of the Norn's more massive legs caught him midair and smacked into him like a giant club, sending him colliding with the cavern wall.

Breath blasted from his lungs.

Everything grew hazy.

Before he could even start to rise, the dís appeared next to him, hefting him up with her human hand. A spider leg plunged through his other shoulder and drove him back against the wall.

Odin tried to scream in pain but couldn't even get a breath in. The dís reared back and slammed her fist into his face. Odin's head cracked against the wall. That fist came back and smacked into his chin, sending him colliding with the wall once more.

A flash of white.

A ringing sound.

More blows landing on his head. His ribs. His gut.

Everything swirling around him. A weightlessness as he fell into oblivion.

29

The narrow tunnel seemed to want to close in around Narfi. On his belly, he crawled forward by his elbows, trying to ignore his injuries and the fresh scrapes along his arms. Sweat and dirt mingled to sting his eyes. Not that he could see a damn thing in here, regardless.

Every so often, a fibrous root blocked the way forward, and he had to wriggle his way around it. If any of those totally barred the tunnel he'd be well and truly fucked, no mistake. There weren't no turning around in here and he didn't even want to think on crawling backward for the next hour or more.

How had it come to this?

Every bone in his body ached now. Hard to breathe, even ... What with his army, he should have been able to overcome the blundering oaf Thor. Instead, he found himself half-dead, crawling through the dark into some warren beneath the World Tree.

Nidhogg's Realm?

Shit. No. The dark dragon weren't down here. Sure

enough, he'd heard it told Odin had encountered the serpents in Naströnd, far below the World Tree. Vafthrudnir knew the dark dragon, too, and feared it more than aught else. But Narfi had to believe that this space weren't so liminal as to allow him to slip through the boundaries between worlds to whatever abominable landscape held that reality. Because if it was, if the Veil had grown so thin …

Don't think on it. He couldn't hardly afford such thoughts. That sort of thing would just get him killed all the faster. Only way left to him was forward, he reckoned, and that meant he had to just keep crawling and hope he weren't edging his way close to the bounds of that place.

Some told it like Naströnd bordered on Hel's domain. An irony that. Would his sister actually help him, if he stumbled up to her gates?

Well, the Sight kept on pulling him forward, which meant, one way or another, his path lay down this tunnel. He reckoned he'd not have seen himself crawling in the dark unless he was meant to do so.

The ground beneath his hands became slick, slimy almost, but harder, like wet rock. Huh. Found a cavern? Narfi patted around until he found an opening, almost too narrow to squeeze through, but it did seem the only way forward.

So.

What did that leave him? Crawling arse-first back the way he'd come, or risking getting stuck in the rock and starving to death. Didn't reckon either option sounded too enticing.

"Oh, fuck it all."

Narfi grabbed the lip of rock and slid himself forward, up until his brow was pushing against that slimy surface. He had to turn his head sideways to manage through it. Cold moisture brushed over his cheek, but the slickness made it easier to squeeze through. Once he'd got his shoulders in, he caught a faint glimmer of light.

If he hadn't been crawling around in the dark for an hour or more, he probably wouldn't have noticed it, not that low. But there was some light source ahead, no mistake. Light had to mean a way out, he reckoned, and aught was better than staying here a moment longer.

Grunting, and wriggling, he pulled himself along the rock surface. His hands kept slipping out from under him, and the path seemed to be sloping a bit forward, water dribbling down along it like—

His hand brushed over open air. Narfi grabbed at the tunnel's side to steady himself, only water had slicked that too, and his hand slipped. He pitched forward, slid down a crack, and then flailed, plummeting through open air for a heartbeat. Enough to catch a flicker of light. Not half enough to figure on where he was.

Then he slammed hard into water. It knocked the wind from him. Shot up his nose, burning. Blackness all around.

Struggling, not half sure which way was even up, he flailed around. His fingers burst through the surface, then his head. Then he set to choking and coughing, scarce able to keep himself from sinking under again.

"Get out of the water!" someone shouted.

Narfi reckoned that sounded wise. Over to his left, a torch on a pole provided the only source of light. Gasping, he swam for it. Something brushed against his leg. Something large and slick, sinuous.

Oh, fuck!

Frantic, Narfi swam faster, trying to ignore his injuries.

Don't let it be a serpent. Not one of Nidhogg's brood. That'd be the last damn thing he needed, no mistake. His legs brushed the rock surface beneath, and then he was scrambling out of the waters and onto the shore.

There was a raft there, tied up, and beside it, two dead guards. Lying in pools of their own blood, ice crystals over their faces, though it weren't over-cold down here.

"Narfi?"

He looked up sharply at his name, and there, chained to a stalagmite in a pool of water, stood Father. The man looked wrung-out ragged, maybe worse than Narfi felt.

Unless this were all some fever dream.

Narfi climbed to his feet and limped his way over to his father. Then he poked him with one finger.

Father grabbed him and drew him into an embrace. "What happened?"

"Shouldn't you know?"

"I'm too far away from the flame to see things. I only know what I've seen in the past."

"Reckon that weren't enough to keep you from getting chained down here. We under a mountain?"

Father nodded.

Narfi blew out a breath. His throat and sinuses still hurt from having saltwater running over them. Grimacing, he planted a foot on the stalagmite and grabbed the chain. Then he called Pneuma to his arms and heaved. The chain creaked but didn't budge.

"It's orichalcum," Father said. "You can't break it."

No. He refused to believe that. He'd already lost half his army, but he'd see the rest of the Aesir paid for what they'd done. Drawing in a deep breath, Narfi heaved again. Pulled until he felt like his guts would spill out, then collapsed to the ground, splashing the water around Father.

Damn it.

Narfi wiped his brow with his elbow. "Has to be a way to sever this."

Father's eyes were red as he looked at him, like he'd wept. Didn't hardly seem like him in the least, not as Narfi knew him.

"For my brother?" Narfi asked. "That's why I'm here. I killed Frigg and I aim to see all the rest dead for what they've done. Where's Mother?"

Father swallowed hard, and sank down to kneel in the pool in front of Narfi. "Gone. Hermod murdered her."

"What? B-because of my attack?"

"No. Old vengeance for a mistake made centuries ago."

Narfi spit. "One worth killing his own sister over?" Father opened his mouth, but Narfi didn't want to hear no excuses. "Don't reckon that matters none. If you're down here, I know who else is, too. And now I know what it meant, me seeing the wolf."

Father reached out to grab his wrist, but Narfi pulled away. "Don't do this."

"You're saying I can't break these chains. You know I would if I could, but I reckon you'd know, one way or the other. Seeing as it stands, I'm gonna find a different ally, and I'm gonna see every last Ás sent down to Hel. They deserve it, whatever she'll do to them."

"No one deserves that. Narfi, please—"

He backed away, shaking his head. "I'm gonna find a way to get you free, too, then we'll see about avenging Hödr and Mother, both. Reckon the wolf is the way to end this dynasty for good."

"You cannot control Fenrir."

"Don't need to control him. Just need to point him at

them trollfuckers what I want eaten, and let him do the rest."

Father grimaced, but Narfi turned away so he wouldn't have to look on it. Grief had made the man weak, maybe. Could be, but it had only strengthened Narfi's resolve. If Fenrir was the way to vengeance, well then, Fenrir was the one he needed to see.

He grabbed the torch first, then the guide pole, and shoved the raft off the shore, steering toward the island in the distance.

It weren't too far, and then the raft scraped up against another rocky shore.

A snarl greeted him. Deep, guttural, resounding over the waters. The object of his search. Still, his own damn feet didn't much want to tread onward. Traitorous feet, truth be told. They had him edging his way forward like he hadn't ridden a varg or fought a war.

The firelight, it glinted red off those eyes. Over there, at the small island's heart, a man stood bound by another orichalcum chain, and that run through a bored out rock. The man wore naught save some rags around his loins, and his hair and beard were long. Fierce and wild.

"The king sends me another meal?" the man said, voice half a growl.

Those chains, they reached long enough Narfi judged the varulf could almost reach him.

He had to reckon that meant he'd gone quite far enough. "You are Fenrir."

"Yes." The man trod forward, to the extent of the chains. Close enough Narfi could feel his hot breath. The varulf sniffed him. "Not human. Not quite. Half jotunn?"

Narfi didn't see much reason to answer that. "I'm looking for an ally."

It began as a chuckle, deep in the varulf's throat, before rumbling upward into full-blown mocking laughter. "And you come *here*? Has the mist addled your simple brain?"

Maybe it had at that. "You're no friend to Odin, that much I know." That, and that the wolf would kill the Ás king and shatter the whole dynasty.

"Ahhh. So the king did not send you. I thought I smelled blood over the water a time ago."

Well, that weren't Narfi, but he didn't reckon it made much difference. "The Aesir murdered my brother. My mother. Bound my father in chains what I can't break."

"Oh. You're *his* son, then. Hmmm." Fenrir jerked on his fetters, setting them to jangling. "You seem to not realize the same bindings hold me."

"Reckoned you'd know of a way to break them."

The varulf chortled again, shaking his head. "These chains are forged from the tormented souls of the damned. Their sufferings resound through eternity. No mortal effort could end that."

Narfi worked his jaw. He refused to believe he'd wasted the trip out here. Fenrir would kill Odin, this he knew. "You must know something that can release you."

The varulf licked his lips. "I can smell it on you. The desperation. The burning need for vengeance even as it slips from your fingers. You've lost, haven't you? You struggled and you *failed*. You teeter on the precipice between glory and wretchedness."

Narfi stepped forward, not caring it brought him into reach of the varulf. "Reckon we *both* want to avenge ourselves against Odin and his kin. Me, I've sworn to see Asgard brought down. So you tell me how we can do that, and you won't never have a truer ally than me."

"Are you certain? You're willing to make any sacrifice for your vengeance?"

Narfi shrugged. After what Odin and Frigg and now Hermod had done to his kin ... naught could matter next to setting that right. "I'll do whatever it takes."

Fenrir snickered. "All right. Do you know what I am?"

"A varulf."

"The varulf progenitor. Stronger than any other varulf. A prince of my kind. But I cannot simply abandon a host, especially not bound by orichalcum. So for four centuries I waited, fettered in this dismal cavern. Do you know why they don't simply kill me?"

Narfi could harbor a guess. "Odin has his sick sense of justice, what would have his enemies suffering for all time."

"No." Fenrir shook his head, his grin exposing teeth that looked a little too pointed. "No. If my host dies, I can move on, claim almost any other mortal in range. They cannot kill me, because destroying my host body would free me to take another."

Oh. Huh. Well, fuck. Narfi glowered at the varulf.

"Oh, yes. You see it now. You cannot break my chains. But you ... *you* do not wear chains." Fenrir's grin was sickening, truth be told. This weren't part of the plan. "Kill this body, and I enter *yours*. And then, I promise you all the vengeance you could dream of against Odin and all who follow him." If that weren't the most Mist-mad plan he'd ever heard, he'd be damned. "You said you would do whatever it took."

Right. Narfi had said that, and meant it too. He still fucking meant it. Hadn't reckoned that included getting turned into no wolf, though.

He sniffed, looking hard into the varulf's eyes.

Odin's followers had killed Hödr. They'd murdered both

of Narfi's mothers. They'd bound Father so that he couldn't be freed. What was Narfi's life, compared to vengeance for all that? The Aesir had wrought their own damnation.

"Your oath," he said.

"I swear to destroy everything Odin has built. I swear, I shall taste his blood."

"Free Father."

"I can't break those chains, but I won't harm him."

Narfi grunted. Well, he'd reckoned as much, but it won't not hurt in the asking. "Kill Odin. Use my body to kill that trollfucker."

"I give you my oath."

"Reckon that'll do, then." Narfi slid a knife free from his belt.

Fenrir grinned once more, grabbing him by both shoulders. So eager.

And why not? Odin's cruelty had bound him here for so very long.

"Send them all to Hel," Narfi said. Then he rammed the knife up under Fenrir's chin and into his skull.

The varulf spasmed and a spray of blood flew from his mouth, splattering Narfi's face. Fenrir took a faltering step back, then collapsed to the cavern floor. There he lay, thrashing slightly, for a moment. The light in his eyes died.

Narfi's ears popped.

He could almost feel it, brushing over his skin. Pushing in through his nostrils, his ears, his eyes. Like a cloud trying to suffuse him, though he couldn't see aught. Like a power, brushing against him.

Slithering up his bowels, writhing in his stomach.

He dropped to his knees, groaning. This was it. This was what he'd bargained for. Come on, then. Let Fenrir come to him. Let him become Odin's fear. His *nightmare*. Let all Asgard tremble before him.

All his bones ached. Like every single one was getting yanked out of socket.

Like his body wanted to turn inside out.

At the back of his throat, a howl built.

PART IV

Year 400, Age of the Aesir
Winter

30

"Was it truth?" Odin asked.

Loki shrugged. "What is truth? Your question belies a simplistic worldview, Odin. Do you ask whether it could have been a mere dream? Of course it could have. But then, even dreams may have meaning, though not always literal ones. If what you saw was not actual reality, that does not discount that it may have held *some* reality worth gleaning."

Hel's icy trench, Odin hated when Loki spoke in such riddles. And by the gleam in his eye, the man damned well knew that. Payback for fantasizing about his brother's woman, perhaps.

"Ymir wanted my father, specifically. *Spoke* to him. Why would he do that? Why—assuming this was literal truth— would a jotunn speak to a Man? Particularly a Man he intended to kill."

Wait ... what? He'd had this conversation before. Everything was ... blurred. His ears kept ringing. Was this a memory? If it was a memory, why was he conscious of it?

Hel sent Ymir to test Odin. To see if he was the Destroyer.

"What did he say?" Loki asked.

"I couldn't understand his language." Odin could feel his mouth moving, as if of its own accord. A thousand questions flitted at the end of his tongue, all the myriad things he'd have wanted to ask Loki, but none of them quite took form. "Something about Hel, I think."

Loki frowned, just a little. "Perhaps he merely threatened to send Borr to her."

How hard *had* the Norns beaten him? He was reliving memories now? He could use the Sight to dive back into the memories, yes, but this felt different. Like he was really there. Like if he just ... pushed a little harder ... he might change something.

Not this.

This wasn't what he needed to change. This was ... his first warning about Hel?

Dreams. He had already glimpsed something out of time, long out.

Waves bombarded his consciousness, threatening to pull him under and drown him in their tide. It was like a profound undertow had caught him and yanked him far out, into a stormy sea, where time roiled around him in a maelstrom. And it was pulling him down ... Down, so deep ...

All breath fled his lungs.

The tidal currents threatened to rip him to pieces.

❧

As HE TURNED BACK to his people, Loki strode up to him. Odin clasped his blood brother's arm. "I suppose I owe this birth to you, in a way."

Loki smiled, shook his head.

That smile. Oh! Damn, but Odin had loved Loki like his own brother back then. Over his own brothers, maybe. He ... he couldn't even well remember Ve or Vili anymore. They had died badly. A few of his so many regrets.

"I wish that I ..." Odin heard himself saying, "well, of course he's far too young for an apple, anyway."

Loki nodded. "Undoubtedly. But, my friend, if it would ease your mind ..." Loki produced a golden apple from a pouch on his belt. "I might have saved *one* more for just this occasion."

No. No. No!

Thor's birth?

Loki had an apple to spare because he'd not needed the one Odin had to offer. Loki had already been immortal, even back then. Long, long before then. He'd buried a daughter in some distant past ... Wait ... had that started the cycle of Eschatons? Hel's death?

He needed to ask Loki now ... needed to know how to overcome the Norns.

Odin took the apple, his hand almost seeming to shake. A hollow opened in his chest. No words seemed worthy of such a boon. "Brother, I ... You did this for me?"

"You're welcome."

No, no, no. This wasn't important. Odin had to ask his questions. He had to know ... wait. This was *the* moment, wasn't it? The one he should have seen, should have understood.

"But if you had an apple to spare," Odin asked, "why did you not give it to Hadding?"

"It would not have saved him. A man cannot change his urd."

Oh.

Oh, fuck.

Loki had told him, back then, before they ever set out for Vanaheim. Was his blood brother trying to warn him? Trying to warn about what would happen?

A man cannot change his urd.

Odin grunted. He'd been thinking about that, about Fate, even back then. He hadn't wanted to believe it.

Instead, he turned from Loki ... wanted to believe his choices mattered.

Or did they matter? Everything had become so muddled before him.

Vili raised a drinking horn in salute, before downing the whole thing in one swig, earning him raucous laughter and cheers from those about him. Odin nodded at him, then passed among the rest of the hall, accepting the well-wishes and embraces of men and women from nine tribes.

Idunn moved in and out of the light of braziers, eyes watching him like a weight on his soul. She ...

Idunn. He'd lost Idunn to the shadows. If he could break free from urd, maybe he could find his way back to her. He had to destroy the Web of Urd, whether Loki believed it possible or no.

Idunn ... she was going to show him something important.

After making sure his guests had all seen him, Odin followed Idunn down the hall and down stairs. The Vanr goddess led him to the room Frigg used to brew her potions and salves and stood there, staring at the wall.

The brazier down here cast the room in heavy shadows that tightened around his throat like a noose. Long ago, someone had worked the Art in these depths, and the foulness of it still tainted these stones.

Odin was about to ask what she did here. But something was ... odd. Those runes on the wall. He couldn't read them, but they ... looked much like some of the runes now wrapped around his chest and arms. After pulling away his tunic, he looked down. Yes, some of the same verses marked his body.

Couldn't read the runes ... back then.

But he could now.

Ragnarok ...

Brother would fight brother ...

Sisters' sons would break the bonds of kinship ...

The World falters ...

Axe time, sword time, broken shields, wind time, wolf time ...

The Destroyer wakes ...

The dvergar had foretold Odin's coming. Coming, in this lifetime, this incarnation.

FROM THE MISTS, Naresh walked toward him. As he drew near, vertigo swallowed Odin, and the whole chamber began to spin. He wanted to retch, though he knew his stomach was empty; regardless, Chandi still held him pinned. More figures drifted out of the shadows, a dozen men. A hundred. A thousand hidden forms advancing as Naresh advanced, converging on him.

Him. Him ...

Each one jerked away his shirt to reveal a glyph over his heart. A rune. The *same* rune as Chandi had touched on Odin's chest. Each subtly different, and yet, always the same lines, the same arcs. Only the flourishes changed. Names and memories and lifetimes changing. But something deeper, the underlying soul remaining ever intact. Always, always fighting against the encroaching urd, against the inevitable return of utter chaos.

Souls. Souls of a thousand men. A thousand lifetimes.

Odin's lifetimes.

But Idunn hadn't known *this*. No, that wasn't what she was trying to tell him. She didn't know ... or she didn't understand the Wheel of Life, even if her grandmother had. Because ... because Eostre had not believed in reincarnation.

Souls born into a life. And in death, returned to the Tree of Life. To be born again, time after time. Given the chance to set right the most terrible wrongs in all the Realms. To stand against the encroaching chaos.

Odin was on his knees, tearing at his hair, his cheeks, his chest. His flesh burned. A thousand lifetimes of memories cascaded through his mind, beating away his senses and his self and binding him to a cycle of destruction stretching back more millennia than even the Vanir had ever imagined.

He was—had been—Naresh. And Matsya and Herakles and Suiren and so, so many more. And he had defeated Hel. Had won victory for Mankind, defeated chaos, even if the cost was the annihilation of an Era. The end of one Era birthed the dawn of the next.

He'd been all these men, always struggling. Always fighting. Willing to do aught it took to stave off the final descent of darkness.

Struggling against Hel.

He'd never really understood.

BORR HELD his newborn son in one arm, the other hand gently rubbing Bestla's forehead. "What shall we name him?"

Bestla laughed weakly. "You're so convinced you can make a better World for him? He's a sign of it, then. Call him Odin—the prophet."

Oh.

Oh, fuck.

His retrocognitive memory of his father. He'd forgotten this. They named him a prophet.

Odin. Odin ... the Oracle.

Why had they named him that?

Borr chuckled to himself, staring at his beautiful new son. Odin. Little Odin, prophet of the World that Borr would build in his honor. In Buri's honor. "Look," Borr said. "I think he likes the name."

"Of course he does," Bestla said. "I have a hint of the Sight."

Because she'd *known*.

His mother had known, all along, on some level, that Odin would have a gift for the Sight. A latent gift, for so long, yes, but it would bloom into something no one else in the World had.

Was that ... was that what *made* him the Destroyer?

If he was in the past, why couldn't he change his choices? Go back. Let him go back, to those days, misspent in rage against Loki, and instead, beg for the answers.

If only he could make it back and change things.

ODIN'S HEAD pounded so hard it felt as though his brain might burst his skull and ooze out the cracks. He lay on the ground, in a damp cavern, illuminated by a single brazier.

He pushed himself up to find he lay beside the Well of Urd, in an empty chamber. Empty, save for a black swan and a white one swimming about the well. Roots of Yggdrasil dangled down from above.

With a groan, he struggled to his feet. Where was Gungnir? Shouldn't it have lain on the floor nearby? Had the Norns taken it when they'd fled?

And what ... what had those visions meant? He rubbed his brow, though it did little to relieve the ache. He'd seen the past, things four hundred years ago. Memories of his first steps along the road that had brought him here.

Had the Norns shown him the visions to prove something to him?

None of this made any sense. If they had given him the visions ... why did they allow him to use those visions to harm them? They'd sent the dís to stop him, but failed, because he turned the visions against her. Turned to them ... when before he'd refrained from looking at the future.

Had they sacrificed their pawn merely to ensure Odin would turn back to the Sight?

He'd failed to kill the Norns, but they hadn't killed him.

Grunting, he stumbled toward the back of the chamber, seeking out his spear. Instead, he found someone rushing down the path into the chamber. An aging man, with streaks of gray in his black hair. A man ...

Odin knew him.

"Who are you? How *dare* you defile the Norns' sanctum?" The man bore a staff, which he thumped on the ground with each threatening step he took toward Odin.

"Did you look upon the well? Did you find what you sought, interloper?"

Where had Odin seen this man before? Where had ...

Oh. Lytir. The Voice of Urd, the keeper of the Norns' well. Before Odin had sacrificed the man to fuel his spell.

But this ... this wasn't a memory. Lytir was speaking to him, though the man clearly did not know him.

Lytir shook his head in obvious chagrin. "I ought to kill you. Cast you into the abyss and let none even realize you'd come here. But, unfortunately for us both, such a transgression must be brought before the queen."

Queen? Hadn't Lytir served Njord? And before that, Mundilfari?

The man roughly grabbed Odin's shoulder and guided him back up the spiraling path, the hollow inside Yggdrasil. It was ... smaller than Odin had remembered. As if the Tree was slightly younger, slightly stronger.

Damn, but his head would not stop throbbing, and trying to make sense of any of this was certainly not helping. First, it was like his mind was flitting about at random through his memories, and now, he found himself in a world before he had any business remembering.

Had he landed in a past life? Was something else going on?

Lytir roughly escorted him across the great bridge, and beyond, all the way to a glittering hall that Odin had ordered his people to tear down, long ago.

Definitely the past. He *felt* like himself, but why wouldn't he?

Lytir took him inside the hall, and into a throne room, though one decorated far differently than Odin remembered. Black drapes covered the mighty windows, deepening the shadows, such that the two braziers provided the better part of the light in here.

Upon the throne sat a woman, dark haired and slender, in a black dress. Dozens of piercings marred her face, intermingled with tattoos that looked like perverse Supernal supplications to powers Odin did not wish to dwell on.

As he drew closer, he realized two figures stood behind the throne, flanking either side of it. Figures with no skin, leaving raw, bloody muscle and sinew exposed.

Odin gagged, wanting to retch. He'd heard ... heard of Mundilfari's perverse punishment. The Living Flayed Ones. Perhaps the darkest use of the Art ever practiced on Vanaheim.

Lytir knelt some distance from the throne, pulling Odin down beside him. "Queen Irpa. I found a trespasser within the Chamber of the Well."

Irpa—had Odin heard that name before?—leaned forward, grinning, biting her lower lip while drumming her fingers on her knees. "Ooooo. Hehehe. Ahhh." Her grin widened. "Did he taste an apple without permission?" She glanced to either side with obvious glee. "I'll gladly add to my collection."

"I do not believe so, Your Majesty."

Odin kept his mouth shut. Of course, he had tasted an apple, at least in his future life.

Irpa grumbled, then clapped her hands. "Oh, well! Maybe force him to eat one! Then he'll have stolen it!"

"My queen, I do not think—" Lytir began.

"And why should we waste an apple on a thief, hmmm, little Nornslave?" Nornslave. Lytir ...? "No reason at all!" Irpa leapt to her feet, screaming the last words. "No, no! No reason to spare a thief! Just have him taken to Mundilfari!

And tell him, this time I want the skin myself!" She sunk back into the chair, giggling. "My blankets are getting old."

Odin couldn't help but gaping at the queen ... the queen of Vanaheim. Who was completely, and utterly mad. Consumed by the Art.

Lytir grunted, whether in discontent or simply in relief at not receiving punishment himself, Odin wasn't sure. "Yes, Your Majesty."

The Voice of Urd rose, pulling Odin to his feet in the process, and then guided him from the queen's throne room.

"She's lost herself," Odin said.

"Silence!"

"The Art has consumed her."

Lytir hesitated a moment before replying. "Not as thoroughly as it will soon devour you, old man."

Perhaps. But at long last, Odin would meet Mundilfari, the famed Mad Vanr.

31

*A*sgard was overrun with jotunnar. Yggdrasil was lost, and the Bilröst, which Hermod had hoped to use to reach Alfheim, had vanished. He'd searched the area, but found no trace of his wife, nor any other living Aesir.

It had left him with no choice but to walk between the worlds under his own power, passing through the shadows of the Penumbra and hunting a way in to the World of Sun.

On that threshold, Keuthos's voice grew dim, until, as Hermod stepped out into the blinding radiance, the Mist-wraith seemed to vanish entirely. If Hermod had not known better, he might have judged the ghost actually driven out of him. But Keuthos had warned him the Sun here would drive him into torpor, the very reason neither himself nor any snow maiden could come here to break a seal.

Rainforest covered much of Alfheim, and Hermod knew precious little of the geography here. The Elder God of Sun, Dellingr, ruled from the city of Gimlé, and Keuthos claimed that south of there lay the Spire of Magec, beyond which he'd find wetlands where the seal was buried.

No one accosted Hermod in the dense, damp forests of

Alfheim. Most of the Vanir had returned to Midgard across the Bilröst and even a good number of the liosalfar—the original ones—had come through, as well. So long as he stayed clear of the city or the islands, perhaps he could manage to cross this world in relative peace.

Well, not counting the bird-lizard things Freyja called dinosaurs, or the feathered serpent that claimed the wetlands which Keuthos had warned him about. The wraith could offer no counsel—or grating commentary—nor any guidance. The sun never set, so Hermod supposed that, so long as it remained directly behind him, he must be traveling south. More or less.

Damp earth squelched lightly under his boots. He'd seen no dinosaurs, though he'd found tracks, impressions in the mud made by creatures as big as mammoths. Or larger in some cases. Having seen those, he continued forward at a slow, cautious pace, careful to make no noise. He'd rubbed mud against his neck to disguise his scent. Between his precautions and his keen senses, he dared to hope he might avoid a confrontation with any animals, giant or otherwise.

He had seen a spattering of frogs, snakes, smaller lizards, birds, and hairy, tree-climbing mammals. Maybe, if one of the Vanr were with him, they could tell him what to call the chittering animals. Didn't really matter, he supposed.

He trod on, crossing a shallow creek, until he came to a slight clearing, within which rose a tower formed from arch-banded paths rising up it in a spiral, all overgrown with flowers and greenery. The Spire of Magec, he had to assume.

For a time, he stared at the tower. Within it, luminous figures moved about. He couldn't make out their conversations—they probably spoke in Supernal in any event—but he could hear their voices, carried on the wind.

"You're an Ás."

Hermod stiffened at the sudden, feminine voice behind him. One of those glowing vaettir had managed to sneak up on him? He turned, slowly, to take in the speaker.

She was clad in a loose, leaf-covered tunic with open sides, and, more strangely, a cap adorned with antlers like a reindeer. She didn't look threatening, though she had a spear in hand.

"Who are you?"

"Given that you are the intruder in this land, I believe I'm entitled to ask first."

He grimaced. He had not come here to bandy words, but nor would getting into an altercation with the locals help his quest. "I'm Hermod. A ... disciple of Odin's."

"Hmmm. You were one of the wounded, treated in Gimlé. My daughter saw you there. Oh, hmm. I'm Beiwe."

He knew that name. A sun goddess, worshiped in Lappmarken and Kvenland. "You're a follower of Magec? Not part of the court?"

She snickered. "Magec is long dead, and I wouldn't go near to Áine's court if Quetzalcoatl himself offered to fly me there."

That was one of the names Keuthos had given for the feathered serpent. "If I wanted to speak with Quetzalcoatl?"

Beiwe shrugged. "So far as I know, he's crossed into Anlang."

"The World of Storm?"

"Storms, wind, sky, whatever. Here, Quetzalcoatl claims everything from his Temple of Winds to the western boundaries with Anlang, and beyond. If you go to the temple, you might find him, yes, but I don't recommend it, unless you're intent to offer tribute or sacrifice."

Keuthos had claimed the seal lay within sight of the Temple of Winds, but if the feathered serpent was away, more the better. Maybe Hermod could achieve his ends unimpeded. Better still, if he could cross into Anlang direct, maybe he could avoid passing through the Roil again.

"What kind of tribute?"

Now, however, Beiwe leveled her spear at him, chuckling to herself.

Hermod raised his hands, not quite sure what was happening. A moment ago, he'd thought they were in pleasant conversation. Now ...?

The liosalf grinned, her eyes glinting with sunlight. "Come along, then." A wave of her spear beckoned toward the tower.

"Why?"

She shrugged. "Because I've got the spear and I'm telling you to? Because we don't let just anyone go and disturb the feathered serpent? Or maybe I plan to feast on your Pneuma." She giggled. "Who knows?"

She twirled the spearpoint in a slow spiral. Fucking alfar. Liosalfar seemed to replace svartalf single-minded viciousness with mercurial whims.

His fingers twitched, tempting him to draw Dainsleif. If this liosalf thought to play with him, maybe he'd offer *her* in sacrifice to the feathered serpent.

Still, given what he'd seen of liosalfar at war, he didn't much relish the idea of crossing weapons with someone who could appear wherever she wanted and move at such speeds.

Grimacing, he marched ahead of her, back to the spiraling tower as she commanded.

The pathway—drenched in light from arches taller than he was—led up in a slow curve, with outlets on landings every so often. Beiwe led him into one such landing halfway up. The lush flowerbeds and shallow pool carved into the floor gave the impression of a garden. A slight incline on the floor must've let rainwater fill that pool during Alfheim's daily showers. Around the garden, a half dozen glowing liosalfar sat, a mix of males and females, clad in leafy outfits similar to Beiwe's. Well, many in fact wore decidedly less, with flowery wreaths around their necks, and—in one female's case—naught else.

The liosalfar ate from platters of strange fruits he had no names for, with the exception of apples and coconuts, such as were found on Asgard.

The naked female tossed an apple to him, and Hermod caught it, shaking his head. "I appreciate the gesture, but I'm not hungry."

She frowned, as if he'd insulted her. In the North Realms, refusing offered food *did* constitute a rather grave breach of manners. Still, it was better not to eat the food outside the Mortal Realm. That bit of wisdom he'd heard too oft to ignore.

Hermod set the apple down on a platter and folded his arms. "Why am I here?"

"We heard so much about the mortals who crossed into our world," one of the males said. "He doesn't look like much, though. Crude and ugly. Scarred."

"I'd lie with him," a female said.

"No surprise," the same male answered. "His is probably the only cock in all Alfheim you haven't ridden."

She giggled. "Don't want to ruin my record, then."

While he couldn't deny he'd hardened just a little at that exchange, the dismissive way they spoke of him as though he were not even there had him equal parts unnerved, and he had to force down the urge to squirm in disquiet. Much as these creatures looked like beautiful women, they were no more human than svartalfar or snow maidens.

One of the others rose, and approached him cautiously, before poking him in the ribs with one finger.

"Bulky," she said.

He couldn't quite contain a snort at that. "Gambeson." She stared blankly at him. "Armor."

"Armor," she said, nodding as if he'd revealed some great secret. "Does he plan to fight us?"

"I'm not here for a fight at all," he blurted. The last thing he needed was to have these creatures decide he was a threat. "I just want to see the Temple of Winds."

The male who'd spoken before glared at him. "What if we tied his left stone and right stone to two different dinosaurs and sent them running?"

What the *fuck*? Hermod stumbled backward several steps, hand going to Dainsleif. "Are you completely mad?"

They all looked at each other and shrugged as if he was speaking a completely foreign tongue.

"What if we made him sing instead?" Beiwe asked. "Sing for us, Hermod of Asgard."

"I don't really sing."

The male threw up his hands. "All right, I'm getting a triceratops."

Hermod's hands shot up in warding. He was taking no chances if a tri-whatever was some kind of dinosaur. "My mother sang, all right? I ..." Shit. He hadn't thought of such things in ages. "Just ... give me a moment."

He drew a few deep breaths, trying to remember songs he'd heard as a child. Centuries ago, Mother had sung for him and Father, and later for ... Sigyn. Mother's songs had always had a sense of sadness, deep and unrelenting, though he'd not even understood all the words. Songs about passing through mist and into light, but always having to return to darkness.

About ... Oh. Well, fuck. She'd been talking about Alfheim in some of those songs, hadn't she?

Seeing this place, its eternal light, it had some of those words flooding back to him. They spilled from his lips without conscious thought. It caught him, seized his heart, his mind, and he hardly knew whether it was himself, or Mother singing once more.

"... Beyond Magec's memorial, I lie and weep, for beauty I cannot hold ..."

The liosalfar were all staring at him, as his voice drifted away. He'd win no contests for singing, that was for sure. He couldn't quite get the rasp out of his voice, nor keep it steady enough. But the liosalfar kept looking at him, as if enthralled.

"A valkyrie's song," the naked female said.

"Who is this mortal?" the other female asked. "Who are you?"

"Hermod Agilazson," he said. A lightheadedness had settled upon him, one he could not explain. Was the song itself responsible, or this feeling, this connection, however fleeting, to a mother he'd lost so very long ago?

Who now might well rot in Naströnd ...

Shit. Mother ...

The naked female rose and came to look deep into Hermod's eyes, craning her head from one side to the other. "You're her son, aren't you? The one who sang as though one of us. We taught her ..."

"You knew my mother? Who are you?"

"Olwen."

The name meant naught to him, but still, he now could not tear his gaze from hers. "You knew my mother?"

"I knew her, after a fashion, some days back."

Hardly aware of himself, he caught her hand—incredibly warm. "Tell me."

The liosalf grinned. "Sate me."

Hermod dropped her hand, shaking his head. These creatures flitted from one thing to the next like moths. "I am a married man and I have never betrayed my wife."

Olwen snickered. "How charmingly mortal of you. Still, I can pass you my impressions of Olrun—it was her, yes?—but only if you draw out some of my Pneuma. And I'll be quite pleased to have a fair taste of yours."

She traced a warm, almost hot finger along his jaw, up to the scar where the better part of his ear should have been. "Unless you find my dripping trench so very repulsive." Her other hand reached down and cupped his stones. "You'd like this more than the dinosaur plan, I imagine."

It was impossible to keep himself down while she worked her palm over his cock.

"I ... have ... a wife."

The male chortled. "By the blistering Sun, mortals are fools, are they not, Beiwe?"

Beiwe, snickering herself, reached around from behind Hermod and began unlacing his trousers, while Olwen pulled at his gambeson.

Stop. His mouth wanted to say it. Yet he could neither form the words, nor make his body resist. Syn ... But he had not seen his parents since the crossing to Vanaheim, ages ago. And these people had known his mother.

Hermod had lost almost everyone he'd ever cared for. His parents. His only child. His ... fucking foster sister.

He shuddered, caught off guard as Olwen's mouth brushed over the tip of his cock. Before he realized what he was doing, he was atop her. Slipping inside. Dimly aware that the rest of the liosalfar were watching, not abashed in the least. It ought to have shamed him, yet he couldn't stop the grinding of his hips.

From the corner of his eye, he realized the others had begun pleasuring one another while looking on him and Olwen.

The liosalf beneath him had her legs wrapped around his back, thrusting her hips in time with his own. Furiously grinding, even as she pulled his head down to her breast.

This was wrong.

He was not the kind of man who ... he couldn't stop himself from ...

Olwen shuddered beneath him. Her energy flooded into him like a bolt of lightning, coursing through him and immediately driving him to climax. Flickering thoughts—visions maybe, though not in any sense he could process—they bombarded his mind. A sense of Olrun—of his mother—as a dying mortal, wounded in battle. A Vall? Perhaps even in line for the throne. Until a spear thrust took all that.

And left her with a choice. To forestall her death and gain unfathomable powers, if she swore obedience to Dellingr and lay with the Sun God. Hardly a choice at all ... until she forsook her oath because of Hermod and his father.

And lost herself ... lost her very soul to the corpse sea ...

Weeping, Hermod slumped off Olwen and lay on his back.

"Huh," one of the males said. "Never saw a man react like that to her trench. Did you grow some teeth down there, Olwen?"

The liosalf didn't answer, just lay there beside him, pensive, leaving him to wonder what she had taken from him. He felt drained, as if some vital part of himself had been sucked out.

❧

"I'LL TAKE you to the Temple of Winds," Olwen said, approaching from behind Hermod.

He sat with his legs dangling out over the side of Magec's tower, staring from the arch at the wetlands to the south, still woozy and uncertain of himself. Certainly, Olwen had not only shared his Pneuma—lying with any woman meant some was shared, and more from those flush with Pneuma from Yggdrasil—but *stolen* a portion of it. Vaettir feasted on Pneuma and on souls, and Hermod was lucky she'd only been after the former.

He rubbed his hands over his beard, stifling a yawn. Fatigue warred within him, yes, and guilt at having betrayed Syn. Shit ... he didn't even know for certain if she yet lived, given the devastation around Yggdrasil.

Urd made wretches of all men, Odin had once told him. Perhaps it was true, though Odin admitted that, acknowledging his misdeeds as part of the Web of Urd did not abrogate one's responsibility for them. Back then, Hermod had found Odin's philosophizing tedious. Now ... now he had to wonder if such thoughts were manifestations of his mentor's guilt, rather than any attempt to assuage that guilt.

"I can use my power," Olwen said, "to guide an animal there, in case the serpent has returned and requires a sacrifice."

Hermod nodded slowly. Whatever Olwen had seen of him, in the Pneuma she'd stolen, now she wanted to help. Because of her connection to his mother, long ago? Or did she know what he planned, and why? He dared not raise any such question for fear she'd change her mind, or that he might reveal more than she already knew.

No, he had to accept her gift and be glad of it. There

would be time enough to brood over his mistakes here later. First ... First he had to avenge himself and Sif both upon Hel, for how the Mist goddess had deceived them.

§

WHEN OLWEN HAD SAID she would use her power on an animal, she meant her eyes would glow and she'd somehow take command of one of the lizards, as Freyja had done to the hydra in the Onyx Lagoon. The animal was a quadrupedal behemoth with a massive, feathered crest, and three giant horns jutting from its head. At Olwen's behest, Hermod reluctantly mounted the overmastered beast, and they rode it together, through the wetlands.

The creature stood tall enough to walk through shallows that would have impeded Hermod's passage, seeming hardly to take note of any of the animals they encountered. Including giant water snakes, and a large-mouthed lizard creature. Perhaps this triceratops—as Olwen called it— lacked the ability to fear predators while under Olwen's thrall.

Either way, she sat behind Hermod, arms around his waist, occasionally tickling his cock, and drawing up memories of their moment together. Intense beyond words, and somehow, though he knew it would mean losing more of himself and his health, he felt drawn to take her once more. This, he would not allow, so he pretended not to even notice her attentions.

Without a word or any means he could see, she guided the animal through the wetlands, until they came at last to a step pyramid of enormous size, situated on a rocky plateau just above the wetlands. Within it, he could hear swirling gales, though he could not understand *how* a storm might rage inside.

The pyramid itself was cut from yellow stone, with gems encrusted in its steps.

"You're in luck," Olwen said. "Quetzalcoatl is not here and, if you finish your business before his return, you'll need no sacrifice."

"How can you be certain he's not inside?"

"Oh." She giggled. "How quaint, mortal. No. The feathered serpent wouldn't fit *inside* the pyramid. He encircles it, or flies above it."

Hermod suddenly found it difficult to swallow. So the dragon ... god ... thing was too big to fit inside that. An unsettling thought.

He slid a leg over the dinosaur's side and slipped down.

"Would you like more sex, before you go?" Olwen asked, and Hermod flinched.

"No."

"Liar."

Well. Whatever he wanted, he knew better.

"It is not given to us to grieve the way mortals do," she said. "But, I would have preferred things turned out different for Olrun."

Having no words—and neither the desire to discuss it— Hermod only favored her with a final nod. And with that, she turned the animal back and rode off into the wetlands.

Hard to say whether he ought to rejoice at the absence of the discomfiting female, or miss her company. Here, in the wetlands, he had only the buzzing of insects and the swirling storm within the pyramid to keep his attention.

No.

He had something else. A mission. He'd come here for

vengeance and, with any luck, a means of defeating Hel. He aimed to be about it.

≈

BEFORE THEY CAME TO ALFHEIM, Keuthos had described a pile of stones on the wetland's edge, not far from the feathered serpent's pyramid. The wraith had even supposed that the dragon may have known of the seal's existence.

Now, Hermod set about pushing stones as big as his torso aside. Thanks to Olwen, he no longer had Pneuma in abundance. Maybe it would have rejuvenated, given many days of rest and proper food, but Hermod had no time for that.

So he'd stripped to the waist and still managed to become drenched in sweat and swarmed by buzzing, biting insects that seemed intent to suck every last drop of his blood out. He drew what Pneuma he still could—there'd be no moving those stones otherwise—and pushed one after another of the huge things out of the way.

Until a hint of blue light escaped from beneath the rocks.

This was it.

Drawing more Pneuma, he grabbed one of the rocks and heaved it aside, revealing part of a glowing sigil not so very unlike the marks he'd seen upon the Mountains of Fimbulvinter in Niflheim. He grabbed and tossed aside the last rock, exposing the rest of the seal. It was a circular design, inset with other circles, inside which lay glyphs of extraordinary complexity. Maybe more complex than even Odin or Freyja could have interpreted.

The circle's diameter was half again his height, and he had to slide down into the exposed pit to reach it.

As far as destroying the seal ... Keuthos had never really gone into much detail on that. Perhaps the wraith had assumed he'd figure it out on his own.

Simply covering the circle had not broken its power. Not here, and not in Niflheim where ages of snow and sliding rock had obscured the massive sigils.

What if he were to more directly disrupt the lines?

Drawing Dainsleif, he paced around the circle's perimeter. As disconcerting as Keuthos's sibilant voice in his mind was, he *almost* missed having the wraith's advice on such matters. Or Odin's or anyone's. Shit, maybe Olwen could have told him how to do this, if she had remained. Not that the liosalfar were like to help him release an enemy of their god.

With a sigh, he dug the blade into the hard-packed earth around the sigil, then slowly pulled it across the circle, breaking it from one side to the other. As he did so, the blue luminance dimmed and finally winked out. His ears popped and his skin tingled, but he saw no visible sign of workings of the Art. Was that it, really?

He grimaced. Sorcery was for madmen and fools. Half the time, other people couldn't even tell if it was real, though clearly *something* had bound Achlys in that cavern. To be certain, Hermod drew another line across the circle, then a third, slicing it every which way in the hopes that would break the seal. Because he had no intention whatsoever of returning to Alfheim.

Finally, he climbed out of the pit.

One down. Now, onto the World of Storms.

32

*W*hen the Aesir had assaulted Vanaheim, rampant slaughter had unfolded all around, enough to crush Freyja's heart. That was naught compared to the devastation that had now befallen the islands. Indeed, the flooding had covered so many valleys, Vanaheim now seemed less two islands than twenty.

What wasn't underwater was blanketed in snowstorms. Or on fire.

"Madness," Freyja said, shaking her head, while standing on the lower slope of a mountain. For thousands of years the Vanir had held the jotunnar at bay, preventing something like this from happening.

Ragnarok, Odin called this.

Every land she had passed through on the way lay embroiled in bloody war. But Vanaheim, her glorious, beloved homeland ... the chaos here surpassed even her worst fears.

To look onto this was to see the end of time. What Odin had feared for so long, he had been powerless to stop. He'd said this was coming, but somehow, not even bringing back the Vanir or the liosalfar had changed it.

Before he'd left, Mundilfari had raved about an unbreakable cycle of destruction and rising chaos. So many of his rantings had seemed born of a tortured, twisted mind. But ... had Freyja's old teacher foreseen the same thing Odin had? Was that why the old king had abdicated the throne in favor of Father?

Twilight had settled upon the islands, though they remained bright enough, given the wildfires that leapt amid the forests. Billowing columns of smoke combined overhead to form a canopy of darkness that seemed deeper than night, making what remained of Freyja's stored sunlight gleam all the brighter.

Freyja had oft needed to Sun Stride to circumvent such conflagrations. She passed from elevated boulders, to rocky slopes, avoiding drawing nigh to the spreading flames.

Could anyone yet remain alive here? Odin had sent her back to join the defense, but she was too late. She'd seen naught but jotunnar and corpses since her return. Maybe Narfi's army had killed all the Aesir, or maybe some had managed to retreat across the sea, back to Valland. Freyja had come via Andalus, and there found the Serklander army had already marched on Valland.

Passing through those lands had proved tedious, always needing to avoid the Serks for fear of encountering the Sons of Muspel.

And all for naught?

Maybe she ought to return to the shore, recover the boat she'd stashed, and retreat from here. Odin now refused to use his prescience, so he hadn't known Vanaheim would look like this.

A choked, dead, wasteland. Her beloved island paradise,

reduced to ashes.

In the distance, a bolt of lightning streaked down, crashing into a tree. So bright it stung her eyes. So close the thunder left her ears ringing, while the scent of burnt air twisted her stomach.

All the forces of nature had turned their wrath upon the World. Creation itself raged against the Aesir. And ... perhaps the Vanir, too. Maybe they were guilty of no fewer crimes than Odin and his people. The hubris ... the failures.

Freyja chewed on her lip, then sighed. No, naught remained here for her to do. She'd have to retreat to the mainland and try to meet up with Odin on his return.

As she turned, however, a man approached, climbing up the rocky slope on all fours.

Narfi? Except, he looked changed. His hair darkened, coarser. His features shifting ...

Possessed? Hadn't she seen this man before?

"Oh ..." The man said. "You still smell the same as you did, centuries ago ... His woman." He chuckled. "I'll enjoy tearing out your throat ... after I've pounded your trench raw."

"Who are you?"

"You've forgotten? You were there, when the one-handed one bound me. You had ... kittens ..."

Kittens? Her lions.

"Fenrir." Freyja twisted her lips into a grimace while she slid her sword free. "I owe you for that."

She'd seen it, when he'd slipped from a dead host to a new one. Spirits so powerful were not easy to cast out of the Mortal Realm. She should run. Stride as far as she could— not so far, given her short supply of sunlight—and escape. But somehow, her feet kept carrying her forward.

Fenrir had murdered her lions and wrought death

among Aesir and Vanir alike. And now, all he wanted, was vengeance on Od. Freyja wouldn't let that happen.

Though he wasn't in range, Freyja slashed with her sword, Sun Striding behind him mid-attack. The varulf's elbow snapped back impossibly fast, catching her in the chin and sending her staggering backward.

The blow cracked her neck too far, felt like it almost took her head off.

She tried to bring the sword back around to bear, but Fenrir batted it aside with a hand. As a liosalf, she had more strength than a Man. Fenrir's casual slap still wrenched her arm. His hand lanced out and closed around her throat, lifting her off the ground like she weighed no more than a child. His other hand caught her wrist and squeezed.

The bones in her wrist snapped audibly, the sword tumbling from her grasp. Freyja tried to scream with the pain, but managed only a wheeze through her closed-off windpipe. He could have killed her like that. But he was keeping her alive just to draw it out.

Desperate, she grabbed his hand, yanking against it just to buy herself one more breath. It was like trying to push over a mountain.

One ... last ...

Freyja looked up, as high as she could raise her gaze. Past flaming trees to the choking smoke above.

She Sun Strode into that black cloud.

Fenrir went with her, but the varulf released her throat with a yelp of surprise. Freyja kicked away from him, pitching end over end. Spinning round, the wind buffeting her. Couldn't catch a breath ...

She tried another Stride, but managed only a few dozen feet, a change in angle, if not in momentum. A change to line her up with a flooded valley.

Her throat burned ... Couldn't catch a breath ...

Falling so fast, like an arrow from a bow, shooting *almost* straight down. The canopy rushed closer and she barely cleared it.

The water hit her like a fist.

Everything went dark.

⚓

THE GROUND BENEATH HER RUMBLED, a violent tremor that jolted Freyja into sudden wakefulness. She lay in snow.

Immediately, she sat up, sending daggers of pain coursing through her veins with such sharpness it blurred her vision. The ground snapped back up to meet her.

"Easy. Slow."

The whole mountainside seemed to spin around her, whirling enough to make her stomach churn.

The speaker leaned over her, placing a hand behind her head to help her sit up, slowly as he had commanded.

Tyr. Odin's champion.

"Owww."

"Saw you fall from the sky," he said, as if she had asked.

Freyja blinked, trying to steady herself, then saw a small group of others had gathered on the slope. They rested on a slope above the valley, one blanketed by a light snow. Which meant frost jotunnar must lurk not too far away.

Scattered around nearby rested Thor, Syn, Bragi, and Mani, along with a few dozen others. All that remained of the Aesir and Vanir?

"You're awake," her brother said, rushing to her side, taking Tyr's place supporting her. "Forgive me ... I had no sunlight left to catch you."

Freyja groaned. Oh. "Fenrir!"

"What?" Tyr leaned in again. "Wolf's loose?"

"Yes. He tried to kill me."

"Fucking varulf," Tyr said.

Behind him, Thor limped over, and, catching sight of him, Freyja could do naught but gape. A third of his foot was gone, as well as a finger from his hand. And he bore more gouges, bandages, and seeping wounds than she'd ever seen in one man. Much less one still able to walk, however slowly.

"Fenrir did that to you?"

Thor grunted. "Narfi. Trollfucker. He fell into the abyss, so I hope Hel has him now."

Oh. Well, maybe an urd almost as bad. "I think ... Fenrir has possessed him."

Tyr groaned and slumped back onto his arse, shaking his head. "Swear I'll find a way to kill that wolf."

"Huh?" Frey asked.

"He can switch bodies," Freyja said to her brother. "If a host dies, he passes to another."

Her brother frowned. "A progenitor of his tribe?"

Freyja nodded.

Frey shook his head, looking to Tyr. "Leave him be, then. There's not a Sun Knight on Alfheim who could challenge a shifter progenitor. It'd be like trying to take on a Prince of Svartalfheim. It's madness."

"Don't figure I've got a choice. Wolf will go for Odin. Me, I won't let the king fall."

Frey snorted. "Look around. The whole *kingdom* has fallen."

"Fuck that," Thor said. "Asgard is ours and always will be."

Freyja blanched as a sudden realization settled upon her. "The Tree!"

"We had no choice but to withdraw," Frey said. He held up his hand to reveal Andvaranaut. "We took the ring to break the bridge, so they can't use it to reach any Spirit World. But we could not hold the bridge any longer."

So they had access to the apples of immortality, but at least they couldn't open another door to Niflheim. For now.

"We have to get off these islands," Freyja said.

"I'm not leaving!" Thor bellowed. "I'll hunt down Narfi or Fenrir or whoever the fuck he is and I'll feed his soul to Mjölnir."

Tyr grunted. "Half-jotunn damn nigh killed you last time. Now he's got that varulf inside him."

"To say naught of an army," Frey added. "My sister is correct. This land is lost. We must regroup with your king. Where is he?"

Freyja frowned. "I ... don't know. He said he planned to ride to the Norns' mountain to confront them about the Web of Urd. He thought ... he could change urd."

Now her brother stared open-mouthed at her, slightly shaking his head.

"What's that mean?" Tyr asked.

"It means he's beyond our reach," Freyja said. "For now. We have to find a place to hold out against the jotunnar and await his return."

Thor grabbed a stone and hurled it out into the water down in the valley. "I'm not telling Father we lost his kingdom."

Freyja winced. "You'll attract attention like that. My brother is right, Vanaheim is *gone*, Thor. The last time Hel made such a move against our Realm, only a few pockets of Mankind survived. We cannot win this by throwing our lives away."

"Hel's not here," Thor pointed out. "Maybe losing the

device is how she gets into our Realm in the first place. Either way, we have to take back Yggdrasil."

"Maybe when your Father returns. For now, we have to escape."

Thor folded his arms over his chest, winced, and dropped them to his sides. "My daughter is out there on this island, hunting for survivors."

Oh. Well, damn it. "I'll find her."

"I can find my own damn daughter," Thor snapped.

"You can hardly walk."

Frey shook his head. "It's still night, even if there weren't so much smoke. No way to replenish your sunlight."

"I'll go," Syn said. "I'm adept at woodcraft."

Freyja frowned. "So am I. And I know these islands better than you. I spent millennia here. We can both go, but the rest of you need to find a way off Vanaheim and to some-place defensible."

"Idavollir," Tyr said.

Freyja looked at him.

"Old jotunn fortress in Valland. Held it a long time against trolls and draugar. Figure it'll hold against jotunnar, too."

Freyja nodded grimly. Oh, she knew Idavollir all too well. "Fine. Then we meet there once I've found Thrúd and any other survivors."

"I don't want to leave you," Frey objected.

Now she rolled her eyes. "If the jotunnar get that ring and understand what it does, we lose. We lose *everything*. You have to get it somewhere safe. Idavollir will do for now."

Frey drew her into an embrace. "Don't you dare die."

Oh, she didn't plan to.

33

*S*essrumnir seemed not so very different from how Odin remembered it, if not quite so overgrown, and not quite so laden with flourishes as it had become under Freyja's tenure here. Now, though, Lytir took him to see Mundilfari, in chambers beneath the great library, lit only by twin wall sconces and thick with Otherworldly energies that had Odin's arm hairs standing on end.

The man was dark-haired and deep skinned, like Eostre, which meant, like her, he must have hailed from somewhere far to the east. Perhaps from the Skyfall Isles, like Eostre's parents, perhaps from elsewhere.

Lytir had not bound Odin's hands, perhaps thinking him but an old man, while he himself had tasted the fruit of Yggdrasil. Instead, the Voice of Urd simply guided Odin to a chair and shoved him in it, then moved to whisper in Mundilfari's ear. The Mad Vanr sat at a desk laden with scrolls and books, his fingers stained with ink.

After a moment more, Mundilfari waved the other man away, and stared intently at Odin, while folding his hands over his lap. "It seems Queen Irpa has ordered I curse you with a penalty normally reserved for those who have stolen an apple of Yggdrasil. Do you know what that means?"

Odin pursed his lips. Was Mundilfari half as mad as his queen? Given his potentially unhinged host, a single mischosen word might send the man raving or invoking the very eldritch powers Irpa had demanded he call upon.

If Odin was in the past—whether in a past life or not—if he were to kill Mundilfari now, would that not change history? Would the Norns try to stop him? Unfortunately, Odin didn't know enough about *when* he was or how he'd gotten here to make an informed judgment. Had the Vanr already summoned and bound Eldr, then his death might not avail Odin in any way, and would certainly carry with it heavy risks.

On the other hand, such a change in history *would* certainly indicate freedom from the Norns' web. If the Mad Vanr died now, he could not meet Sigyn in the future. But would that lead to a worse reality than the one already unfolding?

"You have naught to say for yourself, old man?" Mundilfari snorted, his eyes darting to the side rather randomly. Flitting about. Like he heard conversations others did not. Vaettir. Bound inside himself, spewing their lies and maddening insights, no doubt. "I am more interested, in truth, in knowing *how* you got in the Norns' chamber. You were looking into the Well of Urd, weren't you?"

Odin folded his arms over his chest. Maybe it didn't matter what he did here. So long as it broke free from the Norns' chains, naught else truly mattered. "I looked into the well." If not now. "All the wells, in fact."

"All the wells?" Mundilfari's eyes darted around once more, then he abruptly grabbed a book from a stack, upending the rest unto the floor without paying them so much as a glance. He flipped through the pages of the chosen book with far more care, and Odin could see why. The paper had grown so old it flaked beneath the man's fingers. "You saw the others. The root trails ... Tell me about the others."

He was not mad yet, perhaps, but the seeds of madness already lurked within the man, did they not?

They lurk within all Men ...

Ah. True enough.

"Mediums for divination," Mundilfari said. "Most potent to those already possessing a gift for the Sight, which, in turn I'm given to imagine functions less as a singular vision, and more a web of loosely interconnected perceptions of the underlying layers of reality, yes? All sorcerers—those capable of basic competence—must develop at least a rudimentary ability to gaze across the Veil and perceive extra-spatial realities, while the most blessed or cursed among us also hope to see extra-temporal chains." The man looked to the side once more, head cocked as if listening. "But, but, but ... But! The Sight is not directly a manifestation of the Art, or so many theorize. An internal potential, rather than external one?"

Madness, perhaps, though in his nascent madness, Mundilfari's theories seemed insightful.

In madness lies apprehension ...

Mundilfari thumped his finger on the book. "So, where does the other well lie, then, old man?"

Odin waved his hand dismissively. "Far beyond the Midgard Wall."

"Midgard ... Wall? What wall?"

It took all his control to keep his face impassive, even as Audr's mad cackle reverberated through Odin's mind. The

Midgard Wall didn't exist yet. Mundilfari ... hadn't even thought it up.

"Oh ... They have it! Don't they? *Don't* they? The well to pierce not the past, but the future. It's out there, in the lands still claimed by the jotunnar. That's why we can't win."

Odin couldn't quite keep his mouth from falling open. "Mimir ..."

"The advisor to the Elder Council? Yes ... He ... he controls the well? Of course!" Mundilfari slapped a hand on the book. "Of course. No ... No. Yes!" He flung up his hands wildly, almost as if swatting at an invisible insect. "And it lies beyond this wall?"

Odin grimaced. What the fuck was going on here? Were the Norns showing him something?

Mundilfari had fallen over the precipice of madness—and it didn't seem he had so very far to go—by raising the Midgard Wall. Then he'd journeyed beyond it, abandoned the throne, in a desperate attempt to find the Well of Mimir. Had he ever found it?

Kill him ...

We cannot predict the consequences of such a paradox, Valravn argued.

Odin rubbed his brow. Was it possible ... had he set Mundilfari on his path with this very conversation? How? Mundilfari had already done these things, long before Odin was even born. Before his great grandparents were born. It seemed as if ... not even the Old Kingdoms yet existed. So not even Audr would have existed yet.

A devastating loss to this age ...

Had the wraith just spoken in jest? Did wraiths even *have* a sense of humor? Odin pushed that from his mind. "You're not really intending to carry out Queen Irpa's command, are you? You know I did not steal any apples."

"Oh, she's gone quite mad, yes." Mundilfari again seemed to be speaking to someone else. "My poor student. She delved too deeply into the Art. I warned her. Even Svarthofda lost herself in the abyss. The things out there would chill Hel herself." He drummed a finger on the book. "Oh, the Norns know, but they refuse to answer." From what Odin could tell, the Norns seemed more dire than Hel. "They know ... Hmm. Oh. Yes, well, she'll have to go. Before she destroys all Vanaheim."

"Hel?"

"Irpa! Poor girl. Such talent. Such promise, thrown all away because of her dark urges. Plays with the dead, I'm afraid. Hmmm." Mundilfari blew out a breath and then looked more directly at Odin. "They offered me the throne, you know. I refused, wanted to keep to my research here." He shook his head. "Obviously that was an error, and now I have to rectify it. In her desperation to win the war, Irpa just kept pushing farther and farther into the darkness. She saw something that moved her to it ... maybe it was in the Well of Urd. There's something ... *down* there, I fear."

Nidhogg? The dark dragon. Odin kept himself from saying it, though. Such knowledge would unnerve *anyone*.

"Well. Well, I'll have to eliminate her now. Her self-indulgences are not the only reason we're losing the war, but they are *a* reason, oh yes. Can you believe she wanted an army of Flayed Ones?" He scoffed as if it were more amusing than horrifying. "Her, and Mimir, both. They must go. Ah! Well, I'll attend to Irpa myself. She was my protégée, so it seems only fitting. Then ... then you and I will eliminate Mimir and find his well. Oh. What did you say your name was?"

Odin had made a point of not mentioning one, and he sure as fuck wasn't going to help Mundilfari go hunting for

Mimir. Whatever had happened to him, he needed to get back to the present. This time was ... too precarious. He couldn't predict what ramifications any actions he took in this age would have. Killing Mundilfari, helping him ... No. Whatever the Norns wanted him to see—if they had even intentionally sent him here—Odin wasn't interested.

"I cannot help you," he finally said.

"Of course you can. You must. You *will*." Mundilfari waved Odin's objections away as though he were speaking to a willful child, then rose and stepped around him, out into the hall.

Odin stood as well, but a wave of dizziness seized him, and he slumped back in the chair. The current washed over him, caught his mind, or perhaps his very soul, and rushed it out to sea. The torrent of it had him crashing down, tumbling from the chair.

He never hit the floor.

Rather, the stormy sea of time swept him up, yanking him back into the maelstrom, leaving Odin with only the desperate thought ... a fragile prayer ... to hope he could pull himself back to the present.

Reality melted away.

34

The war band of wood jotunnar had surrounded the hill, moving in and out of the tree line with ease, naturally blending with the environment. The shouting atop the hill left no doubt the jotunnar had cornered victims up there. And, given that woods surrounded the hill on all sides, those survivors could not risk a retreat.

Instead, wood jotunnar would slip in and out of the forest, peppering the desperate Aesir or Vanir with arrows, weakening them and draining their morale. Before a final slaughter.

Below the hill, Freyja and Syn crouched, watching for an opening. The wood jotunnar moved with almost feline grace in their native terrain, despite oft standing six or seven feet tall, with some specimens as much as twice that.

"Thrúd has to be up there," Syn said.

Freyja didn't disagree. "There's no way to reach them without engaging the jotunnar."

"We sneak past them."

"We're not sneaking past wood jotunnar. It'll never

happen. Every jotunn bloodline draws strength from a connection to a Spirit World. The frost jotunnar are the most numerous because they get their power from the mists of Niflheim, which have breached this world. But wood jotunnar, they are keen in places like this."

Syn pursed her lips and eased her sword free, as if to say that, when stealth failed, she had another option.

Freyja could handle a sword, though she didn't consider herself a master. Nor did she like their odds against several dozen jotunnar, with only the two of them, and her without sunlight to burn for speed or Sun Striding.

But what was the alternative? Return and tell Thor they'd abandoned his daughter and all the other survivors? No. Even if Freyja could have done so—and the liosalf part of her was tempted—Syn would never agree. The Ás would rather die, sword in hand, than have her prince think her a craven.

"We wait," Freyja said.

"Wait for what?"

"When they think the camp atop the hill ready to break, they'll charge. That's when they won't be ready for us to attack their flank."

Syn spit in the dirt. "And how many people die while we sit on our arses?"

Freyja sighed. "I met your husband, you know. In Svartalfheim. He was brave, too, and reckless. But not suicidal. If you want to be alive when he returns, this is the way. It doesn't help your people, if you die before they even know you're here."

The shieldmaiden glowered at her, but did settle down on her arse, staring out at the woods.

Freyja did the same. Watching. Waiting.

Trying not to hear the screams from up on the hill.

❦

THEY DID NOT HAVE overlong to wait. A chorus of jotunn war cries drowned out the cries of pain and fear from the Aesir and Vanir hiding atop the hill.

A rush of wood jotunnar charged past, still moving with ease through the woodlands, this time in a wild charge. Now, armed with spears and shields instead of bows.

Freyja and Syn rose together, each grabbing their swords. She looked to the shieldmaiden, who nodded.

And then they were off, chasing after the charging jotunnar.

Freyja dashed between trees, covering ground quickly, but not nigh so quickly as the longer-legged jotunnar. Damn, but she missed being flush with sunlight. She could have Strode out in front of them or increased her speed and raced past them.

Instead, she winced as battle crashed above her. With the tree line, she could not see what was underway, but she could hear it, as wood slapped on wood, as stone spearheads met shields. As Men were thrown down by larger, stronger jotunnar they could not hope to match.

Syn outdistanced her, clearly drawing on her Pneuma to do so.

Freyja might have preferred to save hers for the actual battle, but the shieldmaiden seemed intent to save as many lives as possible.

Without much concern for her own.

Syn ran up behind a jotunn who spun at her approach. Not fast enough, though. Her runeblade bit into the jotunn's side, splattering brown blood even as it looked as though it hit ribs. The jotunn bellowed, pitching over. Syn's backswing half severed his head.

The commotion drew the attention of three other wood jotunnar who broke off their charge and turned to meet Syn's advance. Which was inspiring. Freyja couldn't even hope to fell such a foe with the ease Syn had demonstrated.

Drawing her Pneuma now, Freyja sprinted forward, sword raised in the hopes of pulling one of the three away from Syn.

Another jotunn slammed its shield edge-first at Syn. The shieldmaiden savagely swept Gramr forward and the runeblade cleaved straight through the shield and took off the jotunn's hand in the process.

Freyja winced, but had to divert her attention to the opponent before her. A female jotunn who led with a spear thrust Freyja had no way to block. She fell back, narrowly avoiding tripping over a root, and the spear's point passed within a few hairsbreadths of her face. The next thrust she knocked aside with her sword, but the impact jarred her.

Even as she fell back again, the spearpoint caught her cheek and sliced along the bridge of her nose, gouging her face. Searing pain erupted along the wound, and her brow, and Freyja tripped, stumbling to the ground. Blood streamed down into one eye, half-blinding her. Only when she paused for breath did she realize she'd been screaming.

Before her, Syn went down, a jotunn spear rammed through her chest.

No!

Madness, charging so many jotunnar. They were dead.

She was dead.

She'd never see Odin again. Or her daughter or …

In an instant, the jotunn vanished, reappearing several paces away. Her spearpoint wedged into the ground. A moment later the jotunn stumbled forward, then toppled to the ground as someone hacked at her back. As the jotunn fell, Freyja caught sight of Sunna, auburn-haired and furious, her skin glowing with sunlight, her eyes gleaming white. Her sword sliced into the jotunn again.

A breath later, she was there, yanking Freyja to her feet.

Oh. Syn! Freyja pushed around Sunna, but the shield-maiden was already lying on the ground, abandoned by the wood jotunnar, three of which now closed in on Sunna.

Freyja allowed the other Vanr to interpose herself between the wood jotunnar and her. The bastards had killed Syn and who knew how many others. But Sunna had held the mark of Dellingr even before reaching Alfheim and becoming inundated with sunlight. Now, she was one of the strongest of the Sun Knights.

And those jotunnar would pay for Syn's death.

A slight flash of light, and Sunna was among them, cutting across a jotunn's abdomen. The blood hadn't even began to spray when Sunna vanished cleaving down on the back of another's skull. Moving so fast Freyja's eyes couldn't follow, Sunna was everywhere all at once. A blur of vanishing death, hacking through her foes like they stood still.

Her blade tore through throats, hacked out the backs of knees, and sent blood spraying in all directions. When she paused, five jotunnar dropped to the ground.

Only then did Freyja catch sight of other warriors racing up the hillside, engaging the jotunnar. Not liosalfar, nor Aesir, for they wore strange fashions and wielded shamshirs like those favored by the Serks.

They *were* Serks.

Except, faster than the jotunnar, and at least as strong, by the look of it.

Sons of Muspel.

Sunna vanished again, giving Freyja no chance to even ask how this was possible.

A hand grabbed her arm and she spun, then gaped at the woman before her: Eostre. Dark haired, with wheat-colored skin like so many of the First Ones had.

Freyja found herself stammering, not even knowing what to say. Odin's banishment had not affected the few First Ones still on Vanaheim, but Freyja had assumed Idunn's mother had died in the fighting. Had assumed all the remaining First Ones had.

Eostre pulled her aside, away from the fighting. "Let the Serklanders handle this."

"H-how?"

The other woman guided her down the slope. "There'll be time for that later. When we heard Vanaheim had fallen, I brought a ship here to save who I could. Not even the Sons of Muspel can hold out against so many jotunnar, though. They'll break through the enemy lines, then we can retreat to the sea."

Ignoring all propriety, Freyja threw her arms around her friend's mother.

By the Sun, she'd thought she was dead. She'd thought they were *all* dead.

EOSTRE ALLOWED them no rest on the trek down to the sea. Not even a moment to catch their breath. Ragged as the survivors proved—thankfully including Thor's daughter Thrúd, as well as thirty-seven others—no one complained. No one spoke much at all, so ragged had they become. Panting, they trudged through what remained of the once lush forests, now smoldering embers. They sloshed through waist-high waters separating hills from each other, and plodded through slopes blanketed in frost.

Would this utter devastation last, or would Yggdrasil someday restore the islands to the paradise that had endured for millennia before now? Freyja dared to hope for the latter, even if she never got the chance to see it.

Freyja had paused to claim Syn's sword, Gramr. The shieldmaiden had seemed almost invincible with it. Strange to think Freyja would never really know quite how the woman had fallen. Her rashness, without doubt, but more than that ...

She shook her head. Such things didn't matter. It was her mind racing, struggling to divert itself from the horror around her with inquiries, no matter how useless.

Odin had been right.

Another tremor ran through the ground. They had become more frequent, and she mused that she could hear Yggdrasil groaning from the strain. As if the World Tree writhed in pain, and, in so doing, had begun to rip apart the fabric of the World.

Ragnarok had come to Vanaheim ... or Asgard. Either way, it was lost now. Ravaged beyond hope of repair, even could they have overcome Narfi's army of jotunnar. As for the Moon Lord himself, thankfully no one had seen him. Even a band of the Sons of Muspel would find themselves hard-pressed to overcome such a foe.

Freyja sighed, shaking her head. Od had done so much to prevent this, and he had failed. Four hundred years spent trying to avert this end. And what had he to show for it?

Ashes.

THE MIST HAD INTRUDED into Vanaheim's former sphere of protection, brushing over the beach, as if not even Yggdrasil could hold back the poison vapors whilst the land around it lay so besieged. Standing at the ship's bow, Freyja peered back at her beloved islands and could not even recognize them.

Never, in her thousands of years, had she seen so many leaves fall from Yggdrasil at one time. Nor had she ever imagined this island paradise could lie destroyed.

Visible tremors shook all the islands and sent the waves surging against the ship, tossing her so violently she had to grab the gunwale to steady herself.

Before her eyes, one of the tiny islands created by the flooding—a hill, really—split in half and caved in on itself. A terrible cloud of debris sputtered out.

And then her ship drifted further into the mist, and Freyja could no longer see Vanaheim.

She pushed her palm into the burning cut between her eyes. Part of her wanted to weep, though liosalfar no longer seemed capable of it, or at least not with the ease with which humans could release their pent-up sorrows.

"Freyja," Eostre said behind her. "Let me tend to that."

Freyja turned to see the First One standing close, a strap of linen in her hand. The woman poured water from a skin over the cloth, then dabbed at Freyja's filthy gouge. As an immortal—twice over now she was a liosalf—such a wound would heal, probably with little or no scar. But she appreciated the thought behind Eostre's ministrations.

Thrúd believed Eir, the Aesir's best healer, had perished with Vanaheim.

In the glory days of Vanaheim, Eostre would never have deigned to treat someone's injury like this. Perhaps her time wandering Midgard had changed her.

"What happened to you?" Freyja asked, when the other woman withdrew the cloth.

Eostre leaned her hip against the gunwale, opened her mouth once, then shook her head. Finally, she sighed. "Odin punished me. He claimed the Vanir had failed in their duty to Mankind. He sentenced me to take up my mother's quest to help Mankind." Eostre smiled, shaking her head. "I did, with Bragi at first, before he found his own way to Alfheim." The woman sighed. "For so long I resented Odin, thought him the epitome of arrogance to presume to task me thus."

"But?"

"But I think, maybe he was right. I wanted to try to drive out the mists, as my mother and my daughter had hoped to do. Eventually, I came to Serkland, where the caliphs used Fire vaettir to achieve just that end. An imperfect solution, of course, but I thought it a start. And they honored me, sought my insights and knowledge."

"Hmmm." Freyja's throat was dry. She had to tell her, of course. Only the thought of doing so had her stomach churning. "There's something you need to know. Something ... about Idunn."

35

Quetzalcoatl's Temple of Winds was an enormous step pyramid with—thankfully—no one around it. At the summit, Hermod stared down into a swirling vortex of wind that occasionally crackled with lightning. A walkway below allowed him to drop down and pace the perimeter of that storm.

The buffeting air currents seized his clothes and hair and sent them whipping about the moment he landed on the walkway. The force of it, even below him, tugged on him enough he had to brace himself on the balustrade around the walkway.

Perhaps, had he continued west past here, he'd have found another way into the World of Storm. Anlang, he'd heard it named, but the truth was, Hermod knew precious little about it. Save that this pyramid almost certainly connected the two, and the sick, shifting feeling in his gut told him that connection came through the whirlwind itself.

He did not, however, much relish the idea of jumping into winds of such terrible violence.

He could turn back. Stairs here led downward, inside the

temple, maybe around the storm and to a way out. Of course, if he intended to flee, he ought to do so before the feathered serpent itself showed up and found him intruding in its home.

No. There was no going back. Not without seeing this through. He already stood upon the threshold of Anlang, ready to avenge himself against Hel for her betrayal. If he could not have Sif back, he could at least make the Mist Goddess regret her treachery. Oh, he knew it wouldn't bring Sif back. Naught would now. He tapped his hand on the balustrade.

Naught would ever make this better.

Still, vengeance gave a man purpose, when all else had fled him. Hunting Serks had kept him from madness, back when he'd thought they had murdered Sif. Now ... now he was hunting Hel herself, after a fashion.

"Fuck it."

Hermod heaved himself up on the rail and leapt into the storm.

At once, the gale seized him, strong enough to keep him from falling far. It flung him round and round, stealing his screams, swirling him so fast he retched. The bile whipped back into his face and splattered his clothes. The winds blinded him, beat him like an enraged jotunn, buffeted over and over.

They deafened him.

They stripped his cloak from him and felt apt to rip off his skin. The storm devoured him.

&.

HERMOD WOKE, lying on the temple floor, beneath the still howling vortex. The winds had reduced his clothes to tatters and even now continued yanking on them. With a groan, he pushed himself up onto his arms.

How much time had he lost?

He crawled forward, until he reached a stone overhang that shielded him from the storm, then sat against the wall, head in his hand, willing the pounding in his temples to stop. For a time, he remained like that, resting.

But he had no supplies, and lingering here wouldn't do a damn thing to help his situation. Finally, he rose and made his way through a narrow passage that would never have accommodated a dragon.

This passage eventually led outside.

The temple remained the same, but now grasslands surrounded it on all sides. Howling winds roared overhead, though those held Hermod's attention for a mere moment.

A *dragon* lay coiled around the pyramid staring hard at him.

At his exit from the temple, the dragon lifted its head, then the rest of its body, hovering in the air. Brilliant plumage covered it, a rainbow of vibrant colors, each feather shifting with the air currents swirling overhead. The dragon had no legs but an enormously long reptilian mouth with jutting fangs—more lizard-like than snake-like. It had opalescent eyes that seemed to glow with inner heat, and large spurs that jutted from the back of its head. Despite its bulk—easily two hundred feet long, if not more—it moved through the air with such grace it seemed one with the winds.

His gut demanded he flee. Break into a dead run and keep running until he hit the jungle. Somewhere to hide. *Anywhere* to hide.

Utter madness. A creature like that would snap down

and catch him without even having to move, much less use its obvious ability to fly.

Hermod forced the panic from his face.

Well, he tried to force it from his face. "Great Quetzal-coatl! I ..." Shit. He should have thought about this before he got here. "I greet you!"

The feathered serpent lowered its head, bringing it closer to Hermod. A head bigger than his entire body. This thing could swallow him without chewing. Actually, the way it looked at him, maybe it was considering just that.

"I ... er ..." Hermod paused. Cleared his throat. "Forgive me for intruding. I needed to cross into Anlang." And until just now, the Astral Roil had seemed the more terrifying means of doing so. His bladder seemed to think he ought to reevaluate.

"Why?" The dragon's voice boomed, carried on the wind, and resounded across the meadow as if it came from all sides. It sent Hermod's flesh trembling.

The truth? If he told the truth, the serpent might well eat him. But part of the truth ...

"I seek a means of overcoming Hel, who has breached the Mortal Realm. To fight her ... I need power from the Otherworlds."

"The sirins will tear you apart."

Again, the bombarding force of the serpent's words over-whelmed Hermod, left him wanting to bow down and grovel and beg for mercy. As for sirins ... perhaps the vaettir native to this world?

Hermod swallowed. "How might I earn their favor ... and yours?"

"They live for food and song and revelry that might not be to the liking of a mortal. As for myself, I want ... naught."

Hermod cocked his head. Olwen had said Quetzalcoatl

would require a tribute or sacrifice. Why would he allow a mortal to pass and not a liosalf? "You truly do not require aught of me?"

"No." The word boomed, carried along the wind, leaving Hermod trembling.

Well, he couldn't afford to pass up such a boon. Hermod backed away from the feathered serpent, half expecting the creature to lunge forward and swallow him whole. But the dragon just soared along the air currents around the temple, turning about its abode without further apparent interest in Hermod.

He made his way from the meadow, and up, over a hill that eventually rose to a crag, casting a final look at the feathered serpent. Beautiful and terrible. And Hermod would definitely seek an alternative route back to the Mortal Realm.

The wind whipped over him, just shy of a gale, enough to slow his progress. The scattered trees before the crag all bent in wild angles, twisted, stubborn things that refused to break in this perpetual storm. Somewhere ahead—horrifically close, in fact—thunder rumbled, the sound leaving his ears ringing.

The storms in this world seemed almost on the ground. Hermod needed a better view, so he kept climbing the crag.

The sun was up, though hidden behind clouds, and constant biting winds kept any warmth from reaching him. Had he realized the chill, he might have brought warmer clothes. On Alfheim, the blazing sun meant he ...

Atop the crag, Hermod faltered, gaping. The storms were not closer to the land here.

The land was up among the storms. Beyond the crag, the ground dropped away, with a rumbling storm cloud *beneath* him. He was on a flying island. Across from him, half hidden by the clouds, other floating islands passed in and out of view.

Another gale swept óver him, sending him stumbling closer to the edge.

Hermod dropped to one knee to steady himself. "Fuck me."

Finding it hard to swallow, he turned about—staying on the damn ground—and took in the rest of his island. It was large, maybe a few miles across, though he couldn't make out the entirety because a storm-encircled mountain rose off in the distance. Even so, the island seemed tiny next to the endless sky in all directions.

The World of Storm was composed of flying islands.

"Keuthos," he grated. "*Wraith.*"

A pressure shifted around inside his skull, as if a worm burrowed through his brain. The wraith finally waking from the torpor that had settled upon it in the World of Sun.

"Keuthos."

Yes ...

What madness was this place?

You would have me ... answer self-apparent questions ... to belittle your own ... already limited wits ...

Shit. Slowly, Hermod crawled back from the crag's edge, and down to the relative safety of the weather-beaten hilltop below it. Safety that assumed these islands would not suddenly plummet into the void below.

Not since the dawn of time ...

The wraith had told him he'd find the seal on a mountain in this world. Assuming it was even on this same island, he saw only one real mountain here. One where lightning crackled around a peak he could not even make out for the clouds engulfing it.

The storm ... is not the only concern ...

"What else?"

Harpies ...

Hermod rubbed his beard. Part of him wanted to collapse. To surrender, give up and return to Midgard. Surely Odin would have need of him. Maybe his quest for vengeance against Hel was vanity, and doomed. But ... Odin *would* have need of him. If Hermod could take any action that might begin to break Hel's power, the king's chances of overcoming her would increase.

Knowing Odin, the king might well send Hermod straight back out here to complete the mission if he turned back now. Hermod groaned. No. He'd see Hel pay for what she'd done, and he'd find a way to help Odin. The king had chosen Hermod, above all others, as his apprentice. Not his own sons, nor his trusted companions, but Hermod. Because Hermod alone carried the blood of a valkyrie.

With a groan, he skidded his way down the rocky hillside and back to the grasslands below. "What are harpies?"

Sirins ... Alkonosts ... Bird-creatures ...

Quetzalcoatl had claimed sirins lived for song and feasting. Might Hermod propitiate them with the same song that had pleased the liosalfar.

Doubtful ... It would take music ... or singing talent beyond your ability ...

Huh. Good to know what the wraith really thought of Hermod's singing.

Dreading what lay ahead, he made his way toward the mountain.

NO TREES GREW on the mountainside. It was all cold stone, worn smooth by the constant wind and—at the moment—

slashing rains. The rocks had broken at irregular angles, though, leaving jagged points scattered along the slope.

Hermod made his climb slowly.

Every so often, a howling gale would sweep over him with such force it could have sucked him up and sent him flying, had he not clung to the rocks and held himself flat.

That howl served as Hermod's only warning to seek a safe perch.

Once, when the wind seemed especially vexed, it had torn a chunk of rock clean off the mountain—a great slab, almost as large as Hermod, that had broken from a jutting point and hurtled away on the swirling torrent.

All he could do was lean in against the mountain and rely on his Pneuma to keep him holding on. Keuthos offered sporadic directions, nudging him left or right.

Now, he looked up, trying to gauge the distance to the summit. He could not. He'd passed inside the rumbling storm cloud. A blast of lightning in front of him seared his eyes and left hazy spots of white flitting about his vision. In that momentary flash of light, though, he could have sworn he saw a woman up there. A naked woman with the wings and legs of a bird, watching him intently.

A sirin?

Grimacing, Hermod shifted the angle of his climb. Maybe he could not avoid the vaettr, but he'd at least try to do so.

Slowly, he continued his ascent, until he spotted a cave in the mountainside. A shallow hollow, perhaps, but it would offer some shelter.

There is no shelter from this storm ... But this place ... I know this place ... We are nigh to our ambition ...

Well, the wraith didn't have to worry about being bodily hurled off the mountain by a sudden gale. Hermod drew his

Pneuma and scrambled up, until he could pass the threshold.

Of course, even if Hermod found and destroyed the seal, he'd *still* have to find a way back from this world.

Finally, he reached the hollow, and—gaining his feet—stumbled inside.

Just beyond the threshold, two of those women sat in a crouch, their legs ending in bird-like talons, while great wings jutted from behind their shoulders. He could not well judge whether either was the one he'd spotted from below. Both were naked, with a hungry look on their faces, though he could not say—perhaps for the best, honestly—what they hungered for.

The one on the left began to hum, the sound sweet and, somehow, carried on the wind rather than drowned out by it. Indeed, when she started to sing, all other sound drifted away, and Hermod could do naught save stare in rapture at the woman. Her voice massaged his weary muscles and drew him to his knees, a lover's caress over his mind, promising peace. After centuries of struggle and pain, Hermod might—finally—be freed from all worries. Through the song, he could at last find himself reunited with those he had lost so many years before.

Do not listen ...

The sound became bliss. A promise.

All love could meld into one great love. The utter joy of allowing consciousness to melt away. Of allowing himself to cease.

You will lose yourself ...

A faint voice spoke in his mind, almost buried beneath the all-encompassing melody that soothed his weary soul. A little more, and even that flicker would cease. Hermod swayed in time, smiling, for the first time he could remember, smiling at the total joy of allowing thought to fade.

Allow me to take control of your body ...

Why ... why would he do such a thing?

You are nigh lost ... mortal ... They will consume all you are ...

Yes. But it didn't matter. Indeed, it was relief.

Do you truly wish to forget your daughter ...?

A tiny lance of ice shot through his brain. A discordant note that ruptured the song and left Hermod struggling to shake himself free.

Give me control ...

Yes. Sif. If the wraith was his only chance ... *her* only chance ... then let Keuthos free.

A tightness coiled around his chest and squeezed all air from his lungs. A terrible cold seeped into his limbs, as if his entire body was falling into deathchill. He could see himself moving, but couldn't feel it, even as he stood and drew Dainsleif.

The other harpy cocked her head to the side, seeming bemused. Hermod lunged at the singer, ramming the runeblade straight through her throat. Her exploding blood was hot as flame against his icy skin.

Hissing, he spun on the remaining harpy. The creature shrieked, her face a mask of rage, avian and feral, her hands like claws. She launched herself at him and he swung, hacking off an arm. The harpy faltered, gaping at the bleeding stump of her elbow. She brought her wings up to shield herself. Reflex, maybe.

A bad one.

Dainsleif sheared through wing as easily as flesh, taking half her left wing off in a single swipe. Still hissing—it was *not* his voice—he drove forward, running the runeblade through her gut. He caught the stump of her elbow and pulled it to his lips, feasting on her Pneuma through her hot blood.

Coppery, sickening warmth dribbled down his throat. More and more.

No! Enough! Release me!

Still, Keuthos had the dying harpy, was sucking out her life. Feasting upon it and growing stronger.

We had an accord! You cannot have my body without my permission.

He had given it.

Temporarily!

Snarling, he dropped the harpy, and she tumbled to the ground.

The ease of the pressure around his chest only served to remind Hermod how tight it had squeezed. Now, as if a serpent's coils released, he stumbled to his knees, gasping for breath. A freezing cold presence seeped from his mind, threatening to split his skull in two with the pain of it. He pitched over sideways, clutching his head, unable to get his breath or even form a thought.

MAYBE HE'D LAIN on the cold rock of the cavern a few moments. It felt longer. The howling wind outside filled his ears and magnified the pounding headache the wraith's withdrawal had left him with.

Finally, he pushed himself up onto his elbows.

The two women lay in pools of blood, reeking of ruptured bowels.

Not women ...

Sirins. Harpies. Whatever.

Groaning, Hermod rose to his knees.

This is it … Beyond here lies the seal …

A chill wracked him as he gained his feet. He pushed on, to the back of the cave, some thirty feet deep. There, carved into the sloping ceiling, stood a massive rune circle similar to the last, glowing faintly blue. Similar? Perhaps identical. He could not focus on the individual runes overlong. They seemed to shift and squirm in his mind, as if the harder he tried to understand them, the more mind-rending they would become.

Reaching up over his head, he drove Dainsleif into the rock surface. Slowly, he drew the blade across the circle, until the glow vanished and his ears popped. Then he cut across it once more. Rock dust sprayed into his eyes.

Was it done?

Yes …

Fine. Now Hermod would return to Midgard.

You must destroy the seal in Muspelheim …

He would. But first, he needed to see the king. It had been fool pride—and rage—that had driven him to undertake this mission without informing Odin. Now, he must find his king and reveal that Hel was free because of him. Aught else was shirking his responsibility.

Fool …

Yes. Hermod was a fool, many times over.

But he could at least try to do better.

---

36

*H*is lungs did not work.

He lay upon a cold stone floor, face down. And he could not breathe.

His body convulsed, desperate for air. Unable to catch up to the lurching around in time, perhaps. When was he?

When?

Of a sudden, his lungs opened, sucking down a breath that sent pain exploding through Odin's entire body. He felt rent inside out, torn apart by the tides that had brought him here. To wherever and whenever …

He tried to rise, but consciousness slipped from him, and his face slammed back down onto the stone floor.

❦

LAUGHTER WOKE HIM. Giggling, in fact.

Mundilfari pranced around him, clucking his tongue and shaking his head. "Oh! Oh, he's awake. Waking is good. Almost as good as dreaming. They say dreams bridge the gap between revelation and madness. Did you know that?

Who says it? Well, someone said it, I'm fair certain!" He giggled again.

Now, Odin was bound by chains, in the middle of some cell of stone, perhaps beneath the mountains of Vanaheim. The Vanir had old cells down here, after all.

Groaning, he struggled to his knees.

"They didn't recognize you!" Mundilfari cooed. "Can you *believe* that? A second time a random old man appears where he shouldn't be—in Sessrumnir, no less—and no one recognized you. How absurd. As if they shouldn't know a man, just because a thousand years or so had passed. Oh! Oh, but *I* recognized you, old man. I remembered how you slipped from a closed room with no means of egress. Not this time, no, no, no, no." He waved his finger in denial.

"I see you've gone quite mad, now."

"Mad!" The Vanr lunged at him, seized his tunic, and hefted Odin up to his feet. "Not. *Yet.* No. Ah ... no. But you never told me quite where to find the Well. Oh, I made the wall. I killed Mimir. I made myself king, but you haven't held up your end of the *bargain*."

"We didn't make any bargain to—"

Mundilfari shook him. "Hmmm, hmmm. No. That's the trouble. The rub of it. We are ... powerless, aren't we? Caught in causal loops. They know it. Oh, they know! Maybe they made the loops, who can say! Maybe they just ... uh ... what? Hmm. Enforce them!" He snapped his finger. "Because if time ... time is ... uh." He banged his fist against his head. "Time ... exists. Oracles, prophets, they might see the future. That means there is a future. That means ... means ... the Well! I have to find the Well!"

Odin balked, seriously tempted to kick the madman in the stones and try to break the chains. They didn't look like orichalcum, which meant the Mad Vanr still didn't imagine just what Odin was capable of.

"Causal loops," Mundilfari repeated. "Does the Well create them, or is it created by them? A physical manifestation of the timeline in the most obvious of mediums. Water is liminal, is transitory, is fluid and yet incompressible. A well ... Everything ... everything is a paradox ... Existence itself is a paradox. But ... but ... Redeemability seems to be the key." He shrugged that away. "Why send me to make the wall?"

"I didn't send you—"

"You saw it, in the future, didn't you? Hmm. In the Well? Because of the Well? Or ... Lady Chandi wrote about it. Huh. We thought her mad, you know? Brilliant, but half mad, at least. Or three-quarters mad, perhaps. Five-eights, maybe. I ... I have forgotten the equations we worked out. Is that a problem? Are the answers in the Well? Not the Well of Urd, no. I looked there, so many times, so deeply. Sometimes, even without Lytir's permission. Did you know that? When I thought, perhaps, *they* didn't know. How foolish was that?"

The Norns? Mundilfari was trying to sidestep the Norns' authority?

"Souls! That's what she kept writing about. So much is lost, of course. I don't think she wanted us to know the truth ... Did *she* know the truth?"

A knock on the cell door had Mundilfari spinning abruptly around.

The door creaked open and Loki stepped inside.

Odin couldn't keep the shock from his face. Though neither spoke, both vaettir within him seemed equally stupefied at the man's presence here.

"You're back," Mundilfari said. "Hmm."

"I told you I would return when you needed me."

"Bah!" The Vanr waved Loki away. "I've needed you for quite some time, yes, I think I did. I did indeed, hmm. But now ... now the other one is here. Maybe, between the two of you, you can find the damn well. Yes, you should I think." The Vanr king snorted. "None of this ... this ... *this* matters when the future is such a tangled ball of strings. I have to know, Loptr! I have to *know*."

The man had lost himself, for certain. It seemed Odin's last meeting with him had served as a catalyst to drive him further over the edge. At the moment, though, all Odin could do was stare at Loki—Loptr?—who regarded him without a hint of expression.

"It's beyond the Midgard Wall," Odin blurted. "Beyond even Vafthrudnir's Refuge."

Mundilfari spun and poked Odin's chest with his index finger. "See! I knew it! I knew it!"

"My king," Loki said, "surely you have more pressing duties than—"

"King! King of what, prophet? King of a failing empire in a failing world." He snapped his fingers. "Dust. Dust! All of it, irrelevant. How many times, prophet? How many times ... have ... have they wound us round and round in our loops? The past and future and present ... a mush. Soup! We are drowning in soup!"

"My king ..."

"No more. No, no ... Njord always wanted his mother's throne. Little sister-fucking prince. Well, let him have it. Freyja ought to be pleased, too. Shit, let their entire disheveled family run this faltering island. I ... I ... *I* have to find the Well, Loptr! The Well! I have ... to see farther."

With that, Mundilfari shoved past Loki and stormed from the room. Loki winced as he left.

Grimacing, Odin's blood brother turned back to him,

grabbed the chains, and yanked them free of the iron loop that bound them. Metal grated and snapped.

"Causal loops," Odin said. Mundilfari ... "This is *not* some past life, is it?"

Loki sighed. "Odin, listen to me."

"You know me. You know who I am, even though I still won't be born for centuries."

"We don't have much time." Loki shook his head. "So, listen carefully."

"Not a past life at all."

Loki grabbed Odin's shoulders. "If it was, you wouldn't be asking that question, would you? Focus, Odin."

Odin shoved the man away. "I ought to *kill* you, Nornslave! What utter madness you have wrought. Is this your doing, as well? You sent me—the real me—back in time? What, so I could watch the Mad Vanr become mad in the first place? Why!"

Loki shook his head. "Don't call me that where people might hear it. Right now, here, I'm Loptr."

"Or Loge?"

Now Loki flinched. "Definitely don't use that name, either."

"Or *what*?" Odin stalked closer to the man, chains still attached to his wrists and scraping over the stone floor behind him. "What more will you do to me?"

Loki held up his hands in mock surrender. "I didn't do this to you. The Norns have cracked something open that was already inside you." Wait, what? No. That wasn't ... "Your Sight allows you to glimpse threads from the Web of Urd. But if it were powerful enough, you might grasp hold of such a thread and pull yourself along it, to nodes in the greater tapestry of time. But you're not in control, and maybe it's too powerful for you ever to control, so you're flitting about, both inside your own past, and bodily into nodes that draw your mind. You can, however, learn to guide and maybe even stop the transitions. You have to focus."

We are all of us mad, now ...

Odin clutched his temples, trying to hold thoughts inside that seemed too big for his head. Already, he could feel the tidal forces building again, an almost audible crash of waves at the far edge of his senses, coming for him, intent to drown him once more.

"I didn't change aught ... I thought ... I thought if I brought down the Norns ..."

Loki grabbed his wrists. "They are but symptoms of an already untenable reality, Odin. Manifestations of the force of Ananke, the Chains of Fate. Your rage against them, while not entirely misplaced, is moot, because *if* their chains did begin to snap, if you somehow managed to unravel threads of the web, you'd risk the entire timeline collapsing."

Odin shook his wrists free. "We are powerless. Utterly, and completely helpless before the merciless procession of urd. Deny it, brother. Deny it!"

"You have to get back to your own time, Odin. The future needs you."

"No! I won't betray them thus. I left to find a way to change it."

"No." Loki shook his head, almost seeming terrified. "You don't understand. I needed you, I needed the cycle of Eschatons, even if I didn't know what I was creating, exactly, I knew I needed it. I convinced them to allow it, because the alternative was—"

The maelstrom rushed over Odin, a crash of waves bombarding him, drowning out all his senses. It swept him from his feet and cast him away from Loki, falling through his brother's fingertips.

And vanishing once more into the swirling temporal vortex.

Control it. Focus.

Loki had said ... he said this wasn't something the Norns did to Odin. It was something they unlocked in him. The ultimate manifestation of the Sight. The ability, not only to see the past and future, but to live it.

If he could but gain a foothold ...

But naught Loki said ever made enough sense. He needed answers ... Just like Mundilfari.

Odin *had* to know.

*I*davollir lay buried under a curtain of ice, its doors frozen shut once more. Lucky the Valls hadn't claimed it. Maybe they thought it cursed. Roland said something like that. Way back, when Tyr had fought alongside him. Called him friend. Before he died fighting Serks.

Serks who had now overrun half Valland. Fires raged all over. Villages burned. Cities too. Serks reduced everything to ash. To smoke. To blood and chaos.

Still couldn't say they were worse than the Valls. Not anymore. Valls had always worshiped their Deathless god. Only now, they'd taken to hunting Aesir in his name. Years, Tyr had bled for them. Now, no one remembered it.

Bastards.

A swing of Thor's hammer shattered the ice holding the gates shut. Tyr helped the prince force open the doors.

Odin's son was the first inside. Didn't get far before he was gaping at too tall stairs.

"Weren't old enough to remember this place," Tyr commented.

Thor shook his head. "It's big, I'll give you that."

"Got wells for water. Food's a different story."

Thrúd had gone out hunting, taking several others with her. Including Magni. Thor's son was no hunter, but he said he'd watch them. Just as well. They had to eat. Didn't make this land safe by any measure.

"Start bringing in firewood," Tyr ordered a group of Aesir.

Thor grunted. "Didn't think of that."

Prince probably didn't think of much. Save eating, drinking, fucking, and fighting. Didn't know a real siege. Tyr held his peace, though. Naught to gain, antagonizing the man. The man had lost a lot, back on Asgard. Besides, until Odin returned, Thor held the throne.

Not that they had an actual throne. Or much else.

Still. Didn't much like their chances if anyone actually let Thor lead.

Men and women began piling in, selecting sleeping chambers. Prepping kitchens and forges. Bragi immediately set to giving them orders. Like they didn't know what needed doing better than a liosalf. Skald liked hearing his own voice, Tyr figured. A hair better than Thor giving orders —or failing to.

"Here we make our stand," Frey said, coming up behind Tyr and Thor.

Vanr's sister stood close at hand, arms folded over her chest. Sullen. Eostre had slapped Freyja on the boat. Maybe on account of Idunn, though the old dawn goddess said naught. Tyr hadn't figured she'd have stayed with them, but she did. Even when her Sons of Muspel went off to pillage Valland and kill the Deathless.

Shame, that. Bastards were strong and fast. Would've

made good allies. Not accounting for them being more than half possessed and possibly mad. Eh ... maybe not such a shame.

Thor shook his head, looking at Frey. Prince would never walk quite right again, but still had strength few could match. Couldn't ask for a stronger ally when the fighting came, that much Tyr had to grant.

Now, Tyr nodded at Frey. "It held a good while before. Had draugar swim up the wells, though. Have to guard those."

The Vanr nodded grimly. "Sea jotunnar."

Tyr grunted in assent. "My prince. Care to inspect the defenses?"

"Yes." Thor made his way to the stairs. With that bad foot, it ought to keep him busy a while.

Tyr met Frey's gaze. A grim thing, letting it come to this. Vanr had been his enemy, and a bitter one. "Prince won't know how to prepare for this."

"You do."

Maybe. But Thor wouldn't take kindly to having his authority questioned. Had to make it all seem like his idea. And Tyr hated that kind of trollshit. Manipulating and scheming. Didn't suit him in the least. "You and I. We have to make sure we can hold out until Odin comes."

"Still think he can save you? I'm half convinced we made a mistake in not retreating to Alfheim."

"No," Freyja said. First time she'd broken her silence. "Odin shifted the bridge to open from this side in order to stabilize it. You'd have had to leave the ring in the machine for us to cross the Bilröst. Meaning, even if we shut down the bridge on Alfheim, a clever jotunn like Narfi might have reopened it to any Spirit World he wished. We'd not only damn Midgard, but we'd risk having unending armies pour into Alfheim."

Frey held up his hand, showing off that band. "We die here, they take the ring anyway."

"Comes to it," Tyr said, "you run to Alfheim."

Frey snorted. "I'm not leaving my sister here, even if I was craven enough to follow such a plan. Nor can I abandon any of the other Vanir now trapped on Midgard."

Tyr grunted. "Got to fight then. Got to win."

"The World ends all around us," Freyja said. "Maybe Odin can see a way to stop it. Without him ..."

So strange, being back here. And now, waiting on Odin again. Last time, he'd rode in to save them. Now ... Tyr could only pray the king could manage it a second time.

HE FOUND Eostre atop the ramparts. Staring down at the mist. Grim. Sullen, maybe.

Tyr had spent the past two hours ordering every preparation he could think of. Speaking on Thor's behalf. Sometimes countermanding Bragi who didn't know a defensive strategy from his own arse hole. Skald kept carrying on about epic sagas where men held off armies by themselves. Fought in gatehouses and so forth.

Imbecile might inspire some fools. Get them killed.

Only thing worse than Thor not knowing what to do, was Bragi *thinking* he knew.

"Meant to thank you," he said to Eostre. Woman didn't turn at his approach.

"You saved a good many lives on Asgard."

"Vanaheim."

Tyr grunted. Didn't much matter what they called dead islands, to his mind. "Wanted to say something else, too." Something hard to give words to. He'd almost been tempted to find more tasks to busy himself with. Put this one off. The craven's way. "I was ... fond of your daughter."

Now Eostre did spin on him, glaring.

"Didn't sit well, her cast into Alfheim. Set less well what happened, her trapped in Svartalfheim."

"I can't tell you how much your concern means to me." Woman had an adder's venom when she wanted. He could hardly see Idunn in her, truth be told. Idunn was ... vibrant. Optimistic to a fault, he'd have said.

Tyr rested his hand on a snow-drenched crenellation. "Been thinking on asking Frey for the ring. Trying to go after her."

Eostre scoffed. "All you'd do is get yourself killed and hand an unimaginably dangerous weapon to the denizens of Svartalfheim."

Thought had occurred to him. Problem was, without the Bilröst, only one person could go. Hermod could've gone with him, but the man was most like dead himself, having ridden for the gates of Hel. Utter depths of Mist-madness, Tyr had to figure.

"Can't see abandoning her."

Eostre sneered. "Freyja says she and Odin felt the same. And yet, here you all are, while she rots in the darkness."

"I'll find a way, is all I'm saying."

Still sneering, she turned away. Not inclined to talk more on it, then.

Well, couldn't much blame her. Not after what had happened to her child.

With a grimace, Tyr wandered back to the stairs.

❦

IT WAS JUST AFTER DUSK, a few days later, when Hermod came trudging through the snows up to the gate. Sentries had damn nigh shot him, figuring him a Vall or Serk or even a draug.

But he'd announced himself, and Thor ordered the gates flung wide.

Now, the three of them sat in the great hall, Hermod sipping hot soup made from what game Thrúd had managed. Squirrel, mostly, and a rabbit. All mixed together, spread thin for so many mouths.

They'd told him about Syn's fall, and the man had grown grimmer than ever. Which stood as a feat, itself. Not that Tyr could blame him. She'd died a warrior's death, Tyr had told Hermod. The man only fell silent.

"Where's my brother?" Thor demanded, before Hermod had even finished eating.

Rude, that. Tyr frowned at it. Man had come back from a place Tyr didn't even want to imagine. Maybe the darkest, worst place in any Realm. And here Thor was badgering him.

One look at Hermod's eyes, and you could see he was haunted.

Damn, but Tyr didn't want to know what he'd seen out there.

Hermod swallowed, cleared his throat. "Hel won't release Baldr on any account. She refused any offer I made." Words hung there, like he meant to say more, but didn't.

"What is it?" Tyr finally asked.

"I ... I saw Sif."

Thor stiffened. "Trollshit."

"It's the truth. Hel has her, too. I tried to bargain for her release. I ... I failed."

Now the prince slapped his fist on the table. "Well go back and get her!"

Hermod shook his head. Tyr didn't think he'd ever seen anyone look so tired. Like weariness would make his flesh drip off any moment. "It does not work like that. But ... I avenged her."

"What?" Thor said. "On the Serks?"

Hermod's face grew even grimmer, if that was possible. "Sigyn."

Tyr balked, not quite sure he'd heard that right.

"What?" Thor asked.

"Her own aunt murdered her in her attempt to protect Hödr."

"Fucking *bitch*," Thor snarled. "I'm going to grind her bones into pulp! I'll feed her flesh to a fucking troll!"

"She's dead," Hermod said, almost all emotion drained from his voice. "And suffering under Hel herself."

Thor hardly looked satisfied even at that. Prince just kept shaking his head clawing at the table.

"It's worse," Hermod said, after a moment more. "I ... wanted revenge."

"Rightly so," Tyr said. Time was, he'd almost liked Sigyn. But some things couldn't stand. Besides, that whole family had betrayed Asgard. They'd chosen their sides. Way back, even.

"I killed her in the hope Hel would restore Sif to life. But ... she ... she took Sigyn's body as her own."

"Huh?" Thor asked.

Tyr felt like someone had punched him in the gut. Odin had claimed Hel would find a way back to Midgard. That she was plotting it. Maybe had been plotting it for centuries. Their whole lives, probably.

And now she had done it.

"Hel is here," Hermod said. "She's come back. Whatever Asgard faced, this is only the beginning."

38

*E*ven before Hel had strained her power to engender the endless winter, the snows in these mountains had never melted. It meant the corpse lay frozen, buried under four hundred years of ice. Dead, but not completely unwakeful.

Coming here had stirred up a blizzard, but ice and snow hardly impeded Hel. They fell well within her purview, and thus served her, concealing her steps amid the Sudurberks —as men called these mountains now.

In the back of her mind, the host squirmed, raging against Hel's control. The delicious irony of claiming her father's own wife as a host brought a smile to Hel's lips. Or, to what remained of her lips, since one side of her face had sloughed off.

I am not afraid of you!

Hel didn't even bother scoffing at the host's absurd objection. *Everyone* feared her, and had for Era after Era. In many cases, unaware of the true nature of the Archons or the greater powers beyond them, mortals feared Hel more than they did aught else in all the World. And with good reason, for she alone had usurped the power of an Archon, thus becoming an Elder God herself. She alone ruled Niflheim, and very soon, the Mortal Realm, as well.

Besides which, her host seemed to forget that lying to her was pointless. She could delve through Sigyn's mind, her memories, her deepest fears with ease. Had she truly wished it, she could have glamoured the rot away from her face and even passed for Sigyn herself.

You will never be me.

No. And why should she ever wish it?

Draugar plodded along behind her, silhouettes barely visible in the night, especially given the unending snow and the mist that thickened at Hel's presence. She had called them without even really intending to. Rather, they felt her, the mistress of death, and flocked to her from all corners of the World.

Across the Veil, ghosts flitted, equally drawn to her presence. Wraiths were there, too, though not her greatest assets. For those, she would need to create another breach to Niflheim. At present, though, Hel had another agenda.

Loki will stop you.

Finally, Hel paused—the corpse lay before her now, anyway, buried in the pass—and regarded her host. Sigyn's husband would not dare to raise a hand against her, not while she held his precious wife's body hostage. Even if the man could have brought himself to turn on his own daughter once more, and Hel doubted that, too. Not that it mattered. While Loki had held that hateful jinni inside him —Hel would not deign to even think the vile name—he could not have matched a fragment of her power.

And now?

Well, deprived of the jinni, her father was little better than mortal, if an exceptionally hard mortal to kill. No, he was a fly to be driven away with a wave of her hand so she could tend to more important matters.

Like transforming the Mortal Realm into an extension of Niflheim and heralding the end of time.

None of the draugar dared come any closer when she knelt, placing her palms into the snow and digging in. Hundreds of feet down, that flicker of wakefulness stirred. Yes, draugar came from human souls. And yet, of course, jotunnar were spawned from much the same stuff as Men. Changed, twisted by glorious powers of the Spirit Worlds, but, at their very cores, human.

And this soul, this furious ancient soul, had refused to depart. It had shifted on astral winds, bound to shadow and awaiting this very moment. For Hel had promised Ymir that his sacrifice, should it come to it, would not go unrewarded. All things came in cycles.

Hel clenched her fists in the snow.

The ground beneath her rumbled with a shifting of powder. A fell wind kicked up the loose snow, almost enough that, had she not known better, she might have missed the flakes rising from the mountain slope on their own, rejoining the blizzard and spiraling around her in a whirlwind of bitter cold. Yes, Niflheim drew close here, desperate to pierce the Veil the Destroyer had dared to place between the worlds in a distant Era.

It would not hold her back forever.

And for now, her will alone would serve to pull Ymir's festering soul back into this Realm.

The quakes intensified. Tremors had begun to shoot through all the Mortal Realm, now. The very land writhing in agony at her presence, and at the amount of power the jotunnar had begun to call upon. The World Tree shriveled, gnawed on by the dark dragon who she had bestirred.

When Hel controlled Yggdrasil, she would hold the Wheel of Life in her hand. With that, her power would outstrip all others. Archons would tremble before her. The dark powers from beyond would bow to her. For in souls lay the ultimate sustenance. And Hel would feast on every life and every death.

A hand as big as her body burst forth from the ground. Fingers tinged blue, gaunt, but with only a bare hint of decay. For Ymir had lain beneath the snows, preserved. At least as much as Hel herself, in any event.

The massive fingers flexed, closed, and flexed once more. Then the sickly palm slapped the ground in front of her, digging a foot-deep impression into the snow and flinging up a shower of powder in the process.

What have you done?

Hel didn't answer that. The hand—and forearm—pulled on the ground, slowly digging the fallen jotunn out.

Fresh quakes resounded, beginning an avalanche on a nearby peak. The noise from it drowned out all other sound, a cacophony of plummeting snow headed for her. Hel raised her hand, palm out, and the path of the avalanche shifted, diverted off another slope as if it had hit an impenetrable wall.

Another hand dug itself free.

And then the horn, five feet long and seeming hewed from granite, it jutted from the ice like a breaching whale. The head followed, eyes now gleaming red where the light of life had once shone.

In the back of her mind, Sigyn gasped, no longer bothering with her feeble attempts to conceal her utter terror.

Foot by merciless foot, the corpse freed itself it until, at last, it managed to climb loose. It came to rest on a knee in front of her, the red gleam of its eyes almost lost in the blizzard raging around them.

The jotunn would have stood more than eight times her height. Hel could not help but allow herself a tight, lopsided smile. Here was her champion. Here, was her herald for the end of time.

This time, she would make no mistakes. The cycle would break, and the Mortal Realm would fall, presaging her conquest of the World. Plans begun tens of thousands of years ago would finally come to fruition.

Father had been wrong, back then, though he still might not admit it.

"Come," Hel said to the jotunn. "We have work to do."

IN TRUTH, Ymir was no longer Ymir. Not quite as he had been. As her draug-jotunn, he was something more. And so, Hel had named Hrym, the Decrepit. The taste of such irony —for though his flesh rotted, none compared to his might— offered her a morsel of amusement in her long trek up to Nidavellir.

Not even the dvergar had dared approach the perilous waters of Hel's frozen, underground sea. In this cavernous expanse, the ice was so thick that it could support even Hrym's weight, along with Hel and the small army of draugar now following her.

But she had not delved below the mountains for ice.

Hel knelt upon it, placed her palm on the surface, and pushed.

A crack shot through the ice, spiderwebbing out in an arc away from her, spreading even beyond her view. The crack deepened, beyond great rents in the surface. Blocks of ice thicker than she was tall split and ground together, flinging up clouds of snow dust.

It was there. Sunken so deep it almost scraped the shores of Naströnd.

In the distance, the massive prow of a ship beyond all measure burst through the ice. Living—or perhaps undead would be more apt—and formed from bones and nails and sinew, Naglfar came crashing to the surface once more. A ship, the size of a small city. From its hull, arms and hands of the damned writhed in eternal torment, sucked into service of this vessel that had been denied its proper purpose since the creation of the Veil.

It had waited here, drawing in souls and compounding upon itself for thousands of years.

Men called its jutting bone spikes a grotesque mockery of life. Some had lost their minds at the screeching howls of the damned locked into the slowly growing ship.

It would serve.

"Come, Hrym," she said. "Come and be my helmsman. For in the north, on Thule, lies a city of draugar awaiting us. And very soon, the dead shall outnumber the living."

39

_____

He lay with his head on a desk, sun shining on his shoulders, warming them. Groaning, Odin pushed himself up. How long had he been asleep here? Maybe that question held no meaning whatsoever. Given, relative to whatever time he now dwelt in, he might well have appeared this very instant.

Still woozy, ears thick as though from deep underwater, Odin struggled to his feet and looked around. He knew this place. Back in Sessrumnir, the East Tower.

After steadying himself a moment, he made his way to the door, and then down the steps. It was all too familiar. Mundilfari was gone ... or had been planning to abdicate the throne in favor of Njord. That should mean that Mundilfari's apprentice, Njord's daughter, Odin's beloved, should now be running Sessrumnir.

Assuming, of course, that he hadn't gone further back in time.

At the base of the stairs, Odin faltered. Sigyn sat at a table, staring at him, obviously having heard him coming with those keen ears.

The present.

He'd made it back, hadn't he? Except, she so rarely left Loki's side from where Odin had imprisoned him, and Odin had ordered her barred from Sessrumnir. Almost, almost ... he wanted to release the man. But Loki, slave to the Norns or not, had still allowed the terrible war between their families. Had actively worked toward that war, in order to create Ragnarok.

"My king," Sigyn said. No disdain laced her voice, or not much. More surprise. "I thought you were in Sviarland."

She rose, pushing away from the desk and arching her back in obvious pain. Because her belly was thick with child.

Hödr? As yet unborn. The very instrument of Ragnarok, lying quiescent in Sigyn's womb.

And Sviarland ... so ... so she thought he'd be manipulating Sigmund's defeat of Siggeir Wolfsblood.

"I, uh ..." His head swam with the nonsensical events of the past few ... well, however much time had passed or should have passed or would have. "I needed some information."

"Something I can help you find?"

Shit. He needed to talk to Loki. The man had finally been trying to tell him why ... But Loki wasn't here. Still, his brother had said that Odin was actually the one controlling his own shifts in time. So some part of himself had wanted to know something in Sessrumnir. Something from Sigyn?

No. No, not her. Someone else.

"Lady Chandi," he said.

"Uh, huh. Well, she apparently kept a number of journals, but most were lost, or—Mundilfari suspected—perhaps deliberately destroyed by her. What originals remained, I can't read, regardless. They're not in the Vanr tongue, but he translated a few from what he called the Skyfall tongue."

Yes. Yes, of course. Odin nodded. "Give me ... whatever originals remained and whatever Mundilfari wrote about them."

"All right." She waddled off, one hand to the small of her back.

Odin followed after her, then offered her an arm to make her passage easier. She took it, with a look of mingled concern and surprise.

What if Odin killed her, before Hödr was even born? Would that bring back Baldr? Would it avert Ragnarok? Or would it, rather, enrage Loki and create a yet worse future?

The thought of murdering her before she had done aught, of killing her unborn child, it set Odin's gut quivering.

How magnanimous ... Spare the child even at the cost ... of the World ...?

Maybe Audr was right. Maybe any price was worth it, if it averted the end of time. Wasn't that exactly why he'd gone to kill the Norns?

By his side, his hand clenched into a fist. A Pneuma-enhanced blow could certainly rupture her womb and destroy Hödr. But ...

Sigyn led him to a side chamber where she rustled through a trunk. "Mundilfari makes reference to having translated some additional passages, but those appear lost or misplaced. Unless, of course, he has them in some hidden vault." She shrugged, though Odin could tell the thought thrilled her. Secret, forbidden knowledge. Oh, Sigyn. If only she had learned to leave well enough alone.

Forcing his fist open felt like trying to swim up a waterfall.

Weakness ...

Odin slumped down at the nearest table and, after a glance at Sigyn, began to flip through Mundilfari's annotations.

"So ..." Sigyn said.

"That will be all." For now. Unless he managed the resolve necessary to end her and hope to preserve the future.

Kill her ...

"Oh," she said. "All right, then." Damn her and her incessant curiosity. What Odin needed to learn, she could not know.

Besides, Odin could read the Skyfall tongue. He had known it, long ago, as Naresh, and, if he allowed the memories of those past lives to run through him, he could understand languages that had died in prior Eras of the World.

To say Chandi's musings were missing pages would have been a generous estimation. Rather, Mundilfari had collected a handful of pages with no sense of sequence, thrown them together, and called them a journal.

Sensical ... to the mad ...

Well, then, Odin should be able to figure it out, sooner or later.

... A FUTURE. I know there was, and I saw it, and it left me with hope when despair might otherwise have reigned. The sun was shining, and he told me that alone was supposed to be proof. Maybe it was. I so dearly needed to believe it was, and that Vanaheim was the beginning of that.

They said, also, that the same soul could not exist in the same place, even in multiple incarnations.

I asked the Sisters, but all they'd answer me was that time and souls and the Wheel of Fate were all intertwined.

"Time is a funny thing," the fire priest told me. *"Eras must end and corruption must be abated. And for that to happen, there must be a catalyst. A person, a soul, willing to take up the horrible burden."*

Even now, so many years later, I cannot forget those words.

I feel like ... like he forced it on him. This mantle. This role to serve the needs of the future at the expense of the present ... of himself ...

Fuck. She was talking about the Destroyer. Lady Chandi, fifty-two centuries ago, was talking about the Destroyer. About Odin. Or Naresh, of course. But someone had told her, back then, about the cycle of Eschatons.

"Souls and Fate," Odin mumbled. "The Wheel of Life ... the Web of Urd—the Wheel of Fate."

He rose. Maybe only Loki could finally explain what all this—

The maelstrom crashed into him with such force it sent him toppling over, crashing to the ground and knocking aside his chair. Temporal tides bombarded his mind, stripped the air from his lungs, and shredded his mind into a thousand pieces. They ripped him apart, such that his scream lacked even a sound over the roaring currents.

THE SUN WAS WARMING his face. The ocean waves crashing close at hand, methodical, mesmerizing. Almost enough to threaten to pull him back under once more, to draw him deeper under the current, perhaps never to surface again. Would that be a fitting end to Odin's quest—to find himself lost on the tides of time, unable to ever rise above them long enough to locate himself?

He opened his eye to behold he lay on a real shoreline, bright and warm, and, though it looked little like Vanaheim, he saw not a sign of the mists.

Instead, he found a steep, rocky slope that ended in a short cliff above an impossibly blue sea. The sun beat heavily on the back of his head and he found himself squinting, almost as if he had suddenly woken on Asgard. Across a bay, greenery covered another rocky outcropping, and behind him rose a mountain, atop which lay a spire.

"Naught else here ..."

Blinking, he climbed to his feet, then unslung his cloak to allow the cool breeze to wash over him. Almost, he hoped that wherever and whenever he'd wound up, he wouldn't have to return to the war-torn, mist-shrouded World he'd left. Save that all those he loved remained left behind.

Slowly, Odin made his way to the mountain, only to find a small town lay at its base, nestled around another bay. He had not made it far when a trio of tunic-clad, spear-brandishing warriors came trotting his way, pointing their weapons and shouting in some strange tongue that *might* have been related to Miklagardian. Curiously, despite the bright sun, two of them carried torches in their off hands, instead of shields.

One of them jerked his spear at Odin, motioning him to walk into their midst.

Hands raised, Odin did as the man commanded, forced to turn to keep them each in view.

No ... he knew that tongue ... in faded memories of past lives, he'd known it.

"... Titan spy," one of them said.

"So gut him and leave him to the sharks."

"No," the man who'd first motioned Odin over said. "He said they would come. We have to take him to the Firebringer."

Firebringer ... Did he mean ...?

The men ushered Odin to a path, running up the mountain, steep and somewhat treacherous, enough so that Odin relied on a small amount of Pneuma to keep from slipping, given he had no walking stick. Yes, he missed Gungnir. He'd only just reclaimed his ancestral weapon and now he'd somehow lost it once more.

An unnameable sense of anticipation had built in his chest, as they continued up the path. A tingling prescient insight that, much as he refused to try to seek direct vision, still forewarned him of some momentous shift impending.

{a.

THE SPIRE itself was enormously tall, roughly circular, and covered in greenery and flowers of dozens of colors. Thousands of birds had alighted in great arching windows that composed the upper reaches of this tower, which his would-be captors had referred to simply as the Aviary.

Odin could see why, given that, as they entered the lower chamber, even more birds had gathered inside, squawking and singing and filling the tower with a cacophony. They perched on poles spanning the length of the room, crisscrossed at varying heights. They bathed in a fountain in the tower's center, one that continuously bubbled over its own edge, sending a trickle of water running down into grooves in the floor that ran into grates. Probably accounting for why the tower wasn't absolutely covered in bird shit.

His guards led him up a flight of stairs, past landing after landing, with each home to other wonders of decoration. A rock garden in the sand. An enclosed library with a glass dome that actually did bear streaks from bird droppings. And at the top, a circle of braziers, in the midst of which sat a tall man, cross-legged, hands upon his knees as if in deep meditation. The fires in braziers swayed, slightly in discord with one another and with the wind.

Loki, though his hair and skin were slightly darker now, closer to those possessed by Odin's captors.

"Lord Prometheus," one of them said. "We found this man approaching the village."

Odin glanced around this highest tier. Outside of the roof, a balcony rimmed it, offering a tremendous view over the entire island—for it was clearly an island, he could see now—and the sea beyond, where it looked like other islands dotted the waters.

"Loki," Odin said, turning back to his blood brother.

The man opened his eyes—still crystal blue, even in his slightly altered guise. "Leave me with him."

"But, my lord, we don't know if the king sent him. He could be a Titan."

Loki—Prometheus, whatever—smiled his cryptic, once-disarming smile. "He's not a Titan."

When the others had left, Loki rose and stalked over to Odin, pausing several feet away. "Who are you? Why do you call me that name?"

Now, Odin fell back a step, cocking his head. This ... this didn't make sense. When he'd met Loki in the past, well before his birth, Loki had already known him. As Loptr, he knew who Odin was. As Prometheus ... "This is the first time we've met ... for *you*."

Now, the man glanced past Odin, as if trying to make sure they were truly alone. "You used the box?"

Odin groaned. "I have no idea what that means." Here,

he'd dared to hope Loki might finally be answering his questions, not the other way around. "Titans ... you're at war with them. Jotunnar?"

"We're not at war." Ah, but the 'yet' remained unspoken in his tone.

"They called you the Firebringer." Odin shook his head. It felt apt to burst once more. "You gave them the Art of Fire. Is this ... the first time?"

Loki's crystal blue eyes kept searching, so deeply Odin could almost see him putting puzzle pieces together. "I'm called Prometheus, and yes, I gave the Art of Fire to Man to offer them a bulwark against the Titans and against other, darker forces."

Odin nodded. What did it matter, anyway? "I'm Odin. And ..." It mattered naught, that's what. "One day, we shall be blood brothers. Until you finally betray me."

Now, Prometheus flinched, almost seemed to suppress a shudder. "It's you, isn't it? Yes, of course it is." Not quite so collected as the man would be later, was he? "I believed we would *need* the cycle. I ... for whatever it's worth ... I'm sorry it has to be you, over and over. I didn't have the strength to do this myself ..."

Odin moved up to Prometheus and seized his tunic. "So you *did* create the Eschaton cycle. Why? Why have you done this?"

Prometheus's gaze darted to Odin's hands and for a bare instant, he seemed about to knock Odin away. "I ... I don't know how much I can safely tell you. Not only for your sake, but because speaking it aloud might draw the attention of forces we need to avoid as much as possible."

"You mean the Norns."

"I assume that's just another name for the Moirae, but they're not the only powers we need concern ourselves with

... Odin. They serve a function, holding together the time-line with their Wheel of Fate. But the greater threat comes from powers darker still, consumptive forces that feed upon souls and, if not sated, might burst forth and bring down the foundations of the World. Thus, the only solution, terrible though it was, seemed to be to initiate a cataclysmic struggle to overcome the rising tide of darkness. It ended the World, but at least allowed a new World to rise from the ashes like a phoenix."

"A what?"

Prometheus waved that away. "The point is, the Moirae agreed, perhaps so wholeheartedly that the process became a cycle. It is a means of propitiating the darkness, Odin. A bad solution, yes, but still the only one available to us."

Did he mean ... Nidhogg? The darkness consuming the root of reality. And every Eschaton, the dragon must gorge itself on the hundreds of thousands of corpses sent down there.

Odin wanted to retch. That suffering should so abound simply to keep this *thing* sated, it left his gut churning and his mind reeling.

"You did this ... because you couldn't otherwise hold the World together?"

Prometheus's eyes held all the answer Odin needed.

A truth, at long last. A terrible, soul-devouring truth, that Loki had kept from him for so very long, not out of spite, but out of a desire to allow Odin to truly live. To be freed from the horror that knowledge of the nature of reality must force upon him.

Finally, shaking, Odin sank to his knees, and Prometheus knelt beside him, hands on his shoulders, saying naught, just looking deep into his eyes.

For there was naught to be said.

Because ... if Prometheus was right ... If all the World might otherwise come crashing down, then Odin would have to go back, play his role. Destroy the World so that it could be created once more.

There was never any stopping it.

Ragnarok had to unfold.

EPILOGUE

*T*he tremors had intensified until the entire cavern shook over and over. Stalactites cracked and plummeted, crashing down into the underground lake. One landed so close it sent a rushing wave washing over Loki's chest, drenching him with chilled waters.

Growling with effort, he strained against the orichalcum chains binding him inside the stalagmite. The fetters prevented him from channeling Pneuma and thus manifesting the strength necessary to snap the rock binding him.

Far above, a massive crack shot through the cavern's ceiling, resounding like a thunderclap. A chunk of rock the size of a horse dropped out, pitching into the lake and sending another wave rushing over him. More and more debris fell from above.

Loki could no longer suppress the bitter laugh that bubbled up from his chest. Though he had no mood for irony at present, he could not help but note the potential for it, were he to drown or find himself crushed underground. So many millennia he had served his purpose.

So much anguish.

He'd welcome the end, if it would have him.

Sigyn.

Sigyn.

No ...

He roared, yanking impotently on the chains.

No mere physical torment, not even having his liver repeatedly devoured, might compare to the agony of loss. The knowledge that, no matter how long he lived, no matter what he achieved, still he would never hold her again. Torments of the body were transitory, ephemeral things compared to that. The certainty of *eternal* loss.

A gaping wound that had already begun to fester, until he'd have willingly risked paradox, an unravelling of the timeline, would it have restored to him that which was gone forever.

He knew this pain. *This*, he had so long dreaded. Because he had known it so many times.

And Loki was tired. So weary of it. So, he must do what he always did—the only thing that allowed him to survive that festering wound—bury it with rage, at least for a little while.

Another chunk of rock crashed down, this time a few dozen feet from him. Loki roared at it, letting his wrath suffuse his being. Straining, until it felt his arms would rip from their sockets.

Roots of Yggdrasil now poked down from the gaps left by the falling rocks, roots that slowly writhed in their own twisting agony. The World Tree itself suffered, as the World died again.

These petty Aesir thought to repay death for death until the World drowned in a sea of blood. Well, then Loki would do the same. He would visit his vengeance upon the one who had taken her from him.

"You know I'll be liberated sooner or later!" he shouted into the darkened cavern. Maybe the Norns listened. Maybe they didn't. It hardly mattered.

A stronger quake seized the cavern, driving Loki to his knees. So much debris fell from above that, for a moment, he'd have sworn he truly might spend the next Era buried under a mountain of earth, begging his masters for death that would not come.

And then the stalagmite holding his chains split down the center. Rock ground over the orichalcum links, and one of them snapped. As it broke, a rush of energy surged into Loki, a sudden release of his pent-up Pneuma. He allowed the power to flood into his limbs and took off at a dead sprint, dodging around falling rocks, leaping over chasms now rent into the cavern floor, and dashing like mad for the tunnels out of this place.

Total darkness greeted him, along with the continuing crash of rock and earth from all sides.

With no other choice, he pushed on, stumbling over unseen debris, but always scrambling forward. He had memorized the way out when Odin had led him down here. All he could do now was hope that no cave-in had closed off that path.

Finally, choking on dust and weary, he stumbled out into the light of the setting sun.

All around him, Asgard smoldered.

Ashes carried on the breeze. Great clouds of the stuff, mixed with incandescent embers. In some valleys, the tree-tops still blazed, while a thick layer of dust now covered most else. Several mountains had split down the middle, and one had collapsed into itself, leaving an enormous crater where the sea had rushed in to create a new lagoon.

Rubbing his eyes, Loki made his way around the mountainside, seeking a means of egress from the smoldering ruin. On the far side, though, he had to stop and gape at the World Tree.

A crack now split up the trunk, widening the hollow inside. The rent had severed one of the boughs, pitching it and all the branches into a flooded valley, one laying just beyond the chasm the Tree spanned. What would have happened to those souls? Had tens of thousands of people across Midgard simply dropped dead all at once, with no explanation?

Shaking his head, Loki focused on the hollow at Yggdrasil's base. It grew wider every time. How many more such Eschatons could it survive? Not so many, he had to imagine. If the Tree finally broke apart, the Wheel of Life would falter, and humanity would at last find itself utterly consumed by the darkness that had given rise to it.

Loki pressed a palm into his brow, wanting so desperately to care. After all, he had dedicated eons to this.

But all he could see before him was a haze of red. It demanded he return Sigyn's fate in kind.

From the dawn of time, he had served as a benefactor to Man. He had endured suffering most could never imagine.

And now ... now he would give them reason to fear his rage.

THE CYCLE CONTINUES ...

Next Book: Ragnarok is everywhere. The World is ending. And Odin is lost in time. If he makes it back, can he save what remains of the world?

The Fires of Muspelheim: books2read.com/mlfiresofmuspelheim

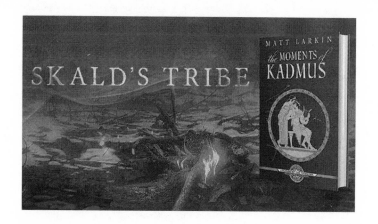

Join the Skalds' Tribe newsletter and get access to exclusive insider information and your FREE copy of *The Moments of Kadmus*.

https://www.mattlarkinbooks.com/skalds/

ABOUT THE AUTHOR

Matt Larkin writes retellings of mythology as dark, gritty fantasy. His passions of myths, philosophy, and history inform his series. He strives to combine gut-wrenching action with thought-provoking ideas and culturally resonant stories.

Matt's mythic fantasy takes place in the Eschaton Cycle universe, a world—as the name implies—of cyclical apocalypses. Each series can be read alone in any order, but they weave together to form a greater tapestry.

Learn more at mattlarkinbooks.com or connect with Matt through his fan group, the Skalds' Tribe:

https://www.mattlarkinbooks.com/skalds/

AUTHOR'S NOTE

So ... the penultimate book in the *Gods of the Ragnarok Era* series. We're drawing close to the end which means more of the inevitable, awful events myth demands are coming to pass.

In the *Poetic Edda* there's a poem called the *Lokasenna* which basically means "Loki's insults." And that kind of tells you how the poem unfolds, with Loki insulting each and every Ás and Vanr in turn. And in a way not at all in keeping with the character we've seen throughout the series.

The answer? The insults are issued by Loki's petulant son, Narfi, of course! Actually, Loki gets blamed for plenty of things he may not have directly done in this series, like shearing Sif's hair.

Speaking of Loki, while previous books have hinted at his nature, called him Firebringer or the like, this is the first time we really start to get the full picture. And that nature ties into other mythologies beyond the Norse.

The Eschaton Cycle exists as part of a cycle of Eras drawn from many different cultures. Within the Ragnarok Era, I have a particular focus on Norse, Germanic, and

Finnish myth (with a few others), but other Eras and myths have been referenced in passing. And now, in more than passing!

I'm sure others have associated Loki and Prometheus. Both are trickster gods who may have been involved in humanity's creation. Both have associations with fire. In Loki's case, this is partly because Wagner used Loge (a demigod of fire) in place of Loki in his opera cycle, which was one of the sources of my work. Earlier in the Ragnarok Era, my Loki even used the alias Loge (also seen in this book).

The characters of Loki and Prometheus are, in my opinion, among the most interesting figures in their respective mythology traditions.

Of course, the greater part of this book revolves around Hermod's ride to the titular Gates of Hel, a tale from the *Prose Edda*. Obviously, given everything that's gone before and the nature of this universe, it turned out to be a horrific, harrowing journey.

One culminating in him learning of Sigyn's long-hidden crime and overcome with rage over it. Even knowing it was coming from a long way off, that was a difficult thing to write. Sigyn was one of my favorite characters in the series.

(And yes, I know nobody really gets a happy ending in Norse myth, but still.)

Rather than ramble on too long, I will just touch on Odin's own journey, a temporal one. Time travel, like prescience, serves as a natural means of examining the question of fate and free will, a prevailing theme throughout this series and the Eschaton Cycle as a whole.

It also profoundly affects Odin, forcing him to reconsider his convictions. And to prepare himself for the final end.

Thanks to my wife for helping me bring this story to life. Also, special thanks to my cover designer and to my Arch Skalds (in no particular order): Al, Tanya, Jackie, Dale, Missy, Bill, Rachel, Bob, Kaye, Mike, Scott, and Regina.

Thank you for reading,
   Matt